This Side of Death

When the Past Comes Back to Hunt You

Andrew Barrett

The Ink Foundry

© Copyright 2020 Andrew Barrett

The rights of Andrew Barrett to be identified as the author of this work have been asserted in accordance with sections 77 and 78 of the Copyright, Designs and Patents Act 1988. No part of this publication may be reproduced, stored in a retrieval system or transmitted in any form or by any means electronic, mechanical, photocopying, recording or otherwise without the prior permission of the copyright holder.

For rights and copyright enquiries, please contact:

permissions@andrew.barrett.co.uk

This book is a work of fiction. Any names, characters, companies, organizations, places, events, locales, and incidents are fictional or are used in a fictitious manner. Any resemblance to actual persons, living or dead, or actual events is purely coincidental.

Praise for This Side of Death

- Spellbinding, hair-raising, and deeply enthralling.
- Don't expect to get much done once you start this.
- Will totally take over your life until you finish it and it will stay with you for days afterward.
- After you've read this, you'll spend time musing about the heart of this character, and what you'd have done were you in his shoes.
- This is another great book, written with Barrett's usual attention to detail and sprinkled liberally with a super-sized helping of Eddie's black humour.
- Having the talent to weave a tale interspersed with humor among sometimes grotesque elements of an edgy thriller, never ceases to amaze me.
- This latest chapter of Eddie Collins' life is a fantastic thrill-ride, full of suspense and just enough gut-wrenching terror to keep you up at night. Unputdownable.
- The ending of this book left me breathless. I was nearly exhausted. My reaction was WOW!!!
- One of Barrett's real writing talents is to put you in the place and time of an event, not to mention in the middle of a scene. You can feel the rain, empathize with the pain, taste the dust, see the stars.
- If you read this book, or any of the books that feature Eddie Collins, you will not be disappointed. You may even, like me, become addicted.
- Despite the dark, dangerous criminal there is quite a lot of humour woven in between the more tension-filled parts.
- I was amazed at how clearly the author described what was going through Alex's mind through colours, voices, spikes, pain.

Preface

Proud to swear in British English.

Foreword

This Side of Death is what happens when an author can't let go of an idea.

I wrote the novella, The Note, and walked away from it, content to put it out there and move on with the next story. I did move on with the next story, but I never forgot about The Note and the very last words spoken by one of the characters in it. "Don't forget me, eh? Because one day, I'll be around the very next corner." It was a chilling sentence.

It was a sentence that I couldn't leave alone. From it grew this book, and in it we learn a lot about Eddie, his psychology, and his past. This isn't a 'typical' CSI Eddie Collins crime thriller (whatever that might be, they're all different), this story centres around him.

This Side of Death includes The Note as Part One – heavily revised, shortened, and turned around until it's a third person rendition, rather than Eddie speaking to you. It is an integral part of the book; it's the foundation. Don't be tempted to skip it (especially if you haven't read The Note), because to do so would be to undermine the rest of the book.

Her Song

In the heart I stab you, dear

And you fall to the ground

To lie in your own blood

As it spreads all around

After your ears go deaf

And after your eyes go blind

Just a box full of memories

Becomes your screaming mind

For a ruined life

Your black eyes cry

But not for too long, dear

You've got three minutes to die

Contents

PART ONE

Then

Chapter One

A Treat for the Slugs

SOMEONE WAS WATCHING HIM. Yet when he spun a three-sixty, no one appeared to be taking a blind bit of notice.

Eddie Collins, CSI, was stumbling through a half-night shift that would have finished at 2am if there'd been no overtime to be had. Right now it looked as though he would sail right past two o'clock without so much as a second glance.

He stood in the car park of the shittiest pub in the shittiest part of Leeds and wondered which gods he'd pissed off recently. And he wondered why CSI Miami never stooped to this level of glamour; because of that crap, people assumed all murders happened in swanky hotel rooms or on a millionaire's yacht. He blew rainwater from his top lip and treated himself to a sigh.

Despite the rain, and courtesy of a dead man found lying on his back near the pub's gable-end wall, Eddie was the free entertainment to a group of toothless drunken men. Life didn't get any more glamorous than that.

Draining from the flap in the dead man's scalp was a pool of blood the size of a welcome mat, and nearby was a length of scaffolding pole.

The drunks kept going inside for more beer and rushing back out to watch him again, maybe hoping he'd done something spectacular like pull a murderer out of a top hat – or found their missing teeth.

It would be no surprise if one of those giggling pissheads was the killer, Eddie thought, just watching the proceedings, proud of his handiwork, maybe wondering if Eddie was smart enough to pull him out of the hat! The only copper at the scene had a brief word with the PCSO on the tape and then waltzed off inside the pub, pulling out his pocket notebook as he went.

The lack of any CID presence suggested they weren't keen to come out and play in case the rainwater dissolved them. They were probably playing cards in the nick where it was warm and dry; loser gets to brave the rain and take statements from the drunken soup-suckers on the set of CSI Leeds.

While his scene was being washed away, Eddie watched the gawping, shouting mob standing behind the thin blue and white tape less than ten yards away. A young PCSO was trying to keep them on the far side of it without getting drunk on their breath, or being vomited on.

Eddie was mesmerised by them; how they could claim to be part of the human race, and how badly he wanted to be away from them. But he was determined to do a thorough job, and to do everything he could to catch the killer and help the victim's family get justice.

It wasn't just public relations bullshit. Eddie didn't do PR – there was a whole department dedicated to that – but he always did his best, because that's what he was paid to do. Anything less would be theft, and Eddie Collins was no thief.

While drunken renditions of Who Are You? echoed off the wet brick walls, Eddie concentrated on the scene. It was a process. And you could either follow it and capture everything there was to capture, or you could just flit around looking for the obvious and miss the subtler clues entirely. That was the difference between a good examiner doing a good job and a shit examiner pretending to do a good job.

Things like the scaffolding pole always leapt out immediately; they were obvious and yes, they could lead to an offender. But if he overlooked something like offender's blood on the victim, offender's hair on the victim, or offender's footwear marks in the victim's blood, the investigation suddenly became reliant upon that scaffolding pole giving them the answer.

"Gil Grissom would've caught the bastard by now," some drunk shouted. His drinking companions thought this was hysterical. Eddie gritted his teeth and ignored them, and got on with taking the initial scene shots, having laid out a few yellow markers next to those pertinent bits of evidence. He wanted to get to the body quickly but had to take care of the preliminaries first.

One of those preliminary things included getting a tent up over the deceased as quickly as possible, but he couldn't do it alone. He hoped CID had finished playing cards by now, and that the loser would arrive before this place succumbed to a drunken uprising, or the corpse floated off down the street.

Once the initial scene photos were out of the way, Eddie squatted by the dead man and shone torchlight over him and the dozens of slugs forming a pincer movement around his head, there to drink of the draining blood. They were capable of ruining blood spatter patterns, and even though there was no danger of that here – it was just a lake, no patterns – Eddie shuddered at the sight of them, and went back to studying the corpse.

There was nothing remarkable about him: mid-thirties, white, short dark hair (now very red towards the back), wearing old jeans, a green t-shirt, and a fleece. His eyes were open, and death had gifted that familiar opacity, like the onset of cataracts. The rain clumped his eye lashes together.

Eddie leaned in closer. There was something familiar about him. That crucifix earring; the mobster moustache. When he stood, he also recognised the red Nike trainers the guy had been wearing the last time Eddie had seen him.

And that's when things turned sour.

A plain car pulled up outside the pub and the longcoats got out. CID. These were the coppers who chased clichés, the ones who saw a detective on TV and tried to imitate him, creating a fake image from a fake image. A counterfeit counterfeit, a self-perpetuating caricature. They were plastic, and they swaggered into the scene, thinking of their image for the crowd.

Morse and Lewis glided under the tape like limbo dancers and nodded as they approached Eddie; the temperature dropped by ten degrees just because they were so fucking cool. Eddie gritted his teeth again. Despite their collars being pulled up against the drizzle, he recognised one of them, and his heart sank.

Eddie didn't like him – never had. He looked like a bad drawing of Officer Dibble, and that's how he always thought of him. They'd worked the same shift pattern for six months, and each time he came to one of Eddie's jobs, Eddie wanted to punch him and never stop.

"DS Trafford," Dibble said to the PCSO, a little too loudly, surveying his audience, hoping to soak up some wows or oohs. Mockery and wolf-whistles hit him square in the face.

Dibble's partner was a stranger but judging by the matching coat he was obviously emulating Dibble in the hope of scoring Brownie points. Dibble didn't introduce him, but he was short, face like a bashed crab.

Eddie didn't like Dibble or strangers showing up at his scenes. "You lost at snap, then?"

Dibble blinked. "I beg your pardon."

"Never mind."

"We're locking it down. Tent it and you can go."

"What?" Eddie growled, prepared to dig his heels in. He wouldn't let someone he didn't respect mess up a scene that warranted a decent job. "My scene. I'm working it." The crowd was getting drunker, louder, just a confusion of noise that chipped away at the edges. "You can't leave a scene on overnight with that lot hanging around."

Dibble wasn't accustomed to being challenged; his face screwed up as though his tongue had turned into a lemon. "We're locking it down till daylight."

Eddie had no intention of locking it down. There were things that needed doing tonight, and if Dibble wanted to leave the stiff until daylight and give the slugs a high-cholesterol feast, fine. But he was going to tent it and process the rest of the scene.

Inside, Eddie grinned – he'd remembered who the dead guy was!

It was every DS's dream to have an identity to work with right from the off, but Dibble had more chance of finding a personality in a box of Kellogg's Cornflakes than of Eddie sharing that piece of good news. Let the prick try to get it out of this rabble, he thought, and see how far he gets.

Dibble's idea was to come here, look cool as he fired off a few orders, take a couple of statements and then prepare a briefing pack for the poor bastards who had to work it the next day. But you only need to lose evidence once and you've got a murderer skipping down the beach singing Oh What a Beautiful Morning. "Just a minute." Eddie stepped closer – not exactly confrontational, just trying to keep his voice down. "You give me a hand to tent it, and then you can go and take your statements and avoid whatever else needs doing. Leave the rest to me."

"Goodbye." Dibble and Bashed-Crab turned and walked towards the PCSO.

Eddie stood there feeling like a prick – but his embarrassment was a pebble compared to the mountain of anger that crashed over him. "Oi, Dibble!"

They both stopped in unison and turned to face him. It was almost graceful. The crowd quietened the way people do when they sense something untoward developing.

"Ayup, Quincy's in a mood." The crowd began laughing, and soon it was like a toothless grin parade at a hick festival.

"Quincy," Eddie shouted, "is a fucking pathologist, you prick."

The crowd jeered, and then Dibble was in Eddie's face, close enough so Eddie could see the flecks of rain landing on his perfectly trimmed eyebrows. "What did you say?"

"Quincy. He's a pathologist."

"What is your name?"

Eddie looked at him, and confusion somehow dissipated his anger. That wasn't a friendly "what do they call you?" question; it was an "I need your name for the complaint I'm about to file" question. "My name?"

"I have dismissed you from the scene, and you have seen fit to stir the crowd with a derisive comment."

"How often have we worked scenes together, and you don't know my name?" Eddie looked at Bashed-Crab. "Is he serious?"

Dibble answered for him. "Last time of asking. What is your name?"

He was serious. Eddie cleared his throat. "Bill," he said. "Bill Gristle."

He took out a notebook and a pencil and actually wrote it down. "Thank you, Bill," he said, nodding towards the body. "You can tent it and go."

The disbelief in Bashed-Crab's eyes was a delight. He nudged Dibble, and then whispered something. Eddie stood with his arms folded and a grin on his face as realisation grew on Dibble's. Dibble looked pissed off and stepped closer. "Funny man, eh? I will be taking this further." He gritted his teeth and hissed, "Stop fucking about and do as I say, or things will get messy for you."

The smile fell off Eddie's face. He unfolded his arms and took a step forward too, just enough to bring his boot gently down on Dibble's patent leather toe and prevent him from reversing. He brought his face down to Dibble's level, curled the man's beautiful silk tie into his fist, and growled, "You wanna put in a complaint because I refuse to compromise evidence? Fine, go ahead, I'll argue all day long with your inspector. But threaten me again and I'll punch your slimy brown tongue so far down your throat you'll be able to taste your own fear. Got it?"

"Get your fucking—"

"And I don't care for rank either, so try pulling that shit on me and see how far it gets you. Now get out of my fucking scene." The crowd was buzzing, even the PCSO looked nervous, and Bashed-Crab cringed as he studied his own shiny shoes.

Dibble tried and failed to straighten his tie. "You haven't heard the last of this."

Eddie smiled, and mouthed "Fuck off".

The crowd parted as the red-faced man with the crumpled tie barged his way through.

Ten minutes later a police van with two coppers on board pulled up and helped Eddie erect the scene tent over the body.

Chapter Two

Just a Blown Fuse

BACK AT KILLINGBECK POLICE Station, Eddie kicked the CSI office door closed and dumped a shitload of exhibits on his desk. His back ached and he was wet through. But he could relax in the knowledge that he'd done his job and helped the day-shift investigators with things that might otherwise have been lost. He made sure that little snippet went into the report.

The dead man was John Tyler. Eddie recalled him quite clearly because he'd photographed him only two days before he was beaten to death in the car park of some shithole pub. Eddie took domestic violence seriously and often photographed injuries to victims, both male and female. This man had been a shy fellow, embarrassed by his predicament, and by the bruises all over his body. Eddie had felt bad for him, as he did with all victims of domestic abuse, and applauded him for being brave enough to ask for help.

But what really bookmarked him in Eddie's mind were the bite marks. He'd had a prominent one spanning the bridge of his nose – fresh too, the bruising not yet fully developed. He remembered thinking what a bastard that would be to photograph correctly, and he also remembered thinking how it must have made Tyler's eyes water.

He had several more bite marks: one on his right shoulder, another on his right wrist. Both of those had bled. It must have been a prolonged attack to get bitten and beaten like that, but Eddie didn't have to imagine too hard – it had happened to him, thanks to an old girlfriend. As Eddie had photographed Tyler's injuries, he remembered being bitten and punched; he'd almost lost an eye thanks to her nails. She was vile.

And so Eddie found empathy for Mr Tyler, and felt more than a little sadness for him now he knew how his life had ended.

It was one in the morning; the chances of getting a flier looked good, considering earlier he'd thought three o'clock was more likely. He'd eaten, brought his computer work up to date, and was about to beat his Inbox down to a level where he could see over it without needing a step ladder. Even after the clash with Dibble, he was relaxed, chilled out, and all was well with the world.

Until he saw the death threat.

They were nothing new; in fact, they were something of an occupational hazard when you worked against the bad guys. And Eddie had received plenty. Most of them were just plain silly, fired off by young men who'd been caught doing something they shouldn't by the nice man with the fingerprint brush. They couldn't handle the embarrassment of being caught, or they were angry with themselves for leaving evidence behind. You do the crime, you do the time, as the saying went.

Eddie filed those threats in the bin – metaphorically speaking, of course. In reality, he handed them over to an equally nice police officer who saw to it that the author was reprimanded for his spelling and grammatical errors.

He opened the envelope, pulled out the letter. It turned out to be one of the not-so-silly ones, the ones that tended to wipe Eddie's ever-present smile from his face. He forgot all about John Tyler, and the hairs on the nape of his neck stood up as a tingling feeling radiated through his body.

He reached for his coffee, only to discover the cup was empty. And now he needed a cigarette. He stared at the note some more.

Your going to die tonight.

The spelling alone should have filed it away into the plain silly category, but what made him take notice was the paper it was scrawled on. It was torn, stabbed, ripped. If you could be pissed off with a sheet of A4, this is what it would look like. And Eddie could imagine the author's fury because those stab marks had been made not by the pen, but by a knife.

How long had it been in the tray? There was no other paperwork on top of it. There was no stamp on the envelope, so it had been hand-delivered, and it was simply addressed to, "Eddie Collins, CSI", in the same handwriting, and using the same pen. He slid the letter inside an evidence bag and sealed it. The envelope went into another bag, and Eddie went outside for a smoke, looking around all the while.

He always walked to his smoking spot with his eyes down to avoid any chance of people stopping to talk to him. But this time he was on full alert, eyes everywhere, scrutinising the faces of the few people he passed along the way.

After the first cigarette, he lit up another and noticed his hands trembling ever so slightly under the lights in the back car park. Behind him was utter blackness as the car park stretched on for hundreds of yards behind the nick. No lights up there – only here by the entrance. There were noises coming from the blackness, and Eddie edged away from them, smoked a little faster.

The rain had slowed to a drizzle as though it were a backdrop to his feelings, a nagging feeling that ran in parallel.

Your going to die tonight.

Back in the office, the silence he usually adored became oppressive, claustrophobic. He heard everything as though he had an amplifier strapped to his head. His boots shushing on the dirty office carpet, the creak of the storeroom door, the echo in the little anteroom as he put the evidence bags away. It was all coming together to make a bad horror movie. Eddie was nervous.

He sat back at his desk and emailed his prick of a boss to let him know about the letter and envelope, and that they needed photographing prior to being submitted for chemical treatment.

It was time to go home. He turned off his radio, put it away in the wall-mounted locker, and collected his house key and his car key. The cool night air and thin drizzle refreshed his face as though someone had just slapped him. And still he wondered if he was being watched.

As he climbed into the Discovery, he submitted to the feeling again, and sneaked a quick look in the back seats before he turned on the ignition. Silly, but he was spooked. And as he let the car wend its own way home, his mind drifted a little, and then BANG! He had one of those moments that almost saw him drive off the road and into a ditch.

He recognised the handwriting.

Only five words. But he was sure he'd seen it before somewhere. And if he recognised it, then he must know the person who wrote it, right? It wasn't like one of those silly death threats where some kid he'd never met before got hold of his name and tried to be cute; this guy knew Eddie. And Eddie knew this guy.

His mind went off at a peculiar tangent, studying the list of people he knew. It wasn't an overly long one, and it didn't get much shorter when he subtracted those who weren't pissed off at him. He wasn't one of life's cuddly sorts. And while his mind played with faces, he'd totally forgotten the obvious fact: if someone was serious about killing him, they couldn't really wish for a better place to do it than his house.

Eddie's house was a single-storey cottage halfway along a dead-end road in the middle of nowhere. And he lived alone. It was the perfect locale for Eddie; his way of telling the world that he preferred his own company. The only visitors he got were the ones he invited, usually to deliver pizza. It was also the perfect locale for an assassination.

Before he knew it, he'd turned off the main drag and followed the lane until the turning for his dead-end road appeared on the left. No time for a recce now; he'd blown it by simply driving straight home.

The good news was that the headlights didn't pick out any vehicle, and there was nobody about – that he could see. The bad news was that the headlights didn't pick out any vehicle and there was nobody about – that he could see. His mouth was as dry as Gandhi's flip-flop, yet his palms squeaked on the steering wheel.

If the note was a tactic designed to scare him, it had worked; the author had scored his little victory and could sleep soundly knowing he'd won... but no, he couldn't. Because he wouldn't know he'd won. Unless he was watching. That strange tingling feeling in the back of his neck returned.

Eddie went to the end of the road, did an eight-point turn and drove slowly back to the cottage. Still nothing. He swallowed, but his throat was as dry as his mouth. He could kill for a beer right now. Two would be better. He lit a cigarette instead.

Now what?

It all boiled down to how seriously he took this threat. If he genuinely thought a madman had sent the letter with the intention of carrying it out, Eddie would have been curled up in a Holiday Inn by now, locked in the bathroom with a coffee and one of those little brown biscuits. So, had he subconsciously discounted the threat or rated it as unlikely to translate into action?

Great. Now his subconscious mind was making decisions that he had to live with.

He left the headlights on and climbed out of the Discovery. There was a dim streetlamp at the end of the road, but even with his head up his arse his boss could still see better than Eddie could right now. Casting a pair of long black shadows before him, he headed through the stillness to the front door, and cursed not having the intelligence to bring home his Maglite. As predicted, the rain had grown heavier; he could hear it pattering on the sleeves of his jacket and could hear the long grass around the side dancing in the breeze.

He was jittery. He wondered if he should just get the hell inside, or go and look around the house first and find a possible point of entry.

From somewhere nearby an owl laughed at him.

Deciding whether to check things out was one of those questions to which there wasn't really a right or wrong answer – just varying degrees of error. He still had that Holiday Inn in mind.

It was while he peeked around the far wall where all the nettles and cow parsley grew that it occurred to him: not only could he see shit-all anyway, but why send a death threat at all?

If you're going to kill someone, you don't want them to prepare. You want them to be oblivious to it; you want it to be a smooth and satisfying experience, surely? If you prepare someone, it could go tits up. "Unless it's me you're threatening," he whispered, "in which case I seem to be doing everything I can to make it go smoothly for you." Goes to show, he thought, how little I know about the complexities of other people's minds.

To Eddie, life was straight-forward. Live it. Get angry. Die.

Anger was therapeutic and pure; it was the medicine that kept him sane. He suspected it also gave him high blood pressure, but you couldn't have it all.

Smoke curled up Eddie's face and stung his eyes, and the glowing end of his cigarette hissed with each droplet of rainwater. He tossed it aside and listened. All that came back was the laughing owl and the swishing of weeds singing in a breeze. There was only darkness.

He continued his analysis. On the other hand, he thought, sending out a death threat could destabilise the victim and make your job as a killer easier. And it's the trap I just fell into arse over tit.

That was about the point when anger took over the situation. He was tired after a long shift, and all he'd thought about for the last couple of hours was how some arsehole had taken root in his mind, making him forget to get milk on the way home – some arsehole who didn't even know the difference between your and you're. Prick!

Time to stop pussyfooting around. Eddie marched around the front of the house, pulling his house key out of his pocket, and used the light from the Discovery headlamps to get it in the lock. Sick of feeling nervous – okay, sick of feeling afraid – he opened the door quickly, letting it thud into the wall with a hefty bang.

Blackness greeted him. Familiar smells of stale coffee and very stale cigarette smoke. Home. He reached in and prodded the light switch, but nothing happened. Still blackness.

Fuck.

He was still angry because this was turning out to be a major inconvenience. But the anger moved aside and fear crept in, nudging its way to the front of the queue with alarming silkiness. This was scaring the living shit out of him.

The fuse had blown, that was all. Or there was a power cut; nothing to get alarmed about.

But Eddie didn't get along too well with the notion of coincidence, so adding that to the death threat made a night at Holiday Inn so very appealing. He was reaching in to close the door when he heard it.

Chapter Three

A Blast from the Past - Literally

"EDDIE."

Breath held, Eddie froze. Across the floor, a faint smudge of yellow from one of the headlights showed nothing. He stared into the blackness beyond it, aware of the Discovery only ten yards behind him lighting him up with a golden silhouette.

In that blackness, the tip of a cigarette glowed orange. Eddie had walked into a trap.

"Come in."

He could be at the car inside five or six seconds. More than enough time to—

The car keys jangled as they hit the floor somewhere nearby. He sighed and mumbled, "Fuck." The first question that sprang to mind was: What do you want? But that would be verging on cliché, and even under this kind of pressure, there was no way he could ask it.

"Step inside and close the door."

It was a female voice. Quiet, just above a whisper. It was so quiet that he could hear the mechanism inside the gun as she cocked it. Eddie went cold from the inside out, like someone had just flushed out his system with tap water. A tremor ran through his body, and it wasn't one that just came and went; this bastard stayed there, buzzing.

It was the same kind of buzz he got after confronting queue-jumpers at McDonald's. A bit of mouthing off that pumped him up; it was the adrenaline, the body preparing itself for a fight over a cheeseburger and large fries. Well, that was the kind of tremble going on right now.

Eddie stepped inside, squinting to see.

"Close it."

Your going to die tonight.

He stared at the orange glow, felt hollow in the chest, like his heart was holding its breath too.

"Now."

He kicked it shut, and she turned on the lamp over by Eddie's armchair. Seemed she hadn't cut the juice to the entire house – just taken out the lounge bulb, maybe, or flicked the fuse for the lighting circuit.

"What do you want?" tried to get out again, but was replaced by, "Can I have one of those?" He nodded to the cigarette, trying to keep things cool. "And a coffee? Would you like one?" The lamp was behind her and so Eddie couldn't see her very well; she was just a glowing silhouette with smoke drifting through it. She was sitting on the arm of the chair, cigarette dangling from her mouth, left hand holding a pistol, pointing right at him. The light glinted off it. The scene looked like something from a gangster movie, somewhere in New York maybe, around prohibition. She was a moll.

Except this was real. It was here, and it was now. Eddie swallowed, and the shaking worsened.

"Go on," she said, "talk your way out of this—"

"Do you mind if I smoke? I mean, if you're going to kill me, the least you can do is let me—"

She stood up quickly, as though she had a spring under her arse, and the speed she came at him almost knocked him off-balance. She was in his face, the muzzle up against the back of his neck, and she pulled him forward by his jacket so she could reach his face. Her lips moved against his cheek, and her hot breath leaked into his mouth as he breathed fast. All the time she twitched the muzzle, boring it into his neck.

Not quite so cool now. He didn't realise it, but his eyes were shut tight. Any hope he had of smoothing his way to a graceful escape vanished.

"Funny man, eh?" she snarled.

Eddie's eyes snapped open.

"Gonna smart-arse talk me? Treat me like shit, Collins?" She screamed in his ear and then hit him on the back of the neck with the butt of the gun. Eddie was on his knees, already in pain, when she kicked him in the kidney.

Any thoughts of being the brave James Bond hero who could talk cool ran away pretty fucking quickly. Eddie was scared. He was submissive. And then it happened: that fucking question that made Eddie as weak and predictable as every other bastard on this planet just fell out of his mouth. "What do you want?"

From behind a shielding hand, he looked up at her as she stood over him, panting. The light was still poor, but he could see she had blood all down one arm, across her face and neck. What the fuck was going on?

One thing that struck him about all this was that it must be personal. That sounded stupid, but if this was a contract killing, she would have done it by now – no preamble, no messing about, no opportunity for James Bond to wrangle his way free, just pull the trigger and hit pay day.

But she hadn't done that; she was waiting for something, she wanted something from him, even if it was only to hear him beg – and hell would freeze over first, he thought.

She wanted something from him.

Eddie had power.

He watched her, and there was something familiar… "Who are you?"

She didn't answer, just kicked him in the back again. This time she got him right on the spine and it sent him into a spasm of pain that made him writhe on the floor. He didn't scream because he was too busy trying to catch his breath; it was like diving into a cold ocean, how it left you breathless for all the wrong reasons. It hurt like a bitch, and Eddie's eyes watered.

She retreated somewhere nearer the lamp and he caught a glimpse of her profile. Eventually the agony lessened, and a silence permeated the room like blood dispersing in water. Despite the pain, he delved inside his jacket pocket for his cigarettes and lit one, staring at her defiantly. He sat up, leaning back on one hand, leg casually bent, trying not to let his fear show.

And she stared at him. Not blinking.

When the penny finally dropped, Eddie gasped. Her eyes, large, dark and deep, gave nothing away; it was as if they were a barrier to what lay beneath rather than a window into her soul. "Funny man" came at him from somewhere distant, a memory that he'd almost succeeded in erasing.

Alex was her name, and she was a fucking psycho.

As she moved around the table to stub out her cigarette, the lamp shone directly on her for the first time, and he saw that she'd changed considerably since he'd last seen her. She'd turned Goth; her smooth brown hair was now a matted black mess, she'd smothered black eyeliner on her upper and lower lids, making her black eyes seem massive, and the black lipstick smeared all down her face turned her into an apprentice voodoo priestess.

But of all the clues – the voice, the familiar handwriting, the propensity for violence – it was the dead guy, John Tyler, who'd reminded Eddie of her the most. The bite marks he'd photographed on some domestic violence victim who wore red Nike trainers. She'd done that to him once. He smoked quickly.

She half-smiled, seeing that he'd finally remembered her. It must have been a buzz for her too.

"Nothing's changed, Alex," he said. "You still can't fucking spell." That would either kill him or cure the situation.

It didn't have the desired effect, and he reflected that it might have been the wrong approach. She walked over, leaned in close and spat in his face. That was enough; frightened or not, that was as much as Eddie would take from her. He dropped the cigarette and stood, despite her pushing him, and despite her throwing a decent punch into the side of his head. He rocked a little but was able to get a grip on her jacket, and, as he began to lose balance, dragged her with him. They teetered and hit the deck in a tangle of limbs that would have been comedic under any other circumstances.

She was breathing hard, almost rasping – her body countering some drugs, he guessed. Everything stopped. Eddie held his breath, mouth open, eyes wide, waiting to see what happened next. The gun felt cold under his chin, and he was back to shitting himself again. His grip on her slackened. Flat on his back now, he raised his hands slowly into the air and watched the crazy look in her dead eyes. His heart stuttered.

The smeared lipstick wasn't smeared lipstick at all. It really was a thick coating of blood that was flaking off like she was shedding a layer of reptilian skin.

Eddie gagged. He had no idea what she was planning to do next, but he seriously doubted he was going to get that coffee.

She pushed the muzzle harder into his throat. His heart rattled, and a pulse of dread throbbed in his temples.

"Close your eyes."

He tried to swallow again, but the gun was so hard into his throat that he could barely breathe, let alone swallow. He croaked out the words, "What turned you into a fucking lunatic?"

The blood around her mouth cracked more as she screamed with all the ferocity of a woman being torn apart, physically and mentally. It was the most horrendous sound he'd ever heard, and it went on and on, her breath streaming hot and sour. Just before she bit into his face, she pushed the muzzle even harder and he braced himself, scrabbling backwards against it, clawing at the carpet.

She fired the gun.

Chapter Four

A Conversation with Madness

AFTER THE FLASH, DISTORTED colours floated across his vision and he screamed at the ringing in his ears. She was laughing and when she lifted her head there was more blood – Eddie's blood – dripping from her chin.

Eddie's face was on fire and his eyes were watering so badly that he could barely open them. Blood trickled down his neck. She really was a psycho bitch!

The bullet had gone straight through the front door.

As she laughed, he blinked away the tears and the distorted colours parted to reveal her front teeth, how the upper canines lay at an angle almost behind the incisors, and the lower canines were twisted to hell like someone had fucked up a card shuffle.

She looked down at him, still laughing, holding the gun with one hand and gripping his jacket with the other as he stared back unbelieving, still in shock. And then she started to grind. Her pelvis gyrated on his dick like they were a couple of teenagers getting randy. Eddie wasn't in the mood for randy.

"Do you think there's a chance for us, Eddie? You know? To be happy, like we was?"

He was shaking. "I think we need to talk," he whispered, wincing as the fire in his cheek grew even hotter. His own voice sounded muffled, as though someone had tuned out all the treble and left only the bass.

Someone else had changed the track from Mad Bitch to Romantic Vampire Slut. She leaned in close, looking at him, studying him. She bent lower and kissed him.

Eddie remembered reading somewhere that some people get off on torture, that they get horny just before the big event – and the big event he was worried about involved her trigger finger, and his brains dripping down the wallpaper. Not an ideal end to the day.

Your going to die tonight.

She slid her tongue into Eddie's mouth and he tasted his own blood.

He nearly freaked out; it was all he could do to keep from vomiting. At least he knew where he stood with the Mad Bitch, but this was scary on a whole new level.

"I could move in. If you like."

She tried to kiss him again. He twisted his head sideways to spit out the vile taste, and got a stabbing reminder of the damage she'd done to his face.

"Hey," she soothed, kindness shimmering in her eyes as she stroked his good cheek with her thumb. He could hear the stubble under her nail. "What's the matter?"

Eddie's first reaction was to laugh, but he choked it immediately, focusing on the death threat instead. This evening wouldn't end well for at least one of them.

Be tactful was the only advice he could give himself. "I could write you a list."

She sat back up and the kindness left her eyes. "What?"

"I mean it's pretty difficult to think with you waving a gun around."

She relaxed, took the gun from his throat and just sat there on his groin with a delightful smile on her wretched face. She was a rose made of arsenic.

Alex got pregnant at sixteen, and her dad had thrown her down the stairs before he threw her out. It was about the same time her mother died. It was complicated, but she had miscarried, and he finally did her the favour of disowning her. She'd told all this to Eddie when she met him a year later, said her dad was ashamed of her, that he didn't talk about her with his friends, and didn't even declare her on some fancy job application he'd filled out.

He didn't want the embarrassment. Eddie had never met him, but he sounded like a prick. It was hard for her, but she'd done nothing to escape the spiral of decay and self-hatred she found herself in. If anything, she'd propagated it, almost relished being inside this maelstrom, and from it had developed a wonderful reputation as a wretched whore who'd cut your throat and guzzle your lifeblood if you so much as farted within earshot.

Eddie last saw Alex when he was eighteen years old, not long after they began dating. At eighteen, you know everything there is to know about the world. Only when someone comes along who isn't on your wavelength do you learn new things. Pain was one of the things Alex taught him. Mental pain to begin with, quickly followed by the physical kind.

"What?" She was staring at him again, obviously amused to find him in thought.

"Nothing," he said, listening as his hearing came back towards normal.

"Go on, whatcha thinking?"

"Get off me, Alex, you're starting to piss me off."

She gripped his jacket, and gave him that look again.

Eddie sighed, and tried to placate her. "I was thinking about us." Her smile returned, and he couldn't keep up with her changing emotions any longer; each comment was a game of chance, a spin of a revolver's cylinder.

"Been doing that a lot too. Thinking about us, I mean." She let go of him. "I was there, you know. When you were photographing him, and it got me thinking."

"Who?"

"Who what?"

"When I was photographing who?"

"Him. My ex, John."

"John Tyler?" He tried to sit up, but it was difficult with a lunatic crushing his nuts. "When? Tonight?"

"I meant when you were at our house photographing his injuries. His bite marks!" She laughed like a banshee on speed, and a fresh shudder skittered through him. She was so fucking unpredictable. "I watched you from the other room. I was remembering you, and how you used to fuck. You were an animal, Eddie. Could've ripped off your clothes there and then." She grinned and winked, but coming from her, it was no compliment. It just added fuel to the misery.

Eddie had wondered why Tyler had been so timid. He remembered pitying the man, but thinking how he really ought to grow a spine. It was no wonder he was timid, if she'd been there watching over him; he must have been bricking himself. If Eddie had known she was there, he'd have bricked himself too. As he was now.

"And yes, I was there tonight too. Watched you arguing with the man in the long coat."

Eddie took a long slow blink. He'd known he was being watched! He tried to remain calm, and asked, "Why do you bite people?" His top lip curled in revulsion, and his stinging cheek began to swell.

She shrugged. "It's hard to dance with the devil on your back."

"Kind of fucking reply is that?"

"What, you my therapist now?"

Eddie said nothing – just stared, demanding an answer.

She sighed, and then her eyes sparkled. "It gives me a thrill. It makes me feel in charge." She sat back on him as though she'd satisfied his curiosity.

"It makes you feel superior?"

She glanced upwards, contemplating.

"You like to be in control of people." He studied her as she stared into him. "You like to be on top."

She smiled.

"It's not funny."

"It is funny when you try to psycho-analyse me. But I'm no subject in a fucking book, Eddie. I'm just me, and I—"

"You love to dominate people. You dominated John Tyler, you ruled and crushed him till he was just a shell with no self-esteem."

The smile vanished. "Bollocks."

Back when Eddie was eighteen, around the time he realised just how little of the world he actually knew, he'd had to grow a spine, and quickly. He finished with her because she bit him on the neck, right where the jugular was. At first, he'd found it very arousing... and back then, it didn't take Eddie long to get turned on. It was such a turn-on that he had her jeans undone in no time at all and was working them over her hips when she'd bitten deeper.

She bit hard enough to stop him dead, fingers paused, not daring to touch her again. He'd held his breath and his teenage fervour had perished pretty fucking quickly.

"I love to see someone in pain that's just the other side of ecstasy. Just before it gets unbearable." She paused and took a quivering breath, brown flakes dropping from her mouth. "But mostly I like to see them on the other side of unbearable."

He remembered how it had begun to hurt, the huge pressure in his chest, how it boiled and how he could do nothing as her teeth cut. How her jaws had clamped so tightly that he wanted to scream but couldn't. Daren't move in case she bit even deeper.

"There isn't no feeling like it. And when I'm pissed off, it's my drug."

And in the same way she'd bitten into his face minutes ago, it had a debilitating effect; it caused complete sublimation, like a paralysis so she could punch and kick. She'd enjoyed that too.

"Coke not in fashion any more?"

Her face changed again and inwardly Eddie groaned. Her eyes narrowed, the silly grin that almost made her endearing faded and vanished. The gun he'd nearly forgotten about reappeared; as he eyed it, she punched him on the jaw, right where she'd bitten through the bristly flesh. Eddie became her rodeo ride for a few minutes as he bucked against the pain.

And just as he'd done all those years ago, he grew a spine again.

There was only so much shit he could take, and Eddie had reached the point where he would rather she just get on and shoot him dead than carry on with this torture any longer. With that feeling came a new viewpoint, one that was prepared to take more risks.

She saw the change in him and recoiled, but it was already too late. Eddie was furious.

He whipped his hips upwards and she tipped forward, releasing his arms from under her knees. She flipped over his head without having time to curse, let alone hit him with the damned gun again. In a frantic scrabble that lasted no more than a few seconds, he positioned himself on his knees at her side and punched her as hard as he could in the side of the head. This was only the second time Eddie had ever hit a woman – and it had been the same woman both times. Both times it had been because she was killing him. He felt justified.

She hit the floor like a sack of shit and Eddie rocked back on his heels, seething at the pain in his knuckles. He rolled onto his backside, breathing hard like he'd just run to the car from the house. She lay there, her black hair a messy tousle over her head, her limbs limp and the gun glinting in the lamp-light a couple of yards away.

That's how he'd grown a spine, and that's how he'd managed to leave her all those years ago, reducing her to tears. He'd hit back – physically and metaphorically. Just as her dad had taught her, that's what life was about: a hitting competition to see who gives in first. And that was followed quickly by abandonment.

Chapter Five

British Standards

"YOU BASTARD!"

Eddie sat on the toilet and dabbed a ball of dampened tissue paper against his cheek. His face was throbbing, and he had a headache. He smiled down at her. "You started it."

She pulled at the kettle cable he'd used to tie her to the copper pipes running along the bathroom wall. She looked uncomfortable, lying half on her side, hands up in the air.

"It's because of you I can't have a coffee."

"Go fuck yourself."

It was three-thirty but Eddie didn't feel the least bit tired; amazing how adrenaline can keep you wide awake and ready to fight again. "How come you got together with John Tyler?" But it was obvious why she'd chosen to hook up with him: he was weak, timid, and she found controlling him easy. And enjoyable.

She ignored the question, stopped struggling and stared hatred up at him. "Can you slacken this off? My hands are turning blue."

"Would you like your gun back as well?"

She pulled at the cable some more, trying to kick him, and it was all Eddie could do to stop himself laughing at her – she looked like a petulant child, bottom lip out, the full works, including tears. She yanked at the cable, and the pipes bent as the veins in her neck stood out and she gritted her teeth.

"You're wasting your time," Eddie said. "I had the plumbing certified to British Standard Mad Cow Restraint Class 1."

"You won't be fucking laughing when I get free."

Another shudder skittered through him. But he shrugged, trying to appear nonchalant. Okay, he'd taken the gun away from her, but she was charged full of nervous energy and a fury that was pure and uninhibited. He kept away from the kicking feet, but he couldn't escape her eyes; they penetrated his to such a depth that he had to push the toilet paper harder into his cheek to break the spell.

It didn't take long for her to exhaust herself. She settled down, panting, recovering her strength, but her eyes remained on Eddie's throughout.

"Why did you write me the note?"

She smiled up at him. Eddie went cold again.

"I'm on a mission," she whispered. "I need to be free of you lot; all the men that have fucked me over all my life."

"What?"

"I'm a mess, Eddie. I am a mess because of you. And them others like you. It's not my fault."

"I've never met anyone as strong as you. You could achieve anything you wanted to achieve. You can manipulate people better than a politician! So how can you say it's not your fault? How can you take no responsibility for what you've become? Why is it always someone else's fault? That's the ultimate fucking cop-out." He didn't want to be so harsh, but it was true; it was always easier to blame someone else than deal with your own failures. "If you'd channelled that strength—"

"What do you know? You don't know me; you don't know what I've been—"

"I mean, that tells me you know you're... you're aware you have mental problems—"

She screamed, "I know that! Don't you fucking think I know that? That's what they told me, that I got problems, that I got to take this drug and that drug..." She stared at him still, eyes on fire. "But it's not a cure."

"So what is?"

Now it was her turn to look away as though she dare not share the secret. But she didn't need to speak the words.

She'd already written them down, once on paper, and now right across her face.

"Killing me won't set you free, Alex. Just like killing John Tyler when he tried to fight back didn't set you free."

She froze.

"I'm not stupid."

It seemed to hit her like a revelation, as though it had never even occurred to her that anyone else might work it out. The tears that came now were genuine; her whole body racked against them, but they won. She gave in and collapsed against her arms, pulling her legs up and curling into a ball.

Part of him wanted to reach out to her. It was only a small part. "I just don't understand it." He dabbed a bit more, speaking now more to himself than to her. "Why not just kill me? Why go through all that shit? Fist fighting, biting a fucking hole in my cheek!" He sighed. "You had the gun on me. Pop," he said, pointing a pistol finger. "Easy as that."

She didn't answer. Why face your failures when you can just cry over them instead?

It was too late for sympathy, though; there was nothing Eddie could do to help her. She'd never be free, and even if she killed him and all the other men who'd abandoned her, she'd forever walk among them, chained to them, and no amount of crying would redeem her. She knew that too.

It was three-forty. What was taking them so bloody long?

"But if you were intent on killing me," he continued, as though chatting casually over a pint in the local, "why send me a note telling me?"

Between sobs, her eyes turned to slits and she snarled, "To make you suffer." A long string of spittle glided to the tiled floor. "You haven't got no idea what it's like to get rejected by everyone you hook up with."

"Biting them probably didn't help."

"Shut up."

"Just a thought."

"Shut up!"

So far as Eddie could tell, there were three men she felt angry towards. Her dad, who'd kicked her out and left her to fend for herself because she was an embarrassment to him; John Tyler, who dared to call the police and enter the domestic violence playground; and Eddie. He was the first boyfriend she'd had who had thrown her away, but he felt no regret over it. Everyone hooks up with people and then parts from them as they find out they don't quite fit together any more.

It was just one of those life-learning things, and you had to get used to it. If you didn't... well if you didn't, you ended up tied to some bloke's plumbing, crying into the crook of your arm.

She glared at Eddie as though he was the enemy, the destroyer of her magnificent dream. Her days of domination were gone. She spat at him again.

Alex put her shoulder against the wall and pulled against the electrical cable. The pipes flexed further and the cable dug into her wrists so much that Eddie thought it would cut right through to the bone. He winced, and knew she was furious with him for not understanding. She screamed in a rage.

Over the coming years, Eddie would often wonder what would have happened next if he'd sympathised with her a bit more. Was there ever a chance he could have convinced her that life wasn't out to get her? It was just there to be lived, and then it ended.

There was an urgent knocking at the door. Alex didn't hear it; she was too busy growling and screaming to notice. Eddie slid out of the room and closed the door.

Chapter Six

We are the Champions

IT WAS ALMOST FOUR o'clock, and nowhere near dawn. In the dimming light from the Discovery headlamps, the reflective stripes of a police car glowed through the patterned glass in the front door. He sighed with relief. When he opened the door, though, the sigh dried up and a groan stamped it dead.

"Where is she?"

The smell of Brut slapped Eddie in the face. "Dibble. What the fuck are you doing here?" Dibble and Bashed-Crab stood under the porch keeping dry; behind them were two armed officers Eddie knew from the nick, Arry and Twiggy. He half nodded at them. They folded their arms and leaned against their ARV oblivious to the incessant rain. Behind it was Dibble's plain car.

"What happened to your face?" Dibble asked.

"Rough sex with an Alsatian." Eddie pulled the door against him so Dibble couldn't squeeze past. He didn't owe Alex anything, except a bill for a new door, but he didn't want to hand her over to this twat.

Dibble would see that she got a rough ride, because that's what made him the big man he believed himself to be. He liked to score off others' misery. For a man with no soul, being a cop was the perfect job – lots of misery within easy reach.

"Is she here or not? If you're wasting my time, I'll—"

"Shut up, you fuckwit. I'm off the clock so show me some respect or get this slammed in your face."

Arry and Twiggy smiled at each other.

Eddie looked over Dibble's shoulder at them and said, "You wanna come in and prove the weapon?" They stepped forward, slid past Dibble, and Eddie opened the door for them. "Over there," he said, "on the little table." He faced Dibble just as more shite fell out of the man's mouth.

"You reported a murder suspect in your house."

"I did. Let the armed officers take her into custody, and you can stay with me and write some lies in your pocket notebook."

"She's mine," he said through clenched teeth.

Well of course she was his; he wanted the collar, he wanted to make inspector before the year was out, and this was a good rung on the promotional ladder. "You shouldn't be here," Eddie said. "You'll compromise the case – you've been to the murder scene. It's called contamination."

"But you've been to the scene too!" Dibble looked at Bashed-Crab for support. How victorious he sounded.

"I didn't have a choice in her turning up at my house, did I? Think about it for a second and when the penny drops, you can piss off back to the nick and ridicule a shoplifter."

"I am duty Sergeant for this Division, so step aside, Mr Collins, and let me do my job before I pull you for obstruction."

As Eddie thought about it, he could hear Alex kicking and screaming in the bathroom behind him. She hadn't calmed down, by the sound of it, and he wondered if she knew they were here for her. Eddie stepped aside and let him in.

Dibble smiled. Eddie wanted to pull his face off and stuff it up his arse.

He licked his lips, eager to get her in cuffs and bundle her into the back of his car. He'd be singing We are the Champions on his way to the nick.

"What makes you think she's the dropout's killer?"

"He has bite marks on him. She bites," Eddie said, pointing to his cheek. "She's also his partner – there's a domestic violence case. His name's John Tyler. I photographed his injuries a few days ago and she admitted to hiding there while I did it."

"That it?"

"She's also covered in blood that I think will come back as his."

Dibble's eyes widened and he looked again at the bathroom door. The noise coming from in there was horrendous, but it didn't seem to put him off. He appeared more enthusiastic than ever, and he was struggling to control that sickly smile again. Perhaps he was hoping for a bit of a tussle, maybe get a bruise or two, maybe a fat lip that could turn him into an instant hero and grant him a commendation.

He made Eddie sick. "She's tied to the pipes with an electrical cable, so there's no need to be rough with her." Eddie stood before him, blocking his way to the bathroom door. "Why don't I go in first and see if I can calm her down a bit?"

"You tied her up!"

"You've seen my cheek!"

"So move out of the fucking way and let me do my job."

"She's distressed, cut her a break."

"Move."

"Don't take your anger at me out on her."

"Last time, Collins. Move."

There really was nothing more Eddie could say or do. Alex was in Dibble's hands now, at his mercy. He pitied her.

Dibble paused at the door for a moment, listening to the riot inside, and then his hand was on the doorknob. Eddie noticed the water trickling out from under the bathroom door, spreading into the carpet by his feet, and realised he could hear it spraying like a fountain in there, as if someone had turned on the shower.

It dawned on Eddie what had happened, and he tried to reach for Dibble as he burst into the bathroom. Eddie was right behind him, had wanted to say "stop", but that word was kind of redundant now.

The broken pipes spewed a fan of water against the wall beneath the sink and right out across the floor. Over the sink was a window, now wide open. The Venetian blind was a tattered mess across the sink, draping over its edge like metal fingers. Toothbrush and toothpaste, aftershave and razor crushed and scattered.

The first fronds of daylight leached through the naked glass, and a little part of Eddie – the part that hadn't received the death threat – cheered her escape. He hoped she got away from here. And most importantly for him and his burning cheek, he hoped she stayed the hell away.

Dibble spun on his heels and glared at Eddie; out of the corner of his eye he'd seen his commendation floating out of the bathroom like a paper boat. "You fucking idiot, Collins." He looked past Eddie and yelled to his sidekick, "After her, Chris! Make sure you get her!" Bashed-Crab and Twiggy ran out of the door; one went left, the other right. To Eddie he said, "I'm gonna have you for obstruction."

"What the hell did I do?"

He turned back into the bathroom. "Stood in my way while she escaped—"

She appeared from behind the open door.

She plunged a knife into Dibble's chest, right up to the handle.

Her ragged hair was wet through. Her hands were still bound together, and now Eddie knew why she'd tried to get her legs up to the pipes where her hands were tied: so she could slide the knife out of her boot.

She pulled the knife out of Dibble's chest and screamed into his face until all the strength left his legs and he just folded, collapsing to his knees on the wet floor like a man made of paper.

There he stayed for a second or two as though unsure which way to fall. Eddie was mesmerised – and not in a good way. His mouth was open, and he stared as Alex screamed her fury into the world, her face taut, anguished eyes closed behind a thousand folds of agony. Dibble's blood soaked her chest, and her own blood dripped from the wound on her wrist to disperse in the shallow torrent at her feet.

Dibble finally made up his mind and toppled backwards, splashing out onto the lounge floor, almost colliding with Eddie. And then he was still, staring up at the ceiling, never quite having made inspector.

She screamed and water gushed.

Then the screaming stopped, and there was just the sound of gushing water. She stood in silence, her face a twist of consternation, a mess of black makeup smeared into contortions. Her eyes were afraid. Terrified, because she was almost free.

Almost.

Water dripped from her clothes and from her face. Red water danced over white tiles, and more joined it in the lounge carpet, swirling from the dead man. She stared at him. "Dad," she whispered, "this is what it feels like to be abandoned."

And then she fixed her attention on Eddie.

Someone screamed, "Get down!"

Eddie didn't turn to ask questions. He just folded his legs and hit the deck as Arry discharged his Taser.

A pair of sparking wires, hair-thin, appeared over Eddie's head and Alex screamed afresh as the barbs pierced her skin. In a spasm of convulsions, she too hit the floor. The knife skittered away.

Eddie lay motionless on the wet carpet, rigid with fear and disorientated, not daring to move. He had never felt more unheroic in his life – and he wasn't ashamed to admit it. This whole evening, from arriving back at the office up to now, being a witness to a brutal stabbing, being bitten, almost being shot… it had been the scariest few hours of his life.

He felt the cold water against his ear, and looked at Dibble, the bloom of blood on his shirt, how it had run across his chest and down to be carried away in the water. But mostly Eddie saw the utter disbelief on his face: How could this happen to me? I'm invincible. I've been alive all my life. And soon I'll know what it's like… not to be. This wasn't in the s cript.

The copper, Arry, was at Eddie's side. "Okay, Eddie?"

He croaked, "Fucking wonderful." He snapped away from Dibble's shocked face and slowly got to his wet feet. Arry grabbed the knife and threw it from the bathroom out here into the lounge. He checked that she was okay, made sure she was breathing, pulled her away from the wall and placed her in the recovery position.

"She played me," Eddie said.

Arry nodded. "You were next, mate."

Eddie could imagine her panting, relieved one of them was dead, but still craving the final retribution – something only Eddie could give her. It was what she'd wanted all along. He imagined standing there, immobile, hypnotised – traumatised – by her black eyes and the streaked black makeup on her cheeks, a look on his face similar to the one Dibble's now wore: of disbelief and incomprehension as she sank the blade into Eddie's throat and twisted—

"Did she say what I thought she said?"

Eddie blinked, and dabbed fingertips at his neck. "She planned it all. All evening I've been wondering why she didn't just kill me. Now I know; she was waiting till her dad came for her." His cheek was on fire again.

"Crazy bitch."

Crazy maybe, but clever, and devious. "This carpet is ruined," he said, trying to fish a cigarette from his jacket pocket. When he did, it was wet through and disintegrated in his trembling fingers. He threw the packet away and looked up hopefully at Arry, nerves wrecked.

Arry shook his head, "I don't smoke."

"Fucking hell, what's wrong with you?" he shouted.

Twiggy and Bashed-Crab ran back inside. When they saw the scene, they gawped at one another, radios blaring all kinds of crap about an escaped prisoner, and about getting the helicopter up and getting the dogs out, and then... then it all got too much and Eddie screamed at them to shut the fuck up.

Eddie found himself in the kitchen, ready to make a strong coffee... only to discover that the kettle had no cable. And he'd run out of milk. And they'd shut off the water.

He closed his eyes at the injustice of it all.

"Two out of three ain't bad, Alex." He felt his neck again, unable to shake the image of her sticking that blade in, and still his fingers came away clean. Trembling, but clean. He gave a snorting laugh, but it couldn't hide how emotional he felt; he'd wriggled out of death one more time, and it almost made him cry. It wasn't like this in the movies. There, the hero picks himself up, refuses medical treatment, and goes on to chase down the last of the baddies to some upbeat musical score.

Well, it wasn't like that for him. He couldn't believe how lucky he'd been as he shuffled back into the lounge.

Dibble was still there, dead on the floor like a fat draught excluder, legs bent beneath him in the last, and best, limbo dance he'd ever do.

It protruded from his breast pocket like a handkerchief.

Eddie stared at it.

Around the room, commotion ruled. Bashed-Crab was asking if he should perform CPR, his voice unnaturally squeaky, and it looked as though Arry was considering whether to slap him out of his reverie. The other armed officer, Twiggy, scratched his groin as he spoke into his radio. Voices everywhere, radio comms everywhere, sirens growing louder. But this time it was all silence to Eddie.

He licked his dry lips and told his stupid legs to get him over to Dibble without buckling beneath him. Dutifully, they did. And Eddie stared down at him as those around him blurred into various degrees of shade, like ghosts drinking ectoplasm.

The handkerchief wasn't a handkerchief. He bent, took it from Dibble's pocket, and carefully unfolded it. It was almost identical to the one she'd sent to Eddie, complete with stab marks.

Your going to die tonight.

If only she'd used a dictionary!

He tried to dispel the nerves with a little humour, but it didn't work. It always had in the past; it was his thing, it was his soothing counsellor's voice, it was the pat on the back, the kick up the arse. It was everything he needed to shake the shit off and get back to normal.

Except this time it didn't work.

Why?

Eddie went cold. He had that spooky feeling of being watched – the one where he'd turn around, but no one would be taking a blind bit of notice. It happened to him just then.

He turned around and looked right into her eyes. They were wide, red-rimmed, inside a void of smudged black makeup. She came at him like a demon, a scream from her twisted mouth nailing him to the spot like he was imminent roadkill. Her talons were almost at his throat, ready to tear it out.

Out of the corner of his eye, he could see Bashed-Crab and the two coppers, their lives on pause, turning to see her rushing at him, powerless to prevent another death.

Eddie was captivated by her. It was nothing more than a reflex action that brought his arms up, probably in a defensive attempt. But the mind and body are marvellous when left alone to get on with things that happen too fast to contemplate.

Without conscious command, Eddie swung a fist at those beautifully horrific eyes and made contact. He threw the blow so hard that he spun right off balance and landed at Bashed-Crab's feet.

Alex spiralled through the air like a dead ballerina and landed in a moaning heap by the damaged front door. Within moments, she felt Arry's restraining knee as he fed her wrists into his cuffs.

Eddie was numb as she looked at him. Her eyes didn't blink. She smiled at him. "I'll never forget you, Eddie," she whispered. "Don't forget me, eh? Because one day, I'll be around the very next corner." She was hauled to her feet, her stare never leaving his.

"Just a minute," Eddie said. He stood and crossed the floor, carpet squelching under his feet. He stared into the chasms of her eyes. "Don't suppose you've got a spare cigarette?"

PART TWO

Now

Chapter Seven

Black Spikes and Bulldozers

BEHIND HER EYES A kaleidoscope of colours merged, light and dark, vibrant and dull, diffused, with scents dancing among them. Predominant was the Brut her dad wore, and the sickly smell of the Tia Maria her mother drank by the bottle.

Despite the headache, the anticipation was a buzz. She'd only ever messed about with cocaine and used a bit of brown every now and then, but this was the ultimate high. Killing someone, a bit of a taboo in today's polite society, was like looking forward to having sex with someone for the first time. The anticipation was killing her and had done for almost a year. She'd been planning this and modifying her behaviour for the last four months.

It would be good to get back into her old ways. She grinned.

I should push you down the stairs again. Knock some sense into you.

For each day of those four months, her parents' voices plagued her. They shouted, soothed, caressed, and beat her until she almost gave in and killed herself. But one thing prevented it: Eddie Collins, and the chance to meet him again. For that chance, she had learned to accept the voices, to live with them, even to ignore them for the most part. She'd taken note of the cognitive behavioural therapy and controlled her violent streak.

But the day had arrived, and the anticipation had gone. Bastard!

In its place was black noise and some kind of growling. It wasn't her tinnitus; that was high-pitched, whereas this was low and mean. She itched, she fidgeted, and she wanted to punch the walls and rip her nails out. She wanted to gouge her arms and her thighs. But most of all she wanted to scream. And scream.

But here and now, the important thing was convincing everyone that she heard white noise. That she felt calm, like she'd just had a spa session or a natter with her shrink. She felt sure that the shrink, Diane Warburton, would be pleased at Alex's serene mental state, headache or no.

And all this without the aid of prescription drugs, never mind illegal ones.

She hadn't taken a full dose of prezimoline for four months. She'd lessened it each week until, over the final few weeks, it finally relinquished its grasp on her, and she had been free of it completely, kissing the tiny tablets into someone else's mouth – there were always takers, and they always paid well. Of course, her empty mouth asked a thousand questions, not least of which was: If you're not a violent psychotic when you're off the drugs, were you ever a violent psychotic at all? That's what they called you – that's what they labelled you. Was it just a state of mind, after all? Just a state of mind to which you let them tie that neat little label? Everyone fucking loves a label, don't they?

Here's a label, and here's a tablet to combat it – we'll have ou normal in no time.

The noises outside her door grew louder. Either that, or the intensity of her thoughts was thinning, allowing real life to seep back inside like noxious gas, stinging her nostrils and tearing up her eyes. She swung her legs off the bed, stood up and brought the shaking under control, sniffing up the accumulating mucus in her nose before it became blocked, nostrils flaring, fingers tingling. She reached for the Lucozade bottle as the hatch in the door slid open. A man stared in, and she smiled at him. Friendliest smile she could muster.

The hatch closed, and the door swung open. "Alex," he said, taking a step inside. "You ready?"

Even though her head was pounding, she nodded, and the buzz crept back up her spine, bringing with it sweating fingertips and a watering mouth. She kept her control and ambled towards him, allowed him to search her before he stepped back into the corridor. He, and the guy by his side, stood back and let her exit the room. The noise of other inmates, of someone's radio playing "Rocket Man", of someone sobbing, of someone yelling "get the fuck off me!" bounced off her like a ping-pong ball off a bat. She barely even noticed. But the heat slowly grew in her chest.

"How you feeling today, Alex?"

Laughter inside her head.

"Good. I'm good." The headache was getting too much to bear, and had brought with it a feeling she didn't like. It was spiky, it was black, and it was growing. It was like the old Alex was coming back, like it could see freedom at the end of a short brick tunnel and wanted to fuck her over once and for all. She wanted to rip this guy's face off.

"You get through today," he said, closing and locking her room door behind them, "and you move up." He looked at her, into her. "You get that, don't you, Alex? You move up to the next level. More privileges, more... of everything."

She smiled, met his eyes. "I get it. I'm ready." She looked away, afraid the black spikes were beginning to show.

"Shall we?"

They walked along the corridor, the man with the keys to her right, his companion behind them. Nice steady pace. She swung the Lucozade between her thumb and index finger like she was taking a stroll with her man along the seafront, not a care in the fucking world; back and forth it swung, back and forth.

But the headache was a bulldozer. The spikes grew longer and blacker.

They moved along through the intermittent shadows between the tiny, deep-set windows, like arrow slits in a castle wall. It seemed to grow darker the deeper they went. The wet mouth had turned dry and the sweating fingertips trembled. Alex had set about trying to conjure up her self-belief when the men stopped. She sighed, closed her eyes for a moment.

He smiled at her. "Just be yourself," he said. "You made some good progress." He touched her arm gently, just a couple of fingertips. "I know you can do this. Have faith, girl, okay?" His smile intensified, and his eyes peered deeper until she was uncomfortable. "I'll be keeping my fingers crossed, and I can't wait to hear—"

"Doc's here, Chris."

Chris's fingertips had prodded her right on the tip of a spike. She wanted to scream and she wanted to smash this fucker's face against the wall and stamp on him. How tough could it be to pretend you were just a mild breeze on a summer's day when inside you were a tornado ripping the world to bits?

Easy does it.

"I'm thirsty."

He stood back to look at her like a proud father waving his daughter off to university and nodded at the Lucozade bottle. "Take a drink."

"Alex, great to see you." Dr Warburton drew a finger of balm across her lips, and then rattled keys in the door to her right, her lanyard swinging as she turned to greet the ensemble. It was the same room they'd been in every week for eight months. The door was painted blue and had a sign on it – one of those that slides between Vacant and Engaged. Above it was a No Smoking sign, and above that was the room number: C210.

Vacant. Engaged.

C210. Here again. The bottle of Lucozade was almost totally red like a bottle of Tia Maria, or like someone had dropped blood into it; it swirled like... like when they'd washed everything away after the birth. She could feel the headache winding up again. They were all laughing at her too.

Oh God, she couldn't do this after all. Her legs trembled, and her knees loosened to the point of coming undone. It was all going to go horribly wrong. She was going to—

"Ready, Alex?"

She snapped out of it, and her breath shivered out through trembling lips. Mrs Diane Warburton, the shrink they all called Doc, was holding open the door. Chris ushered her inside. The Lucozade wasn't red any more. Was it ever?

Alone inside the room, she heard them whispering in the corridor outside. She swallowed. This was the crucial point – would they come in too, the men? Did they trust Alex alone with the Doc? Alex, who had been a raging fucking psycho only a year ago? Why would they? Hell, she wouldn't trust her. Her heart beat so hard that she thought her headache would surely kill her.

Silence. Dim light, like being awake before dawn.

The door closed, the lights came on, and Doc Warburton stared at her, a smile on her greasy lips, and her hand still on the doorknob. Assessing. This is what a dynamic risk assessment looked like, she thought. But it must be good news; if they had decided to keep her here on High Dependency and not "promote" her, Doc would have a fucking shield and two guards.

No headache. No spikes. Euphoria was within reach. Alex arched her eyebrows, widened her eyes ever so slightly and parted her lips in a genuine smile, created from a distant memory and used on occasions like this one. "How are you, Mrs Warburton? It's good to see you again."

Doc Warburton responded with a smile of her own and took her hand away from the doorknob. "Shall we sit?" Doc peered up at her. "Dr Ramsay will be along shortly." She checked her watch. "He's running a bit late. Stuck in another assessment meeting."

Alex nodded, and stood fidgeting. Ramsay, her Primary Doctor, was a twat. She wanted him here now, this instant, or not at all. She didn't want him arriving when things were in full swing, breaking her rhythm. She blinked, cursing her luck, wondering about postponing.

There was a plastic jug of water on the table, with two plastic glasses and a few napkins. Doc put the file on the desk, poured them a water each. Alex sat, quenched her thirst and refilled the glass.

"Didn't know you liked Lucozade."

"Right now I prefer water." Alex looked at her. "That's... that's okay, isn't it?"

Warburton laughed. "Sure it is." She pushed away the file, folded her arms, and said, "If this goes well, it'll be your last day here. You could wake up tomorrow in Medium Dependency. Sound good?"

Alex nodded, replicating the earlier smile for a moment. She didn't believe Doc of course – didn't believe anything anyone told her. Safer not to. But she couldn't show her disbelief, for fear of being labelled "not cured". A big red stamp hit the file. DENIED. Alex swallowed.

"There's no need to be afraid. Dr Ramsay and I have been watching you make good progress recently. I've seen you develop with me, with other people. I'm impressed that you're able to control the more extreme tendencies you used to suffer from. And I'm pretty sure that's not all down to the drugs, either." She sat forward. "Are you employing the techniques we talked about last time?"

"Yes."

"And how often do the... others appear in your thoughts every day?"

I'm here now. Tell her, Alex. Dare you.

Alex shrugged. "A couple." She looked up. "I'm handling him. He don't get too deep any more. I don't let him in." She looked away as her eyes flooded.

Lying little bitch! You can't deny me, Alex. You'll never stop e.

Laughing again.

Be careful, Alex. She's lying to you. You do know that, right?

Leave her alone!

"The therapy is playing a big part. But you're a very strong woman. And I know you have the power to do whatever you want."

Lying bitch!

Alex took more water, eventually allowing her eyes back to Doc. Her breath was getting hotter.

"What do you want, Alex?"

"Sorry?"

"What do you want?" Warburton held her palms open. "Really, what do you want to achieve?"

Alex's fingers fidgeted and she wondered if Doc knew what she had planned; wondered if this question was a stab in the dark, a fishing trip maybe, trying to trick her into giving away her secret. Or was it a genuine question, focusing only on the short term? "I want to get better," she said. Safe answers, well-rehearsed, were the best right now.

Get on with it. Ramsay is coming!

"I know that. But what's your objective?"

"I'm not sure what you mean."

Hurry!

Warburton smiled reassuringly. "Spit it out. What's your objective?"

Alex looked away, sure her eyes would betray her.

No smile now. "Tell me!"

"To be free." That was not a safe answer. That was a dangerous answer. She could never be free. She had murders to pay for. If ever she got better, they'd ship her out into a regular jail to run out her sentence. And that sentence would only end the day she died. But to stay here, in the High Dependency ward, wasn't conducive to freedom – Christ, it wasn't even conducive to mental well-being, fuck knows how they expected people to get better. It was fucking horrible here. It was killing her, suffocating her... This was her one chance. She dug her nails into her leg.

Quick, before Ramsay—

"Free?"

"I mean..." her voice was shaking. "I mean, I want to be free of this mental condition." Back on track, surely.

Fucked it, girl!

Warburton leaned back in her chair; she folded her arms, crossed her legs.

Alex was no demon when it came to psychology, but she knew about barriers, and she knew when someone was putting them up. But it didn't make sense, this was her shrink; this was her analyst, her ticket into another part of the hospital. She was her friend.

No, no, no, she's not your friend. This woman is an analyst, that's all, measuring you up for prison. Do it!

Don't listen to him!

Shut it, woman!

Alex's heart kicked up a gear. Suddenly the buzz was back, the tingling. Suddenly it became clear: the barriers, the hollow smile. She knew!

Warburton said, "You truly are fucking remarkable. You've successfully weaned yourself off the medication and remained mentally compliant." She unfolded her arms and leaned forward, jabbing her in the chest with a pointed finger. "Were you ever psychotic, Alex? Was it an elaborate game you dreamed up to avoid prison?"

Alex's eyes were wide, and her chin quivered. She couldn't believe what she was hearing. "Are you teasing me?"

Warburton glanced up from the file she was reading, hands on the desk before her. "Sorry. What was that?" Gentle smile on her greasy lips.

Alex blinked, brushed a hand over her chest where she'd felt the finger prodding her. "I thought you said... I thought you said something."

"I did. Your recovery has been remarkable. I'm very impressed. The whole team is impressed. Delighted. So long as you maintain your current dose, and continue with the CBT, I don't see any obstacle to your progression." The smile was almost exuberant. "I'm recommending you move up to Medium Dependency. How does that sound?"

Alex closed her eyes and tried to concentrate on her breathing. This was no fucking time for her mind to play games. No, it was time to act.

"You okay?"

Do it!

Alex opened her eyes.

Chapter Eight

The Cactus

EDDIE LET THE MOTOR idle as he stared with hatred at the glass monstrosity.

In the background, Pink Floyd took the edge off his hatred but failed to eradicate it. The building in which he worked was a glass block with a concrete heart and it made him want to hurl every time he saw it. It was like living inside the world's biggest Rubik's Cube. And no matter how hard he tried, he couldn't solve its puzzle.

He snorted, almost amused by his own brilliance. And then he stopped smiling. He was far from brilliant. If he was anything approaching brilliant, he wouldn't be working here at all. It was a shithole, and it robbed people of a third of their lives and gave nothing back in return. And not only that, it represented the most incalculable torture of them all: monotony. Nothing killed a mind quicker than… nothing.

Time measures change; if there's no change, then there's no time. This would be the place where time ended, he thought. The Major Crime Unit in Leeds was where Eddie had come to die for the last four or five years, and each day the building consumed a little bit more of him.

He fucking hated this place.

He lit another cigarette, quietened the nerves in his stomach and shut off the motor. A minute later, he was inside the foyer taking a deep breath in preparation for another day in hell. He acknowledged the rubber plants to his right, and then aimed at the double wooden doors straight ahead. His eyes never strayed left towards the reception desk and... No, his eyes never wavered, they never even glanced at... Eddie stopped; he turned left and took her glory on board.

"Morning, Miss Moneypenny."

"When are you going to start calling me Maggie?" She was smiling at him. She usually smiled at him, but this morning, it was more than a smile – it was like having another sun in the sky, another dopamine injection. "Hi, Eddie."

Eddie looked down at his fly. Nope, nothing wrong there. She was still smiling. "Have you got your furry knickers on again, Moneypenny?"

She giggled like an idiot, and that stalled Eddie's smile. The second sun exploded and when she giggled again, it was like someone had sucked out the dopamine and spat it onto the floor. He felt cold, deflated.

"What?"

"Nothing." She had the temerity to giggle again, and he wanted to tell her to stop, that the silly giggle was spoiling it.

Eddie closed his eyes, sighed again, and punched through the doors. "Another day in purgatory." And the worst part was that he hadn't even copped a swift glance down Moneypenny's top. Maybe next time.

He trudged up the stairs, lost in thought, Glorious tits but an IQ you could measure in single digits. Eddie smiled as he crested the steps, and then felt guilty. "Heart of gold, though," he whispered.

"Talking to yourself again, Eddie?" Eddie's Head of Department, Victor Weismann, rounded the corner at the top of the stairs and hurried down past Eddie, briefcase flapping in the wind.

"The only way to get intelligent conversation around here."

"See you around."

Eddie watched him approach the double doors. "Where are you off to?"

The doors closed behind him.

"Okay, bye. Have fun."

Eddie crept into the CSI office, being careful to close the doors slowly so the creaking hinges wouldn't give him away. From around the corner and further into the office, he could hear a noise. A grunting sound. What he saw caused his mouth to fall open and his eyes to clamp shut.

He opened one eye tentatively and held his breath as he walked slowly up the office. On the wall-mounted TV at the top of the office was a female fitness instructor doing the splits, and it looked like she was praying. On Sid's desk was a Bluetooth speaker; from it leaked a sound like woodland birds with a trickling water backdrop.

Eddie was grinning so wide he was sure Sid would hear his lips squeaking over his back teeth.

Sid wore a bright red leotard, with white ankle warmers, and a pair of black plimsolls. He wore a matching red sweat band and wrist bands, and he had almost achieved the splits. He was grunting, jerking up and down, trying to get his arse flat on the floor, and trembling like a dog taking a shit.

Inside, Eddie was howling with laughter. The sounds, the Lycra-clad woman on TV, and Sid with his arms outstretched and his arse ten inches from the carpet was almost too much. But then he saw it. On a shelf to his left: a cactus. A fat, spiky cactus. This was going to be the highlight of Eddie's day and he almost burst trying to keep the laughter silent. But so far, so good. He held the cactus before him and was creeping forward on his knees, ready to deposit Sid's surprise.

He almost screamed when the office phone rang. He trembled, sliding the cactus the last few inches.

Sid groaned. "Oh phooey! So close. One last go."

Eddie drew back, wondering if he'd gone a little too far, but decided this was too good a jest to ruin by engaging a conscience. The phone continued to ring.

Sid gave it one last go. He put his arms above his head and jerked them down, creating the momentum he needed to force a touch-down.

Eddie held his breath as Sid's arse contacted the spikes like a submarine hitting a mine. There was a millisecond when nothing happened. Sid came to a halt still four inches from the carpet, and then he let out a scream loud enough and high-pitched enough to be heard out in the main CID office.

Eddie collapsed to the floor, slapping his leg, tears rolling down his cheeks and laughing so hard it gave him a coughing fit.

Sid leapt up, screaming and slapping his backside frantically until he saw Eddie – and saw the cactus.

From tear-filled eyes, Eddie peered at him, at his pointing finger, and then screamed with laughter as Sid quietly said, "That was not in the slightest bit funny, Eddie."

Ten minutes later, when Eddie had shooed Benson and a half a dozen concerned people out of the office – and when, by means of an apology, he'd fixed him a drink of Earl Grey in his best china cup together with a side plate laden with Garibaldis and fig rolls, Eddie was able to calm Sid down.

Now dressed in spray-on black jeans, rainbow Doc Martens, and a loose, lacy top that looked like a cast off from a performance of Pirates of Penzance, with his arms jangling because of all the bangles he wore, Sid was staring down his nose as Eddie's smirk continued to flourish.

"You must promise me that you won't do anything like that again, Eddie."

"I won't." Eddie held his breath, screwed his eyes shut and wished he'd been filming it.

"That could have caused serious damage to my nether regions. Not to mention the poor cactus. I've had her five years." Sid bit his bottom lip, and sighed. "I was so close, too."

With a tremble still in his voice, Eddie asked, "Why don't you use a gym? I mean, I would never use a gym because they're full of prima donnas and pricks who love themselves too much, but you..."

Sid cocked an eyebrow. "That's why I don't use them. And because people make fun of me."

Eddie's smirk withered. He started to say that he was only having a laugh, that it wasn't meant as bullying, that he simply couldn't resist... but he couldn't even start the sentence let alone finish it. Instead he said, "I'm sorry. I didn't think—"

"It's okay." Sid smiled, his friendly warmth not dimmed at all. "I can see it was very funny indeed." He sipped his tea, then dunked a garibaldi. "So what have you got planned for tonight?"

"Tonight?" asked Eddie. "What's special about tonight?"

"Today. I meant what have you got planned for today?"

Eddie was confused. "Erm... are you saying I need to attend to the overtime sheets again?"

Sid nodded solemnly. "That's exactly what I meant, yes."

"Are you taking something?"

"Huh?"

"You're weird. I mean you're always weird, but today you're very weird."

Chapter Nine

Impressing Doctor Warburton

ALEX STOOD AND MADE to pour herself more water from the jug. She was sure Ramsay must be on his way. Her fingers tingled.

Warburton watched her closely, her attention coming away from the form she was filling in and landing on Alex. Entirely on her.

Alex picked up the jug and smashed it into the woman's face. Water sprayed everywhere. The jug shattered.

Before she could even raise her hands, before she could even let out a scream, Alex swung an elbow and broke her nose. The swing was violent enough to spill Warburton from her chair. She swivelled as she went down; like a cat, she landed on all fours, but before she could start wailing, Alex kicked her in the ribs. Warburton rolled onto her back, hands blindly outstretched in a blanket of feeble protection.

Alex was on her, punching, biting, slapping as Warburton's hands waved before her in some weak attempt at fending off the attack. There would be no fending off today. Blood splashed across the blue carpet tiles and eventually Warburton's hands fell to her sides. Her breathing was fast and shallow, and from somewhere Alex thought she heard a moan.

There was a broken tooth nestled in the bloody crease of Warburton's chin. Alex listened closer, brought her ear to Warburton's cheek. In the subdued light down here, she could see the golden stud earring glinting, could see the fine golden chain holding the St Christopher; she could see Doc's eyelashes fluttering, getting brief glimpses of the whites of her eyes. She drew back, and Doc's mouth contorted as a scream almost made it out into the room. The broken tooth slid off her face.

Alex put her hand over Warburton's greasy mouth and bit into her nose. The fluttering eyelashes gave way to open eyes, panicking, already swelling. Alex's teeth made it down to the bone but the blood made it slick. Warburton yanked her head away and tried to scream, but Alex punched her again. Water droplets flew from Warburton's eyes. Alex kissed her before she could start sobbing. Her mouth covered the dying woman's, and she straddled her, bringing her weight down on the broken ribs, feeling them grating beneath her backside.

Warburton's head thrashed around, but Alex just laughed. Unable to sustain the kiss for long, she pulled back as a pathetic squeal riding a glut of bubble-filled blood gushed out across her cheek. Warburton seemed to realise how close she was to the end, because despite the busted ribs and the torn nose, she bucked, thrashed her arms, and spat out more teeth and blood.

Alex was entranced as she took one more choking breath and stopped. Her arms fell to the carpet, the throbbing in her neck stopped, and the St Christopher, stuck to her skin by a sheen of blood, became still. Alex bounced on her and laughed as more blood belched from the mouth and nose.

"Are you still impressed, Doctor Warburton? I did well, huh?"

As she reached forward and unclasped the St Christopher and placed it carefully on the carpet, followed by the golden stud earrings, she felt the rush of adrenaline slowing, felt it cooling, and the headache crept very slowly in from around a secret corner, seeping in until it sat proud, front and centre like a figurehead on a galleon.

It was time to get the hell out of here.

Chapter Ten

Lucozade

THIS WAS NO TIME to sit and relax, but that's exactly what she did. If there had been a packet of cigarettes around, she would have smoked one, maybe even two. It was almost ritualistic that once the adrenaline surge had been washed out of the bloodstream, melancholy was likely to fill the void. And if melancholy was unavailable, then retrospection might pop along instead. This whole killing thing, she thought again, was reminiscent of sex. Lying back with a smoke after banging one's brains out was the only way to come back down.

There were no cigarettes. But it didn't stop Alex from taking a moment, because not to do so might invite disaster at this midway stage.

Chill, look around you, prepare for the next phase of the plan.

Don't you feel guilty? I mean, you kill everyone who comes i nto your life, so—

Says you!

"Both of you, shut up."

The next phase involved getting naked. It involved swapping clothes with Warburton there. It didn't matter that Doc was a size or two larger than she was; what mattered was sticking to the fucking plan. It had never occurred to Alex, even through the months of planning, just how hard it would be to strip a dead body of its clothes. But even that wasn't as difficult as dressing it again.

By the time Alex was fully dressed in Warburton's baggy clothes, her dark hair was wet with sweat. She sat to catch her breath, the Doc's jewellery arranged before her on the table. She took a minute to clasp the St Christopher around her neck, and forced the stud earring through holes that had healed up a long time ago. The final adornments were a nice wedding and engagement ring. They looked good on her – they looked great, actually, and it would have been too easy to sit here and imagine wearing them through more conventional methods.

Marriage was something she'd contemplated before. There had been a man – John Tyler, his name was – who was okay, he was subservient to her, and she always liked that in a man. But before she could make him propose, he'd betrayed her, and she'd been forced to kill him.

Alex pulled her gaze away from the rings and their sparkling diamonds, and instead looked at the cooling body of her doctor, at her face – the swollen eyes, the broken nose, the blood that had run down her cheek and into her hair, the broken nails, two of them, no, three of them, in the carpet tiles not too far away. She grinned. What a way to go.

She reached into Doc's pocket and took out the lip balm. It was a tiny round tin, and the lid popped off easily. She smeared a trace of balm into the cracks and tasted strawberry. "Thanks, Doc," she whispered.

The whole experience had been wonderful. And she closed her eyes, replaying it all frame by frame. The best bit was the shock on her face. It was always the best bit; how they thought that previous existence was some kind of guarantee of future existence. The nineteen or twenty thousand times they had woken up on a new day somehow suggested they would wake up again tomorrow, only to find out that this morning was their last. And they didn't even know it. Complete surprise. Shock of shocks.

Get a fucking move on!

And Alex was laughing all over again as she tied up her hair in a tight bun and arranged Doc's lanyard around her neck before reaching for the Lucozade bottle.

It was almost like a ceremony. Almost. Alex stood, cleared her throat as though about to deliver a eulogy. She flicked off the lid of the Lucozade bottle and squirted the liquid into Warburton's face, relaxing her hand once or twice to allow air back into the bottle before finishing the job off, emptying it.

The air turned pungent. The stench was strong enough to make her eyes water, and for a moment she thought she was going to gag. An aroma like nail varnish remover exploded through the air, but Alex didn't move away; she wanted to stand here, wanted to watch the acid do its work.

It wasn't like in the films. There was no smoking, no hissing. It was quiet and dignified, how her face slipped away like a silent mudslide, or like the ice cream sliding off a cone on a hot day. Splat onto the floor. And when the acid hit the carpet tiles, it melted those too and they shrivelled up, creeping away from the pool as it advanced. One of Warburton's eyeballs popped and clear liquid spurted onto her blood-red skull.

It was fascinating. Alex was drawn to it, mesmerised by it, so much so that she didn't even hear the key turning in the lock.

Chapter Eleven

The Visitor

RAMSAY WAS HERE. HAD to be.

Alex dropped the Lucozade bottle and stood staring as the doorknob turned and the door swung inwards. She found herself unable to move.

Maybe it wouldn't be him, maybe Chris had come to check up on them, or one of the other members of staff had been alerted by the noise. Either way, she would be in trouble. He'd peer around the door, see what she'd done and simply lock her in again. Disaster – end of escape plan number one.

This must have been what they were planning in the corridor after they let her in here; coming back after fifteen or twenty minutes just to make sure nothing bad was going on. Of course, they'd said, nothing bad would be happening, Ramsay would be here before long, and anyway, all Alex had to do was smile and give normal answers to a few easy questions, and she'd be "promoted" the next day – there wouldn't be any trouble. It was just a precaution.

But now the fifteen or twenty minutes was up, and they'd come back to make sure neither of them was dangling by a rope. Ha! Even the notion was ridiculous.

It could have been Ramsay, but it wasn't. The door groaned open. In the frame stood Chester, one of the staff members. He was big, and he was muscular – if she didn't know him, she'd be scared. She licked her lips, getting ready to fight. He didn't move. He stood watching her, and she found she was breathing hard – not from exertion, but from a mild case of sudden paranoia. The light dimmed and the colours darkened. Alex was getting angry. She saw his eyes looking first at her, then down to the Doc, back to her. He came in, closed the door, and locked it.

"You can smell that shit down the corridor."

The darkness eased. Alex breathed out and the tension left, taking with it the rigidity that had clung to her. She shrugged and made sure she'd forgotten nothing.

"You said you wouldn't use it unless you had to."

She held out her hand. "Wig?"

Chester pulled it out of his back pocket, rattling the key chain on his belt, and tossed it to her.

"I thought Chris and his pal were going to stay with her. I nearly had a fit."

Chester shook his head. "I put a call out for assistance in D Wing."

She considered him, then nodded her appreciation. "We have to go. Ramsay will be here soon."

"Why did you use the acid?"

She paused. "I had to."

He stepped further into the room, an air of caution surrounding him as though he were approaching a feral animal he'd once petted; his eyes stayed on Alex and took quick glances at Warburton. When he was around Alex's side of the body, he took longer glances at it, which merged until eventually he was gawping at it.

When he faced Alex again, his eyes were watering and he was pale; she wasn't sure if it was the effects of the acid or because of the mess that stared back at him from the carpet.

"That is fucking gross." His throat was tight, the voice barely a squeak. "Alex," he said, "did you really have—"

She adjusted the wig until it felt comfortable. It wasn't exactly the Doc's shade, but it would do. "The longer we stay in here discussing my methods, the more chance we have of getting caught."

"I know, but—"

"Don't fold on me now, Chester. Get us the hell out of here."

He stared again at the melting skin.

"If you don't move now, I swear I'll rub your fucking face in it."

No reply.

"Chester!"

He gasped, and it seemed to shock him back awake. "No need to shout." He was at the door with Alex right behind him. He unlocked it, then turned to her. "The files. Get the files."

Moments later, he'd locked the door and they were hurrying down the corridor, trying to make it look like a casual stroll. "We have to be out of High Dependency and off the wing before the alarm sounds. If we're not" – he smiled across at her, maintaining their charade – "we'll be trapped."

She laughed. "So walk fucking faster."

Between High Dependency and the end of the ward there were four barred gates to get through; they did, without encountering a single other member of staff. There were patients engaged in games of table tennis or pool in the centre of the hub – which was covered well by CCTV – while others conversed by open cell doors. She followed as Chester took a left through an unmarked door and jogged up two flights of stone steps, his key chain jangling, and out onto another floor that was unused.

"Where the hell are we?"

"Ssshhh." He walked quickly. "If we'd stayed down there, we'd have passed one of the staff rooms, and" – he looked at his watch – "it's busy as hell this time of day. Shift change. Up here is vacant—"

"Then why do we have to be quiet?"

"Because this is where staff come to smoke, or to use one of the empty rooms."

"Define 'use'."

He gave her nothing more than a derisory glance and hurried along to the end where there was a set of double doors with a locked gate across them. "Through there," he whispered. "And then down the stairs. Home free." He was panting now; despite his physique, he was as out of shape as Alex was. At the foot of the stairs she was about to ask for a breather – there would be nothing worse than crossing a courtyard or bumping into more staff members if they were both out of breath.

But she was wrong. Just as Chester unlocked the door and opened it, something worse did happen.

It was like something from a WW2 movie. Claxons and horns whooping and wailing, wall-mounted red lights flashing. Alex almost screamed; she expected to see Juniper Hill's equivalent of a SWAT team storming the place any second.

It was cold out here, and the grey skies were preparing to lighten their load.

They were in the main courtyard of gravel and concrete, having just made it out of C Wing and the High Dependency Unit. Ahead of them, some 150 yards away, was a thirty-foot wire mesh fence with iron doors set in it every fifty yards or so. Beyond it was another large complex of Victorian buildings with more modern ones tacked to the far side. And beyond that was more thirty-foot fencing. And then... freedom.

Chester's face was red, his chest heaving, and Alex saw something in his eyes that she really didn't like: panic. "You okay?"

He nodded, head snapping left and right.

She saw officers appearing in doorways, a disorderly confusion among them. And then Chester's radio beeped, and he held his breath as he listened to the broadcast through his earpiece.

The noise was phenomenal, and Alex put her hands over her ears, keeping the file to her right ear as they passed a group of staff officers running towards C Wing; first just a handful, and then the rest of them, like sheep following a leader – maybe thirty or forty in all. Chester was pulling her along. "What's happening?" she shouted.

"They've locked the wing down." He cocked a thumb. "They think there's a dead patient back there."

"Ramsay finally showed up." She followed him at a more sedate pace towards one of the gates, still trying to behave in a casual manner while realising everyone else was on high alert; Alex clutching the files to her chest, and Chester swinging the keys and chatting to her like he was her escort, or a tour guide. "Won't they be looking for Warburton too?"

"You'd assume so, but no mention. Maybe they haven't put two and two together yet, I don't know. But this is good. This is a distraction; it'll help us get out."

There was a controlled panic. No one knew who they were looking for because no one knew what was going on – they had found a dead body, that was all.

The distraction was intense, and not just outside in the courtyard, but inside too; it meant that everyone who was supposed to be vigilant, and watchful for any skulking inmate trying to escape, paid little attention to a guard and a member of staff hurrying out of the rain, and stepping out the way of the rushing officers. They were quick to release controlled doors so they could get back to the gossip coming over the air, so they could get back to monitoring CCTV cameras up the halls and corridors of C Wing, blind to the possibility of psychopathic murderers and their greedy abettors walking right past them and out of the complex in shirt sleeves when it was raining out, and when the wind was picking up.

Their constant chatter, their unhurried stride, and their air of belonging got them all the way through the modern part of the building, into the Victorian complex, and through the air lock. But at the very last door before untainted fresh air, someone stopped them.

"Hey! Hey, you!"

Alex stopped dead. Her wide eyes nearly fell out of her face, and she was reminded for an instant of Doc's eye popping as the acid munched away at it. And her clattering heart, nearly as loud as the incessant klaxons, almost made her keel over. Next to her, Chester was similarly motionless.

It would be easy to see how suspicious they both looked, for any normal person stopped in such a manner would have turned and made eye contact. But these two stood there, not knowing what the hell to do.

"Oi!" the voice shouted again. It was an electronic voice, thrown at them through a loudspeaker above the Perspex window to their right.

Alex turned her creaking neck. A woman with greasy black hair was at the window, beckoning her over with a single curled finger.

On legs that felt as foreign to her as the clothes she wore, she crossed the foyer, and Chester stood by her side, the tremble in his whole body difficult to miss.

Alex leaned forward to the microphone set into the Perspex. She cleared her throat and glared at Greasy-Hair. "'Oi'?"

Greasy-Hair's face became apologetic.

"Is that how you speak to people around here?"

Greasy snarled, her hand hovering over a large red button. She squinted, a grin taking up the full lower half of her face. And she began to laugh. Alex was suddenly afraid. Behind her, Chester stood with his thumbs hooked into his trousers, head lolling, laughter roaring through his mouth. And back to Greasy with her hand over the button, and all of her colleagues gathered around her, laughing.

They all stared at Alex.

Greasy pushed the red button and all the door bolts shot home and everything went quiet. "They're coming for you," Greasy said, "and when they get you, they're gonna pull you apart limb from limb and pour acid down your neck."

Alex screamed, "No!"

"Sorry, love," the loudspeaker said. "But you can't take files off site."

"What?"

She pointed to the file, wet around the edges. "That stays here. Ma'am."

Alex gritted her teeth. "I'm just nipping to the car for..."

Greasy was shaking her head. "Pass it through the tunnel. You can collect it when you come back." There was a question forming on her face. She was just about to ask it when Alex yelled.

"I don't believe this!" She pulled open a metal flap, threw the file inside and slammed it closed again. "There," she shouted. "Happy now?"

Greasy, question forgotten, mustered her best PR smile, glanced down at Alex's lanyard. "Thank you, Doctor Warburton. It'll be here when you return."

Alex turned away from her but the intercom sounded again. "Just one more thing."

Alex swallowed, and faced her again.

Greasy laid a finger on the collar of her shirt and nodded, "You've got blood. There," she tapped her collar, "on your blouse."

Alex feigned embarrassment. "Nosebleed," she said.

Greasy eyed her for a moment, then nodded.

When Alex, followed swiftly by Chester, emerged from the cold, dark vestibule, into the cold, darkening day outside Juniper Hill, she was laughing almost uncontrollably, and still shaking.

"Come on, let's get you safe."

Chapter Twelve

Juniper Hill

JUNIPER HILL STARED BACK at CSI Eddie Collins and filled him with a cold dread – the kind of feeling you get in mid-winter as you clench your jaw to stop your teeth from chattering because there is no warmth to be found anywhere in the entire world, and never will be again. It was a building he summed up in one word: oppressive. Scary, if you wanted a second bite.

Eddie turned the van's engine off and lit a cigarette, put his foot up on the dashboard as he waited for CID to arrive, and pondered his fascination with buildings. How he could hate them so based on their outside appearance. He had exactly the same problem with people. Sometimes.

You can only trust yourself.

The building, Juniper Hill, was a Victorian complex that just screamed for demolition. Actually, Eddie thought, it just screamed, full stop. He shivered, longing to hear his phone ring, longing to hear them say there'd been a mistake, there wasn't a dead woman in there after all, or "there are complications, let's leave it until later". Anything, really; he didn't care what it was, he just didn't want to go in there.

Someone banged on the van window, and he jumped. He turned sharply and saw Benson grinning like a prick. The window glided open. "It wasn't funny the first two-hundred times you did that. And it's not fucking funny now!"

Benson was still grinning. "You know what your trouble is, don't you?"

"Yes. I work with an imbecile."

"No sense of humour. None at all. It's like you're dead inside."

"Well if you do that again, you'll be dead inside. Got it?" He wound the window back up and resumed smoking his cigarette, oblivious to Benson's huffing and tutting, ignoring the exaggerated arm movement as the DI glanced at his watch.

Benson eventually gave up his attempts at subtlety, and just opened the van door. "It's time."

"And anyway, I work for the police. We don't have a sense of humour." Eddie sighed and flicked away his cigarette.

"Really? Two hours ago you were trying to shove a cactus up your secretary's arse, and laughing until you pissed your pants. Now look at you. Miserable git."

Eddie stared straight ahead as he climbed out of the van. "So now you admit it was humorous? At the time you said it was juvenile delinquency."

Benson shook his head. "What's up with you? You usually like a good body."

Eddie grabbed his kit and the bag of special stuff he'd need, locked the van, and followed Benson into the rain and the ever-deepening sense of foreboding. "I'm fine. Or I would be if people would stop asking what's up with me. There's nothing more annoying than people telling me not to be so grumpy. I'm not fucking grumpy, I'm just... me. I'm just me!"

"Alright, alright. Keep your hair on."

There grew from nowhere a third set of footfalls on wet tarmac. Eddie glanced across at Benson and saw him sucking his belly in and sticking his chest out. He swivelled further and his eye fell upon the owner of the third set of footsteps.

The first thing that caught that eye was the blonde hair, how it bounced with each stride despite the rain; its tight little ringlets like uncontrollable springs stapled to her scalp as though she were a grown-up version of Shirley Temple. Or Sid. The next thing he saw was the smile. Actually, he wondered if it was a smile at all. It was as though the skin on her face was so tight it had pulled back to expose her teeth, giving the impression of a permanent grin, or perhaps a permanent grimace. Eddie was reminded of Wallace and Gromit.

He turned back to Benson as they walked. "Did you know we had company? I mean, there's a woman among us, and apart from pretending you don't have a beer belly, you're not acting weird. Yet."

Benson cocked a thumb over his shoulder and turned his face down, out of the rain. "This is Miriam Kowalski."

"Did we join Hill Street Blues?" Eddie squinted. "That it? 'This is Miriam Kazozkizuzz'. What, is she your cleaner? Your carer?" He nodded; that made sense. "Don't think they'll let your carer into a murder scene."

"Miriam," Benson raised his voice slightly. "This is the grouchy bastard I warned you about." As they approached the entrance, he turned back to Eddie. "She's new."

Eddie squinted again. "She's not new. Might have been new when this place was built, but—"

"I'm new to the job."

All three arrived under a fancy curved stainless-steel overhang that was meant to protect people from inclement weather. It looked like a single eyebrow, an angry eyebrow. It was obscene; it was as foreign to this old building as a pair of tits spray-painted on the Mona Lisa. It didn't look good, but it did a fine job of funnelling water onto those approaching, rather than channelling it away down a discreet downpipe and into a drain.

Benson pressed the buzzer.

"When I say I'm new to the job, I actually mean," she slurped through her teeth, and then swallowed.

Eddie cringed, thinking of a horse whinnying. He watched her articulate her words and couldn't take his eyes off her sunken cheeks, at the deep fissures around her eyes. She was two degrees away from being a corpse.

"I used to work in intelligence. Fancied a change." She stared at Eddie, and he was forced to look away. There was just so much on her face to look at that even Eddie would have considered it rude to stare for that long.

"Yep," he said, "if you wanted a change from intelligence, then CID is the place to be."

Miriam laughed.

The door buzzed and then clicked. Benson, chewing on a sigh, pushed it open and led the way into a high-ceilinged foyer that reminded Eddie of One Flew Over the Cuckoo's N est, but everything here was even more dour, depressing, dark, and dingy. This was the kind of building that could have you in tears without a single word uttered or a single person grinning at you like a circus clown. Everything echoed.

Eddie shuddered, and rain dripped from his kit and his clothes onto the grey-painted concrete floor. Cold. Unwelcoming.

And this place was Juniper Hill, a jail for the mentally ill. He wondered if "socially awkward" qualified, then thought better of asking. Murderers and rapists who were not fit for trial ended up here. A hospital prison, if you will. The kind of place your family had you sectioned to, and then left you here. It was a horror film set, a living nightmare. And if you weren't crazy when you went in...

Benson ducked to a Perspex window with holes drilled into it. Aside from the reflection of Ms Temple there, Eddie could see people on the other side of it in some kind of security office; screens across a wall, a comms system in the centre of several desks, radio operator tucked away in the corner. Benson's voice boomed, and then he turned. "They want our phones and radios."

A hatch to a metal tunnel opened. Benson slid the phones through and took a token with the number 13 stamped into it.

"There's an omen if ever—"

"Oi, I've got enough on my—"

Eddie was nodding off to the side where a large, bald man presented himself. "Mr Benson?" The man shook Benson's hand and introduced himself. "Jacob Richardson, Deputy Governor, C Wing."

Benson smiled and shook; for a moment a sliver of jealousy, like walking through a spider's web, touched Eddie's skin and he shuddered. Benson was a natural people-person, seemed to actually like being around them. Not for the first time did Eddie wish he was built differently. Life would be so much easier on a planet full of people if he actually liked his own species. But the shudder and the wish didn't last long, and then he was back to marvelling at what a tosser Benson was with his false smile and his cold hand.

Benson and Richardson walked ahead with Miriam following, clutching a large blue notebook to her chest. Eddie tagged along behind, staring mostly at the floor, but occasionally glancing up as the party threaded its way through gate after gate. Richardson barely took a breath as he pulled the bunch of keys, secured to his uniform trousers on a long chain, in and out of locks every twenty or thirty yards, nodding at colleagues as they passed by.

Eddie felt blessed that he couldn't hear the man's constant chatter, but one word exploded right inside his brain the second it left Richardson's mouth: briefing.

Eddie stopped.

Miriam noticed and turned. And then the two men up front noticed too, and they stopped and turned as well. "Eddie?" Benson said. "What's up?"

"Briefing."

Benson shrugged. "So what?"

"I fucking hate briefings. Why do we need a briefing? You've been on the phone to this place and everyone in it all bastard morning. What else could there possibly be to discuss?"

Miriam stepped up to him. "You okay?"

Eddie blinked at her, marvelling at her puckered lips, sure she could suck a golf ball through a garden hose. He took a step to the side and growled at Benson. "Get me to the cell, let me do my work, and you can go and talk knitting patterns with him, okay? I'll be done in half the time and then we can get out of this shithole."

Benson cleared his throat, smiled an embarrassed smile at Richardson, even patted Eddie on the arm. "No time for you to dick about this morning," he hissed. "Put your petulance in your back pocket for a bit, eh. Let's get this done."

"I...er," Richardson was next in line; another one suffocating Eddie. "It won't take long. We've got to hand over officially. It's a death in custody, needs special treatment. Forms to fill out. You know."

"Fine. Go ahead." He stared at Benson. "Why couldn't you have got this crap out of the way and then called me?"

Benson came in close. Too close. "I don't know what's bothering you today – more than usual, I mean – but whatever it is, you'd better get a grip. The prison service are close colleagues, and we work together on stuff like this, okay? Enough of your childishness."

Eddie watched Benson's eyes flitting back and forth between his own. That little flit always fascinated Eddie: why couldn't they just pick an eye and stare at it, why must people continually inspect both eyes?

He nodded.

"Come on, then." Benson and Richardson were soon back in step, back in the groove. It wouldn't have looked out of place if they'd hooked arms and begun skipping along the tiled corridor.

"I don't like being here, either. Gives me the collywobbles, this place. And the people in here." Miriam hurried to catch up to Benson, and left Eddie staring after them.

She got it. In one. The collywobbles, indeed.

As predicted, the briefing lasted an hour. Eddie sat in the furthest, darkest corner he could find. They were gathered around a desk with no fewer than three telephones on it, and a pair of computer screens. The screens were black, the phones mercifully silent. Eddie watched them: Miriam and Benson listening to Richardson like he was Richard fucking Branson giving out financial advice. If it hadn't been so jaw-clampingly cold in here, they would have their tongues tucked inside his trousers by now. Eddie smiled at that. He watched the other officers gathered in the shadows around the table too, listening, giving their own findings.

The business was interspersed with personal chat, where prison staff compared shift patterns with police officers, grumbled about their respective IT systems, about how stretched they were, and where the best all-inclusive holidays were. Eddie almost fell asleep.

If it wasn't for the occasional forays into business, he would have been snoring long ago. And the business side of this was a dead woman. Death always interested him, especially when it was something he was about to be involved with. You could keep all the corporate bollocks and all the inter-disciplinary smooching and arse-sniffing; just give him the body. Especially this body. There were accounts of last contact from several staff, from those the deceased had recently mingled with. There were logged accounts of security checks, and meds checks.

Towards the end of the briefing, there was an overview of the path taken by inmates as they progressed through the system – for a system it was.

And then there was the doctor.

Rebecca Charlesworth, her name was. She was mid-forties, wore round gold-rimmed spectacles, and a turtleneck sweater in grey. She was of interest to Eddie. She didn't speak much, was quiet when she did speak, and she was annoyed at being here. Her tapping fingers told him so. "I really must—"

"Yes, yes," Richardson said, palming away her semi-formed protest, as though discussing shit with Benson was more important. Then he looked at her, and said with regret, "you're right. Sorry, Rebecca. We've held you up too long. Please, go ahead." He smiled warmly.

"She'd been hiding some of her anti-psychotic drugs."

"That's interesting," Richardson said. "Make a note of that in the records, Julie." He pointed to a collection of papers and then to a woman, his managerial finger connecting the two together in an intricate and well-paid wag.

Eddie was impressed by that wag. "Does she have an alias?"

Richardson looked at Eddie. "Who?"

Eddie blinked. "Margaret Thatcher," he said.

"Sorry?"

"He means Alex Sheridan." Benson laughed and elbowed Richardson gently while giving Eddie daggers.

Chapter Thirteen

Onward to the Briefing

EDDIE COUNTED ELEVEN PEOPLE in this entourage. It was like the Fellowship from Lord of the Rings. Benson and Miriam up front, carrying bags of kit, along with Robinson and two guards – called staff members so as not to freak the inmates out. Inmates, by the way, were called patients. In the middle bunch were four staff members who were directly involved with the dead woman, having either befriended her on a professional basis or been directly involved with supervising or caring for her; one of them had been the team leader when the body was found.

Bringing up the rear were Eddie and Rebecca Charlesworth – the most interesting person there by far. Eddie stared between the floor at his feet and Rebecca's face, always content to just follow the noise of the group as they walked corridors and shuffled through gates and doorways, ascending stairs, interacting with other members of staff as they went. It was a long and slow journey – one so tedious that he hoped he didn't need to go back to the van for anything.

The background noise of voices and footsteps, of sporadic laughter and jangling keys, faded to nothing and Eddie zoned in on the quiet voice and timid smile.

"There's a member of staff who has relational security with her," Rebecca said. "Her Primary Doctor."

The confused look on Eddie's face gave her the chance to explain further.

"When you've worked with someone for a long time, you become so involved with them that you almost know what's going on inside their heads. You get a feeling for them. You build up trust to such a level that it can be as strong as the bond shared by siblings."

"You never know what's going on inside people's heads," Eddie said. He knew what she meant, but he'd never experienced it. His own sibling, Malcolm, was a twat. They hadn't seen each other for the better part of twenty years, and for Eddie, that was just the kind of relationship he liked. "Where is she? This staff member?"

"Oh, you'll need to speak with Mr Richardson. He knows the shifts inside out." She looked across at Eddie. "I'm more of a people person."

"I hate them."

"Hate them? People?"

"Shifts," Eddie said.

"That's a relief—"

"And people." He smiled at her apologetically. "Not so keen on people." Although she smiled back, Eddie could tell she'd taken an emotional step away from him. He breathed easier for it and resumed his inspection of the shiny, scored tiles as they slid backwards beneath his boots.

A small free addition to the constant chatter and the shiny corridor floors in here was the claustrophobia. That feeling didn't disperse when they arrived in an atrium, despite it being larger than the corridor. There was a high domed window from which hung an impressive chandelier of spiders' webs that had caught dust and muck over many years. Ribbons of it hung down the walls like frayed curtains until the light from the dome ran out of breath and relinquished power to a couple of sixty-watt bulbs.

Beneath the permanent twilight, and about ten feet up from Eddie's boots, were strips of artificial light. Blanked off between them were the old gas pipes from an era when a patient's death would warrant not much more than an entry in some logbook, and shipment to a local cemetery.

The walls were painted magnolia; a twelve-inch blue 'skirting' board had been added to give it that homely feel. The bare bricks had been painted over a thousand times until each had lost its definition – its individuality. He wondered whether that was how it worked in places like this: a patient would be moulded, kneaded, and drugged so much that they were no longer the person they had once been – that they were not even the shadow of who they once were.

"We've relocated the patients from here." Richardson stood at the head of the small entourage, like Gandalf lording it over those with smaller beards and sticks. "So you're free to work without worry. And we're leaving Ruby and Carmichael here to make sure you're taken care of. They have radios with them, so please don't fear for your safety."

Eddie's eyebrows dived. Don't fear for your safety? I wasn't, until you said that!

Within a minute, after yet more hushed conversations that reminded Eddie of the time he went to the library once, Benson and Miriam were at his side. Rebecca took a step back to allow Miriam entry to the tight little circle. "You ready?"

Eddie snorted. "Have been for about two fucking hours."

Chapter Fourteen

Taking the Piss out of Miriam

WHENEVER A PRISON CELL is locked down to preserve it for CSI, or some other police investigation, the prison service put a locking bolt through the keyhole secured with a padlock – the key to which is locked away and signed in, only to be signed out with the authority of a governor and the police liaison officer, or appointed CID. It was much the same here at Juniper Hill on the more violent patients' doors. But here in the atrium, there was no fancy padlock facility, because these doors were glorified office doors, not cell doors.

Instead, there was simple biohazard tape across the door, and a guard stationed on it all night. He'd done a pretty good job of pretending he hadn't slept through most of his shift, eating his yawns before they could force his mouth open. Richardson unlocked the door, pulled the tape off, made a note of the time, and stepped back.

Eddie unpacked a scene suit, and when he looked up again, Richardson and half of the Fellowship had vanished, taking with them a good portion of the noise that had become normal throughout the journey up here. Now it seemed unnaturally quiet. That quietness, as talking and laughter plummeted into whispers and giggles, allowed Eddie to contemplate the real fear that had turned him quiet and contemplative instead of sarcastic and loud. He stood and tossed a plastic-wrapped scene suit at Benson. "It's triple-XL, you'll be fine."

Benson threw it back. "I'm staying out here. But thank you." His expression was calling Eddie a bunch of names not permitted in current company, and that made Eddie smile despite his worrying who might be behind that door. "Shame," Eddie said. "Who am I going to take the piss out of?"

"Me." Miriam held out her hand. "Medium, please."

"You?"

Her face was still glued into a permanent smile/grimace. "Unless you don't know me well enough to take the piss out of."

Eddie tossed her a suit. "Here's a large, dear; don't flatter yourself."

"And so it begins."

"What? So what begins?"

Benson came in closer. "Why do you always have to be a prick?"

"I don't. It's a life choice that comes from being surrounded by idiots and arseholes."

"Thanks," said Miriam.

Eddie nodded at her. "Consider it an advance payment. If you're not an idiot or an arsehole now, working with him will get you a ticket to their AGM."

"Cretin," Benson whispered. "Just go do your shit, and then maybe we can get—"

"Get out of here? You've been hanging onto Richardson's arse like a cluster of piles since we got here. We could have had this done by now—"

"Protocol, Eddie. And yes, politeness too. We like to keep a good working relationship with other agencies."

"Fuck your—"

"Wait!" Benson closed right in, glaring at Eddie, his face tinged with crimson. He took Eddie's arm and walked him away a few yards. He faced him, anger still stoking the flames. "What's wrong?"

"Nothing."

"I've got used to you being fiery over the years. I expect it. I kind of like it, actually. But you've been especially bad today. Why?"

Eddie's eyes lost contact with Benson's; they tracked the atrium and those now looking on at them. They included Rebecca. She was staring not out of curiosity like the others, but because she was psycho-analysing him. Eventually, gravity won and he looked at the ground. "I don't like these places."

"Prisons? Hospitals?"

"Yup."

"That it? You sure there's not more?"

Eddie's eyes climbed to meet Benson's again. "I'd just like to do my job and fuck off out of here, okay?"

Benson sighed, and his body deflated slightly, the colour leaked from his face and took with it the anger. "Okay. You know if there's anything... You can talk to me."

"Are you kidding? Couldn't throw a stone in this place without hitting a shrink." Rebecca's stare sent a chill through his body.

It was a good-sized office. You could probably fit a snooker table in here and still have room left over for a bar in front of the window and a dart board in the far corner.

Underneath the window, a large Victorian radiator leaked orange stains onto the carpet tiles. Before it stood a desk; nothing special, just a regular office desk, a couple of chairs this side, facing a couple more in front of the radiator.

This was some kind of assessment office. Green walls designed to calm the patient, light blue carpet tiles to make them feel more at home, rather than the shit-brown tiles running throughout the rest of the building, designed to hide any number of stains.

Eddie took in the whole room, its furnishings, its colours and its smells. He took it all in before he allowed his attention to creep towards the body. When he finally did, the smell seemed to get stronger. It was like battery acid, stinging and sharp, cloying and penetrating.

"I think we might need respirators, Eddie."

Eddie nodded, and pulled at the face mask currently residing under his chin. "Go on. Go get yourself one."

He heard Miriam move, but she stood her ground, aware that he'd offered her a get out of jail free card – one she was disinclined to accept.

"What do we do about the floor?"

"You don't like it?" Eddie turned to her. "You're right. This needs to be laminate, oak effect. Maybe with a few scatter rugs to break it up. What d'ya think?"

Miriam sighed. "I meant footwear marks, Eddie."

"Oh. I see." He tapped his lower lip.

"You didn't waste any time taking the piss out of me."

"Keeps the boredom at bay." Eddie circled around the body while Miriam stayed barely a yard inside the room, hands behind her back, obviously determined not to get in the way, and not to disturb anything... except Eddie himself, apparently; she felt it was fine to disturb him.

The deceased was indeed a female – so they'd scored well so far. And yes, he reckoned the murderer had used acid, so they'd got that part right too. They were doing well—

"I'm just trying to learn. I'm trying to help, too."

Eddie growled to himself. He stopped looking at the face, at how it had melted right off the bone like cheese from a clumsy man's pizza, and had slid onto those wonderful carpet tiles, to join them in holy matrimony, dissolving together. He looked up at Miriam. "Come here."

"Look, I'm not trying—"

Eddie held up an index finger to his lips. "It's okay. Come here."

Tentatively, she brought her hands from behind her back and slowly strode around the body to stand next to him. In the doorway, Benson stared on.

"What looks odd?"

"Odd? About the body?"

"No, about Benson. Yes, about the body." He muttered behind a gloved hand, "We'd be here all day if we were listing odd things about Benson."

Benson folded his arms and shook his head.

Miriam laughed. Her mouth opened even further around the sides of her face. "Well," she said, "her face is missing."

Eddie nodded. "Good start." And he whispered, "This is why Benson stayed out there. He doesn't enjoy the grotesque." He stared at Miriam's lips again and felt a needle of guilt for doing so. "You're doing better than he would already. What else is odd?"

Miriam took her time getting closer to the body, looking at each facet, not seeing them all at once – and so missing or ignoring them. "Her jeans are undone."

"Why are they undone?"

Miriam stood upright again. There was resignation on her face that told Eddie she was bowing out of the game right now. She had exhausted her cache of oddments, had achieved a bronze star. "That's my observational powers exhausted."

Eddie bit his lower lip. "What's her name?"

"It was mentioned enough times in the briefing, Eddie."

"I was asleep. Humour me."

"Alex Sheridan."

Eddie took a long blink. An enormous relief flooded through him, like someone had just sucked out a poison. His fingers stopped tingling almost immediately, and the fog inside his head seemed to disperse as though a wind had picked it up and scooped it away.

"You okay, Eddie?"

He took a long time to answer. Eventually he said, "No. I'm not alright at all."

"You know her, don't you?"

Eddie blinked. "No, I don't know her."

"What then?"

"What's going on?" Benson called.

Miriam looked across, waved a hand. "Nothing. We're cool."

"Get a move on, Eddie!"

Eddie smirked. "Cool?"

"Come on. What's bothering you? You're acting like you knew her."

"How the hell do you act like you knew someone?"

"You've been anxious all day. And seeing her has made it worse."

Now Eddie turned to her. "Fuck. Are you clairvoyant? Or maybe you're yet another fucking shrink in a house full of them!" He wasn't smiling at her.

"No need to have a pop at me."

"Well, then, stay out of my fucking head!"

Benson was about to shout again from the doorway, but Miriam waved him away. "I'm sorry," she said. "Let's just concentrate on her. Whoever she is."

Eddie said nothing. Miriam said nothing. She moved from foot to foot as the tension crept up a notch. She folded her arms. Still Eddie said nothing; just stared at the dead woman and her melted face.

"I knew someone who was in here. Years ago. Probably dead now. Or in mainstream prison. She was an 'Alex' too, not Sheridan though. Can't remember her surname."

Miriam was staring at him when he eventually looked up at her.

"She wasn't the kind of person I ever wanted to see again. Dead or alive."

"And you came here thinking it might have been her?"

"I had a job to do." Eddie shrugged. "Doesn't matter now, does it?"

Benson called out, "If you two could get a move on we might make it out before it gets dark."

Miriam sighed.

Eddie noticed Rebecca standing next to Benson, watching what he and Miriam were doing. He nodded towards the body, and said to Miriam, "Want to know what I find odd about her?"

Chapter Fifteen

What's Wrong With This Body?

THERE WERE A LOT of things wrong about this scene. And the more he looked at it, the more wrong things he saw.

"Well, I got the jeans undone bit."

Eddie folded his arms. "Didn't get the 'why' though, did you?"

"That's why you're CSI and I'm... not."

"What are you, exactly?"

Miriam swung her DNA mask by its elastic strap. "Shouldn't we be wearing these?"

"When we get closer. For now, I'm happy we're not spitting at her and ruining anything the acid hasn't eaten. So what are you?"

She hesitated, and then deflated slightly. "I'm his boss." She nodded at the door where Benson was leaning against the doorframe, engaged in quiet banter with Rebecca the shrink.

"You are taking the piss?"

She shook her head. "Nope."

"This place goes through new gaffers quicker than Breaking ad goes through villains."

"Sorry," she said, "lost on me."

"Never seen Breaking Bad?"

She ignored the question. "Anyway, your department isn't exactly overpopulated right now, is it?" She wiggled an eyebrow at him. "More chiefs than Indians, last I heard."

"Sore point." Eddie cleared his throat. "Shall we get back to the matter in hand?"

She laughed, and Benson turned to look at what was so funny. Eddie just stared at him and gave him the finger. Benson mouthed, "what?"

Eddie asked, "So is this like a get-to-know-your-staff kind of thing?"

"Yes, it is. I like him; he's good at his job, and he's good with people."

"Are you fucking kidding?"

"And I'm getting to know you too. You are also my staff – via Weismann, of course."

Eddie sighed. "Shit."

"Never mind all that office nonsense," she said. "Tell me what's wrong with this scene."

Eddie sat in one of the chairs on the far side of the desk. A weak, grey light fell onto his white scene suit and when he pulled back the hood, it shone on his hair, damp with sweat. Miriam took the other chair, crossed her legs and looked at him.

"She was dead – probably – when the acid was poured on her."

"How can you tell?"

"Well, when I say dead, I mean she was horizontal. The acid has drained straight down off the side of her face, taking the face with it, and into the carpet. Had she been standing for any length of time, there would have been evidence of her neck coming away too. And her hands, look – there's no acid on her hands. If someone had squirted acid—"

"You'd raise your hands."

"Of course you would." He leaned forward. "And there are no acid splashes on any part of her clothing."

"Which means?"

"Which means the offender killed her and then swapped clothing, and then poured acid on her face."

"What? Why would—"

"If you need those clothes, you're not going to spoil them first, are you?"

"Premeditated, then."

"Quick. I like that in a boss."

"I'm still learning."

"Hurry up. Learn faster." Eddie returned to the body. "And to back that up, there's no acid on any of the other carpet tiles. She was sprayed where she laid, lay, lie, or whatever."

"Sounds disgusting, whichever it is."

"Have we changed subjects all of a sudden?"

Miriam smiled, waved at the body. "What else?"

"The jeans aren't fastened because the clothes don't fit her. They're all too small. The attacker was considerably slimmer than her."

Miriam raised her eyebrows, impressed.

"And see how there's a lace missing from one of the trainers? The offender probably used it to tighten up the waistband of the trousers or skirt or whatever she took from this lady. Then she doused her face in acid to keep her identity a secret for as long as possible."

"Are you saying what I think you're saying?"

Eddie turned to her. "Has anyone checked on Alex Sheridan's cell?"

"How long do you think this might take, Inspector? Only the patients... they get restless very quickly. It makes taking care of them even more difficult than usual," the nurse said. The name badge dangling from his lanyard proclaimed him as Chris Armartie.

Benson nodded as they walked. "I appreciate that, but we're dealing with a suspicious death, and if it takes all night, then it takes all night."

Eddie looked across at him. "Better bloody not."

They came to a halt and Chris selected the key from a bunch. "We always keep them locked."

"From the time she was escorted to her meeting this morning, no one's been in this cell?"

"Room. We call them rooms."

Eddie rolled his eyes.

"But you're right. This room has been locked the whole time."

Eddie asked, "How come there was no one with them?"

"How do you mean?"

"It's not a trick question. Is it usual for a doctor to be left alone with a patient?"

Chris looked uncomfortable as he leaned forward and unlocked the door. "It's being looked at."

"I bet it is."

Around him, as if to affirm his concerns, the volume increased. Miriam, though she was perfectly safe out here with the others, stood with her back to the wall, keeping an eye on the doors around this echo chamber. She jumped when one of them banged as a chair or a bed or something – might even have been a person – hit it from inside.

"Isn't this cross-contamination, Eddie?"

Eddie, torn from watching Chris unlocking the door, turned to her. "You're right. Let's go back to the van, call up for another CSI, and wait for them to arrive, shall we? Shouldn't take more than a week." He saw her raise her eyebrows. "There is no one else!"

She was about to apologise, when her chin quivered. Someone screamed from inside their room, and Miriam squealed.

Benson took hold of Eddie's arm, and Eddie just yanked it free. "Get the fuck off me."

"Eddie—"

"If I came down with something right now, you lot would be screwed. And it's about time you realised that we're not an unlimited resource; you can't just click your fingers and somewhere a new CSI is born. Doesn't work like that. You don't go on Amazon and get a new box of CSIs the very next day."

"I'm sorry," Miriam said.

"Enough," whispered Benson. "Let's go take a look."

Chris turned the handle and pushed the door open, then stood back, allowing them access. His face said it all: he was more scared of these coppers than he was his own patients. This kind of reaction from supposedly sane and professional people was clearly not what he expected.

Benson cleared his throat, and said, "Sorry, Chris. Long day. We won't be long."

"You told him we might be all night a minute ago." Eddie was in the doorway. "We'll be as long as we need to be. Stop lying to him."

Benson smiled at Chris, excused himself, and stepped in beside Eddie. He whispered, "I'm telling you one more time..."

Eddie said nothing. He just looked into Benson's eyes, and Benson took a hasty step back.

He swallowed and said, "Eddie? Are you alright?"

"Fuck off." Eddie turned and walked further into the room.

He'd prepared himself for a brief search; something that might indicate premeditation, something that might suggest involvement at least, maybe even a diary, however unlikely that would be.

He reached forward to a shelf, his freshly gloved hands trembling, his heart rate accelerating. He just knew this search was going to end in bad news, could feel it in his water.

"Eddie." It was Miriam.

She nodded at the wall above the simple bed. Eddie swivelled to look and nearly fainted.

Chapter Sixteen

The Past is Only Inches Away

THROUGH THE WINDOW, THE last of the light was dying, and the sky was just a mass of grey spinning in random patterns that might be described as a swirl – it reminded Eddie of how his stomach felt.

He was back in the meeting room. Room 101, or at least it felt that way. The heating was on, the radiator dripped hot water onto the brown stain and leaked heat into the room with ridiculous efficiency. Sweat ran off his face and collected around his chin, sealed against his skin by the respirator, and his fingers squelched in the thick gloves he wore. He'd gathered a dozen PVC bags, and was busy cutting the upper clothes from the deceased.

She had been provisionally identified as Dr Diane Warburton by deduction – and by a small device used to read a single fingerprint from a body. It was a tiny scanner, and once it had the ridge detail from an index finger loaded up, it fired that information across to the Police National Computer. Once there, it scored a hit – not against the regular database where all the known criminals were lodged, but against another, more discreet database of professionals engaged in sensitive healthcare.

It took less than four minutes to have it confirmed on Eddie's tablet. This had been Dr Diane Warburton's final day at work.

"Why are you cutting her clothes off?"

Eddie was shocked out of his reverie. Benson, as usual, stood in the doorway, well away from anything that smelled of work. Eddie nodded towards the corpse. "I want to see her tits."

"What!"

The respirator collected his sigh. "Why do you think I'm doing it?" Even though Eddie was shouting to be heard, his voice was still muffled. "Go on, have a really good think. You can do it, Benson, go on, give it a try."

"Look, I understand why you're—"

Eddie pointed the scissors at him. "Leave me the fuck alone!"

"Eddie—"

"Last chance, and then I throw these at you!"

Benson left. And now he'd gone, Rebecca peered in. Eddie felt that prickling sensation of more sweat being pumped out of his body, and looked away from her, ready to scream at her too.

Why was everyone suddenly so interested in him? Why couldn't they all just piss off and leave him alone to do his job? If there was an easy exit here instead of a mile of corridor, you wouldn't see Benson for dust. But, because he was trapped in here, Eddie was the only show in town.

By his side were a stack of PVC bags with the trainers and the lower garments in, all duly photographed before packaging. The T-shirt was next, once he'd finished slicing it. Most of it would probably be left behind in the gloop anyway, but he was being as thorough as the conditions allowed. It was horrid work. Each time he touched the corpse, he got a whiff of acid, despite the respirator. And every time he moved her significantly, a bit more of her flesh cascaded into the slop on the floor.

An hour later, the pile of empty PVC bags was depleted, and the pile of bulging PVC bags had grown, each identified by its own yellow exhibit label: right trainer, right sock, left trainer, left sock... He had decided to bag her hands with PVC, along with the remains of her head – which he double-bagged. Her feet would go into normal plastic bags because the chances of them being damaged by acid moving about during transportation was minimal.

Once he'd rolled her into a PVC sheet, and tied it top, middle, and bottom, he manoeuvred her into a body bag, zipped her up and tagged her; he even bagged the damaged floor tiles after photographing them.

He stood and arched his back, digging his thumbs in until it hurt enough to take away the general dull ache. Predictably, that was the same time Miriam came back into the room. She wore no suit this time, but there was little use for one now the forensic work was out of the way.

"You okay?"

Eddie closed his eyes and whispered, "Fuck off."

"I heard that." She approached him. "I don't want to get in your way, but I'd like to know what you've done. I'll be giving a briefing at the PM tomorrow."

Next came the Lucozade bottle. He photographed it in situ, then made sure the pop-up cap was securely closed, and inspected the outer surface to see if it was contaminated by acid. He wanted to try it for fingerprints, but knew the chances of it being dry enough to examine were slim. Instead, he dropped it into a stout plastic tube and sealed that inside a PVC bag, hoping the exhibits officer would get it shipped to the Fingerprint Development Lab first thing in the morning.

Once the bottle was safe, he pulled off the mask and gloves. His face was ringed where the rubber had contacted his skin and a gallon of sweat trickled onto the carpet from inside the mask and gloves. His fingertips were white and corrugated, shiny with sweat.

Miriam skirted the body bag and took up residence in one of the office chairs. And still Rebecca peered on from the doorway.

Eddie pulled and ripped himself out of the white suit. He looked like he'd just stepped out of a shower, clothes and all. His face was red and shiny, his hair matted and sticking to his scalp.

"Bet you can't wait for a smoke."

"Say it. Don't beat around the bush with shite small talk. Say it and then we can both move on."

Miriam licked her lips. "She was the girl you once knew."

"Enlightening. Thank you." Eddie rolled up the suit and rammed it into a paper sack along with the mask, a pile of nitrile gloves from the floor, and his booties. He dried his hands as much as he could, then pulled on another set of gloves so he could remove the carbon canisters from the respirator and chuck those in too.

He sat on the floor, knees up, arms around them. "I'm sorry."

"What?"

"How come you didn't hear that, but you heard the 'fuck off'?"

"I heard it. I just don't know what it's for."

"I got shitty with you, before, at Alex's cell. I shouldn't have. I... I'm not built for these things."

"What things?"

"Places like these. People... especially people. I'm feeling a bit out of kilter, too."

"Understandable." There was a long silence, and then Miriam asked, "How long ago was that photograph taken?"

Eddie thought about it. He looked at it again, in his mind's eye – it was now in an evidence bag along with other stuff Benson had seized. He focused on it; there he was, maybe eighteen years old, dark-haired, smooth skin, no wrinkles, and even a smile in his eyes. He wore a moustache back then, in the early nineties – porn-star style.

"Her name was Alex. I can't remember her surname. Just Alex. We were both into Pink Floyd. Got talking." He forced himself to remember. She was in her pre-Goth days but still wore lots of eye makeup like a punk, big earrings, big hair, and was sticking out her tongue at the photographer. The photographer, Eddie remembered, was a guy called Mike Freestone who was in a rock band called Chrysalis. Dead within two years, the lot of them.

Everyone who had anything to do with that fucking photograph was doomed. Including himself. Despite how happy he looked back then – and he looked happy because he was happy – something had drifted away and got lost, and somehow never returned. He was just an empty shell now. A bit like a chrysalis; he smiled at the irony. "Early nineties, I guess. It was taken backstage at a gig."

"Anyone I've heard of?"

Eddie shook his head.

Another long moment passed, and then Miriam asked, "How do you feel about it? About her?"

He looked up from his twitching fingers and said, "I often think about her."

"You do?"

"I imagine us going to McDonald's together, maybe take in some face-painting and a Disney flick." Eddie went to stand. "Might even ask her to marry me."

"Come on, be straight with me."

"Be straight? That was a long time ago. I have no feelings for her. None."

"Really?"

"What is this, Question Time? I told you—"

"You freaked out when we went to her room."

"Wouldn't you have? It was like waking up and hearing Wham on the fucking radio all over again. Those are days I'd rather not revisit, thank you. And to find out that those days were here all along, just inches away, like I was walking on ice and beneath it was the world I left and never expected to see again. It was a shock."

Miriam said nothing for a long time. And then, "You haven't seen her since then?"

Eddie paused mid-stand. He sniffed and wiped his forehead with his bare arm. "Once—"

"Come on, Christ's sake," shouted Benson. "Body recovery is here, we can finally bail out."

"Coming." Eddie grabbed his kit and marched towards the door.

Alongside Benson in the doorway, Rebecca winced.

Miriam gritted her teeth and her face said she could have cheerfully slapped Benson. She said to Eddie, "Any idea where she might be? Where she might have gone?"

Without looking back, he said, "I'm not Google Maps."

"We need to find her, Eddie. We really need to find her."

Chapter Seventeen

More Black Spikes

SHE KNEW IT WAS a mistake coming back here. A huge mistake. How long would it take the staff at Juniper Hill to realise Chester was missing, even amid all the chaos? Eventually someone would work out who the body was in room C210. And from there they'd work out who the body was not.

It wouldn't take them long to check the CCTV, and bingo – they'd turn up Chester and a woman in clothes that didn't fit, just waltzing right out of the front gate as though they were going for lunch in town. In their shirt sleeves. In winter.

It had taken them twenty-five minutes to drive here to his piece-of-shit flat in Woodhouse with the intention of clearing out his bank account and clearing out of town. The bank account was supposed to have been emptied yesterday so they could just leave. But now he was having second thoughts. She screwed her eyes up and tried to keep black anger away; how could you have second thoughts when you'd been party to killing someone in order to break a murderer out of a secure hospital? Any second thoughts should have happened months ago!

In one corner of the lounge was a part-built set of shelves, and a pile of books on the floor. A drill, a hammer, other tools, and screws; it looked like a display at Ikea. "How come you never finished the shelves?"

He didn't even look up from picking his fingernails. He was trembling. "Just never got around to it."

That was plain crazy. Everything was there, ready to go, ready to finish what he'd started. Twenty minutes' work, max. Those shelves were like a metaphor for this whole fucking crazy show she was involved with right now. What the hell was wrong with this idiot? Along the wall in the other corner was an electric guitar. Fender, it said across the top. Next to it, a practice amplifier, also Fender. Covering both of them was dust – lots of it. "You don't play it?"

His eyes tracked along to the other corner. "I'm waiting."

"What for?"

He shrugged. "Motivation, I suppose. I love the thought of playing it, just not the learning."

"You get nothing unless you work for it." She turned and he was sitting on the sofa, smoking a cigarette and chewing his nails, like the weak streak of piss that he was. She could see out of here along the hall to the front door, maybe fifteen yards away. Half an hour ago the pane of glass in that front door had been light grey, but now it was dark grey. It was time to act, but how to broach the subject?

"I think we acted hastily," he said.

Back here in the lounge, rain hit the window, seeped between the frames, pooled on the sill, and dripped steadily onto the damp carpet. Yes, Chester was a prick with no spine and no motivation; a man who couldn't blow his own nose without a set of instructions and careful supervision. But those faults were precisely the faults she'd been looking for in an escape buddy. Stuck within the walls of Juniper Hill, she'd seen them as attributes. Now they were faults again. She just wanted to slap him. Until his face fell off.

"We needed more time," he whined. "We shouldn't have rushed it, Alex."

A wind pushed droplets around the pane, whistling like a tune inside her head, and she was mesmerised by the beauty of it all. She stared out of the window, absorbed by the show in the dying light of a winter's day. But it couldn't last, this beauty. She could feel it fading already like the daylight, and she was drawn back into the room by his incessant talking.

Some people didn't know when to shut the fuck up. "I can feel one of my heads coming on."

"I'm sorry, but I need security."

She blinked. There it was: the selfishness. "Is that what this place is? Security?" She took a breath, prepared to placate him for the time being. "Calm down. Everything's going to plan. None of that other shit... it just doesn't matter." From somewhere nearby, a spiky black headache crept in.

"That's easy for you to say. They'll hunt me down."

"They're probably starting their engines right now." She enjoyed the fear on his face. "They'll hunt me too, remember? I'm a bit of a murderer, in case you forgot, and they tend to frown on that shit these days." She shrugged. "You knew all of this when you agreed to help me. When," she reminded him, "we agreed to start a new life together." She dug her nails into the arm of the chair. "None of this matters now, so stop being a prick."

He grabbed her arm and pulled her towards him. She showed no signs of fear, no signs of discomfort. If anything, her eyes glistened a little bit more than they always did, her lips curled into a smile. And she hoped it annoyed him; she hoped this might provoke him into being a man instead of remaining a coward.

He bared his teeth and anger narrowed his eyes. When he saw no fear in her, his grip tightened, his rage deepened. He spat, "Nothing matters to you, does it?"

She shook her head. "Every day is a blessing."

He flinched at that. Slackened his grip.

Was that it? Really? Was that the sum total of his manliness? "Got any idea what them drugs do to you?"

"What?" he said, caught off-guard by the change of subject.

"Antipsychotics. They're a lobotomy in a fucking bottle, Chester. They numb you to everything. Everything. And that's what they want, like. They want you compliant, so you won't fight back when the brainwashing begins."

"I don't know—"

"Ssshhh." She put a finger to his mouth, felt his lips trembling. "I know you don't know what I'm talking about. But I want you to understand what it's like." She took away her finger, stood, and stared down into him. His hand fell away from her arm. He was a shallow man, easy to read and even easier to despise. "When you understand what it's like being on the other side of them cell doors, you'll realise that you had the easier part in this deal. Get it?"

"Deal? Is that what you call it?"

She almost growled. "You got a hard on when I mentioned my two-million quid. Remember that? That was the 'deal'. Us, and my money; a joint force. You were practically drooling. Now look at you, frightened of your own shadow." She scooted forward, teetering on the edge of slapping him, and stabbed a pointed finger instead. "You are complicit in killing someone, Chester. You aided a murderer in her escape from a government facility. Now, answer me this: do you think they'll discipline you and expect you back at work promptly tomorrow morning with your lunch packed up and your boots all shiny? Or do you think they'll lock you up and pop back to see you in about fifteen years? Huh? Pick one. And do it fast."

"And now that you have no drugs?"

Ah, that was the question she would have asked about three months ago, when she suggested this plan to him. Shallow indeed. "Now that I haven't got no drugs, I'm free to be me. At last." It had taken months to come off them. It had taken willpower so strong that she surprised herself. It was easier being on them, of course; it was easier letting the world float by on a ripple of fluffy cloud, waving to the people who sat upon it waving back with happy smiles and cooing voices. Coming off them was like having your eyes torn out by short jagged lengths of barbed wire. It was like having your brain spit-roasted over a flaming fire – hellfire, perhaps.

"Does it scare you? Seeing me... naked?"

"Naked?"

"Off the drugs, Chester. Does it scare you? Do I scare you?"

He shook his head and stood. "No. I don't think you're like the others. I think you have issues, sure, but you still have the ability to reason. You're not just violence on legs. There's more to you than that."

She nodded, impressed by his rationale. And he was more or less correct; she did still have the ability to reason, but reason swung on a scale, like her mood. Didn't take long for a mood to change. Pale colours meant happiness, dark meant anger. Moving through the spectrum could take hours. Or seconds.

The black spikes grew.

And her sacrifice coming off the drugs was reason playing its part; but she knew that it had been just a process, a pathway to trek along until the barbed wire blunted and the fire dimmed to warm ash. It was a process. And through it all, throughout the agony, even as the barbs tugged and her mind fizzled and popped, she'd had to pretend to smile at the happy cloud people, and wave back while suppressing the need to kill the fuckers.

No one took any notice of you as long as your lobotomy still seemed to be working.

And now... well, now she had no shackles, no pain. Just the freedom to do what she wanted, when she wanted, and to whom she wanted. Sometimes it was hard to conceal her excitement at that prospect. But looking at Chester now, looking square on at his Adam's apple with the stray whiskers surrounding it, her enthusiasm dulled. The sooner he was out of the way, the better.

He drew his hands through his hair and then buried his face in them. "I didn't know it would do that. The acid, I mean."

"Is that what this is all about? The sullen mood?" She laughed, "It was acid, what did you think would happen?"

"You said you would just threaten her with it."

"I lied." She blew out a sigh. "If I was just going to threaten her with it, then I wouldn't have asked you to bring it in for me; I would have just used actual Lucozade, wouldn't I? Calm down, Chester. They haven't got no idea you helped me, yet." She watched him reason it out inside his head, saw the slight nod as he played back her words and convinced himself she was correct, that she knew what she was doing. "And by the time they realise it, we'll be long gone – if you get your sorry arse in gear, that is. But we really need to make a start, don't we? On getting away from here, right?"

He relaxed, and even managed to brush cold fingertips down the arms he had grabbed only a moment ago. He stood and sighed. "I'm sorry. You're right."

"Yes, I am. The acid will give us a longer head start." She moved in closer to him and stroked his cheek, gazing into his eyes. She leaned in and kissed him. "You have to believe we can go abroad. Huh? Start again, new identities. Okay?"

He nodded, wrapped his arms around her.

"So. How much money do you have?"

He let her go, took a step away. "I don't understand why we need my money. You said you had—"

Alex kept calm, at least on the outside. "I have more than enough money; I told you all this, remember? I told you a dozen fucking times. But not here! It's in Whitby. Hidden."

"Well, then—"

"Chester, listen to yourself. You think I'm trying to rip you off? For what, a couple of grand, maybe? You think I went through all this shit for a couple of grand? You... you don't trust me?"

"Of course I do."

"Then we take all of our money with us; yours and mine. No sense in leaving anything behind." She looked up at him. "Do you trust me, Chester?"

"Of course—"

"Then start acting like it. We are one, you and me, okay? And we stick to the plan. Go and get your money; we'll need cash. When you get back, pack only whatever you can't live without, leave the rest. We're going in an hour."

"An hour? But—"

"With or without you. I'm going in one hour."

Just put him out of his misery. You don't want to be s hackled by him.

Yeah, you could just kick him down the stairs. It's your a nswer to everything!

Shut up, woman!

"But—"

She stopped him with nothing more than a stare. "We head to Whitby, we get my money, all two million of it."

He gasped again at the thought of it. "And then what? Have you planned further ahead?"

"It's all sorted. I told you. Christ's sake."

"You never did. You never told me any of the plan after we left Juniper Hill."

She sighed. "I know some men at Whitby who can get us across to Zurich. Fast but uncomfortable."

"Zurich? Switzerland?"

"Zurich, Netherlands."

His excitement wavered.

"A private dock. No police, okay? We can get new documents there. We fly from Groningen to Barcelona."

His eyes softened again. "Barcelona."

"All of it under the radar, Chester. All of it, just like I planned."

"Two million's enough to set ourselves up?"

"Are you fucking kidding me?"

"Sorry, I meant—"

"Plus whatever you have."

He blinked as though pulled away from the romance of the forthcoming adventure, right back to here, back to Leeds and the rain and the greyness. And his savings. He shrugged. "Six hundred quid," he said. "Or thereabouts."

She nodded, contemplating something. "Go and get it. Take your ID into the bank and withdraw it all, every penny."

Chester was excited. Suddenly so. He'd gone from scared, through cautious, to daring to imagine a new freedom with sunshine and cocktails, and now he could see how it could be done. "Alex," he said but then fell quiet.

Her eyes shimmered with tears. "I killed someone today so I could be with you, so we could be free of that stinking shithole, and so we could be together at last." She swallowed, and her voice cracked. "Do not let me down now, Chester; don't leave me all alone now I've broken us free of that place. I'm not sure I could cope on my own. I'm not sure I could cope without you. But I'll try. One hour."

He seemed to grow a foot taller, his chest inflated, and he stroked her chin, nodding. "Gimme half an hour."

Chester barged through the front door thirty-seven minutes later, closed and locked it behind him, and stood with his back to it, breathing like he'd run a marathon, his face glowing red. "I got it," he panted, eyes closed. "Cash. Eight hundred and seventy-four quid."

"Where is it?"

He patted his coat pocket.

"Great!"

He opened his eyes, squinted.

Even though she'd drawn the curtains to keep light to a minimum, she could see the fear in his face smash any residual excitement out of the way until he was nothing more than a pair of slumped shoulders and damp eyes.

"Are they here? Are we surrounded?"

She laughed. "Don't be daft; did you see any coppers on your way back in?"

"What, then?"

She smiled at him, unbuttoned Doc Warburton's blouse and shrugged it off.

"Wait," he said, licking his lips. "What are you doing?"

"We're having our first sex session."

"Eh? Now? Right now?"

"It'll release the tension. It'll give you new motivation, Chester."

"I thought we were in a hurry."

"We are. So run to me, Chester. Bang my brains out."

Confusion mixing with anticipation mixing with fear coloured his face. He took off his coat, hung it up on the hook behind the door, and stared at her again.

Alex took off her bra. "Run to me," she smiled, holding her arms out.

Chester licked his lips again.

Chapter Eighteen

The Trap

IT WAS ALMOST FULLY dark when Eddie got back to MCU and emptied the van of its rubbish. He leaned against the skip around the back of the building where the fire exit stairs and aircon units were. A cigarette dangled out of his mouth, eyes closed to the smoke rolling up his face, hands in his jacket pocket trying to keep them warm. Amid the humming of the aircon units, he was in deep thought again.

It had been such a strange day. And he hated it when the past came back, totally uninvited, to bite him on the arse. If he'd wanted a trip down memory fucking lane, he would have bought a ticket, but for some bastard to haul him there without so much as a "fancy it?" was beyond ignorant.

Alexandra Sheridan.

And then it hit him, where she'd got the name Sheridan from. It was the—

His mobile phone rang, and his eyes snapped open. He held the thing in his pocket and curled it into a fist, wishing he could crush the thing until it shut the hell up. Instead, he pulled it out and read the screen. Benson.

Moneypenny had gone home. The reception area was only dimly lit, but he could still smell her aroma; whatever kind of perfume she wore was such a pleasant change from rotting flesh and faeces, he found. And much better than being in the same room as Benson.

He climbed the stairs to the CID floor and marvelled at how busy the office still was. What the hell do they find to do? Surely they couldn't all be absorbed by their own games of solitaire or noughts and crosses, or whatever they played while pretending to be busy, claiming overtime for beating their best scores.

His derision was cut short, his attention grabbed by Benson standing in the doorway of one of the farthest offices along the right-hand wall – one of those glass-fronted offices with the Venetian blinds that screamed of the occupant's self-importance. Benson was waving at him, and Eddie found it impossible to pretend he hadn't seen him – it was too late. The price you paid for daydreaming when you should have been plotting your escape.

"I hope you've got me a coffee lined up," Eddie said as he neared the office.

"I have."

He followed Benson inside; sure enough, there was a mug of coffee on the desk. Three of them, in fact. He looked at Benson. "Did you spit in it?"

Miriam laughed and gestured at them to sit.

Eddie was suspicious. "Listen," he said, "I had a curry last night, and my ring piece is like a dragon's nostril. So if we could keep this brief – I think you'll thank me later."

"Eddie, we just want—"

"I knew I should have legged it while I had the chance. If I'm not home in thirty minutes, my old man will start—"

"Eddie. Shut up." Benson creaked into the seat next to him and slurped his own coffee.

Miriam leaned forward against the desk; her perpetual smile seemed threatening to Eddie now – predatory, almost. "I wanted to thank you for showing me the ropes today," she said.

Eddie, on his guard, nodded. "No probs."

"It was good to get acquainted. As the new Head of MCU, I want to get—"

"You lot don't seem to last too long around here. Big gaffers, I mean. The last fella barely even got that seat warm let alone put up any certificates to impress his minions. Photos of the kids, stolen police memorabilia, that kind of thing."

"Eddie," Benson said, "give her a chance, will you? Don't start with the ridicule and defences just yet, eh?"

"I like to save time."

Miriam cleared her throat. "Tell me about Alex."

How had he not seen this coming? He'd walked into this trap, sweetened by one of Benson's rare offers of coffee without the slightest inclination of why they wanted him. Had he given it some thought – any thought – he'd have been better prepared, more able to give a quick put-down, and piss off quickly. Now they had him; now he was searching the walls for something to say. Bastard!

"She likes to bite people."

Miriam blinked. She looked to Benson to see if Eddie was taking the piss, but Benson appeared equally stunned.

"It makes her feel good. It makes her feel like she's in charge of people. She's narcissistic." He almost enjoyed the shock on Miriam's face. "But worst of all, she would never share chocolate digestives. Ever."

"Stop dicking about," Benson said.

"It's true. She'd snatch biscuits right out of your hand!" Inside, Eddie grinned.

Benson asked, "How did you meet her?"

"We were on Blind Date, with Cilla Black."

"How did you meet her?"

"Why?"

Miriam almost managed to close her lips, but instead did that sucking thing like she was pulling in orange juice through a bucket of gravel. "We're asking these questions for three reasons. One: I need background info on her that Juniper Hill simply doesn't have; it'll help me to catch her. Two: I need to know if you're in danger—"

"Ha, come on! Really—"

"Eddie, shut up."

Eddie turned to Benson, and was half out of his seat, pointing a finger in Benson's face. "If you tell me to shut up once more, I'll knock you out of that fucking chair."

Benson recoiled, hands out in defence. "Whoa, there's no need—"

Miriam raised her voice. "I need to know if you're in danger, Eddie. Someone has to take this seriously."

Oh, Eddie was taking this seriously, alright. Eddie knew Alex from years gone by, and she'd never been absent from his thoughts for more than a day or two. Alex was special. Alex was—

"And thirdly: I need to know why she escaped."

Eddie's mouth was dry. He took a sip of coffee. "Isn't it obvious?"

"Not to me."

"You seen the décor in that place? It's disgusting."

Benson and Miriam both breathed out. Eddie's smile collapsed, and he found himself staring at the mug, a thumbnail tracing the rim. He whispered, "Maybe her neighbour snored?"

Benson tutted. Not brave enough to tell him to shut up again, Eddie noted.

Eddie looked across at Miriam. "She'd stopped taking her drugs."

Miriam didn't move.

"Oh, come on; isn't it obvious?"

"Fill us in," Benson said.

"I'll fucking fill you in—"

"Eddie!" Miriam shouted. "Stop it. I'm trying to do my job here. I'm asking for your help."

Eddie noticed the angst in her eyes. She was almost pleading. Most gaffers didn't want to hear your opinion outside of the crime scene. To them you were a necessary evil, an added extra; you were the heartburn after eating onions, and your opinions were never sought. Your opinions were discouraged, drowned in Pepto-Bismol.

He took another sip of coffee. "That doctor, Rebecca whatever, said Alex was getting better. She said Alex was getting so much better that she was climbing the ladder, off to pastures new, a new ward, more privileges.

"Once she starts on that ladder – and unless you're completely off your trolley, you're going to progress because they will push you onwards – once she started on that ladder, she would reach a point where she could enter the general prison population.

"And once she got there, she'd be there for the next thirty years or so."

"Double murder," Benson squeezed a couple of words out.

"No, a triple murder," Eddie said. "She wanted out, and this place, the pre-whatever ward, was the easiest place to escape from. Had she moved up, the rehabilitation or whatever they called it would have been much more intense; she'd have less opportunity to escape. They fucked up big time by not having anyone staying in that room with her and the doc. Big error. Never trust Alex Sheridan. Never."

"She stopped taking her meds in order to escape?" Miriam said, echoing Eddie's early words.

He nodded. "She needed to be sharp if the escape was ever going to succeed. Those drugs keep you blunt, malleable. She needed to be in charge. And also," he said, "she wouldn't get those kinds of drugs on the outside without taking risks. Better to just wean herself off them a few months in advance."

"But surely she'd risk becoming psychotic again?" Benson said.

Eddie shrugged. "I'm no doc. Maybe she didn't need them, the drugs, I mean. Maybe she wasn't psycho-loopy to begin with."

"Acting?"

Eddie shrugged again. "You should be asking the professionals these questions, not me."

"You knew her. Was she 'psycho-loopy' back then?"

Eddie sighed, closed his eyes for a moment, and memories of her swamped his mind. And this made him angry all over again. They had no fucking right to make him dredge all this shit up, when he'd done his level best to keep the worst of it buried. He clenched his teeth. "Yes."

"In what way?"

"Well for one thing, she liked Marmite."

Benson sighed. "Not again."

Eddie cleared his throat. "She once said to me that she enjoyed hurting people. She enjoyed seeing someone in the kind of pain that's just the other side of ecstasy, before it gets unbearable." He looked at Miriam, then swivelled to face Benson. "But most of all, she said that she enjoys seeing people in the kind of pain that's on the other side of unbearable."

The office was silent for a moment.

Eddie spoke again. "She had a gun at my throat at the time. And she said it just after she bit into my face."

Miriam's mouth fell open.

Benson coughed, eyebrows raised to Miriam. "Mind if I get off?"

She nodded, "See you tomorrow."

Eddie watched him leave and thought how strange it was that he wanted to go home early. After the door closed, he said, "I still have the scar." He rubbed the stubble on his cheek.

"Are you sufficiently distant from this girl to be involved with the investigation?" Miriam watched him carefully.

"I am. But I won't be doing any investigation anyway. You're the detectives, not me."

"You know what I mean – you're a part of this circus too. And your demeanour says you're not distant enough."

"It does?" Eddie slurped coffee, put it on the desk and leaned forward. "Makes no difference, Miriam, cos I'm all you've fucking got." He smiled. "Is that all? I have a father to ridicule."

Eddie watched Miriam; she was deep in thought, eyes down, face expressionless. Then she looked up. "Do you think you're in danger?"

He swallowed. He could remember the last words she ever spoke to him: "I'll never forget you, Eddie. Don't forget me, eh? Because one day, I'll be around the very next corner." He smiled at Miriam. "I don't think so. I mean, she broke out of that place to get away and be free. I don't think I feature in her plans." He looked away.

Chapter Nineteen

Two Nightmares

– One –

IT WAS GOOD TO see that the streetlamp at the end of Eddie's road had been repaired. Yesterday at this time – almost 6pm – it was utterly black around here. Eddie's little cottage was out on its own at the entrance to a dead-end country lane. It looked like a gatehouse, and maybe that's what it once was; there was a manor house a quarter of a mile away, Leventhorpe Hall, and it wouldn't have shocked Eddie to learn his humble home was a building with a purpose, instead of what it was today – a building to contain an introvert who pretended to be otherwise, and an old fella who thought he was still a teenager.

The new streetlamp cast a weak and sickly yellow glow just as the old one had. You could almost hear it groaning "Well, if I must".

Had the light been stronger, perhaps Eddie would have seen the car parked at the far end of the lane, near the bollards that turned it into a dead-end.

He parked as usual down the mud and gravel track at the side of the cottage and reached for the door handle. But he didn't pull it. Instead he sat, peering through the windscreen into a narrow slice of total darkness. Feathered at its edges were the branches of sycamores that waved in a barely noticeable breeze against a lighter blue patch of sky. It was almost as though they were warning him, trying to push him away.

To the right was the cottage, a single-storey, eighteenth-century stone building with a white plastic door and central heating – just as the architect had intended. The light came on in the hallway, and that plastic door opened. Into view came Eddie's father, solemn face with solemn creases stared out at him.

Eddie climbed out, locked the door, and headed over to Charles. "What's with the long face? Soiled yourself again?"

"Very funny."

"Not if you have a sense of smell." Eddie stopped walking. Charles's face didn't lose the creases but remained serious. And the sycamores still clattered together above his head as if warning him. "Okay, you have my attention."

"There's someone here to see you," Charles said.

Eddie's eyes widened. You are fucking kidding me, was his first thought. His second and third thoughts merged into one long cacophony that said Grab Dad and get the hell out of h ere! "Okay, keep calm, Dad. Walk slowly with me to the car and we'll—"

"Come inside." Charles turned and walked back into the house.

Eddie tried to snatch the old man's cardigan, but missed, leaving him growling and whispering all at once. "Dad!" Eddie's mouth went dry. "You stupid old..." He gritted his teeth and ran through the door.

– Two –

There was something altogether peculiar about Chester that had first attracted her to him – as an accomplice, of course. There was never anything else besides that, despite what Chester might have hoped for. That something peculiar was a strange sense of propriety; he was a gentleman, not likely to take advantage. She had needed that propriety because inside Juniper Hill, he was in a position where he could have taken advantage of her lots of times. She had encouraged it in him and was surprised to see him remain professional despite the look in his eye and the twitch in his trousers.

It was an important facet of their relationship that she had nurtured. It was the carrot for him to help her. She had promised him everything: money, sunshine, all the sex that his gentleman's imagination could possibly crave. And in return he had given her life back, her freedom. She owed him big time. And that's just what she planned on giving him – a big time. The biggest of his life.

She had sought something else too. Ever since she woke this morning – her last morning in Juniper Hill – she'd kept an eye out for it; when he left for the bank, the perfect tool just slid into her hand. The perfect opportunity. She wanted only one more thing from Chester, and she counted on his explosive release of sexual tension to give it to her.

Alex rubbed her nipples, and Chester licked his lips again as he stood at the front door, some fifteen yards away. "Come on, then," she said, grinning. "Run and get it, Chester."

He needed no further encouragement.

Chester took to his heels like Usain Bolt chasing a medal, and he was sprinting by the time he saw it. But by the time he saw it, it was too late to take evasive action. She knew he'd seen it because in a millisecond his focus changed from her breasts to something immediately in front of him, making him appear cross-eyed. His eagerness faltered and he almost managed to bring an arm up, almost managed to slow down a fraction.

All to no avail.

Chapter Twenty

Eddie, Sid, and the Bronx

EDDIE STOPPED DEAD IN the middle of the lounge, prepared to fight.

"Surprise!"

He didn't know whether to scream or feign a heart attack.

Charles patted him on the shoulder and almost doubled up with laughter at the shock on Eddie's face.

"You old twat!" Eddie was white, and his mouth hung open so far that you could see his breakfast. There must have been a dozen people in his lounge, all laughing and pointing, all shouting, and Eddie felt his chest tighten. His eyes tried to gather who they were, but didn't scan each person in turn, instead zapping across the room and back again in shock until all the faces melded into something that looked like Doc Warburton's face. They all looked the same; they all looked foreign, scary. For a moment, Eddie thought he might actually pass out. How fucking embarrassing would that be?

His mouth clamped shut, his eyes went dry, and it seemed as though his skin was suddenly made of Velcro, the way it prickled and itched.

Within a few moments, he was surrounded by people. Some thrust their hand in his and shook it, some clapped him on the back, others ruffled his hair like he was a teenager who'd had a growth spurt.

And as quickly as the noise had erupted, it fell almost silent. A dozen pairs of smiling eyes all stared his way as though expecting something. Eddie was utterly glued to the spot, and he thought now might be a good time for that heart attack. "What the fuck?"

"Happy birthday!" they shouted.

"What? Wait, wait; it was my birthday last month, you freeloading cretins."

They looked at him. They looked at Charles, and then back at him.

"So you can all piss off home and watch Britain's Got No Fucking Talent."

There were several moans, a little bit of laughter from the back of the crowd, and then one guy in front took focus. It was Benson. He stepped forward and waved a bottle of beer at him. "Lying. Little. Bastard."

"That's why you left early."

Benson winked.

There was a substantial pause in which no one was sure if Benson was right or drunk, knowing that Eddie would always try to lie his way out of a straitjacket. A moment later, everyone was laughing again as though good old Eddie – the life and the soul of the god-damned party, man! – almost got away with it.

Eddie's toes curled, and he closed his eyes. Bastard. The background noise hitched up a notch as conversations bubbled and popped like mud on a geyser. Suddenly there was music. Party music.

Things could only be worse now if someone attached electrodes to his scrotum.

"Nice try, Eddie." Someone patted him on the cheek, and Eddie opened his eyes.

"Sid?" Eddie stared him up and down. "What the hell are you wearing? You look like a warthog's ballbag."

Sid was wearing something that wouldn't have looked out of place in a pantomime – a large knee-high dress, stripy tights, tall hair, and outrageous makeup. "I am an Ugly Sister."

Eddie blinked. "You're not too far wrong."

"It was my last stage ensemble. Thought I'd get one more wear out of it."

"Before you grew up, you mean?"

Sid grinned. "I almost gave the game away, didn't I? When I asked what you had planned for tonight, remember?"

Eddie nodded. "No idea what you're talking about."

"Well, happy birthday." Sid pushed a little parcel into his hand. "Thanks for being the best boss I ever had." And then he threw his arms around Eddie and hugged him, and the crowd cheered.

"If you don't get off me right now, you might find that your next boss will be better. And you might find out as soon as Monday fucking morning. Alright?"

Sid released him, laughing. "Aren't you going to open it?"

"Wasn't planning on it, no."

"Aw, go on!"

It hadn't taken long for the bubbling geyser to escalate into something like a pub in here. A busy pub, where everyone was talking and laughing all at once – mercifully drowning out a Bee Gees track where the combined noise was just a fraction more tolerable than having a helicopter in the room.

The box was tied with a pink bow. "Is it your resignation letter?"

"Open it, you miserable git." Benson was in Eddie's face, shouting, halfway through what must have been his third bottle of beer.

"Hope you're getting a taxi?"

Benson tipped the bottle towards him. "Staying over. Hope you don't mind."

He was about to allow his tongue full rein over whatever came out of his mouth, but he pulled up short. Benson was in turmoil at home, and it didn't take a genius to see how he was coming apart; bits of Benson-stuffing were leaking out of the sides. He needed to be away from his problems, even if it was just for one night. So a comment about his 'wife feeding him Pedigree Chum out in the doghouse' probably wouldn't go down too well. Instead, Eddie just smiled, and ripped into Sid's package.

"Hope you like it." Sid was hopping from foot to foot, the anticipation dangerously close to ruining his panto underwear. "Took me an age to choose it."

The wrapping paper fell to the floor, and Eddie's face brightened up. He held it aloft and smiled this evening's first genuine smile. "Hey," he said, "thank you, Sid. This is very kind of you." It was a Pink Floyd mug. Maybe a throw-away gift to anyone else, but it meant the world to Eddie. Someone had taken the time to understand what made him tick, and they appreciated him for it, didn't try to change him. And that someone took the trouble to get him this. "It's perfect."

"You have to bring it into work and use it there."

"Nope. This is staying at home. Besides, Kenny would probably use it, and I refuse to put my mouth anywhere his has been."

Sid almost burst.

"Thank you."

"Happy birthday, Eddie." An arm appeared from around Benson's bulk, and Moneypenny followed it into centre stage. She came closer and kissed him on the cheek. "I'm so glad I could be here."

"Well," Eddie squirmed and lied politely, "Moneypenny. So glad you could make it." He tried to look away, at Benson, at the Pink Floyd mug, at Sid, who even now was shrinking away into the background, but he couldn't; his eyes fought to get to hers and lingered there, taking them in, drinking them like Benson supping his beer. She was beautiful. Demure.

And she knew it, breaking the stare, and breaking the wish that was forming on Eddie's lips. He took her hand and was about to pull her a little closer, maybe to ask her out again.

They'd tried dating a while ago, but it never amounted to anything; it had been like a comedy sketch, with Eddie always the fool.

But he couldn't do it. Not only was it too busy in here, with no privacy, but he'd left his bravado in that restaurant all those months ago. It had never managed to find its way home again.

And there was another reason not to ask Moneypenny out again. He was attached to her other hand and now he stepped forward and looked down on Eddie. "Ayup, pal."

Eddie looked up at a gorilla. He was well over six and a half feet tall, wider than a phone box, biceps poking out of his skin-tight sweater – something that would have been positively baggy on Eddie – like he'd been shrink-wrapped. He had designer stubble that made Eddie's look like a tuft of old carpet. "Hi," mumbled Eddie, searching for a non-derogatory response. He settled on the ultimate lie. "Pleased to meet you." He snarled and pictured himself smashing the Floyd mug across his perfect fucking face and gouging his blue eyes out with the shards, just before he went and kicked his father up the arse. Hard.

The gorilla was staring at Sid, struggling to keep a laugh to himself. But he lost the struggle, and didn't possess the tact to keep quiet. He blurted out, "Is the little skinny queer the entertainment?" He winked at Eddie, but Moneypenny yanked his arm and shushed him. The gorilla laughed.

Eddie didn't.

Moneypenny said, "Eddie, this is—"

"No. Let me guess." Eddie stared at the man-beef for a full thirty seconds. "Brad. He's a Brad."

"Close," she said. "Bronx."

"Say what?"

Moneypenny cleared her throat, and said again, "Bronx."

Eddie handed the mug to Benson. "Take care of that for me, please." He looked back at Bronx, tipped his head back and laughed so hard he thought he'd grown a hernia. "That's the funniest name I ever fucking heard. That has got to be a piss-take, surely?"

Neither Bronx nor Moneypenny found it very funny. Moneypenny shuffled her feet and stared down at them. Bronx's eyebrows formed a perfect frown, and he glared at Eddie.

Eddie found that hilarious too. "Your parents must've hated you. And I can see why."

"I beg your pardon?"

"No need to beg, mate." Eddie clicked his fingers, and pointed to Bronx, a realisation clearing his face. "Hold on, wait a minute; your parents didn't choose that name, did they? You chose it. You chose your own name, and the name you chose wasn't Dave or Mike. You chose... Bronx. Bronx is so hard and muscular, a tough-man's name! You self-centred twat!"

"Eddie!"

"So how long have you been in love..." – he glanced at Moneypenny, and she put her fingertips to her lips as usual. But he was speaking to Bronx – "with yourself?"

Bronx ignored the taunt, yanked on her arm. "Why did he call you Moneypenny?"

Eddie stuck a finger between them. Moneypenny closed her mouth, and Eddie said, "None of your beeswax, Steroid Boy. That's my name for her. You're not allowed to use it."

Moneypenny looked aghast. "Are you drunk, Eddie? You're being very rude."

"Nope. These are all my own words." He didn't take his eyes off Bronx. "Is your IQ the same size as your biceps?"

Bronx smiled. "I often come across men like you. Jealous and small-minded."

Eddie nodded. "Better than being small-penised, though, eh?" It was the best he could come up with under the circumstances.

Bronx snorted, and Moneypenny was already trying to pull him away. "Actually, Eddie, he's a maths lecturer at Leeds Uni."

Eddie was pointing a finger, ready to launch into Bronx with something to cover up his insane jealousy, but he stopped dead. "Wow," he whispered. "He really is perfect. Apart from his small penis and his fucking huge ego."

Around him, the thunderous noise of a new party quietened. Eyes turned.

Moneypenny was going red through embarrassment, Bronx through anger, and Eddie because he was pissed off at Moneypenny. He was pissed off at her for being dumb enough to bring the twat here in the first place when his own failed relationship with her was still a bleeding wound. But what pissed him off even more was that Bronx was nothing like Eddie. Bronx was his polar opposite, and that begged the question what the hell had she seen in Eddie to begin with? Had it all been a lie? Or was this visit here tonight just to rub salt in that wound?

Sid stepped forward again, painted smile now a crooked line of black lipstick that complemented the worry in his eyes beautifully. "Eddie," he said, "come over here, eh?"

Bronx's mouth fell open and he laughed at Sid again. "What the hell have you come as?"

A snarl ruptured Eddie's tight lips. Moneypenny saw it and tried to pull Bronx back, saying, "Don't laugh at Sid."

"Get the fuck out of my house and take your ego with you."

"Beg your pardon?"

"Only I take the piss out of Sid. You do not have that privilege."

Bronx turned his nose up at Sid as though there was an unpleasant smell wafting from him, and then sneered at Moneypenny, "You really do keep the strangest company."

"Out now or I'll rip your fucking face off and stuff it down your mouth."

It was Bronx's turn to laugh. He took a step forward, craning his neck to stare down at Eddie, but Eddie stood his ground. Moneypenny was sobbing. Sid had his face in his hands. "Whenever you're ready, old man." He smiled. "I could crush you like a... like a packet of crisps."

Eddie blinked. "A packet of crisps? Is that your best fighting talk? A packet of fucking crisps?"

Moneypenny grabbed him by the funky sweater and pulled, her face wet with tears. "Come on, Bronx, it's not worth it."

"And you," Eddie said to her, "I'm surprised at you stooping so low. Is he a rebound from Tinder?"

"Don't be so rude!" She pulled harder and Bronx yielded.

"Just be careful," Eddie shouted as they made for the door. "He's got dodgy eyes. You can't trust him!"

The door slammed and the room was silent. Eddie turned around, all eyes on him again. He grinned. "Best fucking party I've ever had."

The door opened again and everyone assumed it was Bronx come back to finish it off, but instead it was Eric from McDonald's who walked in clutching a bottle of red. "Am I late? I parked down the road like you said."

Despite himself, Eddie burst out laughing, and pretty soon the helicopter noise was back again.

Chapter Twenty-one

Three Minutes Left

THE ONLY THING TO stop Chester's instant death was a slight twitch of his head before his neck enveloped the hair-thin wire across the doorframe.

His head whipped backwards and his feet left the ground. He landed heavily on his back. The wind burst from his lungs and took with it a spray of redness that painted the wall all the way down to the skirting board. The wire had caught him, not on the Adam's apple with its stray whiskers as Alex had intended, but on the chin; the momentum had scraped away the flesh beneath his jaw to reveal a shiny red and white U-shaped mandible.

When she had planned it, Alex had expected it to take his head clean off, but she was disappointed. The wire had got as far as his neck and then snapped.

He lay like a dying fish half in the lounge and half in the hallway.

She pulled the bra back on, fastened up Doc's blouse, and dropped the knife on the sofa. "I didn't know if you'd see it," she said. "The wire, I mean. Couldn't risk you ducking under it and coming to take your revenge. Or whatever you would've called it." She smiled, friendly, and walked to him.

Chester's arms had stopped flapping around and his legs were still. She watched his wide eyes, wondering what he could see. Was it getting darker? Was he growing colder?

Now it was Alex's turn to lick her lips as she knelt by him. She was wrong; the wire hadn't stopped at the neck but had travelled through the trachea. Spots of blood bubbled from his throat. It had partially scalped him. The wire had slid under Chester's right ear and sliced it neatly up the side of his skull. It was still attached to his face but just by the skin up at the top; the loose end of the wire poked out like an aerial.

If you saw him from the left side, you'd think there was nothing wrong, except for the blood. On the right, it was like looking at a skull.

It was marvellous.

He tried to say something. She leaned in a little closer, but all she could hear was the bubbling breath in his throat. Disappointing really. And then, "You and me..."

It came out sounding like "ooouneee".

Alex snorted, and feigned bemusement. "There never was no you and me. I wanted you to get me out of that place, and I wanted whatever money you had because I'm penniless. Did you really think someone like me would have two million quid?"

She pulled aside his legs and lay down next to him, propping her head up on one hand as though engaging in the one and only bout of pillow talk they would ever experience. Tears tumbled down what was left of his cheek, and blood trickled out of his neck. It was beautiful, she thought – like a water feature. "Are you cold?" she asked.

He blinked and squeezed out more tears.

"It'll soon be over." She dipped a finger into the growing pool of blood and drew a doodle in the carpet. Before long the blood stopped running out of his neck and it just dripped like a tap with a leaky washer.

He wasn't up for a conversation, she could see that. And in truth, neither was she. She had things to attend to. There was a reason she wanted out of Juniper Hill, and not all of it was because she liked the idea of freedom. Alex was about to get busy.

The Doc had asked what her objective was; what did she want to achieve? And in a moment of weakness, Alex had blurted out that she wanted to be free. She looked around at the dim hallway, the cobwebs floating in a breeze high up in one corner. And she considered that question again now. "I want to be free," she whispered.

But was she? On the surface, yes, she was – providing she could evade the police. She was not caged up any more, therefore she was free. But she remembered saying to someone years ago that she wanted to be free, and he'd said, "the only way you'll ever be free is if you kill all the men who've ever fucked you over". Something like that, anyway. At the time, she had believed the same thing – and her voices agreed with her.

"Can you still hear me?" She leaned in closer. "Can you still see me?" She held her free hand in front of his mouth and felt no breath, could hear no more bubbling from the gash in his throat. "They reckon you can still see and hear for about three minutes after your heart stops. It's a fact. So, I'll leave you with this one thought to pass away the remaining minutes: how does it feel to know you trusted the wrong person?"

Chester's eyes stopped seeing.

Chapter Twenty-two

The Protective Suit

BENSON'S EYES FLICKERED OPEN and the over-exposed daylight closed them again. His head echoed a groan that seemed to come from somewhere outside. The smell, and a crackling noise, forced his eyes open again. He shielded them from the light and sat up, rubbing his head.

"Morning."

Charles was standing in the kitchen doorway, wearing a pinny and a smile. "Someone enjoyed themselves last night."

The grin was almost too much to bear. "Morning, Charles."

"Coffee?"

Benson's tongue clacked against the dry roof of his mouth and the taste of old beer made him nauseous. "Yes please."

"I'm doing a full English too."

"How come he didn't wait for me?" Benson was showered and had just finished breakfast, feeling better but still not ready to take on the world.

"Eddie's not what you might call a morning person. We avoid each other before midday; it's like a ritual. Actually, it's more like a safety net." He took Benson's empty plate. "He's so not a morning person that we only just manage to get along in the evenings." He laughed. "Come to think of it, he's just not much a people person, full stop."

"Well, anyway…" Benson stood, took his cup out to the kitchen. "Thanks for this; best start to the day I've had in years." Benson was smiling, but there was something approaching regret as he thought about home, and how true that statement was. "My wife isn't very…"

"She going to rattle your arse for being out all night? It's like being a teenager all over again, eh?"

"Yeah, something like that. She's not a people person, either. Actually, she is – she's just not a Tom Benson person."

"Ah. I see." Charles filled the kettle. "It's not easy being the one waiting at home, though." He looked at Benson with understanding in his eyes. "You become a different person when your other half leaves for the day. It's like wearing a suit or a second skin; having something to shield you until they're home and you don't need it any more. You wonder how you're going to get through it. And you start looking forward to them coming home just so you have some company. And that feeling grows into an itch by about three o'clock."

Benson raised his eyebrows.

"It's true. Could set your watch by it. And if they're late, that itch gets a bit painful, like if you've been sitting too long in one place and your leg turns to stone, know what I mean?"

Benson nodded politely. He hadn't a clue what Charles was talking about.

"And when they do get home and you can turn back into your old self, they're tired, and their mind is still on whatever they've been doing all day. You try to fit in, and you try to show an interest in something you can't understand, and you know then that you're an outsider and you'll never be allowed into their thoughts.

"Even though you've climbed out of the suit that got you through the day, you start feeling the need to keep it close by in case they won't let you in again." Charles wasn't even blinking, eyes out of focus, mind somewhere else. "And so you eventually keep it on, that shield, even when they're back home. You both walk around the place wearing your own suit and not letting the other one inside any more. And it…" – he smiled a little – "and it's like you're growing further apart."

Benson stared at Charles, bolted to the spot. As Charles poured water into their cups, Benson thought about his wife. They were growing apart, and Benson did keep her locked out. Cold. Unemotional. Repetitive. Distrustful.

"So what have you got lined up for today?" Charles slid the cup of coffee towards him.

"Is that why you had a party for him? I mean, he doesn't strike me as being the party kind of person."

Charles nodded. "He gets really deep inside himself. And sometimes I just want to prod him with a pointy stick, the little git. If he goes too deep for too long... well, it's not healthy, is it? He won't thank me for it – the party, I mean – I know he hates anything like that, with people involved. And I don't want his thanks; he just needs help sometimes and last night was my way of giving it to him. He needs to know that people care about him." Charles cocked an eyebrow towards Benson.

Benson didn't miss it.

"Thanks for coming. He will have appreciated it. He'll never tell you that, though, but he will have."

"You've become his stay-at-home person?"

Charles nodded. "Suppose I have. I get to wear that suit, waiting for him coming home, making meals that end up in the bin, eating alone." His eyes glazed over again, and Benson, embarrassed, looked away to give the man some privacy. "I can't grumble. He's a good lad, Tom. He really is. And if it wasn't for him, I'd be cooped up in the old family home, waiting to die."

Benson sipped the coffee, and before he knew it, the question he was thinking poured out of his mouth without ever going near the brake pedal. "What happened to Mrs Collins?"

Charles flinched. He glared at Benson for the shortest of times; those kind eyes turning feral for a millisecond.

Benson cringed. "I'm sorry. I shouldn't have—"

"No, it's fine, really." Charles busied himself scraping food off the plates and stacking them by the sink. As he worked, he said, "She found life very difficult. Steph, her name was. I talk to her every day." He paused as though thinking of how to proceed without offending the memory of his wife. "That suit I was telling you about, the one we wear till our loved ones come home at night? Well, her suit was paper thin, very fragile; she couldn't take bad news well, and it gnawed at her.

"She loved her boys, lived their happiness and their pain as though living her own life wasn't enough." He sniffled, smiled at the memory. "Eddie has a brother – Malcolm. He was into something bad enough that he... well, he made a mistake, that's all. And it hurt us, the family, and Malcolm did a runner. It played on Steph's mind. She convinced herself that she'd let him down, that she'd let the family down, and..."

"It's okay." Benson rested a hand on Charles's arm. "I don't want to rake up old—"

"She killed herself. To get away from the pain." Charles tore off a sheet of kitchen roll and dabbed his eyes. "I always thought killing yourself was selfish." He cleared his throat. "And I was right, Tom. There was nothing we couldn't have got through as a family. But she took the burden on her own – or tried to – and couldn't handle the weight of it. Her suit wasn't up to it, see?"

Benson leaned back against the worktop. He didn't feel quite so happy any more, and cursed his tongue for wrangling that particular story out of Charles. The nausea was back again, bringing a dose of heartburn along for the ride.

He didn't want to hear the story, and he was pretty sure Charles didn't want to relive it, either. It made his own domestic woes shrivel up by comparison.

"And when Eddie lost Becca... Well, it damned near cut him in two. She was a smashing lass. They don't really speak any more. It's like they've grown an independence that's as thick as a cow hide, and they've lost the ability to pick up the phone and reconnect. It's sad, really. And Ros, too. I think that hit him particularly hard; they were very close, had saved each other's skin for years, and had grown into a couple by all accounts." He nodded to himself, then shrugged."

Benson nodded; he remembered Eddie splitting from his family, had witnessed it from afar, sliding the well-worn shield of detachment into place before any of the shrapnel could get near. And then he wondered how he'd come to be so close to a man he'd once despised – the bastard, Eddie Collins – that he could spend the night at his house.

"He's had a shit time of it, has Eddie. I guess it must've felt like he was responsible, the common demonator or whatever you call it. Every woman he's ever known has topped herself or bailed out on him. It must hurt something awful."

Benson was almost in tears driving to work. He got stuck in traffic by a parade of shops. One of them was a florist.

Chapter Twenty-three

Beelzebub and the Unremarkable Sid

EDDIE REMEMBERED HIS FINAL words to his dad before they turned in after the party: "You ever pull a stunt like that again and I'll drown you in a bucket of piss."

This morning, he didn't regret saying them, but he opened the door to Charles's room and smiled at the old man's bare arse as it poked out from under the duvet, just the same. He crept through to the lounge and saw Benson sprawled on the sofa, his belly draped over its edge like a slow motion replay of flowing lava.

He was tempted to pour warm water on his trousers or just kick him in the balls – for old times' sake – but resisted the idea. Having to converse with Benson first thing in the morning was not something Eddie could tolerate just now.

Better just to leave quietly, grab breakfast at Starbucks.

After the usual ritual of sitting in the Discovery listening to Floyd and staring at the glass shit-box of a building he had to work in, while smoking his third cigarette of the day, Eddie took a breath and walked into the foyer. He'd tried to prepare himself for the graze along Moneypenny's starboard side as he hurried through the reception area and punched a hole in the double doors.

It was going to be awkward; he might have been a touch rude to her monster of a boyfriend last night, and he expected a bit of backlash this morning. You see, he thought, that's what comes of mixing business with pleasure. But then he thought about it some more: you couldn't exactly call the surprise birthday party pleasure, just as you couldn't call his relationship with Moneypenny business.

Still, he wasn't looking forward to the encounter. Eddie might be known for his aggression, but he didn't enjoy conflict – not with women, anyway. It didn't seem right.

He exhaled as the door creaked shut behind him. A face looked up from behind the reception desk and Eddie gasped.

He walked toward it, feeling worried. "Where's Moneypenny?"

The face was confused. "Who?"

Eddie stuttered. Even after all this time, he still didn't know her name. Perhaps he once had, but he'd been calling her Moneypenny for so long that he didn't remember it now. Discomfort cooled his mind and, in the distance, he could hear panic climbing out of its box. "The woman who usually… the woman who sits where you are now."

"Maggie?"

"Yeah, yeah, that's her. Maggie. Where is she?"

"Called in sick. Code brown, I think."

"What? She's never sick." He remembered the bruiser she was with. Bronx. Ripped like Atlas, arms like tree trunks, ego like Mount Etna. "Are you sure?"

The woman standing on Moneypenny's patch of floor folded her arms. "Look, given a choice I'd rather be in my own office, okay, not stuck out here smiling at idiots like you as they saunter past me like I was a bad smell. So yes, I'm pretty sure she's sick otherwise they wouldn't have prised me from my own chair, alright?"

Eddie blinked. He liked her. "What's your name?"

"Beelzebub."

Eddie nodded slowly. "Okay, Beelzebub. Don't suppose you have her number, do you?"

"Just a moment." The woman stood there looking at Eddie, face blank, eyes bored. "No."

He squinted at her, noted she showed almost no cleavage whatsoever, sighed at the appalling customer service! "Thank you for your time, you've been most helpful."

"It was almost a pleasure."

Eddie scanned the CID office, wondering if Benson had beaten him into work while he'd been enjoying his full English prepacked reheated sandwich at Starbucks. But Benson's seat, like his head, was empty.

The CSI office was unusually quiet this morning, too. Kenny was in the far corner, head stuck in a newspaper. And if Eddie had expected to see Sid getting on with his yoga, he was startled for the second time this morning.

But this time Sid wasn't trying to do the splits.

This time Sid wasn't Sid at all. Eddie stopped walking and stared at him. "Sid?"

Sid raised his eyes from the computer. "Morning." He looked at his screen again.

Eddie approached his desk, concerned. "You okay?"

"Why wouldn't I be?" He didn't even look up.

Sid was wearing a shirt and tie. Black trousers. There was no eyeliner, no lipstick. He wore no jewellery, no nail polish. He was bland.

"Have I woken up on a different planet this morning?" Eddie swallowed, the worry sinking slowly deeper until it occupied the whole of him. He wasn't sure how to approach this. Sid had joined the ranks of the unremarkable. And Eddie found that desperately sad. Something was wrong. But how should he ask what the matter was?

Sid pushed his chair back and stared up at Eddie. "Everything okay?"

Eddie scrambled for the words. Panic looked up hopefully again, and Eddie had to beat it back into its box. "My office," he said. "Bring coffee."

"What about me?"

Eddie stared at Kenny. "It's a private party."

"You're just pissed off because I didn't get you a present."

"I'd be pissed off if you did get me a present. It would have been second-hand or stolen or an old Christmas present that your Great Auntie Doris knitted for you. Or it'd be something you bought for yourself but didn't like."

Kenny considered this. He shook his newspaper out. "Fair point."

"There's a PM at ten with your name all over it. The acid woman. Try not to lick her face, eh?"

"Oh, come on! I always get PMs these days!"

"Kenny, you're looking at the entire squad of MCU Forensic United. Of course you get them!"

"Well, why don't you do one for a change?"

"Because I don't like them. They bore me. And I'm your boss, so I get to politely decline." Eddie turned and marched down the office. "And you didn't get me a birthday present."

"Twat!"

"I heard that."

"We need some new staff."

"Only because the old one is shit!" Eddie closed his office door.

Chapter Twenty-four

A Lead

BENSON SAT HEAVILY IN his chair and nudged the mouse. The screen remained blank. "Bastard," he said. "Who turned off this bloody computer again?"

No one looked up.

He hit the power button and waited, arms folded. "Fucking thing takes a year to boot up!" He stood, took off his coat and marvelled at the newly ringing phone on his desk. "Christ, I only just sat down." He also marvelled at how no one else picked up. "No," he said, "I'll get it. You lot sit there; wouldn't want to disturb your gossip or your game of Ludo, would we? I mean, it's only work, isn't it?" They stared. "You're all fired. Get the hell out." Everyone cheered, and Benson grabbed the phone. "DI Benson, Major Crime Unit."

Benson sat up straight, listened to the caller, and made no attempt to speak, except to say goodbye. When the call ended, he dialled the Force Operations divisional control room, tapping his fingers until they answered.

He got the preliminaries out of the way, then rattled instructions into the phone. "Two ARVs to 48 Foster Square. Preliminary RV point will be the university car park on Woodhouse Lane at," – he looked at his watch – "0930 hours – strike at 1000 hours. One will assist divisional units with containment, one to enter premises after MOE. Code 21 granted by me. This is a P1 so there's no briefing pack; if there's any aggro, point them in my direction. Oh, and better get in touch with ambulance, I want one on standby at the uni RV as well, same time."

"Who's heading up?"

Benson thought for a moment, heart banging around somewhere in his stomach, heading for the nearest exit. His pro-active days were long behind him, but it was good to feel the blood squirting around his veins again; it was like riding a bike, you never lost it. "Gold will be DCS Miriam Kowalski. I'll be Ground Bronze, and I'll brief at the RV. And you can pick your own Silver – dump it on a firearms inspector, I don't care which one."

"Okay. I'll set you up on Incident Talk-group 1."

"Fine. Oh, and see if we have a dog unit free. And Xray-99 if it's available – I want it hovering above the uni at 0950, paying specific attention to the locus."

"Anything else?"

"I'll let you know." Benson hung up, stood, and hurried to Melanie's desk, dragging his coat from the chair as he went.

She looked up as he approached, and so did the others. Khan joined him there.

Benson said, "Get me Nominal Links and create info packs for one Alexandra Sheridan."

"The woman from Juniper Hill?"

"That's her. Keep an eye on MCU email because Juniper Hill nuthouse is sending through a pack for Chester Layman, an employee of theirs. Check PNC and Niche for him too. And make sure we have the make and model of any vehicle he drives, the VRM, colour, blah, blah."

Melanie was already hitting the keyboard, taking Benson's instructions in her stride.

"We might not have anything on him, but if we do, copy the whole lot across to the divisional Duty Inspectors at Weetwood and City Centre, and a set to the Firearms Unit."

Melanie nodded and got down to her work.

"Boss?"

Benson turned to Khan. "Incident 1. Two pairs in plain cars – the shitty old ones, not the ones that scream CID."

Khan nodded. "What we got?"

"A lead. Chester Layman escorted a killer out of Juniper Hill yesterday."

Khan raised an eyebrow. "They've only just found out?"

"This isn't a Bourne movie, Khan. There's four-hundred staff working there. And there was a lot going on, a lot of staff movements caused by the alarm, so a lot of CCTV to watch. Anyway, get down to his flat; it's in a terrace off Woodhouse Lane. One front, one back; keep your eyes open, but keep out of the bloody way. Status report to me as soon as you land, and Melanie will update you regarding his vehicle. I want to know if it's still there. Okay?"

Khan nodded, already picking his officers.

"Tom?"

Benson looked across the office; Miriam beckoned him over.

"I was just coming to see you."

"She surfaced?"

"We have the name of a guard who escorted her out of Juniper Hill. We're doing obs and then a full tac-move on his place. I think we'll find out they've already gone."

Miriam nodded in thought. "You have a containment proposal?"

"It's in hand, yeah."

"Need anything from me?"

"You're Gold Command. Grab a radio. Incident 1. I'll be in touch if I do."

"Sit down, Sid."

Sid put the tea tray on Eddie's desk, took his favourite cup and saucer, sat down, crossed his legs, and took a sip.

Eddie stared at him. There was something unnerving about someone changing so dramatically. This wasn't just a haircut, or a new tattoo. This was... well, this was a stranger to Eddie. "Explain this."

"Explain what?"

Eddie waved a hand. "This. Where's the old Sid?"

"He's gone."

As Sid brought the cup to his lips, they trembled ever so slightly. But Eddie saw them. He paused for a long time before saying, "Well, I miss him. And I'd very much like him back, please."

Sid's eyes widened. "You would?"

"Why would I want you when the proper Sid is the real deal?" Eddie said. "Bronx is a shallow arsehole, Sid. Please don't pay people like him any attention at all. You're worth a thousand of him, and I don't want you to change who you are or how you feel comfortable because someone with wide biceps and a narrow mind laughed."

"But he's a maths lecturer. He's bright; he's intelligent."

"He's a wanker." Eddie cleared his throat. "Listen, just because he's good with equations doesn't make him a decent person. And it doesn't mean you should treat him as the gold standard of the human race and take everything that comes out of his mouth as gospel."

Sid smiled, but looked away.

"This is a man who changed his own name to Bronx, Sid. Bronx."

"I know, but—"

"And not only that – there are two other angles to this that you seem to have overlooked. The first is you being true to yourself; you told me when you first joined this office that you felt comfortable in feminine clothes and it suited your persona. I admit I thought you were a bit of a prick to begin with."

"Thanks!"

"But it didn't take me long to admire you and what you stood for. You were being true to you. And there aren't many people who can say that. Everyone, me included, walks around behind a façade all day, every day. We interact with people from behind that façade, because if we were true to ourselves, people might laugh at us. People like Bronx, for example. So I admired you for taking it on the chin and getting on with it."

"Thank you, Eddie."

"And the second angle you seem to have overlooked is me."

"What do you mean?"

"While you're comfortable, you're giving me your best work. You're happy, you're smiling, you're affable, and you're capable of performing at the top of your game. If you dress for people like Bronx, you're miserable, and you're unhappy. If you're unhappy, you perform like a chocolate fireguard."

Sid smiled up at him.

"Go home and get your glad-rags on, eh?"

"Well..."

Eddie grinned. "You've got some here, haven't you?"

"I always kept a spare set in case of accidents. I have burgundy chrome nail polish, too – it's to die for."

"Go to it, my man. Oh, and while I remember, I just thought of a third angle to consider: why let the Bronxes of this world win? If he had his way, we'd all be clones of him, and that's not a world worth living in, is it?"

"You can be very poetic at times."

"Yes, I can. But if you tell anyone, I'll smash your teeth in, okay?"

Sid stood, swapped his cup and saucer to his left hand and held out his right. "I know you don't like contact with other people, but I think a handshake is in order."

Eddie looked at the hand.

"I have some hand sanitiser in my drawer."

Eddie grasped it firmly, and shook.

Chapter Twenty-five

The Compromise

SID CRUSHED HIS LIPS together, and that was the finishing touch to his makeup regime. Lashes were on, nails were on, Dolly Parton wig was on, and an outfit right out of a Bugsy Malone production finished the ensemble. "What do you think?" He turned to Eddie and found a woman standing beside him. "Oh," he gasped. "I'm sorry. I—"

"That's better," Eddie said. "What do you think, Miriam?"

Miriam sucked air in through her teeth. "Fancy dress?"

"Nope. This is Sid. The best secretary in the whole Wild West."

Sid squinted. "It's not a cowboy theme, Eddie. It's a mixed creation. It's all I had here."

Kenny belched and barged past Eddie, making sure to knock him out of the way as he passed. "I'll just go to that PM then, shall I? You lot can stay here and play Strictly Come Dancing."

Eddie waved. "Have a good one, Kenny!"

"Up yours."

Eddie grunted at Miriam. "He loves me, really."

Her eyebrow twitched. "Can I have a word?"

"Should I prepare coffee? Ma'am, would you like tea?"

"Not even my kids call me ma'am, Sid. Miriam will do."

Sid curtseyed.

"You really are a knob sometimes, Sid." Eddie walked Miriam to his office, and called back, "More coffee. And don't spit in it."

When he had closed the door and sat down opposite her, she was sniffing the air. "Smells of alcohol in here."

"Hand gel. I have an obsession." She nodded; Eddie pretended to smile at her. "I expect you think this is an office full of weirdos, eh?"

"It had crossed my mind, yes."

"They make the best forensic officers; didn't you know? A little out there, a little on the wild, untamed side. We're artistes, every single one of us."

"Really?"

"Yes. And right now, we could use another one or two artistes. We're a little on the short side, if you know what I mean."

"How many staff do you have?"

Eddie looked at the ceiling and began counting on his fingers. "One... Erm. That's it. One."

"One?"

"Plus an admin."

Miriam fell silent, her fingers tapping on the chair arm. Eddie began to think something really bad was about to happen. But eventually she looked up at him. "I have a deal for you."

"You're giving me Benson, aren't you? I knew it; I just knew today was going to be a bag of shit."

"Benson? No, that's not the deal."

"Then what is?"

"Mr Weismann is your Head of Department."

"A very big head for a very small department, yes."

"I'm not sure how much he's told you, or how aware of his situation you are, but he might not be coming back."

Eddie raised his eyebrows, intrigued. "Assume I know nothing and you won't be far wrong."

"He's had to leave and return to Nottingham. It's a family thing, I'm afraid. And I would be surprised if he returned to work. At all."

Eddie's eyebrows nearly slid over the top of his head. "This place is like a merry-go-round for gaffers. I tell you, it's jinxed."

"This is, by any standards, a very small department."

"Size isn't everything. Fortunately."

She nodded. "It doesn't need another tier of management. It's got enough with you. How are you with budgets?"

"Me?"

"You."

He shrugged. "Not had the bailiffs in yet. How much?"

"Half a million or so."

"I could get some pretty cool shit with half a mill. I'm thinking new van, fifty-inch TV with surround, office outing to Camber Sands—"

"I hope you're taking the piss."

Eddie winked. "Okay, forty-eight-inch and a trip to McDonald's."

"Listen. You agree to attend a senior management course focusing on budget control, and I give you instant promotion to Forensic Manager at MCU."

Eddie was shaking his head. "Nope."

Miriam was taken aback. "What? You're turning down a promotion?"

"I get it, you don't know me very well. So let me explain something. I hate courses; they're full of wannabe arseholes taught by has-been arseholes, and I couldn't make it through a single day without getting bruised knuckles and a disciplinary record."

"But—"

Eddie held up a hand. "And if you think I'm your typical alpha male who wants to climb the ladder to success, you're very wrong indeed. I didn't even want to be a Supervisor, but some bastard forced me into it."

"There'll be a substantial pay rise to go with the new title."

Eddie hung his head. "What would I want with a wage rise, Miriam? I don't give a toss about anything enough to spend money on it, and I definitely don't give a sideways shit about status. Do I really strike you as that kind of man?"

Miriam studied him for a while, and slowly the confusion left her face. "I get it. But the terms still apply. If you want to keep this job, you'll go on that course. You'll get the bloody pay rise whether you like it or not – hell, give it to charity, you sanctimonious idiot – but you get the rise, and you get the new title." It was her turn to hold up a hand and stop Eddie from talking. "I haven't finished. Shut up."

Eddie growled.

"And with Weismann not coming back, we can save a lot of money. Some of that will go on your new role, and some can go towards another member of staff for your office."

"But—"

"Shut up!"

"No. The last time they sent me new members of staff the world collapsed."

"Now that I do know about, so that's why I'm giving you free rein to choose someone, or at the very least to sit in on the interview. You pick someone you can get along with—"

"I don't get along with anyone."

"Enough. That's the deal. Take it or take it." Miriam stood. "And by the looks of your man who was heading out to the PM, I'd say you should take it."

"Do I have a choice?"

"Eddie, I need someone with good knowledge to run this place, and that person is you. Your management skills aren't the greatest, so we'll strengthen those points with a course. The rest is up to you. There's nothing to stop you still attending scenes – I know that's your passion. But the rest needs work. This is a great compromise, Eddie. Both sides win."

"I need time to think it over."

Miriam raised her arm, studied her watch. "You have twenty seconds."

"I want Sid to have a pay rise, and Kenny."

"You can raise them a scale point each."

"How long do I have left?"

Miriam dropped her arm.

Eddie groaned. "Okay, okay. If I must."

Miriam shook her head. "I've been in the police for twenty-five years. Never have I seen someone accept a promotion in such a disappointed fashion."

"Me and disappointment are close acquaintances."

"I'll get a new contract to you and enrol you on that course – details to follow."

"I'll have a digestive to celebrate."

"Have two. Right, now that's out of the way, you'll be pleased to hear I have a scene for you to attend. And when it's done, I want you and Tom back at Juniper Hill. He'll explain everything."

Eddie sat up.

Eddie waited until the door had fully closed behind her before walking up to Sid. "Looking much better, mate."

Sid's smile was so big that his skull almost fell out of his mouth. "I feel a million dollars, Eddie! Thank you!"

"Okay, now listen, I have a proposition for you."

Sid's face clouded. "I already told you, I'm not that way inclined."

"Neither the fuck am I."

"Sorry."

"Now listen. I put a lot of trust in you; I think you're good at your job, and I'm going to give you a chance to get even better at it. I'm going to hang so much responsibility around your neck you'll think I chained you to the floor."

"Ooh, sounds exciting."

"I'm putting you forward for a management and budgeting course."

"A what?"

"Ignore the management shit, just take note of the budget stuff."

"I'm not with you."

"I'm offering you a pay rise to go with the extra responsibility. Okay?"

"Er, yeah. Sounds great."

"Good. I have to go out now. Behave yourself."

Chapter Twenty-six

The Dew Drop and the Ticket

EDDIE STOOD IN A light drizzle and filled his plain blue van with diesel, thinking about the job offer until the pump clicked off, and he had to fill out the vehicle logbook. How each successive gaffer had forced a promotion on him that he didn't want. And he had to question whether he was the right person for each of those promotions, or whether it had been their own way of getting what they wanted quickly, circumventing the system and making do.

On the way from the Major Crime Unit out to Woodhouse, he had more time to think. His office had been subject to so much change recently. Every member of the team – all three of them! – was feeling the effects of instability.

And speaking of instability, he believed he might be suffering from a little mental instability too – albeit perhaps in another portion of the spectrum. But he reflected on his behaviour at the party, and specifically at his behaviour towards Bronx, and how rude he'd been; something that had not been lost on the delightful Moneypenny. Eddie hung his head in shame. He didn't want to upset Moneypenny – ever. There was something wrong in his head. Had to be.

The road was closed.

Well, one lane was closed. There were so many police vehicles crammed into one small area that they'd needed to set up traffic control – a pair of PCSOs, who were frantically waving the late rush-hour traffic around the obstruction they'd caused. Eddie was about to add to that obstruction and about to add to the PCSOs' burden.

He swung the van across a line of approaching traffic to park along the kerb in front of a dog van. A crowd of students and men with brown briefcases and black umbrellas filled the pavement, some of them spilling onto the road. Eddie watched them. The incessant throng made him anxious to be in the silence, the serenity, of a murder scene where he could be alone with his thoughts, where he could wonder about death and when his own would be.

Where the hell was Benson?

A moment later, as he was about to light up a cigarette, the PCSO who had been directing traffic knocked on the van window. Eddie lit the cigarette, took a drag, and wound the window down; the chill from outside crawled inside, and sucked out the comfort. He stared at the PCSO, at his red ears, and at his red nose with a dew drop of snot quivering on its end.

"You can't park here. There's a police operation under way."

Eddie held up the van's logbook, the one with the police crest on it, and shoved it towards the PCSO. His face simultaneously relaxed and grew tense; relaxed because that was an end to the parking issue, but tense because a new issue had now arisen. "You can't just cut across a line of traffic like that. It's very dangerous, especially—"

"Sorry." Eddie began to close the window.

The PCSO's tense face grew concerned and then angry. He banged on the ascending glass.

Eddie sighed, dropped it again. "What now? You're letting the cold in."

"I'm so sorry about that. I just wanted to ask you something." There was still anger there.

"What?"

"Why are you so fucking rude?"

Eddie took a drag on the cigarette. "Beg pardon."

"You think you're better than me? You think you're above the law, that I'll just let your bad driving, your disrespect for me and for other drivers go because you're a... what are you, exactly?"

"CSI."

"Ooh, get you. A CSI. Wow!" The PCSO feigned fandom, then set his face into anger mode again. "Do you? Think you're better than everyone else?"

"Look, I don't have time for this shit."

"Shit? It's shit, is it?"

"Mate, there's a dead body in that house—"

"A dead body, you say? Dead? So it's not going anywhere? So it could wait an extra minute while I got you across a line of traffic safely? I mean, it's not going to get up and piss off, now, is it?"

"Okay, you made your point."

"No. I don't think I have. You're getting a ticket, sunshine."

"Well get a fucking move on, I'm growing old and cold listening to the bollocks coming out of your mouth," Eddie spat. He could see the PCSO's jaw grinding as he considered writing the ticket. Eddie leaned towards him. "Write it. And then fuck off before I turn you into a dental emergency."

The PCSO's eyes narrowed and his chapped lips tightened. He ripped open a Velcro pouch on his stab vest and pulled out a book.

Eddie saw Benson approaching, took a drag on his cigarette and sighed again, amazed at how shit a day could get without him actually having to do anything.

"What's going on?" Benson asked.

The PCSO turned to him. "And you are?"

"Detective Inspector Benson, Major Crime."

The PCSO licked his lips. "I was going to offer this gentleman a ticket for a traffic violation."

Benson raised his eyebrows and stared at Eddie, the humour only thinly masked.

Eddie closed his eyes. "Let him get on with it."

"On your way," Benson told the PCSO.

"No," Eddie said. "He's right. I fucked up." He flicked away the cigarette, turned to the PCSO. "Write it."

The PCSO looked between Eddie and Benson. Benson shrugged. With one more look of hatred towards Eddie, the PCSO walked away, putting the book back inside the pouch.

"Prick," Benson whispered after him.

Eddie said nothing – but he didn't think the PCSO was a prick at all. He thought the guy had done a remarkable job of putting him in his place.

So far, he'd met two new people this morning, and both had walked over him like he had "Welcome" written on his forehead. He allowed himself a moment to wrestle with his confusion. What was happening to him?

He wondered if this was a pre-cursor to his new place in the pecking order; and the only way he had been able to rise above it all in the past was by being aggressive. Should he start lashing out again?

"Excuse me?"

Eddie looked up.

Benson was pointing to a house with a busted front door. "Don't suppose you want to do your bastard job, do you?"

Moments later, the two of them filed up the pavement, arms full of kit. At the gate, alongside an officer with a clipboard, was an armed officer. It was Arry – the guy who'd tasered Alex a few years ago.

He nodded at Eddie. "How you doing?"

"Haven't been shot yet, then?"

"There's time."

"Okay, okay," said Benson. "Can we save the reunion for when it's not minus ten degrees; I'm freezing my tits off out here."

Chapter Twenty-seven

And the Dead Don't Talk Any More?

"SO HE JUST WALKED out with her?"

"I spoke to Richardson this morning—"

Eddie looked up, one leg in a scene suit. "Who's Richardson?"

"Richardson. The governor. At Juniper Hill. Remember, he gave us the briefing that you ignored and whined all the way through."

"Oh, him."

"Yes, him. And yes, Chester Layman waltzed right out the front door with her."

"I wonder what she promised him."

Benson stared at Eddie as he zipped up the suit.

"I fucking hate this weather," Eddie said, arms folded, watching his breath curdle before his eyes like sour milk in coffee.

Benson nudged him. "Above the clouds, it's always sunny."

"Comments like that make me want to kill people. Usually the people who say them."

"You're a ray of sunshine, you know that?"

"Your Miriam Whatserface said we need to see a shrink." He nodded towards the house. "Up at Juniper Hill, after we've done here. Why?"

"Maybe they'll do us all a favour and keep you in this time."

Eddie was quiet for a moment, and then nodded. "I think I'd like it there. Just me, one room, and maybe a decent stack of books. Some Floyd on the turntable." He smiled, imagining it. "No more people. Ever."

Benson was wide-eyed. "You actually mean that, don't you?"

"Is that so incredible?"

"Is that a real question, or is it bait for another sarcastic comment?"

"I didn't say 'no more you, ever', did I?" Eddie pulled on a pair of overboots. "I'd go there on holiday if I could. Well... not there, exactly – it's a fucking horrible place. But I could live perfectly happily in solitary confinement."

Benson had become completely still. He was looking intently at Eddie, obvious worry on his face was.

"What? What's up?"

"You've got a multiple personality disorder, I'm convinced of it."

"Yep. And none of the fuckers like you."

Benson licked his lips and tried to look nonchalant. "We're going to see Alex's therapist. Find out what we're up against."

Eddie groaned. "Yippee."

"I can see this will be a thrill ride," Benson said. "It'll be just like Alton Towers!"

Hands on hips, Eddie stared at the busted door. "Why do they always have to smash the door in?"

"Maybe no one answered it?" Benson was shaking his head at Eddie. "His car's nowhere around."

"No, I mean, look at the state of it – I've got to examine this shit."

"MOE isn't about it being pretty. It's about getting inside quickly."

Eddie tutted at Benson. "And why can't you just say method of entry? What's with all the abbreviations?"

Benson put a finger to his lip, thinking. "Well, gee, I don't know. Maybe it's because" – he looked around as if about to share a secret – "this is the fucking police!" He turned and walked back towards the roadside. "Just get a move on!"

Eddie shouted after him, "Bring coffee!"

Within half an hour, he'd commandeered some help and had the scene tent rigged up outside the front of the house, wedged between the bay window and the hedge that separated the house from the one next door. He closed down all the flaps and weighted the feet to stop the wind carrying it off down the street. Inside it, he'd erected a small table that he could put his kit on.

And then, fully suited in white, fingers numb under his nitrile gloves, he stared at the door – or what was left of it. The central panel was lying on the hallway carpet, a thousand muddy footprints on it from the coppers who'd run over it in their haste to get inside.

The hallway, and the lounge beyond, were carpeted, so Eddie wasn't too concerned about destroying any footwear evidence that might have been left after the charge of the blue light brigade. He took out the Nikon and fired off a series of shots along the hallway to where the deceased lay.

Eddie put the camera on the floor behind him. The dead man stared at nothing. His whole body, feet first, was in the lounge, laid on his right side, his right arm crushed beneath him. Eddie squatted down and peered at the face.

Both eyes were open. There was no fear in them, no terror. No scream. But they had something in them that Eddie recognised. They wore regret like an old overcoat, as if taking cover in the emotion... no, no, they wore regret like a comfy pair of slippers, like it was good to be home in them once more. This man lived with regret like it was his wife.

Beneath his chin was a clean cut up under the jaw that had gone halfway through his tongue before the blade had suddenly changed direction and taken his face off, all the way past his ear. That flap of skin – the side of his face – was cut with precision, almost surgically clean. And almost random.

The blade wasn't a blade at all.

Poking out from beneath the flap was a length of wire no thicker than a hair. Eddie squinted at it, then looked up into the lounge. The curtains were closed; fans of weak light sprayed the wall above them, and pooled below them in timid puddles by the skirting board. The room was grey with shadows; gloom had built a nest here. It crept and filled each void, turning the further reaches black until the scene was a monotone image from decades ago.

Eddie followed the wire back to the sliced cheek, out the other end, and up at a steep angle towards the doorframe. He stood, took a step into the lounge and turned. The wire was wound around a screw in the doorframe. Across in the other side of the frame was another screw that held more turns of wire, with a snapped tail no more than a couple of inches long hanging from it.

"A garrotte?" But surely, he thought, you couldn't walk fast enough for it to take your head off – if that was the intention – or to even cause more than a superficial cut. "You had to be running. At least. Sprinting, even." But why would you be running in your own house? He turned, and the sofa stared back at him, and shrugged its arms.

And how come he didn't know the wire was there in the first place?

In the lounge was a guitar. The thinnest string, the E string, was missing. On the floor next to the guitar was a pair of pliers. And nearby was a set of shelves that looked like they were still under construction; screws like those in the doorframe in a neat pile, and a small power screwdriver on the floor by the lounge door.

Someone knocked on what was left of the front door.

"Eddie?"

He took a breath and closed his eyes for a moment. "What?" He stepped back to the lounge doorframe and peered along the hall to see Benson illuminated by the diffused light of the tent.

"Coffee's out here."

"Ta."

"Well? Have you done your séance bit?"

"Is that what you're calling it these days?"

"Well, I think it's kind of creepy, if I'm honest."

"Does this face say I give a fuck?"

"Why are you so uptight all the time?"

"Why am I always forced to do shit I'm not qualified to do? Like being nice to fuckwits like you?"

Benson rubbed his face. "Okay, enough. Have you got anything for me?"

"Besides a blunt chainsaw, you mean?"

"Stop it!"

Eddie smiled. "Spoil sport. And while we're on the subject, how come your new gaffer promoted me to Weismann's seat this morning?"

Benson did a horrible job of trying to conceal a smile.

"You put her up to it, didn't you? You twat!"

"Twat? That's a bloody good promotion, is that."

"But I didn't—"

Benson wagged his head and put on a whiny voice. "I didn't want it." He straightened up. "You're an ungrateful little bastard, Collins, do you know that?"

"Honestly, I don't even play an active role in my life any more. Shit just happens and I go along with it."

"I've put my faith in you, and so has she. And all you can do is moan about it."

Eddie was about to reply that it would have been nice to have been consulted first, that Benson had no right to put in a good word for him; he was about to rant about how selfish Benson was; indeed, he even raised a sharp finger in Benson's direction, got the swearing mechanism engaged, and was about to ask whether Benson was always so stupid or if he was making a special effort today, when he stopped. The hot tide inside his head receded, the finger curled up and fell away, and Eddie said, "I'm sorry." And mouthed, "Not sorry".

Benson jerked his head forward like a pigeon, in a way that said he was top dog again. He went on to flip the subject as if proving to Eddie that he didn't dwell on the errors of others. Inside, Eddie was laughing his nuts off. Benson began again. "We found out that he withdrew his savings from the bank at four-thirty yesterday afternoon."

"How much?"

"Nearly eight hundred quid."

"Not really worth the effort, was it?"

"Depends how desperate you are, I suppose."

"Nah." Eddie strode over the corpse again, and picked up the camera. "She's not the desperate kind. She has everything under control. She got this idiot to walk her out of Juniper Hill, and then she got his money, and then she got rid of him."

"You sure she did this?"

"What? Are you on stupid pills? Who else?"

"Alright, alright. I only asked." Benson took a step into the hallway. "How did she do it, then?"

"I know how she did it, but I don't understand how he fell for it."

"I don't follow you."

Eddie approached him. "Look, go get a suit on, and I'll walk you around what I've seen so far. Maybe we can find other stuff that'll help you locate her?"

It took Benson five minutes to squeeze inside a suit, and by the time he joined Eddie in the lounge, Eddie had found a knife between the sofa cushions.

"There's only two reasons why he would run the length of the hall."

"How do you know he ran—"

"He had to be running. The wire across the doorframe did some deadly damage. If he was walking, he would have seen it and avoided it altogether. So she's either sitting here where this knife was, goading him—"

"Or beckoning him," Benson said.

"Exactly. And if, by some miracle, he made it as far as her unscathed, it means he saw the wire."

"That explains the insurance policy." Benson nodded towards the knife. "Can you get prints from it?"

"It's on my list to try. I'll get DNA from the pliers too, more from the screwheads, hopefully."

Benson grimaced at the corpse. "That's gotta hurt."

"He won't have screamed much. But there's a lot of blood, so he was alive for a while after she opened his throat." Eddie walked across to the dead man and knelt beside him. Rustling from Benson's suit suggested he was over by the drawers, looking through them. "I don't think we'll have a problem putting her here."

"I'd like to prove she was the cause of his death."

"The DNA on the screws will do that."

There was a pause in the conversation as Eddie stared at the blood on the floor and Benson stared at a receipt he'd found.

"He bought the acid for her. Look – a delivery note from BritChem Ltd. It was twelve quid including delivery." He looked across at Eddie. "That's scandalous. A litre of acid is twelve quid!"

Eddie wasn't listening. Eddie was staring at the carpet next to the blood. The blood had clotted into lumps of snot-like red goo, but Eddie saw something near it that he really didn't like. A clean piece of carpet next to the doorframe – and letters in blood: EC.

"I say, twelve quid!"

Eddie brushed his gloved hand over the letters and they blurred into just another meaningless red smear.

"Why would they sell acid to people?"

"Drain cleaner." Eddie stood. "You also get it in car batteries... that kind of thing."

"Photograph this for me, will you?" Benson looked at Eddie, and concern appeared on his face. "You okay?"

"Where's his computer?"

"You look pale. Are you okay?"

"Lack of vitamin D; don't worry about it."

"That's a very sudden lack of vitamin D. You were fine—"

"Where's the computer?"

Benson reluctantly turned around, looking for one. Eventually, he asked the obvious question. "How do you know he had a computer?"

Eddie pointed at a small table under one of the lounge windows. On it was a computer mouse.

"She took it?"

"Looks like it."

"But why?"

Chapter Twenty-eight

Tricks of the Mind and Killing Time

SHE HAD PUT CHESTER'S money to good use immediately. For starters, she'd got herself a room well away from anywhere that could reasonably be connected to Alex Sheridan, either by deduction or by means of relevance to her past. She paid thirty-nine pounds a night in a budget hotel within walking distance of the city centre.

The best thing about The Bohemia Guest House was that it had no CCTV – none that she could see, anyway. It was clean, it was quiet, and it was anonymous – perfect for someone who, similarly, wanted to remain anonymous. Her name, for the register, was Alex Collins, a name she liked to slide into when the mood took her. She'd even practised the signature, just in case she ever needed to use it in anger. She never really had.

She paid for the room for a week; the owner, a Mrs Dee Groocock, who reminded her of Sybil Fawlty, had smiled widely and welcomed her to The Bohemia Guest House as though she were long-lost family. And when that was settled, she hid Chester's laptop under the bed, and went out to buy some clothes that actually fitted her: good jeans, boots, a hoodie and t-shirt, and a warm overcoat, some new underwear, and some basic toiletries. Another ninety-five quid down the swanny.

She also bought a screwdriver, found a car that was almost identical to Chester's grey VW Golf, and stole its number-plates.

Next on her list had been a good meal – and that, as far as she was concerned, was all of her basic needs fulfilled. Which meant she could concentrate on the next most important thing in her life right now: the future.

And the future began with sitting in a local coffee shop, Full o' Beans, with Chester's laptop – now rechristened Alex's laptop – on the table next to a latte and a blueberry muffin.

It was after three o'clock and the place wasn't exactly heaving; there were two other customers at a table not far away, their conversation flattened by Sia playing over the ample music system. In a mirror on the opposite wall, Alex could make out a bored barista staring out of the shop window at the drizzle, playing with her earring and daydreaming.

Alex's table was in a strangely shaped alcove by what she supposed might once have been a chimney breast, as far out of sight as it was possible to get in here. She was busy searching LinkedIn, for someone special, when Eddie Collins himself walked in the shop.

Life was on hold. Heart in her throat. Her fingers poised over the keyboard.

He ordered a coffee and looked around as the barista snapped out of her daze and got busy. He saw Alex, smiled, and – she thought – half-winked at her. Her heart missed a beat or two, and her mouth watered like she was about to throw up. She sat back in her seat, breaking direct contact with him. Doc's words stuttered around her mind as she stared at him: so you want to be free, Alex? She closed her eyes and put her fingers to her temples as the music ground its way inside her brain like a corkscrew.

It was supposed to be an enjoyable evening listening to some New Age band called Hypersonic; instead, some rock band, or grunge or whatever the hell they called it, had shown up as replacements and practically made her ears bleed. But it was still better than being at home with her father turning her eyes black and making her lips bleed. Bastard. It's why she wore so much makeup; a difficult habit to break.

The band were called Chrysalis. Chrysalis, a new beginning; for the time being, she gave them the benefit and let them play another song to her.

He came up to her head on, smiling like he'd smiled from up at the bar just then. He sipped his drink and said, "Is anyone sitting there?"

Alex shook her head, chewed on her bottom lip.

"Mind if I do?"

His eyes were stunning. They weren't that stunning deep blue or sparkly like David Bowie's were, but they were still stunning; dark brown and so charming that they could disarm you in an instant, especially combined with that smile. He was just magnificent, Alex's natural defences crumbled and washed out to sea when he sat right next to her.

She was in awe of him and she found herself incapable of speaking. The music didn't exist any more, the grimy floor and the smoky atmosphere drifted away on a cloud of fear and Alex smiled at him and tried to peer inside those large brown eyes. She was sixteen years old, and this was the first time she had met Eddie Collins. It was also the sweetest.

"What's with the laptop?" He winked. "Looking at porn, are you?"

The large brown eyes had turned green and they were slits, lizard-like. And as if to confirm his reptilian heritage, his tongue ran across his top lip as he grinned inanely at her. His thick eyebrows rising in a question that she had to rewind and play again to fully understand.

Chrysalis turned out to be Sia again and she was telling Alex that Big Girls Cry, and the smoky room was suddenly clear and clinical and plastic; the waft of coffee hit her like a cricket bat and the laptop cursor blinked at her impatiently. The Doc implored that she didn't throw up, and the non-Eddie's moustache seemed to move of its own accord.

Alex's breath caught in her chest, and she almost shrieked. It felt like stepping back into a room she'd left only moments ago to find it was now the middle lane of a motorway or an aeroplane's wing at thirty thousand feet. The shock was paralysing. She said to the not-Eddie, "Who the fuck are you?"

The moustache lifted, the lips parted, and "Mick Turton, at your service," slithered out through yellow teeth, spreading its stench in her face.

Her toes curled inside her shiny new boots; a small lump of bile hit the roof of her mouth and caused her words to stall. She swallowed, and said, "Go away. Now."

"Oh come on, there's no need to be like that. We're both just after a good time." He crawled closer along the bench, fingers seeking her, eyes picturing her naked, ears hearing her groan; just a regular pervert thinking a regular pervert's thoughts, she knew.

Alex's eyes softened, and her lips acceded to her apparent willingness to engage with him, with Mick Turton. "Come closer, Mick," she said, closing the laptop down and pushing the latte out of the way.

Mick obviously thought his luck was in. He'd probably cast this hook a thousand times and this was the first time anyone remotely pleasant had given him the nod. The lizard licked his lips again and drew even closer to her.

Alex held her breath; not because she was afraid, but because she didn't want to breathe in what he was exhaling. She looked up into the mirror to make sure she wasn't being scrutinised. The shop had another couple of people in it, sitting at a table on the far side, near the counter, and if anything, they obscured her even further.

Her attention landed squarely on the unfortunate Mick Turton and the bulge in his stained trousers. She pulled down the zip on her hoodie and smiled at him, inviting attention. "Tongue only."

His hands were inches from her chest, dirty fingers writhing in anticipation. They stopped and he looked at her, a questioning in his eyes, a kind of longing that eventually receded and grew into a new and more potent lust. He didn't need a second invitation. Mick curved his spine, craned his neck and brought his face in towards her chest. His eyes left hers only at the last second as they sought the curves of her breasts and perhaps the merest hint of nipple. A groan fell out of his mouth, no doubt similar to the one he'd imagined her creating not so long ago.

Alex grabbed his head, getting flakes of greasy scalp under her fingernails, and twisted. A sharp, sudden, and powerful movement.

She closed her eyes, and that feeling of witnessing someone's passing gave her such pleasure that she did, in the end, moan because of something Mick had done for her. His wish came true.

A sudden fear grabbed her and shrieked inside her head so loudly, like Chrysalis up on stage, that she screwed up her already closed eyes even tighter. Dread, so palpable that she could taste it as a sour heat, flooded through her. For a moment, she wondered if she'd open her eyes again only to discover that she was once again standing in the middle lane of the motorway or clinging to an aeroplane's wing – or whether she'd open her eyes to find that she hadn't killed some street perv at all, that she'd killed Eddie Collins instead.

He let out one final groan that was cut short. And then he became limp. Her eyes slid back open, millimetre by millimetre. She was here, in some inhospitable coffee shop. The relief almost had her in tears. Fear had its own quarters inside her mind and seemingly came out to play at its own whim.

Alex had to grip him tighter to stop him rolling off the bench and crashing to the floor, bringing the table and drinks and laptop down on top of him. If that were to happen, it might make walking out of here unnoticed a good deal harder.

She peered at his bristly face and snarled. "I reckon you have three minutes or so before your brain shuts down like an old diesel engine running out of juice. Three minutes to die, you fucking pervert. I hope you take that time to reflect on how disgusting you are, and what you've accomplished with your time on earth. I reckon we'll all be a lot better off with you out of it."

She manoeuvred him upright and folded his arms, tried to make it appear as though he was having a nap, rather than suffering from a broken neck. She stood and brushed away a red flower from her lap, gathered her laptop, zipped up her hoodie and left with her coat draped over one arm.

Chapter Twenty-nine

When Push Comes to Shove

– One –

IT WAS FULL-ON DARK when Eddie parked the van in the very same spot he'd parked it yesterday, next to Benson's car in the front yard of Juniper Hill. The home for the mentally disturbed, Eddie thought as he switched off the engine. He looked at the building, lit up like The Town Hall with floodlights every forty yards, raindrops twinkling on the barbed wire. It sent a shiver pinballing up his spine. "I hate that place." It was cold out here. A crisp wind rattled the flags and whipped the overhead wires, and it made Eddie's eyes water.

He locked the door and fell in step with Benson. "You know I think this is a waste of time, don't you?"

Benson huffed. "No," he said. "I didn't know. You've never mentioned it before."

"Oi, I do the sarcasm around here."

"Let's just get it over with."

"I had to get Kenny to do his PM."

"Chester's?"

"No, Kenny died; he's doing his own PM. Yes, Chester's. Who else?"

Benson stopped and turned to face Eddie. In the glow from the spotlights hitting the old black stone, Eddie could see that he might not be in a jolly mood. In fact, Benson was not in a good mood at all.

Eddie took a step backwards. Benson filled the expanding void between them by stepping forwards, and his voice boomed in the dank air. "I've had about enough of you and your fucking juvenile attitude. I'm not here so you can play your stupid mind games with me." Benson shoved Eddie hard enough to unbalance him; he staggered and almost fell. "If you don't wrap it up, me and you are going to seriously fall out." He didn't stop the advance, and was in Eddie's space again a moment later. He grabbed his arm.

A stranger seeing Eddie Collins for the first time at this moment might say he wore a hurt expression on his face; maybe it was even shock. But he shook it off quickly, or he hid it well. "Fall out? To fall out, you first have to be friends." He shook his arm free and pushed Benson back.

Benson stopped. "And we're not?"

"Friends don't push each other."

"You've been pushing me for years."

Eddie shouted, "It's supposed to be fun! It's supposed to be what friends do—"

"But it's only fun for you!"

Eddie opened his mouth to shout, but realised he had no defence. He said, "It is fun for me. Taking the piss out of you and everyone else is what gets me through the day." He began walking towards the entrance. "I ain't going to stop, either. Like it or fuck off."

"I'm serious. Pack it in, Eddie. The next time you dick with me will be the last."

Eddie flipped the finger.

– Two –

While they were waiting in the foyer of Juniper Hill, ten yards apart with their backs to each other, Eddie's phone rang just as he was about to hand it over to security.

It was Sid. "They thought he'd just had a heart attack and keeled over."

"You're going to tell me he had a poison dart sticking out of his neck, aren't you?"

"Broken neck. I don't mind telling you, Eddie, it makes me cringe just thinking about it."

"In a coffee shop, you say?"

"Dancing Bean, yes. No, wait – Full o' Beans, that's it."

"Best place to croak. Listen," Eddie went on, "I'm about to go inside Juniper Hill again, and I might be a while. Has Kenny finished at that PM yet?"

"I'll ask – hold on."

Eddie listened to Sid covering the mouthpiece, heard him ask Kenny if he'd finished the PM yet. He heard all this on the office phone. Eddie didn't know whether to laugh or cry so settled on covering his eyes with his spare hand.

"He says... Kenny, I can't say that."

In the background, he heard Kenny yell, "Fuck off, whatever it is, just fuck off."

"Sid? Sid?"

"Eddie, yes."

"Tell him I'm offering a pay rise, just like the one I gave you this morning. One whole scale point."

"Really?"

"Yes, just tell him. I want the scene doing, and he'll have to follow up—"

"With the PM?" Sid finished for him.

"Erm, yep, with the PM. Tell him I'm sorry, but I can't get out of this meeting. And tell him—"

"Eddie, it's me, Kenny."

"Kenny, my man!"

"Whatever you want, the answer's no."

"Listen, you take this, I'll give you a full scale-point pay rise."

"What?"

"You heard. You take the whole job, start to finish, and do the PM. I can't get out—"

"A full point?"

"Yep. And it's indoors, nice and warm. Coffee shop. Come on, it's the perfect place to work a murder."

There was a very short pause. "Okay, I'll do it, but I want that raise pronto." Kenny killed the line.

The guard was standing the other side of the Perspex with his hands on his hips. Eddie passed the phone into the tunnel.

Chapter Thirty

When the Danger Sinks In

"CAN I GET YOU both a drink?" Rebecca Charlesworth clapped her hands like an unsure hostess as her office door creaked closed behind her, smiling as Benson and Eddie stood at opposite sides of the long oval table, ready to sit.

"Coffee, please," Eddie said. "My colleague will have strychnine. Two sugars."

"Just tea, please," Benson said, fingers tapping the table.

Rebecca smiled politely and left the room.

Eddie stared at the desk over by the window, the one with a computer on it – its screen blank because of patient confidentiality, no doubt, or perhaps they had a functioning clear desk policy. He wondered what Alex would need with Chester's laptop, and that led him back to the time in his house when she was sitting against the bathroom wall with pure hatred in her eyes.

"...till we're done here."

Eddie blinked. "Sorry, what did you say?"

"Can we put our animosity on hold until we're done here."

Eddie gave it some thought. "No."

The door opened and Rebecca brought in a tray. "I'm afraid we only have instant coffee."

"I forgive you." Eddie smiled at her, ignoring Benson shaking his head, and then noticed the biscuits.

When everyone had settled at the table and the polite smiles had been passed around like a tin of Quality Street, Benson cleared his throat. "Thanks for agreeing to see us, Rebecca. We – that is Miriam and I – wondered if you could shed some light on Alex's condition; whether there might be something that could help us get her back quickly. Before..."

"Before she rearranges someone else's face." Eddie said, staring at Benson's tapping fingers, and pursing his lips.

Benson stopped tapping and reached for a biscuit.

Eddie closed his eyes, slid his chair back as far away as he could.

Rebecca took her seat and watched Eddie. Then she pulled a notebook closer and flipped to the first page. "I'm not Alex's Primary Doctor; that is a Dr Ramsay, I found out. However, he's been on leave since the... since the incident. Dr Warburton acted as a kind of consultant."

"You're like an area manager?" Eddie said.

"I oversee many aspects of patients' progress, yes, so I have a good understanding of Alex and her condition. I have access to the CBT sessions, too."

"We appreciate that. Anything you can tell us might help."

"Alex is a very complicated individual. She suffers from psychotic episodes, has violent tendencies brought about by borderline personality disorder. We think there are signs of psychopathy, too. It's very rare to a get a crossover of those disorders, but she shows signs of impulsive behaviour, and emotional instability. She also engages in unstable relationships. She feels isolated and guilty; she had acute—"

"Excuse me, Doc." Eddie glared at Benson. "Can you stop chewing? I'm trying to listen, here, and all I get is your munching, so if you're not actually hungry..."

"But I—"

"I bet you're one of those people who just has to take snacks to the cinema, aren't you? Can't go ninety minutes without rustling wrappers and chomping on crisps."

Benson, embarrassed, put the biscuit back on the plate, pushed it away, and swallowed.

"Thanks," Eddie said. Then he turned back to Rebecca. "Why's she feel guilty?"

Rebecca was staring at Eddie.

"So why does she feel guilty?"

"It could be for killing her father, or her ex-boyfriend. Or it could be for almost killing you."

"I wouldn't have thought she'd feel guilty for that." Benson muttered.

Both looked at him.

"Sorry. Do go on."

Eddie continued. "But what was the source?"

"Of the guilt?"

Eddie nodded.

"We never got that far back. There was probably an issue in her childhood, some trauma that we've never managed to get anywhere near."

He snorted. "There's a team of a million doctors here, and not one of them managed to get back to the baby she lost."

Benson looked appalled at Eddie. "Hey, you can't—"

"Shut up," Eddie said.

"We got back to the baby, yes."

Eddie's eyes widened.

"But there was something else, we think."

"What else?"

"Are you deaf?" asked Benson.

She smiled. "We don't know, Eddie. But she's scared."

"Scared? She's one of the most confident women I've ever met."

Rebecca nodded, smiling. "She's a tremendous actress. And if she wasn't burdened by her mental issues, she'd make a very powerful leader. But her fear comes from inside, from never knowing what tricks her mind is going to play on her next; never knowing if it's reality or not.

"It can be frightening to realise you're not in control of your own thoughts; it can be terrifying to realise you're not where you thought you were, or you're not talking to who you thought you were. Her interpretation of reality is different to other people's.

"She hears voices that don't belong to her. Think about it; think about how terrifying that would be. It's like waking up in a different foreign land each day and having to find a way to cope. She chooses violence to keep her safe."

"Then why come off the drugs?"

She turned to Benson. "I've been giving that a lot of thought. Most of the time people stop taking their drugs because... Well, if you don't believe you're ill, why would you take medication? But that's not Alex. She knows she's ill. But hers are powerful anti-psychotics. As well as dampening down her desire to fight, and keeping her mind subdued in order to minimise the risk of it lying to her, they also cause nausea, feelings of depression, and frankly they can dim the personality until there is barely anything left.

"It's sad, but effective. But she'd need her wits about her to escape, and that's exactly what she did, gentlemen."

"She must have had to fight the fear and the violence and pull the wool over everyone's eyes."

"As I said, she's a superb actress. It must have been hell for her, though. It must still be hell. She has no help from people or from drugs in the outside world."

"Just going back to the guilt thing for a minute. Could she be feeling guilty about losing the baby?"

"I think she does feel guilty about it, yes. I also think she blames the baby for her current mental state. It's complicated, but she hates it and loves it at the same time. She feels unworthy, and she feels the baby rejected her. And these aren't superficial feelings; these are very deep-rooted emotions that she can't just snap out of. They follow her around; they have become part of her, I'm afraid."

Benson absorbed her words. After a short pause, he asked, "What I want to know is what she'll do next. I mean, will she run to the highlands or try to get abroad, or will she stay around Leeds, where things are more familiar?" He looked at the half-eaten biscuit, and then at Eddie. Eddie was shaking his head.

"I think we need to analyse why she broke out of here, firstly. If she did it to avoid an eventual custodial sentence in mainstream prison, then she'd be wise to get as far away as she can. If she did it just to be free of Juniper Hill, then she'll probably find comfort in familiar surroundings."

Benson leaned forward. "And what if she broke out of here for some other reason?"

"Such as?"

"She killed her ex, as you said, and she killed her father. I know, from reading the case files, that she considered Eddie as her third target. So what if she broke out of here to get to him?"

Rebecca switched her gaze across to Eddie; Benson was focused on him too.

Eddie blew a sigh of exasperation. "You don't really believe that bollocks, do you? Pardon my language, Rebecca."

No one spoke.

"Oh, come on."

Benson said, "It's something we need to consider, Eddie. She's a killer, and she's got her hooks in you, like it or not. We'd be negligent if we didn't take it into consideration."

"I've considered it for you already, and I think it's shite, so you can forget all about it."

"Why do you think it's not possible, Eddie?"

Eddie gritted his teeth as he stared at Rebecca. And then he looked away.

"Eddie?"

He nodded slowly, as if finally understanding. He stared at Benson. "That's why you brought me here, isn't it? You and Miriam had a go at this yesterday, and you thought it would be a good idea to have a shrink back up your cockeyed theory that she's after me, because once a shrink agrees with you I've got to take notice. Is that about right?"

Benson said nothing.

"For what it's worth, Eddie, I don't think it's something you can just dismiss out of hand like that."

Eddie's mouth tightened, and so did his chest. Suddenly he'd lost interest in being here. He stood up to leave.

"You might as well sit back down," Rebecca said. "You'll need an escort to get out, and I'm not about to summon one for you."

Eddie's tight mouth fell open.

"You might get that cell you always dreamed of."

Rebecca said to Benson, "You're not helping." Then, to Eddie, "I want you to consider the ramifications of that possibility."

"Of you keeping me here?"

"No, of her coming after you."

"You were lucky last time, Eddie."

"No one asked you!"

Benson stood. "No, you're right, no one asked me. But I'm going to tell you anyway—"

"Oh, here we go."

"Yep, here we go. She beat Tyler to death. She stabbed her own father in the chest. She poured acid on her own doctor. She almost decapitated the man who freed her from here."

Eddie closed his eyes, but not before he saw Rebecca's hand cover her mouth in horror.

"Christ," said Benson, "I'm sorry, Rebecca, that was—"

"Insensitive?"

"Shut it, Eddie."

"Please, I'm sorry," he said. "I'd appreciate it..."

She shook her head. "I won't say anything, don't worry."

He turned back to Eddie angrily. "So what makes you think you're so fucking invincible?" No effort to apologise to Rebecca this time. "What makes you think she will spare you? What makes you think she'll spare your dad?"

"When she turns up at your door, do you think you'll be able to talk her round?" Rebecca asked.

Eddie sat with a thud. He stared into nothing. He noted how Rebecca chose the word when, and not if. And it was that one word that brought him around to their way of thinking. When she turned up at his door a few years ago, he hadn't been able to talk her round then, had he?

"What was your relationship with her?"

Eddie cleared his throat. "It was private, that's what it was."

"No one is going to judge you, Eddie." Rebecca's face was blank, but her eyes showed concern. Possibly even genuine concern.

"We met at a gig. A band called Chrysalis were playing. We both got rat-arsed, got along well, I suppose." He sighed, drinking the years and the memories like a man dying of thirst glugging spring water.

His face clouded over as though something unpleasant had taken a shit in that spring water. "One of the band members, the drummer I think, was found dead the next day. Drug overdose, they say. That was the big news, that was what people were concentrating on; that's what I was concentrating on. I was mates with the lead guitarist, and it hit him very hard. I forgot all about Alex and her wild eyes. We didn't see each other again for a year."

When he looked up, Benson and Rebecca were quiet, contemplative – sympathetic, even.

"So what do you want me to do?"

Chapter Thirty-one

Almost a Storm in a Teacup

– One –

Before he'd even taken a step inside his home, Eddie could feel the atmosphere, he could feel the coldness. The fire was on, the TV in the corner was talking shit to itself, but there was no Charles.

The kitchen too was cold, no signs of any cooking going on, no smell of burning food, no smashed plates, or pans with holes in the bottom.

"Dad?"

"Oh, so you're home, are you?"

"Where've you been?"

Charles looked at Eddie with disdain, walked straight past him, and headed for the kettle. "Checking the windows are locked."

"Wow, I have a real ability to piss everyone off today! You know, this is just like being married. Coming home to a cold shoulder and a stern word. At least if I was married, I'd have a pair of boobs to look at. All I have with you is a wrinkly forehead and a neck like a saggy foreskin. Not much of a welcome, is it?"

"It's all over the news."

Eddie's eyebrows scooted up onto his forehead. "That I've been pissing people off? Wow, talk about a slow news day."

"What? No, I mean—"

"Your foreskin neck?"

"That girl, that old girlfriend of yours. She's escaped, hasn't she?"

The laughter in Eddie's voice crackled and burned, singed his throat and made him cough. "I was going to tell you."

"So it's true? I knew I recognised her from somewhere."

"Have you ever known the news people to lie?"

"Eddie. She's a psycho. She'll be through that door like a, like a... you mark my words!"

"Okay, consider both like a's marked."

"Don't get clever with me, boy. She'll be there with an axe. She'll be screaming, 'Here's Tony', like in Psycho."

"It's 'Here's Johnny' in The Shining, Dad."

"Nonsense. You want a drink?"

"Please. Anyway, why are you laying all that at my feet like I had anything to do with it? I knew her once, briefly, a long time ago. That's it – the end."

The kettle clicked off, Charles clanged mugs together, and soon the aroma of coffee filled the kitchen. Eddie killed it with cigarette smoke.

"Does she know where you live? Where we live?"

Eddie shrugged. "She might have an idea."

"Oh, Christ." Charles was trembling.

"Why are you so worried? Why would she break out of a loony bin just to break into another one? To come and get us? She'll have better things to do with her new-found freedom than to come and get us. She'll be on her toes right now. She might even be in a different country already."

Charles threw a teaspoon into the sink and handed over a steaming mug of coffee. "If you're hungry, we'll have a pizza delivered; I'm too exhausted to cook. Too fraught to cook!" Eddie was about to open his mouth with a smart remark about his cooking when Charles gave him the side-eye.

"Pizza it is." He walked through into the lounge. "How come the TV is on, talking shit to itself?"

"Because, if she's outside casing the joint, she'll hear conversations. She'll think there are lots of us living here."

"'Casing the joint'? Have you been watching Starsky and Hutch again? And did you stop to think that all that conversation is constantly interrupted by adverts for lawyers and sanitary towels?" Eddie thought about it. "Same thing, really. Anyway, it screams daytime TV. Wouldn't fool anyone for a second."

"Hey, better than doing nothing. We have to be prepared, boy."

"We are prepared."

While Eddie stood facing the window, Charles sank into the sofa. "How so?" He slurped a mouthful of tea.

Eddie turned and said in a low voice, "Don't panic, alright? There's armed cops front and back."

Charles spat tea across the floor. "Armed coppers!" He took a moment to absorb it, and to question how he felt about it all, and then he finally arrived at the obvious question, the very same one that Eddie had arrived at in half the time. "Wait, wait, wait. Why aren't they sending us to one of them safe houses?"

"Because—"

"Too expensive?"

"No, it's because—"

"They haven't got any spare?"

"Will you shut up so I can actually tell you?"

"Sorry. I'm worried, Eddie."

"You don't say. Think about it; why are they not moving us to a safe house?" Eddie finished his cigarette and stubbed it in an ashtray. His eye began twitching.

Charles coughed out something that could have been a scream mixed with a gasp and laced with a yell, and then shouted, "Bait!"

– Two –

After fresh drinks, Charles had calmed down enough to be told a little more of Eddie's past. They sat on the sofa, which Eddie had dragged closer to the fire. It was cosy, reminiscent of telling ghost stories around a campfire – not that either of them had ever been near a campfire.

"We had a bit of a spat a few years ago. Before you moved in."

"A spat?"

Eddie considered his choice of words, tutted, and said, "She tried to kill me. A bit."

"Here? In this house?"

"That repaired hole in the front door? It's a bullet hole."

More tea hit the floor and sprayed into the fire.

Eddie cringed.

"She had access to a gun?"

"Only a little one."

"She fired through the door!"

"She was a bad shot! She missed me – see, I'm right here. Nothing to worry about."

"You always said that was caused by plastic worm."

Eddie screwed his nose up. "Yeah. Bit of a fib." Eddie had started out with the intention of telling Charles everything that had happened here, the dead Detective Sergeant who had turned out to be her dad, after the dead guy in Middleton who had turned out to be her ex.

And he was going to tell Charles that she only had one target left before her mission in life was complete. But he thought better of all of that. The old man was teetering on the edge of a breakdown as it was, and one more revelation might be just enough to see him float gracefully over the precipice and into a black oblivion.

Eddie did not relish the prospect of having to call an ambulance tonight.

When the bang came at the front door, Charles tossed the cup of tea right over his head. It smashed somewhere near the kitchen doorway.

"Relax," – Eddie got out of the chair and scrubbed tea from his jeans – "it's the pizza." He walked to the door, pointing at the dead cup. "And that's coming out of your pocket money."

Chapter Thirty-two

Morse and The Fingerprint Cometh

– One –

EDDIE OPENED HIS EYES, wondering if he'd actually had any sleep at all. It was as dark in his bedroom now as it had been when he turned out the light last night, and the fatigue clogging his brain was still there, a stupid grin on its face, eyes half closed like in a cartoon.

He took a glance across at the dazzlingly bright red digits of the alarm clock to confirm that it was morning; six-thirty in the morning, in fact.

"How can you possibly wake up more tired than when you went to sleep?"

From under the door a slice of yellow light glided across the floor. And then it went out and came back on again. It did this over and over, and eventually it stopped, and Eddie heard his father enter the lounge and from there the kitchen.

After his shower, Eddie somehow made it to the kitchen and turned off his autopilot. "Thanks." He brought the coffee to his lips and took a long swallow. No sooner had the mug hit the worktop than he took out a cigarette and lit it.

Charles folded his arms and took a breath, ready to commence his public health warning for the day.

"Save it. Not interested."

He picked up his jacket from where he'd left it on the floor the night before, and almost made it all the way to the front door before Charles said, "Eddie."

Eddie closed his eyes. "What?"

Charles approached and put a soft hand on his shoulder. "Should I take them a brew?"

Eddie's eyes popped open. "Who?"

"The coppers. The armed officers."

Eddie turned. "No, Dad. They're covert. No one is meant to know they're there."

"Oh, right."

"And remember, they are there for our protection. If you give the game away, they're not going to be able to perform their duty. Are they?"

Charles thought about it for a moment. "No. S'pose not. But what if they need the loo?"

"I'm sure they'll manage." Eddie turned away. "See you tonight." He got his key in the lock and was about to turn it.

"Eddie."

"What, Dad?"

"If I need to go out. Do I let them know?"

"No. Just pretend they're not there, okay. They're professional; they've done this thing a thousand times before."

"Right. Ignore them."

"Ignore them."

Eddie swung the door open and was about to leave when he turned to his dad, a cockeyed grin on his face. "It was you, wasn't it? You were doing it on purpose."

"What was me?"

He raised an eyebrow. "The hall light flashing on and off."

"You saw that?"

"Like someone had installed a lighthouse in my bedroom."

"Right."

"Well?"

Charles sighed. "It was Morse code."

"You are shitting me."

"I just wanted them to know we were okay. I sent 'SAFE'."

Eddie closed the door and laughed all the way to the Discovery.

– Two –

When Eddie tossed his cigarette into the bushes outside MCU, and squeaked into the foyer, the smile had completely left his face. Beelzebub stared at him as he walked towards the double wooden door, her head tracking his movement.

He smiled at her again.

Nothing.

"No sign of Moneypenny yet?"

"Take a wild guess."

He smiled at her. The doors took an age to arrive and they opened agonisingly slowly. By the time Eddie had finally escaped Beelzebub's glare, he was sweating.

– Three –

Kenny's smile was the first thing that greeted Eddie, and he stopped dead, suddenly feeling vulnerable – the way you feel when there's a practical joke around the very next corner and a crowd has gathered to watch you fall into it. "What?"

"Nothing." Kenny grinned.

"You have three seconds, and then I start shouting. Five seconds later, the punches arrive in your ample midriff and work their way north to your face."

Kenny laughed. "I made you a coffee. Come and sit down; you'll love this."

Eddie followed him cautiously up the office. Even Sid was smiling. "What's he done?" Eddie said.

Sid said, "Nothing, really."

"Then why is he grinning like an idiot who just found his dick?"

"The coffee shop killer, remember?" Kenny said.

Eddie shrugged. "Look, I'm not very good at guessing, I'm hopeless at those silly mind games, and I'm useless with Mensa stuff, so... Justfuckingtellme!"

"Alright, keep your hair on." Kenny sat on his desk, folded his arms.

"Are you trying to piss me off? This isn't Jackanory – just tell me."

"The dead geezer in the coffee shop – broken neck, by the way. Ouch. Well," – now Kenny's arms were flapping as though the story sounded better with visuals – "he was called Michael Turton; local charity worker, very highly thought of, out and about for the Royal British Legion selling poppies. He was found sitting at a table with only one cup in front of him, part empty. Blueberry muffin completely untouched – such a waste."

"Nudge me if I begin to snore."

"Also on the table was his charity collection vessel."

Eddie looked at him. "Google has a lot to answer for."

"He was selling poppies, Eddie. I fingerprinted the cup, took DNA rim swabs from it too, just in case. I also printed the charity..."

Eddie growled.

"...the charity box."

Eddie nodded.

"Then I processed him and shipped him out, along with his tray of poppies. Come to think of it, there was one stray poppy on the floor. Anyway, to cut a long story short—"

"Trust me, you already failed."

"The fingerprints on the part-drunk cup came back as one Alex Sheridan. Your escapee." Job done, Kenny folded his arms again and waited for the accolades, buffing his fingernails on his sweater. "Don't forget my pay rise."

It was like someone had opened all the windows and turned the AC up to max. Eddie's heart paused. The colour fell from his face as though that same someone had opened a tap in his anus and let out all the blood.

"You won't be surprised to learn that the fingerprints you found on the Lucozade bottle were hers too. Eddie?" Sid waved a hand. "You okay, Eddie?"

Sid's voice was like an echo from a distant room. Eddie sat down on the desk next to Kenny, knocking and spilling the drink Kenny had made for him. It washed across the desk and poured onto the carpet, and Eddie stared at it; it reminded him of the blood from Chester Layman's neck. Sid ran down the office towards the kitchenette, no doubt to find the carpet shampoo.

"This is body number three." Kenny was grinning. "This makes her a serial killer."

Eddie blinked and snapped his attention away from Chester's blood/Kenny's coffee. "Who's next?" he whispered, rubbing his twitching eye.

Chapter Thirty-three

Prey

"Judging by your face, I'd say you already know that Alex got busy in a coffee shop."

Eddie didn't look at her. "I'd heard, yes."

"And how does it make you feel?"

Now Eddie did look at her. "Did Rebecca Whatsherface give you a bunch of questions for me? Was that seriously top of the fucking list?"

Miriam put her hands up. "No, I—"

"Stop asking stupid fucking questions, then," he growled.

She sat back, slowly lacing her fingers together. It took precisely the same amount of time as counting slowly to ten might. "Need I remind you that I am your..."

Eddie's eyes snapped to her. "Say 'boss' to me and all favours are off the table. I mean it; I'll play nice and I'll go along with your schemes and I'll make sure you have a top-notch forensic ally just down the corridor. But if you say 'boss' to me now, then I start sulking and I take all my fucking toys home."

Another ten seconds. "I was going to say 'friend'."

Eddie gave her the look – the one that says, yeah, whatever.

"I was. Really." She leaned forward, elbows on the desk. She rested her chin on her forearm, so she was looking up at Eddie through the tops of her eyes. "You're right. I'm sorry; it was a dumb question. I didn't realise how hard this thing with Alex had hit you."

"I was kind of hoping she'd escaped Juniper Hill to go to New Zealand and hide. Maybe start over under a new name." He looked at Miriam, and decided she was okay, that she'd become acceptable to him. Comfortable. "I expected her to disappear. But she hasn't. She's sticking around, getting acclimatised again. Maybe cooking up some plan. But whatever she's doing, she's coming for me."

"I have to be honest and say I hope she's quick about it."

Eddie glared, and she smiled at him.

"Those armed officers, and the others that are out following you two all the time... costing a fortune."

"I'm worth it. And so's the old man."

"Of course, Eddie. I'm just joking. But what I'm not joking about is the press. They're all over it. The press office has been given instructions, but social media and public interest is escalating. They're putting her alongside Myra Hindley and Rose West. Honestly, it's becoming a gruesome competition, and the world is beginning to take notice. They are looking at us, at me, as the new head of Major Crime—"

"Asking if you're up to the task?"

Miriam nodded. "We pull out all the stops for this, Eddie."

"I always do."

"I know, I know. But if there's anything you need that will help... you only have to ask."

"I will. But you have to wait until she's seen or she shows herself. I certainly don't think she'll make the coffee shop mistake again. She'll try to stay hidden now she knows the world is looking for her. And she's got herself a disguise."

"The wig? Yes, to look like Diane Warburton – I'd heard." A sigh rippled the cuff of her blouse. "And it's not easy sitting here, either. I'm not saying I want sympathy or anything, far from it. But I have meeting after meeting with the SLT; I have the Home Office on my back, too."

"How come Leeds Watch haven't tracked her back to wherever she's living yet?"

"Not known. I suppose she's good at avoiding their cameras, changing her disguise on the go... who knows?"

"I'm sorry I gave you a hard time," Eddie said. "Though don't tell anyone I said that."

Miriam smiled, "I won't. Got to keep up the pretence that you're a bastard, haven't we?"

"I feel threatened and I feel embarrassed. I feel worried. She's a fucking psycho, she's not afraid to kill, and she's bloody good at it. So I feel bad, and I feel selfish too – like I'm only thinking of me all the time."

"I'm used to it."

"Touché."

She sat back, straightened herself out a bit. "Well, don't feel selfish. I need you to focus on you and your dad. You can't afford to slip up, not even once."

"Thanks," Eddie said. "I feel so much better now."

Miriam cleared her throat. "Well, this'll cheer you up. You're interviewing next week. We have five candidates who've passed vetting, and all are available to begin as soon as you choose one."

"I get to interview them?"

"That's what I agreed to. But to make sure you don't just pick the one with the biggest tits, I'm sitting you alongside someone from Personnel, okay?"

"You saw right through me!"

Smiling, Miriam pulled out a slim sheaf of papers. "And this is your new contract. Take it home, look it over, put in the bin or the shredder, whatever you want. You're officially Head of Forensic Services at Major Crime now. Congratulations."

He stared at her for a moment. "I'm not going to any meetings, you know. I hate all that shit."

"You'll be answerable to me only, so don't worry."

Eddie was quiet for a moment.

"What are you thinking?"

"Makes me wonder what I could have achieved if I'd been ambitious."

Miriam gasped. "Well, your Business and Management course begins tomorrow, so maybe we'll see a new you."

"Whoa, I'm not doing a course while all this shit is going on. I can't concentrate as it is."

"You don't think it'd help to take your mind off things?"

Eddie laughed. "You're joking, right? I won't take any of that crap in while I've got crap of my own going on. I'll end up staring out the window. And if I stare out the window, I'll be thinking of Alex Sheridan and wondering who she's going to knock off next."

"It'll be just the right time to take your mind off it all. Few days away, learning something new; it'll be perfect for you."

Eddie sighed.

Chapter Thirty-four

The Bravest Coward

– One –

EDDIE HAD ENDED THE meeting. It was going nowhere fresh – they were just batting shit back and forth and his twitchy eye was annoying the hell out of him. He knelt on his desk and leaned out of the window to have a cigarette, and watch the traffic jam out there on the motorway. Even when he'd finished, he stayed there, elbows on the sill, eyes gazing into nothing, mind playing with the end of his days, wondering when she'd show up with a knife in her hand and a smile on her crazy face.

Back in the office with the window shut, he set some questions he thought might make him sound like he was interested in the forthcoming interviews, and shoved them across his desk, so indifferent that it actually hurt.

On the plus side of things, he felt able to leave early and go home without needing to ask permission first. He was the bossman. The Big Bossman!

He snatched the car keys from his desk and was about to leave without saying goodbye to Sid, when Sid gave one of those "excuse me" kind of coughs.

"What's up?" Eddie asked.

"When am I going on that course?"

With slumped shoulders, Eddie made his way up the office putting the idea of another cigarette out of his mind for the time being. "It was for this week – but I told Kowalski I couldn't make it, but she..."

Sid's eyes latched on to his own and right there, Eddie knew he'd dropped himself in it.

"Excuse me?" He used words this time.

Eddie licked his lips – caught, hook line and sinker. He could tell Sid to like it or lump it, or he could just walk away laughing and let him deal with it in his own way – fretting and crying probably. Or he could level up with him and see how it went. "You are better at office things than I am, Sid. Yes?"

"That's not the point."

"It's exactly the point. I dick about at crime scenes and you love the wonderful world of paperclips and numbers. You thrive on it, Sid. You love talking to people, and you adore finding my errors in overtime sheets. Tell me I'm wrong."

"That's all true. Except the paperclips. But you should have told me the truth. They want you to go on a management course but you fobbed it off on me – so you wouldn't have to do it but you'd still get the benefit. Is that right?"

"No. Absolutely not right," Eddie lied.

Sid looked confused.

"Okay, okay. Forget it. I'll go on the course myself, and you can forget the extra responsibility and the—"

"You can't take back the wage rise now, Eddie! Please!" He swung his legs off the chair and stood. "I'm about to enrol on a calligraphy course on the back of that money."

"Calligraphy?"

"It's swirly writing."

"Yes, I know what calligraphy is, Sid. What I don't know is why you'd want to bother."

"Because it's artistic."

"So is dancing. I thought you—"

"Ssshhh." Sid put his finger in the air. "Dancing. Yes. There's a Samba class just starting in Woodlesford village hall." His eyes searched the room, looking for details, looking for reasons not to attend. "I could enrol today. Samba. Eddie, you've got to give me that raise."

"Who says I don't know you, Sid, eh?"

"I have a new black number that would be perfect. Red sequins."

"So, the course?"

"Yes, yes, put me down for it." Sid began swirling around the desks. "I need to brush up on my Carioca Runs, this is an ideal time."

"I sometimes get that after a curry. Soon clears up."

"Go away, Eddie. I need to find the lesson details."

"The course details, you mean? It starts at nine tomorrow morning."

"No, no. I found those out already. The lesson details for the Samba class."

Eddie smiled and rubbed his twitching eye. "Right. Well, I'll leave you to it, then."

"Bye." And then he was dancing again and singing too. "Bom bom, bom bom aaaaaa..."

"One more thing."

Sid tutted. "What?"

"I lied. About the course. I did fob it off on you, and I still want the benefit."

"Yes, I know, Eddie. I'm not dumb." He stared at him, eyebrows raised. "Anything else? Busy."

Eddie was by the door when he remembered why his eye was twitching. It was twitching because he was nervous. It was twitching because he was stressed. And he was stressed because of Alex Sheridan. "Sid?" He walked back up to Sid's desk. "Do you know Moneypenny's address?"

– Two –

Somehow the day had been a slippery little fucker; it had disappeared in the space of twenty minutes or so. At least, that's how it seemed as Eddie watched the gates trundle open, his fingers drumming on the wheel, biting his bottom lip. His back tingled with nerves.

The headlights shone back from the wet road surface and rain fell through the beams at an angle that meant the wind was picking up again. All of these things careered around Eddie's mind and dimmed his focus as he hit the motorway and brought the Discovery up to eighty, mind already at Moneypenny's house, already fearing the worst.

Another twenty minutes hurried by, dragging in its wake a dusk that was thick with rain on the hills and thick with fog in the valleys. Full dark had crept in like a villain by the time he reached Moneypenny's place. The tingling nerves in his back had spread and turned darker, turned almost as black as the night, as it fell down the pit into something nearing dread. He swallowed and turned the motor off, more nervous than ever.

Rain mixed with hail pelted the car windows and he looked at number seventeen Ashby Mews. Her car was parked on the small driveway to the side. The mud up the sides of the tyres said it hadn't moved for a while. The house was a tiny semi-detached thing, fastened to a neighbour whether it liked it or not.

Lights blazed next door in number nineteen, and he could see people moving about inside. Someone approached the window and looked out. They pulled the curtains shut and the light diminished as Eddie's gaze drifted to number seventeen again. No lights on. No windows open. Eddie swallowed and lit a cigarette, fighting the wind and rain to do it.

Eddie Collins: the world's bravest coward. Eddie Collins: the man who delayed seeing his dead mother because he couldn't face her; facing her in life was often difficult enough, but in death it would be too much to bear.

He'd seen hundreds of bodies, most of them not in the best condition, quite a few almost unrecognisable as people. Yet to step inside the old house and see his dead mother had filled him with a fear so strong and pure that it made him immobile.

He'd loved his mother, of course he had. He'd loved her more than he had the vocabulary to express. But right then he hated her because she made him this way, and she'd highlighted his inbuilt cowardice all over again.

If he went inside and saw her lying dead on the sofa, it would overwrite all his other memories of her. It would become the default memory. Each time he thought of her from now on, he'd see her body there, empty. No more mother inside, smiling, caring, loving. No more talking and laughing together, no more arguing. No more tears.

It filled him with something approaching hysteria. He remembered his sweating palms and his nausea, but most of all he remembered the excruciating feeling of loss, agonising emptiness, and the overwhelming sadness that lay on him so heavily it squeezed out tears by the thousand. This was real pain. The hole inside him where she had once been was already a ragged cavern. Nothing inside it now but cold blackness.

He'd been late. He could have been on time; he could even have been early. But the coward in him eased off the accelerator pedal, the coward in him prolonged the journey home. Perhaps he'd done it to allow his father time to realise he'd fucked up. He'd made a mistake; she had just nodded off, fast asleep.

The mind will grab at any straw to make a fact become an error, a truth become a lie. Perhaps that's what they called grief. When he discovered that the fact was indeed the truth, he found another emotion had barged its way into the living room – an ironic term for the place his mum was found dead – and that was hatred. Not simply the how-could-you-leave-me-alone-in-this-world kind of hatred, but one tinged a strange orange-red colour and smelled of sulphur. This hatred added another string to the base emotion and created a chord that sounded like it had escaped from a horror movie: it was how-could-you-kill-yourself-bitch! How could you choose to leave me?

That had been the day when hatred stepped up front and centre whenever he thought of his brother, Malcolm. Thief Malcolm. Not only had he stolen all eight grand of his parents' savings, but he'd stolen away his mother, too.

He scrubbed away a tear and stepped out into the rain, welcoming the coldness of it as it ridded his mind of his mum and brought him back here to number seventeen with the blank car.

Holding his wet and shaking hand, dread walked with him across the road. Moneypenny was dead.

Chapter Thirty-five

Looking for a Real Live Person

– One –

EDDIE STOOD LOOKING AT the front door. Above it was a dusk-till-dawn lamp that was lit right now. The cobwebs around it fluttered in the wind but were largely protected from the elements by an overhang, there to keep the rain off homeowners desperately searching for their house keys. There were more webs and cottony balls of spiders' nests in the top corners of the front door where it met the doorframe.

Like the mud spatters on the car tyres, this was an indication that life at number seventeen was not all that active.

He knocked anyway. And then he banged.

Nothing.

Eddie bent and opened the letterbox flap and pulled aside the black plastic brushes that kept out the draft and the spying eyes of nosy neighbours. He could see a fraction of the tiny hallway, and nothing more. He smelled nothing and he heard nothing. Most importantly, he thought, there were no bluebottles. He brought his mouth up to the flap and called, "Alex!"

And then he stood, letting go of the flap.

Did he just shout Alex? He felt the little muscle under his right eye twinge again.

He put his mouth back to the letterbox and called, "Moneypenny?" No reply. He banged on the front window and made his way past the little red Toyota and around into the back garden. It was black around here too, except for a cluster of streetlamps in the near distance. There was nothing closer to shoo away the shadows.

The little LED light on his phone showed him that nothing looked disturbed around here. It all looked as lifeless as the front of the house. Perhaps she'd fallen madly in love with Ego-Boy and was now at this very moment shacked up under the duvet watching Coronation Street and choosing engagement rings from Argos. Maybe. Perhaps all this panic was for nothing, just another illustration of how Eddie Collins thinks: illogically.

He trudged over damp grass to the kitchen window, put the phone's torch against the glass, and peered inside. He could see nothing of interest; it all looked clean and neat, there was no sign of a struggle, no legs sticking out of the lounge doorway.

Well that's a relief.

He went to the back door and knocked, stepping back and looking up through the rain to the upstairs windows, hoping to see a light come on or a curtain pulled aside. He squinted as raindrops bounced on his eyelashes; nothing there, either. The feeling of dread deepened. Tonight was not going to end well.

Eddie bit his lip again and sighed through his nose.

Decision time. Leave and just hope everything was okay; keep banging until the neighbours got pissed off with this love-sick Romeo serenading his woman by banging on her door and reported him to the police, or... Or put the door in and go looking for her.

He banged again on the back door and wondered if he should try to trace Bronx. The trip to Leeds University might be worth it – but not now, not in the evening time. He had reached forward to bang again when the door swung inwards and Eddie screamed.

– Two –

He always liked how she laughed. Her green eyes sparkled, and the shape of her mouth was like an elongated love heart. "I'm sorry," she said. "It's rude of me to laugh, but you look awfully pale."

"It's what happens when the bomb doors open and your arse falls out."

She laughed again. "Are you sure you wouldn't like a drink?"

He shook his head. "I was just worried. Hadn't heard from you since the party—"

"Ah, yes, the party..."

"Look, I'm sorry. I behaved atrociously. When I see Ego... When I see Bronx, I will offer my apologies."

"No need. Not on my behalf, anyway. We had a curry after we left yours. It was like a farewell dinner. We split up."

Eddie sat forward, "You did?" He grinned, and then killed it, replaced it with an off-the-peg version of sadness. "I mean, you did? How awful, I'm so sorry."

Moneypenny put her hand to her mouth and giggled into it. "Anyway, I think it was that curry that..." – she patted her stomach – "you know."

"Ah yes. I was just telling Sid I had a curry like that once, my ring-piece was like a dragon's nostril for days."

Moneypenny howled with laughter and then, almost comically, stopped immediately, hand again over her mouth and eyes wide with some kind of unpleasant realisation. "Would you excuse me for a moment?" And then she was gone, mincing her way across the lounge and up the open-plan stairs.

Eddie watched her go. If you held up a white bath towel behind her, her face would disappear. It was like the best snow camouflage ever. She was so pale, so thin, feeble.

He wondered if there might be a chance for them again. He'd screwed it up last time because he'd chosen to leave his mobile phone switched on during their date, knowing full well that the calls he received were always from CID telling him another body had been found and please would you mind putting your social life on hold and popping over.

And there it was again: that old work/life balance debate. Hadn't he promised himself that he wouldn't get involved with another real live person after she blew him out the door the last time? Hadn't he agreed with himself that he was no good with people and he shouldn't be around them? It hadn't been a pleasant experience for either party.

But...

For now he would play it cool. He'd come here to check she was safe, and she was. Now he could put her to the back of his mind, and perhaps reappraise the situation when this Alex thing was dead and buried.

Miss Moneypenny descended the stairs and a cloud of pine fragrance descended with her. "How's work?" she asked, sitting down gingerly.

Work is horrible. I'm being hounded by a crazy bitch with killing on her mind. So far she's despatched three people, and I was shitting myself in case you were number four. I don't care about your upset stomach; I just care that you're not dead. "Boring," he said. "Apart from the woman who's standing in for you on reception."

"How come she's not boring? I thought it was a prerequisite for receptionists."

"Short black hair. Round black-framed specs. She called herself Beelzebub and she's scary as hell."

Moneypenny pointed and shrieked, "Marcie! Marcie Hamilton from purchasing!" She laughed again. "She's got no personality. Everyone wonders how she got a job in the police."

"I thought that was a prerequisite?"

Another half hour whisked by. Whoever said that time flies when you're having fun was spot on. He imagined it as a kid on a bicycle like the one from ET, a small wheel at the front under a wicker basket. Only this kid controlled Eddie's personal time and was fucking red-hot at pedalling fast when Eddie just wanted him to take a chill pill and relax for a while, maybe get an ice cream and watch a flick. Little bastard.

At the front door, he said goodbye. "I'll pop back and see you again in a couple of days if you're not back at work. If you need anything, give me a bell."

"I would, but I don't have your number."

"It's the same number I had when we..." Ah – she'd burned it, of course. Eddie wrote it out for her again, and said a hearty farewell, resisting the temptation to lean in and peck her on the cheek. To his credit, he even resisted a quick glance at her cleavage, on display through the gaping dressing gown. *I'm growing up!*

With a smile, Eddie turned into the rain, and ran across the road just as a small grey car set off from the kerb, twenty yards away. He happened to glance up at the driver as she turned away from him.

When he looked up again, doing a double take, she had gone.

Only the rain was left.

Chapter Thirty-six

Where There's a Will There's a Pair of False Eyelashes

SOME MIGHT CALL HIM a pessimist; in fact, he was just a realist with the occasional depressive cloud raining down on him. Eddie Collins was one of that pragmatic breed who shrugged their shoulders more than most, but behind the shrug was planning. And today's planning involved sitting in the Discovery and smoking his third cigarette in a row. He cracked a window to help his stinging eyes, and watched as the smoke curled its way outside lazily, like it didn't give a shit. One more drag and he tossed out the cigarette.

Through the remaining haze he looked across Austhorpe Road in Crossgates. Dobson and Perkins the sign said. Solicitors.

This was the planning. The name of that depressive cloud was Alex, and she could rain any time she chose – no amount of protection would keep him safe, and that's why he'd elected not to remain under house arrest for his own safety. They'd known better than to even suggest it to him. He'd be guilty of murder within twenty-four hours if they tried to do that to him.

So he'd elected restricted freedom – a sort of halfway house, a compromise. And a further compromise they'd made was to have no protection living inside the house with Eddie and Charles. There could be few worse punishments than not being able to just lift a cheek and fart in your own living room; having to consider the company would be too much to bear.

With compromise came risk, though, and that was Alex's speciality, that was the crack she'd crawl down, knife between her teeth, gun already cocked. No getting away from it.

Eddie got out, closed and locked the Disco, and played Dodgeball with the traffic. He entered the office. The receptionist looked up; her white teeth glowed at him and her false eyelashes suggested someone was missing a couple of sweeping brushes. "Welcome to Dobson and Perkins – how may we assist you today?"

He couldn't remember a time when he'd wanted to strangle someone so fucking much as he wanted to strangle her right then. She couldn't have been more false if she'd been made of plastic with silicone chips for eyes.

Eddie cleared his throat, put his fingertips on the fake wooden counter, and said, "I want to make a will."

Chapter Thirty-seven

A Hearty Slice of Past

EDDIE HAD MULLED OVER the Alex situation so much on his way home that he didn't even experience any of the journey. He remembered putting the key in the ignition, and the next thing he knew he was home and taking it back out again. The miracle of time travel by thought.

With the engine off, he sat in the darkness, listening to the rain on the roof. It was quite relaxing, like one of those mood CDs – only in true surround sound. As his eyes grew accustomed to the dark, the hall light suddenly appearing to his right was like a firework going off in a library. It made Eddie jump.

When the door opened, a wrinkly face peered out and its eyes found Eddie's.

Like déjà vu kicking him in the nuts, Eddie sighed and knew that was the end of his me-time. He got out, locked the Discovery, and trudged through the rain, letting it sting the back of his hot neck, and approached that wrinkly face as the wrinkly body appeared in the doorway.

Eddie stopped. "You going to let me in or do you want to see my ID?"

Charles smiled and some of the wrinkles pulled out tight. Those around his eyes grew a little deeper. "I have a surprise for you."

"It wouldn't be a dry towel, would it? Only I'm getting piss wet through—"

Charles held out his hand, palm towards Eddie, and his tongue slobbered around his lips.

"Dad? Have you got a lady of the night in there?"

A nervous laugh.

"You'll catch—"

"Someone's here to see you."

"You pulled this trick last night, you old fool."

Charles looked at him blankly.

"You don't remember? The birthday party to end all birthday parties?"

Charles's lips pulled tight, enough to make them disappear altogether. He turned and stepped back into the hallway, leaving Eddie on the step with the door wide open.

It didn't look good. Eddie's eyes widened for a moment, and somewhere deep in his chest, his heart kicked and threatened to do a runner. He felt like turning around and getting back in the car. "Why me? What the hell have I done?"

"Malcolm's here."

If the hall light coming on was like a firework in a library, that little statement, hurried out and hiding inside something like a sigh, was like being hit between the eyes by a wrecking ball.

Malcolm – or as Eddie preferred to call him, The Twat – was Eddie's elder brother. They were not the best of friends. They were not even close. Apart from the fact they were tied together by the word brother, they'd have been happy to remain complete strangers.

Eddie felt his heart kick again, and for a moment he wondered what to do – not about the heart, but about Malcolm being here. There were options: go inside and stab him in the chest, or get back in the car and drive away, or... well, that seemed about the limit of his choices. Eddie looked back over his shoulder at the car.

"Come in, Eddie," Charles said.

"Eddie!"

Eddie stopped breathing. That was Malcolm. Shouting from the lounge. It was true, then. It was horribly true. "Just when I thought life couldn't squeeze out another turd in my direction, it gives me a shower in shit."

"Eddie," whispered Charles. "He's your brother. Clean slate, eh? For me. What do you say?"

"I say you're a fool."

Charles swung the door open and Eddie stepped inside, already on guard and tense.

"I made us a lovely family meal." Charles closed the door. "Cauliflower cheese."

"You know I hate French food, Dad," Eddie said.

"Still shit at sarcasm, I see." Malcolm sat in Eddie's chair by the window, arms folded, legs draped over the arm of the chair, posh cowboy boots dangling. He wore a smile that might have fooled an observer, at a casual glance, into thinking it was friendly. But it wasn't friendly. Eddie could see the razor blade-edges in it, and he could see the barbs in his brother's stare. The whole ensemble was puckered up and ready to brawl, and the sarcasm comment was just the opener.

Eddie took off his coat, threw it somewhere near the coat hook inside the door. He glared at his brother. "You're in my chair."

"Don't see your name on it."

Eddie growled. "What? Are you serious? Are you still eight years old?"

Malcolm smiled, and his eyebrows rose, declaring that possession was still nine-tenths of the law according to the schoolyard.

"Dad. Tell him. He's in my chair."

"I've done chunky pork chops as well! How about that, eh?" Charles's enthusiasm was but a drip of warm water on an inferno. You couldn't even see the wisp of steam.

"Please get out of my—"

"Eddie," said Charles, "why don't you sit with me on the sofa?"

Eddie swivelled slightly and gave Charles the briefest of glances. "Because I'd rather shove wasps up my arse than sit within spitting range of you while you eat. It's called an exclusion zone for a reason, Dad."

"Oi, don't talk to him like that."

"Boys, boys! Come on—"

"And anyway, that's my chair. Let him sit next to you."

"Fine!" Malcolm stood up. "There. At least one of us is all grown up."

Eddie curled a hand into a fist and was about to step forward. But he looked down and there was his dad's hand gently resting on his arm. Charles was smiling up at him. "Tonight, we chat like civilised people." He looked across to Malcolm. "Okay?"

"But tomorrow I can smash his face in?" Eddie whispered.

Malcolm swept an arm towards Eddie's chair. "My lord," he said, and slumped onto the sofa.

Eddie nodded, then turned to Charles. "You need a hand burning anything?"

"Already burnt to perfection, thank you. Go sit down, and ask him what you've been aching to ask him since you got here."

"You mean, why is he still alive?"

"Go on, sit. I'll bring coffee. Food won't be long."

"Ah, even calling it food these days?" Eddie strolled past Malcolm, dropped into his chair and lit a cigarette. "I admire your optimism."

"Can you spare one of those?"

"No."

"Fine. Didn't want one anyway."

"I've no doubt you'll steal one later." He stared at his brother, his long greasy hair, his beard that was probably a nest to some family of small rodents, and the moustache he kept chewing on. It wasn't the component parts of Malcom that repulsed him; it was the man as a whole. "How long have you been here?"

"An hour or so."

"Dad, check the silver candelabra drawer."

"Wow. Still as funny as ever, Eddie."

The outer parts, he could forgive – he could forgive and he could understand anyone wanting to dress like that, it was a free world, after all, just like he'd told Sid earlier. But he couldn't stand what crawled beneath the posh boots and the skin. "What the fuck are you doing in my house? We've got no money for you to steal."

Malcolm nodded, raised a hand. "I asked for that, I suppose. I even expected it."

"Then you're not disappointed."

"I'd hoped you might have forgiven me by now." A smile that just didn't fit with the sentence blew onto his face, and then just as quickly fell off it again.

"We all need hope. Carry on."

"Can't we talk about something else?"

Eddie stared. "Nice weather for the time of year."

Malcolm sighed. "Dad's forgiven me."

"Dad's a fool. And old men don't like disharmony among their children. It's a fact." He paused, staring at him. "It's bollocks, too." He leaned in a little closer, eyes flicking towards the kitchen and the old man scooping something onto plates. "Out with it."

Malcolm stared. He sighed and hung his head down low.

"Out with it, or I start guessing."

"Guess away, little brother." He sat back, arms behind his head. "This should be fun."

Eddie smoked and Eddie stared. When he stubbed the cigarette out, he said, "You're on the run, aren't you? Your shady past finally caught up with you. You're being chased by a drugs gang."

Malcolm said, "Nope. But good effort. Try again."

"You owe money to a landlord?"

"No. Next."

"Just tell me, you tosser!"

"Here we are," Charles brought a tray of cauliflower and white sauce over to Malcolm. "I'll bring the salt and pepper."

Eddie and Malcolm stared at the plate, then stared after Charles, who shuffled back into the kitchen, trying and failing to whistle some happy ditty.

Malcolm whispered, "Where's the meat?"

"Get used to it. He's got dementy."

"Seriously?"

"Do you know anyone else who'd serve cauliflower cheese and nothing else?"

"No wonder you're so thin."

Eddie looked over at him. "Stop trying to make small talk. I don't do small talk. I hate small talk."

"Fine."

"Yeah, fine. And when you've finished your vegetarian meal, you can fuck off and hide somewhere else. You're not welcome here."

Malcolm put down his fork. "Now, why am I not welcome at my brother's house?"

"I don't entertain thieves."

"You're such a self-centred wanker. Did it ever occur to you that I might want to see the old man?"

"It occurred to me that you might want to steal from him again."

Malcolm took a breath, obviously trying to remain calm. Staring at his food, he let it back out again as a long slow sigh, and then smiled. He picked up his fork as Charles walked back in.

"How is it?" He nodded towards the plate.

"Brilliant, Dad, you haven't lost your touch."

"He never had a touch."

Charles tutted and sat next to Malcolm with his own tray, picked up his knife and fork.

Eddie cleared his throat. "Dad?"

Charles looked over.

"Aren't you forgetting something?"

Charles looked around. "Don't think so."

"Mine?"

Through a mouthful of cauliflower cheese, Malcolm said, "You lazy git. Go get your own."

"Sorry," Charles said, "my mind's all over the bloody place. If you want to know, it's all becoming too much for me. Psychotic women and armed men everywhere. Plastic worm and bullet holes. It's no wonder I don't know my arse from my elbow these days."

Eddie stood up and headed for the kitchen. He heard Malcolm ask, "Are you alright, Dad?" but couldn't tell if there was an answer.

He came back in with a grill pan. On it were three burnt chops, smoking like they'd been in a barbeque for a fortnight. "Anyone for chipped teeth?"

Charles put down his knife and fork. "See what I mean?" There were tears in his eyes.

Eddie glared at Malcolm. He didn't like anyone to upset his dad, and he knew exactly where to lay blame for that upset right now. The cause was staring right back at him with white sauce clinging to its beard.

Chapter Thirty-eight

When Forgiveness Hides

EVENTUALLY CHARLES DISAPPEARED FOR a soak in the bath while Eddie used an angle grinder on the burnt pans, and washed up. He was dismayed to find that not only was Malcolm still there when he walked back into the lounge, but that he'd helped himself to one of Eddie's cigarettes. "Knew you couldn't keep your thieving hands to yourself. That's another quid on top of the eight grand you owe us."

Malcolm produced his own packet of cigarettes and threw them to Eddie. "Help yourself."

"I'll smoke my own, ta. Never a borrower nor a thief be."

Malcolm gritted his teeth, blew smoke out through his nose, and looked away.

"How did you even get in here?"

"You mean did some scary-arsed bastard stop me entering the road until I could prove who I was?"

"You met my friends then."

"What the hell is going on, Eddie? Why's Dad talking about psycho women and bullet holes?"

Eddie sat back, lit a cigarette and breathed out a long plume of grief. "An old girlfriend of mine – I'm talking twenty years ago – has come back to haunt me. She's mad as a fucking hatter, and she quite likes killing people."

Malcolm coughed out smoke and had to gulp coffee. "Alex?"

"You remember her?"

He was quiet for a long time. And then, "I remember her, alright. I thought she'd gone forever in the mid-nineties."

"She came back and nearly snuffed me a few years ago. She just broke out of a secure mental facility."

Malcolm stared, nodding as though agreeing with some thought he was having. "Not that secure, obviously."

"She's clever." Eddie watched him. "What are you thinking? You don't seem overly shocked by the news. Do you know something?"

Malcolm shook his head and sipped his coffee. "No. It's all news to me."

"I'm on her list of candidates." Eddie had a feeling Malcolm wasn't offering full disclosure; he couldn't work out what he might be hiding, or why that would be. But he wondered whether Malcolm's return and Alex's escape were wholly unconnected. Too coincidental. "You going to tell me what you've been up to? And why you've come back?"

"I'm a journalist. A music journalist for Classic Rock, among others." He fidgeted with his beard. "And I just wanted to see Dad. That's all."

"Forgive me if I think you're talking bollocks."

"Forgiven. But it's the—"

"How did you even know where he lived?"

"I went to the old house, and he'd left. So I hit the net, and it brought me here."

Eddie was confused. "Wait a minute. You found him on the internet? And you found my address on there too?"

Malcolm swallowed. "Come into the twenty-first century, Eddie."

Eddie stared into the distance. "Fuck me." He stubbed out his cigarette and went to make more coffee. He handed one to Malcolm and said, "When he gets out of the bath, you say your goodbyes and naff off, okay?"

"Christ, I was hoping to spend a couple of days—"

"Not here, pal. Have you forgotten what you ran away from? Have you forgotten what a fucking bombsite you left behind? I swore if I ever saw you again I'd break your legs, and here I am feeding you chops and giving you coffee. Not the good stuff, granted, but still."

"But—"

"Have you the slightest idea what you did to him? He was close to death after Mum... She killed herself because of you and your fucking drugs. You ripped a good family to bits, blew it to smithereens, almost killed him too, you selfish bastard. And because of the money you stole, we didn't even have enough left to give her a decent send off."

Malcolm didn't meet Eddie's eyes. He sat there holding the cup too tightly, nails trying to dig into the porcelain. When he did look up, his eyes were wet and he had snot leaking into his moustache.

Eddie sighed. Although his anger was still growing, he was doing his best to keep it in check because his dad would be back out soon, and he didn't—

"It's in the past, Eddie."

Both looked at Charles.

"It's time you learned to leave it there. Look at that girl, that Alex, she couldn't leave things in the past, and look at her now."

"She's got a mental illness, Dad."

"Yes, she has. And you'll end up with one too, if you keep dragging your past around with you like a ball and chain. I mean it, Eddie. Let it go." Charles went into the kitchen. "I'm taking a brew to bed with me. And when I wake up in the morning, I expect Malcolm to still be here. And I expect you to have moved on and forgiven him."

"No fucking—"

"Is that clear?"

"I'm not—"

"I said is that clear, boy!"

"Dad, I can't just let what he did to Mum go."

"So what are you going to do to resolve it?" Charles stood there, an old man with thin skin, thin hair, thin blood, and a thin temper. "This needs putting to bed. How are you going to do it?"

Eddie looked at Malcolm, and his nostrils flared. "I'll..."

"Forgetting about him doesn't work, does it? What he did to us still happened. He's still alive, and he's here," – Charles threw his arms into the air – "as if to rub our noses in it! How dare he?"

Eddie thought on it. "Is that your attempt at sarcasm?"

"Shut up, idiot. And listen for once. The only way you can settle this problem is to forgive him, okay? That's the only way, boy. Killing him won't take away what he did, hating him won't change it either. Forgive, and move on. And stop hating; it's the only way to stop hurting, boy."

"Pffft."

"Just stop blaming him. It's over, it's gone, it's in the past, dammit. I heard you, what you said to him about your mum's death and him legging it nearly killing me. It's true, it did nearly kill me. And now you're killing me." He stared at Eddie, grey eyes unblinking. "Think long and hard on it, Eddie."

Malcolm sat there looking magnanimous – noble, even.

Chapter Thirty-nine

Dead Man's Warning

– One –

"WILLIAM, WILL YOU GET your feet off the bloody table?"

With a grunt he slid his feet onto the carpet, bare toes feeling for his slippers, fingers reaching for the remote control.

Dee put the tray down and poured them a cup of tea. "I don't know why you do it. I mean, it's not as though we're newlyweds, is it? You know I don't like it and you still—"

"Alright, alright, woman."

"Don't you 'alright, woman' me, William Groocock. I polished that bloody thing only—"

"Shush a minute."

Dee's mouth fell open. "Well, I must say—"

"Look!" William was pointing at the TV, and specifically at the news item that now flashed onto the screen. It was twenty-past ten, and it was the first time either of them had sat down all day. Both were exhausted and irritable, both wondered if this venture of theirs was actually a coffin in disguise.

William had caught a brief snippet of the national news while Dee was in their kitchen, but now the regional news team, with their cardboard sets and creaking presenters, were on, doing their bit for Leeds. There was an image of a woman just over the presenter's shoulder.

"What? Are you saying she looks even rougher than usual?" Dee grinned. "Bet she puts her foundation on with a trowel. I've seen plasterers do a better job. You'd think they'd put the poor woman out to grass, wouldn't you? Get someone under sixty to take over."

"Not her." He pointed to the image. "Her!"

Dee's grin melted. She pushed her glasses further up her nose and peered down through them as though scrutinising a guest's bar of soap for hairs. "What am I supposed to be looking at, exactly?"

"You really need your eyes testing. The woman in that picture."

"What about her?"

"That's..."

"That's who, William? You're starting to distress me."

"Don't you think it looks like," – he clicked his fingers – "her? The one who came to stay yesterday? Room Four."

"What? Nah, it's nothing like her."

The image showed a woman in her early to mid-forties. Her face was relaxed but her eyes were wild, and her black hair was a nest of pythons. The image went, replaced by another, this time a photofit, of the same woman wearing a blonde wig.

Dee and William looked at each other.

"I can see a similarity," Dee said. "But really, William, you have such a poor sense of shape."

"Eh? I have a poor sense of shape? As in square, triangle, hexagon, that kind of thing?"

"Now you're just being obtuse."

"It's her."

"Rubbish."

William stared at the screen until the weather came on, and then he switched the television off.

"Are you in a mood with me?"

"No," he said. "I'm not in a mood." He stood, ready to take out the tray. "It's... I was certain, Dee."

"Make sure the balcony door is locked before you come to bed."

– Two –

When she opened her eyes, the room was not there – just a bright yellow glow, and the smell of Brut. She blinked, screwed her eyes up again, and this time when she opened them, everything was normal. Except for her dad.

"Who let you in here?"

He sat on a crooked old chair by the window, holding a curtain aside, and said nothing to her. He just stared out into the blackness of a Leeds night. Traffic noise wafted into the room; he stood and drew back the curtains, then turned to her. "You did."

Alex sat up in bed, pulled the quilt up to her chest. "How come you're never around when I need you?"

He looked down at her with no expression on his face at all. He took his seat again. "Because I'm ashamed of you." He rubbed a hand down his face and sighed into the room. "I always was."

She turned away. Counted to ten and breathed deeply. When she looked again, he was gone and so was the crooked chair. But the curtains were still open. A shiver sent her cold body into spasm, and she wondered how

"Go kill yourself, you mad bitch."

she could get through the day without getting pissed or giving up her goal and handing herself in. The voices were real. There was never any doubt about that. But they were only real to her, and she had to use all of her acumen to remember that – just like she'd taught herself during the latter stages of her stay at Juniper Hill. She'd taken everything those counselling sessions had given her and used it, fighting the rebellion that exploded in her mind, and fighting it without the help of antipsychotics.

Yesterday, at breakfast, Mrs Groocock asked if she was going to go and kill herself this morning. Because if she was, then she ought to put on a good coat, and maybe a scarf and gloves too – it's only just above zero out there, she'd said, and you don't want to catch a chill. All with a polite smile on her face.

It was a shock that she would never get used to. Hearing people speaking like that bumped your heart, made you take a sharp breath. And then her acumen kicked in: would a landlady ask one of her guests if she was going to kill herself today? And do it with a friendly smile on her face? No, of course not. So she'd asked Mrs Groocock to repeat her question, "Sorry, say again?"

"Are you going shopping this morning, dear?"

She had almost laughed the sharp breath back out again. But this was the middle lane of the motorway, and she was getting used to living on it, dodging the traffic.

Alex crawled out of bed, keeping an eye out for her dad again, and dressed in the same clothes she'd worn for the last three days. Is that why Mrs Groocock asked if I was going shopping? Bitch has been snooping in my room.

A cold prickle ran through Alex's body like a spider infestation. It all suddenly became clear to her: why her dad had chosen to visit her and wake her up at one o'clock in the morning. And why she had that cold feeling of dread again. Okay, she lived with that feeling like some people live with tinnitus, but today it was even angrier than usual; louder. It was as if it, and the other things too, were combining to tell her something.

Something bad was happening. And she needed to be ready for it.

– Three –

The clock said 02:43. William stared at the ceiling, knowing he had only three hours left until the alarm sounded. He also knew that he would stay wide awake until five, and then fall into the deepest sleep imaginable.

This place, The Bohemia Guest House, was supposed to have been their ticket to Florida. It would earn them close to sixty grand a year, net. Back when they had put their savings into this place and taken out a mortgage, they reckoned five years would see them about ready to fly to America and take up residence in the Sunshine State.

Twelve years and a total of sixteen grand in the savings account made him – and Dee – more than a little resentful. That the previous owner had lied about his takings and profit by approximately eight million bloody percent chapped a little bit!

Before he knew it, his mind had switched channel and was watching that news item from last night, the one with the wanted woman, Alex something. He was utterly certain she was staying just a couple of doors away in room four. Utterly certain. "I know my shapes," he whispered.

"If you're so certain..."

"Jesus, Dee! You scared the hell out of me!"

"Well, I mean, if you're so certain, then go and call the police."

By ten past three, William and Dee were sitting in their dressing gowns with a fresh pot of English Breakfast on the table before them, fast-forwarding a replay of the news. Before long, the elderly presenter appeared, looking just as rough as she had the first time around. The photo popped up over her shoulder, and when the image changed to a woman with blonde hair, William whooped.

Dee cleaned her spectacles on her dressing gown, shoved them on good and tight, and leaned forward, squinting. "Bloody hell!" she yelled. "Get a pen, get a pen, quick; write the number down."

"I told you! That's our ticket to Florida. Right there!"

"Pen!"

The presenter was winding the story down but inserted a few choice keywords to keep the tension in her voice, making the most of having something exciting to report on for a change. "Alex Sheridan suffers from mental problems and is thought to be extremely dangerous. Police are urging members of the public not to approach her, but instead to call the special hotline at Elland Road Police Station."

"We don't need a pen, I'll just pause it. Grab the phone, Dee."

Dee sat down next to the telephone table and rubbed her face, excitement and apprehension blurring her eyes. She held a new cordless phone, which meant she could have made the call from the sofa, she could have made the call from outside, even – but old habits die hard. She bit her lip waiting for the detective, or whoever, to pick up.

William's eyes never left her face. "Play it cool, remember."

She closed her eyes and shook her head. "I am on the phone, William."

"Ask them about—"

Her eyes tore into him, and William retreated quickly. "Oh, hello. I'm calling about the news item on Calendar at ten o'clock last night. The woman, yes, Alex Sheridan. Are you a detective? No? A call-taker." She rolled her eyes at William. "Well I'd very much like to speak with a detective, please, young lady. This is most urgent."

"Ask about—"

Dee covered the mouthpiece and pointed at him, "If you so much as utter one more word—" She sat up straight. "Ah, Detective Price. Hello. I have some information about Alex Sheridan who was on Calendar news— Well, yes, actually, some very good info— I know precisely where she is. She's just along the landing from me right now."

Dee's eyes fluttered almost closed and she raised her chins as though suddenly speaking to the lower classes. She nodded, and said, "I presume there will be adequate recompense for my information? Yes, a reward, Detective Price, a reward. I'd be helping the police put this woman back behind— I know it's my civic duty, that's why I'm calling you, at my own expense, may I point out.

"But I should be grateful if the state would recognise my part in closing this investigation without further loss of life. Yes. Pardon? What name did she book in under? Erm, it was Alex Collins." She looked positively regal just then, but the charm fell from her face a moment later. "No. No. No, not until we've discussed the reward. Call me back? But, but don't you... Listen, this is not a hoax, you know, Detective Price, I— What? Very well; I shall expect the call" – her face changed back to regal; it was obvious to William that Detective Price had hung up, but Dee was too self-important to acknowledge that little fact in front of him – "at your earliest convenience. I bid you good morning, Detective."

Dee put the phone down and drained the English Breakfast.

"How will they ring you back if you didn't give our number?"

"It comes up on their display, apparently." She shrugged.

"You really told him, love. I'm very proud of you."

"They don't mess with Dee Groocock, William, let me tell you."

"So we can finally ditch this craphole and move to Florida?"

"They're coming up with a figure, I expect. Right now, that Detective Price – apt name, don't you think – will be negotiating with his inspector."

"Chief Inspector, I shouldn't wonder."

Dee nodded. "Chief Constable, probably. He'll want to meet us, William. To thank us personally." She chewed her bottom lip again. "There'll be press there, and television too."

"That wrinkly lass from Calendar, her with her makeup?"

"I'll need a new dress. A hat, too."

Chapter Forty

Khan and the Chipolata

STEAM ROSE AROUND BENSON'S head and sweat ran into his eyes. He'd made it too hot, hot enough to make his skin prickle, but he'd be damned if he was going to waste that heated water by adding cold into the bath. Nope, he could suffer. It'd soon cool down, anyway.

Benson had a Bluetooth speaker on a shelf behind him, and he set it playing Frank Sinatra, while his wife was downstairs watching Strictly Come Dancing, no doubt planning a new and exciting way of killing him. Frank was well into The Best is Yet to Come, and it set Benson off thinking about what was to come with the Alex Sheridan case.

Alex was a top drawer nutjob, and it was no surprise to learn she was aiming to collect Eddie Collins's scalp to go with those of her dad and her ex, as well as the recent ones, the poor Doc, the stupid Chester, and the poppy seller. Why the hell would she top a poppy seller?

The only thing he could come up with was what Rebecca the shrink said: Alex was prone to hallucinations and voices in her head. It was as likely to have been something as random as that. She was what they used to call psychopathic. Now she was what they called a person with a personality disorder – borderline personality disorder. "Well past borderline if you ask me." Benson preferred his own title for her condition: fucking nuts.

Fucking nuts she might be, he thought. But she was intelligent enough to break out of a high security hospital. She was sharp enough to top the accomplice and take his money. But she wiped a poppy seller, so she was still fucking nuts.

But Eddie Collins's murder would be well planned. For sure. Her intelligence was in no doubt, and Benson wasn't taking anything for granted.

They had armed officers pointing their guns at Eddie's place because that's where she was most likely to try and get her claws into him. He was safe at work, so that just left the scenes he was working – safe there too – and trips to Sainsbury's and McDonald's. They were covered but were weak spots. Benson had tried to close those down as much as possible by getting other people to do the fetching and carrying for him. And of course, Eddie had refused to have an armed officer in the house with him. Stupid man.

He could have made everyone's life easier by insisting Eddie stay home, but he had as much chance of finding success there as he did of getting his marriage out of the shitter. Collins was only a degree or two away from being a fucking nutjob himself. He had something going on upstairs in his head too, maybe even something like Alex, only much milder; no chance of Eddie throwing acid in your face. But still, there was something buzzing away in Eddie's head that would certainly place him on the spectrum.

Eddie had got things more or less correct: Miriam and Benson had wanted Eddie to hear how dangerous Alex was from a professional, because he certainly wouldn't listen to anyone else. Stubborn. But there was another reason why he wanted Eddie to go and see the shrink. And that reason had taken root at Doc Warburton's murder scene: she couldn't take her eyes off Eddie. Benson was sure it wasn't anything physical, nothing of a sexual nature; he thought Rebecca was professionally fascinated by Eddie.

And during their first meeting, she could barely take her eyes from him again.

Benson smiled, but it was no smiling matter. What was wrong with Eddie? Maybe he'd pluck up the courage to ask Rebecca for her opinion one day.

Frank took flight into They Can't Take That Away From Me and the speaker promptly declared its battery was dead.

"Fuck."

Silence was a heavy thing. And without him even knowing about it, the bath had cooled to something less than comfortable. How a simple train of thought could occupy so much time was something he was about to ponder when he heard his mobile ringing next door in the bedroom. Benson tapped his fingers on the edge of the bath. Who the hell was it? What the hell did they want?

He pulled his bulk out of the tub and threw a towel around his waist. It didn't wrap in front of him like it would on, say, Brad Pitt. His tackle was on full show. Sometimes he hated life as much as Collins appeared to. Sometimes, he marvelled as he left the bathroom, he thought Collins was the sanest person he knew; certainly, the most switched on to life's incessant shit storm. Everyone else lived through it without noticing or caring, but Collins felt it all and saw it all. No wonder Rebecca was interested.

He reached for the phone just as it stopped ringing.

"Fuck."

Benson began to secretly appreciate Eddie's rantings: how the lights always changed to red as you approached them in order to let no waiting traffic at all go through. How the phone always rang off just as you got it. How the wife always bailed out when she'd squeezed you dry for twenty years. Bitch. How Frank's batteries died when you weren't in a position to do anything about it, but the fucking phone still worked!

"Who was that?"

Benson jumped. He looked at the screen. "Khan." Speak of the devil. "I thought you were watching—"

"I got bored."

He chose to say nothing. It would have only started a fight, but it didn't stop him thinking it all the same, how that word applied to more than just watching TV. His face must have given it away.

She smiled, and only bowed her head as if to confirm it all. And then she pointed at his gaping towel. "You letting him out for good behaviour?"

Benson didn't know what to say. Was she joking? Was she poking fun at him? And then he said, "Yep, go on and have a good laugh at the fat man with a chipolata for a dick."

She took a deep breath, and then sat on the bed. "I've been thinking, Tom."

He straightened up, bracing himself, and the phone rang again.

He looked at her as if needing her permission to answer it. But he had the sense this was one of those pivotal moments. He was filled with uncertainty.

"Answer it if you want." She was staring at him with something approaching a purpose in her eyes, a hidden meaning. "I'm going to bed, Tom."

Benson had always been poor at reading women, even his wife. Especially, it seemed, his wife. It was easier to read someone like Alex Sheridan; at least she followed some kind of logical pattern, even though she might not know it. If she had a purpose, she would find a way to get to it while taking the most direct route. Whereas most women, his wife included, took the scenic route, the most obscure route, the most infuriating route! Why couldn't they just say what they meant?

"I wanted to thank you for the flowers. You could join me. If you like."

Benson's eyes sprang wide just as the towel fell. He threw the phone out onto the landing.

"Tom? Tom?"

Benson opened his eyes and he could hear music. "Brenda? What's up?"

"Your phone's ringing again."

"Bollocks." He threw the quilt back and stumbled out onto the landing, heading for the glowing screen. He predicted it would ring off just as he made contact with it, but as if to piss him off completely, it didn't ring off at all. One of life's little sideways swipes.

"You have no idea how good this had better be."

"Boss. Sorry to disturb you."

"Get on with it!"

"I think we found her."

Chapter Forty-one

Battle-ready Sleep

– One –

"The phone number comes back to a guest house called The Bohemia. It's in The Calls, city centre."

Despite Benson's optimism, he stared at Khan with no expression on his face. "Have you been here all night?"

Khan nodded. "I wanted to track any leads that came in."

"The call handlers passed how many to you?"

"They filtered a hundred and eighty-three calls and passed along twenty-seven to us."

Benson sighed. "One hundred and fifty cranks."

"Or mistakes, yeah. The call-taker had to pretend to be a detective, he says, otherwise she wouldn't have spoken with him."

"What makes you think this isn't a mistake?"

Khan sat next to him. "At first I thought they were full of shit because they waited like six hours after last night's appeal before ringing us. It sounds like they weren't sure, but the more times I listened to the call, the more I'm convinced they just wanted to be sure it was her."

"And what's your gut say?"

"It's real. The callers are greedy, but she insists Alex is just along the landing from her. She's a paying guest. Booked in as Alex Collins."

Benson's heart fluttered. "I don't want this to be another Foster Square, Khan."

"With any luck, she'll still be asleep."

Benson looked at his watch, wishing he was still asleep. It was four-forty-five. "Mrs Groocock expecting a call back?"

"The call-taker said it would wait until daylight, and someone from CID would ring them."

"Okay, make the call to FSUP, and let's get things rolling. I want them on perimeter watch only, no Code 121. And let's have divisional backup too."

"Want me to ring Eddie Collins?"

Benson looked at Khan, surprised at the question. "Why?"

Khan shrugged.

"Why?"

"I just thought... he's very close to the investigation... very close to you... that you'd want him informed."

Benson stood, looked down on Khan. "There are two implications in that series of semi-statements; neither of which I like and neither of which is true."

"Sorry, Boss, I thought..."

"Having problems finishing your sentences recently?"

"I thought he'd be relieved to know he's out of danger." Khan stood. "I've been up all night. I'm tired. So forgive me if I speak my mind. Boss."

"He's CSI. He's reactive, not proactive, so we won't be needing him tonight, okay?" Benson stepped closer, taking up Khan's challenge. "And if you're insinuating that Collins is somehow in cahoots with Sheridan and is feeding her information to make sure she stays free, let me tell you that he's the one least likely to survive any encounter with her. So he's the least likely to tip her off, wouldn't you say?"

Khan took a long breath, and it was easy to see he was choosing his words carefully. "He's had relations with her. I thought—"

"She's mentally unstable. She's not the person she was when they had a relationship. And that relationship ended twenty years ago. He has no feelings for her. And if you're worried that he's my star investigator and not you, then you have nothing to worry about. Okay?"

Khan bowed his head. "Sorry, Boss."

Benson resisted grabbing Khan by the shoulders and shaking him. "And he's not safe until she's behind bars. Get it?"

Khan nodded.

"Ring the cavalry, okay?"

"Cavalry?"

"Infantry, then. Smart arse. I want to be outside The Bohemia at oh-five-thirty hours."

"They're not going to be pleased, Boss."

"Who aren't?"

"Firearms inspectors."

Benson felt like just going home again; it was getting ever more tedious working with Khan.

"They don't like short notice jobs like this. It's not exactly responding, and it isn't exactly a planned firearms operation."

"Let me see; you're worried that this operation falls between two stools?"

"Kinda, yeah."

"I'm completely sure they'll have plans for events such as this too."

"Right, Boss."

"Oh-five-thirty." Benson walked away, unsure that he could keep his mouth closed if he stayed there any longer.

– Two –

Alex stared at Doc's watch. The little fluorescent tips on the hands told her it was just after three in the morning. The house was silent. Her eyes roamed the darkness and eventually found a faint orange glow seeping in around the curtains to focus on. Once she had latched on to that, she found it easy to latch on to any sounds in the house, too.

Turns out it wasn't silent at all.

She could hear floorboards creaking, and she was almost certain she could hear voices.

And then she checked herself: were these voices in her head or were they real?

She remembered the first time she heard "fake" voices. She had been in the shower, seventeen years old. Over the hum of the water, she heard a noise outside the bathroom door. It was faint, unrecognisable. And so she stood perfectly still, head cocked over to one side.

It came again, a shushing kind of noise, velvety like thin mud, but there were sharp bits in it, and the sharp bits were glass poking out of the top, like spikes on a dragon's back. Except they weren't spikes at all, they were the edges and corners of words. They were the parts of speech she could catch over the sounds of running water. They were the parts of the dragon she could see protruding from the mud.

The edges and corners broke through again and once more she paused.

This time she caught a full word, not the just the edges or the corners.

Slut.

It had made her stand up straight, wide eyes searching the steamy room, trying to catch more. "Hello?" She'd shut the water off and stepped out of the cubicle. Aside from the drips of water from the shower head hitting the floor, there was no other sound.

Slut!

She ripped open the door. Steam rushed out over her and condensed on the wall mirror opposite. She and her misty self stared at each other, like two people reassuring each other that they were not in danger. She took solace in her own scared reflection, and together, they listened. Nothing. "Hello?"

Alex.

Her eyes searched again, and her reflection's eyes were wide, and they were scared. "Who's there?"

It hated you.

Where the hell was it coming from? Alex had raced downstairs, through into the lounge and the dining room, growing colder by the second, wet skin dripping on the floor.

"Dad?"

The house was empty.

It's better off without you. Slut.

Alex screamed and covered her ears.

It had grown from there; that was the birth of it all. And she remembered how scared she became, how she wanted to pull her face off, rip her ears off and gouge her eyes out just to get rid of it. The Doc once asked her about the voices – what they sounded like, how they spoke.

She'd replied that her favourite track was Shine on You Crazy Diamond. She'd smiled in what she hoped was an ironic way, but the Doc didn't respond – just asked why. My voices, she'd said. They sound mono. In Shine On, she'd said, Floyd play with stereo, and that's how most people sound to me – to everyone, I guess. But in the beginning of that track is a mono piece. It sounds as though it doesn't belong, and that's what those voices sound like – foreign, illegal immigrants, if you like. They're a skinny mono voice in the middle of my head.

There were two of them back then, she said. My mum, I think. She was the first one, and the second one was me. Sensible me. Sane me. That one didn't come to me often. And now I don't hear from myself, my own voice, at all. But a few years ago, she smiled, another voice came along. My dad. He's always angry, filled with hate. They always fight, she said, as the tears came.

And Alex found herself now, lying in some stranger's bed in The Bohemia Guest House, crying all over again as the sounds that filled her head were the edges and corners of partially hidden words. Someone was inside her head, again invading her, violating her privacy.

At five o'clock, as armed officers got themselves ready and prepared to leave for the RV, sleep and nightmares came and paralysed her.

Chapter Forty-two

And Closer They Creep

– One –

THEY WERE READY AND assembled in Hunslet by a quarter past five.

It was still nowhere near dawn. This was the quietest part of the night. The revellers and drunks were home or heading there, and even most of the early risers were still sleep's prisoners. Benson had become almost detached from the gathering as divisional officers dispersed among the shadows and made sure their radios were set to Incident Talk-group 1 as designated. Now they were all on one channel, and through their earpieces, each could hear the others when they pressed-to-speak.

The Lamb and Flag pub sat quietly with its windows black, and behind it few lights were on at The Bells apartment block. High Court Lane swung around to The Calls with its cobbles and the stacked apartments squeezed into its prime land along the River Aire. Fronting it all on Kirkgate was Leeds Minster, where three people still slept out of the cold wind in the shelter of a buttress.

Across the grass behind the Minster was a short row of Victorian terraces that began on The Calls and ended on Chantrell Court. All cobbles. At the end was The Bohemia Guest House. The crooked sign out front stated it was a four-star establishment. The faded paintwork, the crumbling bricks, and the weeds growing from the guttering suggested otherwise.

In all, the area was four acres of secluded walkways, old structures, rat-runs, hidden car parks, modern apartment buildings that were, for the sake of being interesting, arranged in a scattered, almost haphazard way. If you wanted to surround this place, you'd need a thousand officers.

Benson had twenty-five: a single serial from the Operational Support Unit – one-third of West Yorkshire's entire overnight resource – three double-crewed units of authorised firearms officers, six divisional officers (all that could be spared), and Khan.

He licked his chapped lips and despite the cold, his palms were clammy with sweat. He knew there were more holes in this than you'd find in your average sieve and his earlier optimism looked foolish now. Benson climbed back into the car. Khan, sitting behind the wheel like a man made of wire, almost too afraid to move, dared to ask, "All set?"

In the near-darkness, Benson nodded. "I want this bitch tonight." He swivelled towards Khan. "And I don't care if she walks into a cell or she's carried to the mortuary. Either way, I want her."

Khan swallowed. Nodded.

The radio screen lit up and an officer said, "2854."

Benson cleared his throat. "Benson, go ahead."

"I think I've located the vehicle. A grey VW Golf on Maude Street." There was the sound of paper being unfolded. "VRM is not the same though."

"Have you done a PNC check?"

"Comes back to a VW Golf in grey from Methley, no reports."

Khan spoke up. "Got to be Chester's car. She's changed the plates."

Benson nodded, and spoke into the radio. "2854. We believe it to be the suspect's vehicle but run the chassis number anyway. Keep it under obs and be prepared if anyone approaches it. You double-crewed?"

"Yes, Boss."

"Stay near it. Out." Benson swallowed again; the odds just hitched up in his favour. She was still at home. Probably. The relief that he was on the right track calmed him slightly. He blew out through pursed lips.

"How you going to play it?"

"If it's a guest house, the kitchen will be the first thing to light up. We'll know the Groococks are up and about." He faced Khan. "That's when you and me go knocking."

Khan sat upright. "You're not sending AFOs in first?"

"This isn't a fucking film, Khan. Do you really want Mrs Groocock screaming her tits off and waking everyone up? No, we'll play it cool, quiet; get inside first, keep the element of surprise."

Khan nodded, and Benson could see the apprehension in his red-rimmed eyes.

"We'll have a couple of AFOs behind us. Don't worry." Benson folded his arms, gritted his teeth and looked out across the underbelly of Leeds city centre.

Only a few minutes passed before the radio lit up again. "4110. Ground floor lights are on black side. Door one-two opening. Male stepping outside." There was a pause. "He's lighting a cigarette."

Benson looked at the dash clock: 0530. He pressed the radio button. "Received. Is anyone not ready?"

No reply.

He nodded at Khan. "Okay, we're moving to black."

As Benson and Khan walked along the cobbles, past the designated white side – the front of the building – and then left, along the red side, they were joined by two silent authorised firearms officers who escorted them to the rear of the building – the black side, where lighting was poorest – and through a low gate. They stepped aside and let Benson and Khan take the lead.

Up ahead, they walked along a short stone pathway that led to the kitchen door. A man there, leaning against a wall, and smoking a cigarette, suddenly stood straight and tense.

Benson showed the palms of his hands, and whispered, "Mr Groocock, it's okay, we're police officers. Nothing to worry about."

William Groocock's shoulders rounded, and he patted his chest. "Frightened the life out of me." He dropped the cigarette into a bucket that was already full of cigarette ends. It smouldered in the cold air. "Are you here—"

Benson shushed him with a finger over his lips.

"Can we speak inside?" asked Khan.

Groocock nodded and disappeared through a chain curtain over the doorway and into the kitchen.

– Two –

"Where's Mrs Groocock?" Khan asked.

"How did you find us? I mean, we didn't—"

Khan looked over William's shoulder. "Is she about?"

"So do you have a figure in mind?" William looked from Khan to Benson and back again, a friendly but business-like smile on his face. "I've never done this before; do we sit down with a negotiator and barter, or what?"

"What are you talking about?" Benson stared down at him.

"The reward. For information leading to the arrest of Alex Whatsherface."

Benson moved forward and William swallowed, took a bigger step back. "There is no reward. We're about to save the public more loss of life by taking her into custody. You and your wife will be so grateful to us that recompense won't even enter your heads. Am I right?"

William chewed his bottom lip. "I don't think Dee will see it that way."

"She will. Eventually."

"Where is she?" Khan asked again.

"Dee? She's having her shower." He looked at his watch. "She'll be down in four minutes. She's front of house, and a stickler for punctuality, is Dee."

Benson waved the armed officers inside. “One by the stairs door, and one by the front door.” He turned to face Groocock again. “Which room is Alex in?”

“Four, I think. But really, gentlemen, please – let’s wait for Dee to get here. Won’t be long.”

Chapter Forty-three

Bad Timing and a Lack of Vigilance

– One –

THERE WAS SOMETHING QUITE delicious about being in someone else's room illegally. Alex had almost leapt out of bed, dressed, and silently stalked across the landing, because the police had arrived. From behind the net curtains in her room, she'd seen them organise themselves across the cobbled lane down there, even seen two of them in plain clothes enter the rear garden with two armed officers, all dressed in black.

From down the stairs and in towards the reception area, she could hear hushed voices.

The door to the Groococks' room was unlocked. Mr Groocock was not inside; Mr Groocock would be the owner of one of those hushed voices she'd heard. She stepped in and closed the door behind her. And locked it. There was a background noise that blended in with her tinnitus, a constant hissing noise like air escaping from a leaking tyre.

Ahead of her was the lounge, and off to the right, she guessed, was the bathroom. As she crossed the lounge, her eyes were drawn to the TV in the corner, by the curtained balcony window. The screen had been paused and on it was the face of a worn-out newsreader. Over the newsreader's shoulder was an image of her.

Now you know why the police are here.

"Leave me alone."

Conspicuous by its abrupt ending, the hissing noise stopped. Alex looked towards the bathroom door and licked her strawberry-flavoured lips. Mrs Groocock would be out any second.

– Two –

William looked at his watch again. He smiled at Benson; the kind of smile two strangers give each other as they're waiting for a train. "She'll be down any second."

Benson nodded.

"I'm going to start making breakfast for the earlies – that's what we call the early risers."

Benson nodded again, tapping his fingers on the reception desk.

"Would you like anything, Inspector?"

"No, thank you."

"I could murder a coffee," Khan said. "Been up all night."

"Coming right up. Sure you won't have one, Inspector?"

"I thought you said she was a stickler for timekeeping?"

"Give her a few more minutes."

Benson held out his hand. "Key."

"What?"

"Key to room four."

"Dee usually handles—"

"Now." He wagged his fingers, and William dropped the key to room four in his hand. Benson walked towards the stairs, saying, "Come with me," to the armed officer.

"Boss? What about—"

"Stay there, Khan."

1784 was cold. He was shuffling from foot to foot, wishing he'd put on a base layer because the cold was eating him alive with its sharp little teeth. He was watching Green Side but the streetlights around here were those from the sixties – dull orange things that grudgingly gave up a small pool of bile-coloured light.

And anyway, Green Side was like a no man's land with overgrown bushes, brick walls that had part-collapsed, surrounding what once might have been a garden. It was almost impossible to say that for certain, of course, since the whole scene, apart from his own puddle of bile, was just a vision of blackness.

He'd only glanced away for a moment, beginning the ritual of looking for somewhere discreet to take a piss before this thing got going – if it ever did get going, or before daylight came along and ruined any chance of discretion he might have.

He'd been in the job long enough to know that ninety percent of these operations came to naught, and everyone would file away contemplating a certain mixture of relief and frustr—

"And we'll be having no more birthday parties there, Jeremy. The catering was abysmal..."

She came from nowhere. A woman wearing a three-quarter-length trench coat and a head scarf, carrying a laptop bag and something you might call a carpet bag. The need to relieve himself forgotten, he watched her walking along the cobbles, oblivious to his presence, phone wedged against her shoulder.

"And I'm no fan of Trisha, either. I won't be inviting her around for Christmas drinks..."

1784 clicked his radio. "Any news, Boss? I have a female walking along Green Side."

Benson quietly turned the key, twisted the doorknob and pushed. The door squeaked a little. There was a glimmer of orange light seeping in around the curtains, but it was sufficient to see the mound lying under a duvet on the bed. He stepped into the room as his radio lit up.

"Any news, Boss? I have a female walking along Green Side."

Benson turned on the light and felt relieved to see the mound was human-shaped; he was almost delighted to see the hand of a female poking out from under the quilt. "Let her go. We have who we came for."

The woman didn't stop talking the whole time. She put down the bag and fumbled in her coat pocket for keys. The car, a white Mini, flashed its lights. She opened the passenger door, tossed the bags inside and walked around to the driver's side.

Once inside, she started the engine and drove cleanly away.

As Benson stepped further into the room, he noticed the hand – how old it looked, how wrinkled it was, which was fine for a sixty-year-old lady, but a bit strange for someone twenty years younger. And as if to accompany that oddity, there was the blood.

Chapter Forty-four

Lady Penelope and Earl Grey

EDDIE DIDN'T LOOK UP as he marched through reception. He hoped Beelzebub wouldn't spot him. He also hoped that Moneypenny would be back soon; he didn't like starting off the day under scrutiny, being taunted by the devil herself. He liked it when he had something divine to look at, not something with scales.

It would be good to see Moneypenny again.

And then it happened. Involuntarily, he flicked his eyes up in her direction. There she was standing behind the reception desk, arms folded, glaring at him. Eddie suddenly felt two feet shorter – and vulnerable. He was sure the foyer had grown another mile or two, and the doors were now just tiny little things in the distance. And he knew when he got there, he wouldn't have the strength to push them open and she'd start to laugh at him and...

On the other side of the doors he rested, could feel little beads of sweat on his top lip. That woman had to go.

He crested the stairs and saw how empty the CID office was. He looked around for Benson, someone he in turn could make feel small and so regain some of his lost composure, but Benson wasn't there. The few people in the office were busy on the phone, or scratching their heads, or studying their computers. There was an unusual air to the place; Eddie christened it diligence.

In the CSI office, Sid greeted him with a mug of coffee and a plate of bourbons.

"Bourbons?" He looked at Sid. "Is it Monday already?"

"No, but today could be just as stressful for you, so I thought I'd break out the good biscuits."

"I didn't get bourbons!" Kenny shouted.

"Stressful?" Said Eddie.

Sid whispered, "She's in your office."

Eddie whispered in return, "Who's in my fucking office, Sid?"

"A lady. Penelope."

"Lady Penelope? She's here?"

From behind Sid, Kenny was laughing. "I want to sit in, please let me sit in."

Eddie bit his top lip. "I'm going to punch you in the stomach in a minute, Sid. Now tell me!"

"She's from Personnel. Said she was here to assist you."

"With what?"

Sid shrugged.

"You are as much use as a deckhand on a submarine. You're supposed to be on my side, protecting me, making sure these arseholes don't stab me in the back."

Sid pulled a face and walked off.

"Traitor." Eddie kicked his office door open and spilled his coffee all in one graceful movement. "Fuck." And then the biscuits slid off the plate. "Fuck." He looked up and saw a woman sitting in the guest chair, legs crossed, pad and pen already in her hands. She looked at Eddie and the biscuits on the floor and the coffee soaking into his trouser leg, and smirked. Beside his own chair, another chair had appeared. This place isn't big enough for one chair, he thought, let alone three. What's that doing here?

"Can I help you with those?"

Eddie stared at her. She was looking at his biscuits. "No. I got it. Thank you." He put his coffee and the empty plate on his desk and went back for the biscuits, shoving one in his mouth before he even got back to his seat. He stared at her some more and realised it must have come across as incredibly rude that he didn't accept her offer, and he hadn't introduced himself.

He dusted off the bourbon on his plate, took the other from his mouth and put that on the plate too. He looked from the biscuits to the woman. She shook her head, and Eddie breathed out.

She's going to want to shake hands, he thought. I know it, I can see it in her eyes. He licked the crumbs from his lips, thought he'd better get it over with, and stretched out a hand in her direction.

To his utmost surprise and delight, she only looked at it.

"I don't shake, I'm afraid."

He smiled at her, relaxed a bit, and said. "It's so nice to meet someone else who dislikes contact with people as much as I do."

"It's why I chose a career in personnel."

Eddie nodded. He didn't have a clue what the hell she was talking about. "Indeed," he said. "I'm Eddie Collins."

She nodded. "I know. Shall we get started?"

"Started?"

"Interviews for CSI?"

Eddie almost burst. "Ah! That's why you're... I'd forgotten... that's today?"

She nodded and offered a smile that suggested she felt sorry for him.

"Calendar's all messed up. I'm normally very organised." He pointed to the door. "It's Sid; he's supposed to be... he's my..." He picked up the phone and shouted, "You're sacked!"

"Shall we get on?"

"Let's, yes."

She stood, opened the door, and called, "Sid. Can we have the first one, please?"

Eddie heard Sid say, "Certainly, Penelope."

Who the fuck is called Penelope these days? All he could think of was Penelope Pitstop and her pink jumpsuit. He looked at her and could easily imagine her in a pink jumpsuit. And then he could easily imagine her climbing out of a pink jumpsuit.

"...Eddie?"

Eddie snapped out of it, looked up, and there was Penelope with a young man standing beside her. "Sorry, was thinking about... scene work."

"This is Jason." She turned to the young man. "Come in. I'm Penelope from Personnel, and this is Eddie Collins, Head of the forensic department."

Please don't shake hands, please don't shake hands. "Sit down, Justin."

Jason sat down, looked between the two, wondering whether to correct Eddie or not, and decided he should. "My name is Jason." He held out a hand.

"Jason, sorry." Eddie ignored the hand, picked up a pen, and pretended to write it down.

"Eddie has prepared a few questions for you. Haven't you, Eddie?"

Eddie stared at her, stared at the kid, and wondered just what the hell she was talking about.

"I think I saw them..." Penelope pointed to Eddie's desk.

"Thank you." He wondered if she had been politely curious when she was in his office all by herself, or just plain nosy. And then he wondered why he'd forgotten that he'd even prepared any questions. Was he losing his mind? He dragged the sheet over, shielding the coffee cup stains from Jasper.

The kid cleared his throat. "I expect you'd like to hear about my qualifications for the position, and what work I've done in preparation for our meeting?"

"Have you brought your application form?"

The kid looked worried; he said to Penelope, "I sent it through to the MCU Mailbox as the instructions said."

"Yes, yes, of course," Eddie said. "I've got them on the system, but I don't want to hear about your qualifications, thank you. I want to know about you as a person." He sneaked a quick glance at Penelope and thought he'd recovered quite well. "What makes you want to work here?"

Jason stuttered and almost smiled. "It's on my form."

"But you can still speak, can't you?"

Penelope coughed.

Eddie noted the cough, and smiled at the kid. "I'd like to hear it from you."

"I... I like the thought of piecing puzzles together. I like the thought of working out a problem until we have a solution. Of course," he went on, his sweaty hands pressed tightly together, "I would use the NDM, and have studied the Standard Operating Procedures and Best Practice manuals, so I would..."

Eddie stared at him.

"I would..." He rubbed his hands on his suit trousers. He swallowed and looked up at Eddie. "I just like working with dead people."

Eddie ran a hand over his chin. "Have you thought of a career with CID?"

"Sorry?"

He ignored the frown on Penelope's face. "Or even Personnel?"

"I'd be an asset to the team," Jason obviously sensed the interview grinding to an end. "Prepared to work all hours. You know."

"Well, Julian, thanks for coming in. Really appreciate it. We'll be in touch."

The kid sat there, smiling at Eddie.

"The door's behind you."

"Oh. Is that it?"

"I think Eddie might have another—"

"No," Eddie said. "Eddie has made his evaluation, thank you. Goodbye."

The kid looked at Penelope for some kind of reassurance. Maybe the big bad man was playing a trick on him. Maybe it was part of a role-playing exercise, and they just wanted to see how he reacted when someone was being rude to him. He grinned. "You almost got me there." He straightened in the chair. "How am I doing?"

"Goodbye." Eddie stared at him. "Sid will give you a garibaldi on your way out."

When the kid stood and turned, Eddie noticed a damp patch on the arse of his trousers. Sweat. He'd been really nervous. And for a moment he wondered how it must feel for them, the candidates, as they sat there hoping Eddie might change their futures for the better. It must have been terrifying. But it is what it is, Eddie thought. I have to get this right; I'm going to be working with them.

"I thought you were very rude."

Eddie raised an eyebrow. "I don't care what you think. You're here to observe. So observe. And shut up, keep your opinions to yourself, because I don't really give a shit what you think. Okay, love?"

He expected her to take offence at that, to start crying or to storm out, angry and full of thoughts of Grievance Procedures. But she didn't. Instead, she grinned, nodded in what almost looked like respect for him, and said, "It's so nice to meet the real Eddie Collins at last." She uncrossed her legs and leaned toward him. "I've heard a lot about you."

"Send in the next one, Penny."

"Why didn't you like him?"

"Plays life by the book. I don't like that kind of behaviour; shows a complete inability to think for oneself."

Penny nodded discreetly.

"And anyway, what the hell is the NDM?"

The next one was called, "Trudy Truelove, pleased to meet you both." She sat in the chair without being invited and turned to face Eddie, with her back almost full on to Penelope.

Eddie almost pissed his pants right there. Trudy? Jesus wept. "And tell me, Trudy, why you want to work here?"

"The money is good."

Eddie nodded. "That it?"

She shrugged. "You get to be on telly every now and then."

"That's not quite the answer I was looking for."

"Oh right, sorry. You're after all them buzzwords, eh? Erm, hold on," she turned her hand over and read from it, "I like to work the forensic strategy, I want to be involved with furthering forensic—"

"Where do you work right now, Trudy?"

"I'm in the evidence stores at Weetwood nick."

"Thanks for coming, Trudy," said Penelope. "We'll let you know."

"Oh, is that it?" She stood. "That was easy. They said it'd be much harder than that; I did a load of reading for this, and I even watched CSI: Miami. I'll be in for the rest of the afternoon if you want to call me. But I'll be out in Leeds tonight; it's Mandy's leaving do and I'll be holding her hair out of the toilet bowl by eight. My turn."

Eddie had finished his second coffee by the time he learned from Sid that two of the candidates hadn't shown up. One had called in to say they didn't want the job any more because they'd found out who was in charge, and the other one had sprained his wrist.

"Wankers," Eddie said.

"One left, then," said Penelope. "Send them in, Sid, if you wouldn't mind."

"Time for another tea first," Sid said. "They're not due for another hour."

"She doesn't want tea," Eddie said. "She'd like to get this torture out of the way and piss off back to Personnel. Wouldn't you, Penny?"

Sid shrugged. "I can't help it if you're so popular, Eddie."

"I could think of better things to be doing," Penelope said. "But thank you, Sid, I'd love another."

"I'll get the Earl Grey. Twinings," he whispered. "Very nice. And the reason the tea fund owes me thirty-five quid." He stared at Eddie. "Just saying."

Penelope caught Sid by the arm. "I love the nail varnish, by the way."

"It's Chanel Le Vernis. Classic Burgundy, it's called."

"Alright, alright. Sid, bugger off and get the drinks." He sighed. "God, I'm bored."

Chapter Forty-five

A Shit-Fest and Seeping Lavender

Eddie was leaning out of the window, smoking a very welcome cigarette, passing it back and forth to Penelope as they talked about the candidates and how using a proper interviewer would perhaps have been a better proposition than merely making it up as he went along, when there came a knock at the door.

"Not yet, Sid! We're still working on the questions."

Irrespective of Eddie's command, the door creaked open an inch and Sid whispered, "Eddie, Miriam's here. She looks... pensive."

Eddie flicked the cigarette, climbed down off the desk, and sprayed Scent of Lavender until it was lying as thick as fog. "Send her in," he coughed.

"I think it would be wiser if you came out, really."

Eddie waved away some of the fog. "Yep." He coughed again. "You might be right."

Out in the main office, Miriam paced a patch of floor until she was wearing out the carpet, arms under her pits, looking like someone was pointing a gun at her.

"It's not good news, is it? I can tell; I'm very perceptive of the human emotional spectrum now. I can recognise most of them."

Miriam watched him. Her eyes said – Is that it? Can I speak now?

"Go on."

"We have another death. At the B&B she was staying at."

"Who, Alex?" He closed his eyes. "Of course, Alex. She's top billing these days, isn't she? Every fucking day."

"It's a mess. Briefly, we got a call from the news appeal last night. The landlady of The Bohemia Guest House in The Calls said that Alex was one of her guests. Tom arranged an operation…" Miriam sighed. "She got away. Left the landlady dead in her bed. In Alex's bed, I mean."

Eddie was wide-eyed. "What a shit-fest. She has to run out of luck some time."

"It's not luck. The operation was shoddy; she was smart, almost like she was expecting us."

"How's Benson taking it?"

"He's beside himself."

"Christ. Imagine that: two Bensons."

Miriam did not smile.

"Sorry."

"The scene needs processing. I can't hang about trying to find a solution for you; I've got an important meeting this afternoon. I can't get out of it."

"I can't leave this." Eddie nodded towards the layer of lavender seeping through the gap under his office door. "Not now. God knows when I can arrange for candidates to come back again. If we don't get this sorted today, we won't be getting any more staff, and we need more staff."

"What do you suggest?"

Both of them turned around and stared at Kenny.

Kenny looked up from his newspaper. "What now?"

Chapter Forty-six

New Pain in Old Wounds

MALCOLM CRADLED THE CUP as he sank into Eddie's chair. The smell of bacon burning in the kitchen was divine. He took a sip, put the cup on a small wooden table next to the chair and reached for the remote. He pressed the power button, but nothing happened.

A purple cloud roiled slowly from the kitchen; as Malcom pressed the power button even harder, the smoke alarm sounded. He rushed to the kitchen and took the pan of burning bacon off the gas. His Dad wasn't there.

The side door opened, and Charles whistled his way into the hallway and grimaced at the noise and the smoke. He stopped whistling and rushed into the kitchen. Malcolm grabbed the open door and wafted the smoke out. Eventually, the alarm stopped.

"They make those things too sensitive."

Malcolm stared at his dad, mouth open in shock.

"Seriously, that's the fourth time in as many days. It's going to need new batteries soon. Stupid thing."

"Where did you go?"

"I just took the armed coppers a cup of tea and some toast. I would've taken them a bacon sandwich but we're nearly out.

Nice lads – Arry and Twiggy, they're called. I think Twiggy is a vegetarian."

"You're feeding the undercover officers?"

"It's only polite. Manners cost nothing, Malcolm." He turned to the frying pan. "Love crispy bacon."

They sat in the lounge and devoured the sandwiches. Malcolm tried the remote again. Still nothing.

"You'll be there all day trying to get that thing working."

"Why? What's wrong with it?"

Charles took the empty plates back into the kitchen and refilled the kettle. "Eddie cut the plug off it."

"He...Why did he cut the plug off?"

Over the boiling kettle, Charles shouted, "He said there was too much sh— He said it was rubbish, polluting my mind."

"I'm worried about him," said Malcolm. "Sounds like he's losing the plot to me."

"If I want to watch anything, I just use the laptop." Charles came back in carrying two mugs of coffee. "He's under a lot of strain right now with work. That girl. Did he tell you they'd promoted him? Head of Forensic Services at Major Crime Unit. Hell of a title, eh?" The proud smile straightened out. "But he said there's only three of them works there. Not much of an empire, is it?"

"Hefty responsibility though."

Charles nodded, thinking. He looked Malcolm right in the eyes. "It's great to see you again, son." He licked his lips. "But why are you here? Really? What's your responsibility?"

"Woah, can't a man come home to see..."

Charles was shaking his head. "Come on, out with it. You've been gone for years. No Christmas cards, no birthday messages. Nothing. And then, poof, you're suddenly back as though nothing has happened."

"I missed you."

Charles stared.

"Seriously. I did."

"What, it just hit you after twenty years of not missing me?"

Malcolm looked at the television.

"Seems a bit coincidental. That Alex girl and you turning up in the same week, more or less."

Malcolm shrugged. "Coincidences happen, Dad. That's why there's a name for them."

"There is, but I prefer the term Eddie uses for them: bullshit."

A smile ruptured Malcolm's discomfort. "I know I've been a bit absent lately."

"As understatements go... I'd forgotten what you even looked like. Do you have family? Wife, kids?"

"Nope. I'm still young, free, and egotistical. I got a comfortable life, Dad; no responsibilities. I do what I want when I want. Don't have to answer to no one."

Charles was quiet for a time, then asked, "Don't you want those things? Kids are a strain, but they're wonderful, son—"

"I'm happy just the way things are. I see people getting married, divorced, sharing out the booty of a short life together, maybe harming some kids in the process. It's not for me. I don't do family stuff."

Charles was nodding. "Yeah, I noticed that. You never got to finish your family life with us before you upped and left." He was gritting his teeth. "I did all the hard work. We did all the hard work, bringing you up, turning you into a man. And I never got to see what you did with it all."

"You feel cheated?"

"I feel robbed."

Malcolm gave a big nod. "Ah. Now I see where this is going."

"You do? Well, you're wrong. I know you took that eight grand. But it's in the past now; I'm not losing sleep over it, son. But I do feel robbed of knowing you." He sighed. "I don't suppose you understand, but I put a lot of time and effort into you... because I loved you. And I wanted to carry on loving you for years and years.

"But you took it from me, all that time, all those experiences. You stole them from me, Malcolm." He smiled and looked down at his feet; a tear fell from his eye. "And I suppose once you've caught up with me and Eddie for a couple of days, you'll go again. Once you've had your fill. You'll just go. Poof."

Charles looked.

There were tears in Malcolm's eyes too. When he heard the story of their lives like that, it was upsetting. He'd always just got on with it; never had a voice in his head telling him to contact home; never gave those he ran away from too much thought. And looking back on it now, and having his father enhance his own thoughts, it was clear that he'd been very selfish all this time.

But the decision to leave hadn't been a difficult one. It had been thrust upon him; the course of his life had been changed by something out of his own control, like a river redirected by a dam. It hadn't been his fault.

And making people see that dam, way upstream in his life, would be too difficult a task. It was easier just to let people think what they wanted to think. No point upsetting everyone all over again. It would look to them like he was just trying to shift the blame for what happened with Mum. No point in inflicting new pain on old wounds.

"What?"

Malcolm looked at his dad.

"What else have you got going on up there? You have something unfinished that you need to share. I can see it in your eyes, boy."

"There's nothing there but regret, Dad."

Charles chewed his lip. "You sure?"

Malcolm nodded. "I'm not a bad man. No matter how it might appear. Okay?"

Chapter Forty-seven

Skid Mark

KENNY WOULD COPE. HELL, Kenny would more than cope – he could do simple murder examinations in his sleep. It wasn't that; it was the guilt Eddie felt at pushing jobs onto him all the time. He'd asked him to take general shots, and Eddie would join him just as soon as he could.

"Yeah, like I've never heard that before. Don't rush, eh? Have another bourbon."

"Sorry, Kenny," Eddie had said. It didn't appease Kenny, who almost tripped over his bottom lip on his way out of the office.

Eddie felt drained. Alex was inside his mind right now just as much as if she were in the room, just as much as if she had her teeth in his cheek again, or a gun pointed at his head. He dragged a hand down his face, and wished he were at home watching some shit on telly with his Dad and Malcolm. But of course, no one was watching any telly today.

The only way out of this is to forgive.

Eddie checked his watch. "Send in the final victim, Sid."

The last victim came in behind Sid and held his hand out to Penelope as Sid left. When Eddie looked up from his sheet of questions and saw the man leaning in hoping to shake hands, he nearly screamed.

The last victim's hand dropped back by his side, and the polite smile on his face fell off and landed on the carpet flipping about like a dying fish. "Well," he said. "I'll not waste your time or mine. Bye."

He turned to the door and had it halfway open before Eddie said, "Stop."

The victim turned again, head canted to one side as if suggesting Eddie might like to play for a while first.

"Sit down. Please."

Penelope asked, "What's your name?"

"My name is Mark Strange. I'm a PCSO out of Centre." He glanced at Eddie, and then back to Penelope. "I have no chance of getting this because I almost gave him a ticket for being a... for cutting across a line of traffic at a scene."

Penelope raised her eyebrows at Eddie.

"I was being a dick." Eddie shrugged. "Please, sit down. Strange, eh?"

Mark sat, shoulders rounded, hands flat on his lap, and it seemed an effort to even lift his eyes to meet Eddie's. "Seriously, why don't I just walk now? No way are you going to give me this job."

"I would have given it to you already—"

"If I hadn't threatened you with a ticket."

"If you'd written it."

"Eh?"

"You bottled it. You were doing your job, and a DI asked what you were doing, and you backed down."

"Well, of course—"

"No 'of course'. You do your fucking job. I don't care who's in your face."

Mark began to get up.

"Sit down, Mark. Tell me why you want this job."

"So you can just tell me to naff off?"

"Tell me why."

They sat there in silence for a while. Mark was breathing hard, and his hands began to fidget; he took a breath and stared Eddie in the face. "I want this job for two reasons. I want this job because I've been searching for something worthwhile my entire adult life. I've been searching for something that makes an instant difference. I've been searching for something that... that helps."

Eddie took a breath in through his nostrils, already refreshed by the meeting. Hell, this man didn't know what he was letting himself in for yet, but he spoke with passion. "And the second reason?"

"I've been searching for something that I give a damn about. I've been from shitty job to shitty job all my life. I landed PCSO and I thought I'd struck gold, but I hadn't. I missed it by a country mile, and still had a shitty job. I want to care about something; I want a job I care about." His face softened.

Eddie stared at him, his fingers tapping the desk.

"Plus I really like those white suits."

Penelope laughed. "How old are you, Mark?"

"Is it a problem?"

"Not to me," Eddie said. "I like people who have wool on their back. This isn't a university-leaver's job I'm offering. I want someone with life skills."

"I'm forty-eight," Mark said.

"I don't care," Eddie replied.

Penelope's eyebrows rose; she smiled, and nodded.

Eddie asked her, "Please pass over my alcohol gel." He held out his hand to Mark. "Welcome aboard, Skid."

"Really?"

"I want to read your application—"

"You haven't read it yet?"

"Why would I? Five people came for this job, I was only taking one or two on. Think of the time I've saved by not reading any of them. I choose people because of who they are, not what they've written about themselves. Or what other people I don't know have written about them."

"Then why bother reading them at all?"

"Because I'm nosy. If I like yours, you've nothing to worry about. Now shake."

Chapter Forty-eight

Three's a Crowd

THERE WAS SCREAMING.

A lot of screaming. It was vile, tortured, harrowing, and incessant. And in among it, hidden like a timid creature running from the beast, was a whimpering sound; something scared crying quietly, afraid of death, but petrified of life.

The petrified thing was Alex.

It was noisy and it was happening inside her head. She sat with her hands against her ears and an inaudible scream issuing from cracked lips, curled up in the seat, foetal, closed in, arms up, protecting herself as if from a physical attack, eyes screwed tight against the vision. The pain was deafening. And the noise was agony.

It took half an hour for them to stop, by which time, Alex was in tears, stunned and afraid. It was an invasion, and it left her feeling weak and vulnerable, head buzzing, black spikes moving in.

For the first time since she'd run away from Juniper Hill, she wondered if it was all worth it; if the pain was worth the gain. The gain, after all, was in her imagination anyway – probably.

She came out of it panting, her heart tripping over itself, standing again in the centre lane of the motorway with cars rushing past either side, and waited for the impact. Eventually, she opened her eyes and found the screaming had stopped, the light was dim, painless, and there was blood on her hands. It was from her lip – she'd bitten it again, almost all the way through.

So what's the endgame?

She jumped, and realised the voice was in her head again. She calmed down, paid no attention to her shaking hands. "The what?"

Where is all this leading? You must have given it some thought.

She closed her eyes and thought through the plan again. "Of course I have."

Tell me.

Alex tapped her fingers on Mrs Groocock's steering wheel and turned off the windscreen wipers. "No." She stared at herself in the rear-view mirror, mopping at the blood with a tissue, and tried to smile but her smile muscles weren't responding. All by themselves, as though the message to the smile muscles had been re-routed, the tear muscles kicked in and a couple of drops rolled down her cheeks. Just seeing them upset her.

"What's up?"

The smell of Brut made her sigh. "Leave me alone."

"What are you going to do?"

Alex refocused her eyes to the owner of that new voice. Her father was sitting in the back of the car. "Why can't you piss off and leave me alone? I don't want you with me. Either of you!"

Don't listen to him. He's just here to make trouble. He pretends to care—

"You think I don't know that?"

Just saying.

"Yeah, well, you can keep quiet as well."

"Who is that? That your mother?" Her father leaned forward, and she could smell his cold breath on her cheek.

You were about to tell me why you're crying.

"I'm not crying, Mum...Yes, Dad, it's my I-couldn't-give-two-shits, gimme-booze mother."

Don't fucking talk about me as though I'm not here! And don't bullshit me. Get in there and get it done. This is the only way through it. Ask your father, he was always good at taking care of problems by force. Bastard.

"Alex, what's she saying to you?"

This is the only way to that endgame we were talking about.

"You were talking about an endgame. Not me."

"What's she mean by end-game?"

"Why the hell can't you hear her? You're both inside my fucking head!"

"Don't get shitty with me, Alex. I'm trying to help you."

"Since when have you tried to help me? Huh, go on, when was the last time you did anything helpful for me?"

Tell him, Alex. He's a fucking nuisance, is all he is. You know he kicked—

"I haven't been the best father, I know that—"

Not even on the scale!

"Shut up, both of you."

"Everyone abandons you, Alex. Have you noticed that?"

She could see him smiling at her.

"Doesn't that tell you something? Take the easy way out. Stop it all now. Go on. Slut."

Alex rubbed the heel of her hand against her cheek and suddenly the tears were gone, and she felt much better. Her father sat back, and Alex managed that smile in the mirror after all. She stared at the red door through the melting windscreen.

Go on. Go do it. It's the only way you're ever going to get him back.

Alex climbed out into the rain and left the voices behind. She closed the car door and walked across the road, through the spray thrown up by passing cars. The red door was shiny. The little Toyota parked next to it was also red, and the rain ran off it and dripped onto the ground, flicking mud up against the tyres.

She wrapped the coat tighter around her and noticed how those drips turned electric blue when they hit the pavement, like that bioluminescent algae in the sea. It was fascinating.

Alex?

Damn, why couldn't they leave her alone? "Okay, okay." She turned to the door and knocked.

What are you going to say to her?

"I don't know yet. It'll come to me. Just be quiet, please. For ten minutes."

You don't have anything planned? Come on! This is important; think of the end game!

The door opened before Alex could make a reply, and her attention landed on the pale face that greeted her. Her hair was long and mousy brown.

The same colour as pig shit. Do her, Alex. Do her!

She looked tired. She looked ill. And after a second or two, she looked afraid.

Alex saw her tense up, preparing to slam the door, and so rammed it open with her shoulder.

The woman fell back inside, tumbling to the floor as Alex stepped in and calmly closed the door behind her. The key was still in the lock; a keyring bearing a photo of a small black dog swayed back and forth. Alex locked them in. "What dog is that?"

The woman looked up, tried to sit up and fell back again.

"I said what dog is that?"

She's fucking you about, Alex.

"What do you want?"

Surely the first question should have been "Who are you?"

"She already knows who I am, stupid."

"What?" The woman struggled to her feet and scooted back around a sofa, trying to put something between them. "What do you want with me?" There was panic in her voice.

Alex cocked her head towards the door. "I like the fucking dog! What is it?"

"It's a spaniel."

Alex leaned in to take a closer look and cooed. "Aw, lovely. What's his name?"

The woman pulled the dressing gown tighter around her body. "He was called Tyrone. He died last year."

What a shit name for a dog!

"Shame, sorry for your loss. I like it, the name. Shut up."

The woman looked as though she was on the verge of screaming. "I didn't say anything."

"Not you. What's your name?"

"Maggie."

That's a nice name for a dog!

"Maggie what?"

"Maggie Darlington." She swallowed, stood up straight. "Now. What the hell are you doing in my home?"

"I'm sorry for the intrusion," Alex said. "I have a question that I need an answer to, that's all. Nothing..." – she smiled reassuringly – "nothing sinister."

"You're Alex, aren't you? Is that right? Alex Sheridan?"

She's playing tricks. Be careful.

"I know!"

"From Juniper Hill?"

"Yes, I am."

"Sit down, won't you?" There was a tremble in her voice; the reassuring smile that grew on her face was a lie. "We can soon have this sorted out. We need to get you some help."

Ever heard the term red rag to a bull?

"I don't need your help, okay? I need you to call someone for me, and I need you to ask them a simple question. And then," – Alex moved around the sofa – "I'll leave you alone. Okay? Do we have a deal?"

The tremble had moved from Maggie's voice onto her face. Her chin was wobbling, her teeth clattering. "Please," she said. "I'm not well, I—"

"Two minutes. That's all. Just two minutes, and I'll be out of your life."

Nicely put!

"Who? Who do you want me to call?"

"Sit down, Maggie. Get comfy." Alex tried to ignore her father sitting on the end of the sofa. He looked up at her and laughed.

Chapter Forty-nine

The Horror of Loss

EDDIE PULLED UP TO the cordon, shut off the engine and reached across for his cigarettes. The rain was still falling; it was perpetually raining these days. It reminded him of that old movie, The Crow. "Needed some serious drainage in that fucking thing," he whispered to himself.

Outside, the cordon tape tried to escape, and some copper chased it along the cobbles, losing his hat in the process. It wouldn't have been polite to laugh, Eddie thought, and then laughed anyway as he noted his arrival time for his report. He could see Kenny's van parked a little further along the street, where the copper was chasing the tape.

Thoughts turned more serious then. Alex was so far out of control that she was likely to do anything to anybody she came across. She was wild, feral, and the only way she would stop was when she reached her target.

And Eddie was that target.

It made him shudder, and all humour washed from him like the rain down the gutter. Cigarette ash fell onto his lap, and he came around as though from a trance. He'd been away thinking for minutes, and the cigarette was spent without him taking a drag. He tossed it out of the window towards a drain and lit another.

He stared at it, and thought of Alex again, pointing a gun at him. He saw her, as she stabbed Dibble in the chest and watched him fall. "Now you know what it's like to be disowned", she'd said to his corpse. Is that what she thought Eddie had done to her: disowned her? Abandoned her?

He'd done no such thing; he'd chosen a different path, that's all. She wasn't on the guest list. He had that right; he hadn't signed anything bonding them both together.

"I'm free."

He gave his name at the cordon, ducked under the tape and headed for the front door of The Bohemia Guest House. With its gothic wallpaper, black sculptures, and blood-red carpet, the dark reception area was like something out of the Addams Family. Benson was there, studying that carpet for all he was worth.

Eddie sat next to him.

"Fuck off."

"Yeah, good morning, Tom. Thanks for inviting me to your ultimate fuck-up."

Benson swung around and took Eddie by the jacket. "I mean it. Leave me alone while you still can." He let go. Resumed studying the carpet.

Benson's eyes were red-rimmed, as though he'd been crying. Or he was just very tired, been yawning a lot, maybe. Eddie straightened himself up. "I'm sorry."

"Again. Fuck off."

"No. Tell me what happened."

"Eddie—"

"If I have to examine this scene, I need to know what happened. So cut the feeling sorry for yourself shit and speak to me."

Benson sniffed, sat up straight and folded his arms. "Had a tipoff that she was a guest here. We had the place surrounded. She must've seen us. She pulled a switch – out of the balcony and into the overgrown garden at the far side, over a low wall and just walked away. She took the landlady's car and just..." – he made a whooshing noise – "went." He swallowed and took a breath. "Meanwhile we're waiting down here for the landlady to show. She's upstairs in Alex's bed, dead.

"I let her walk, Eddie. I thought we had her, I thought we had Alex in bed, asleep. But it was the landlady. Dead."

Eddie sat quietly for a moment. This looked bad for Benson; he was in for an arse-kicking, no doubt about that. Simple protocol: don't take anything for granted. But worse than that, as far as Eddie was concerned – the fucking lunatic was still free when she should have been banged up in a cell. The ramifications of this were almost incalculable. Eddie was dead – almost a certainty, just a matter of time. But what worried him was who else would get taken out along the way. "Any idea where Alex is now?"

Benson just stared at him. "Go upstairs, Kenny is working the scene."

Eddie nodded and stood.

Benson stood too, cleared his throat. "I'm sorry."

"Don't—"

"I set her free. That was the best chance we'll ever have, and I blew it."

Eddie thought Benson was going to cry, and that was so very unlike him. He'd cocked up before, but nothing like this – nothing with such dire consequences attached. Dire for Eddie, mostly.

He shrugged. "Don't beat yourself up, Tom. We'll get her."

Eddie hadn't even reached the top of the stairs when the phone in his pocket buzzed. He was tempted to ignore it and just go and see how far Kenny had got, but he took it out and looked at the screen. It was Moneypenny. "Hey – hope you're feeling better."

"Eddie?"

She didn't sound better. "You okay?"

She sniffled, tried to speak and her voice cracked on the first word.

"You sound awful. Got a cold as well as the shits?" He was still smiling, but now there was concern in there too, ready to roll over into fear if called upon. He had a feeling it would be called upon. He stopped walking. "What's wrong?"

"I have something to ask you."

Eddie saw Kenny wave at him from the other end of the landing. He held up a finger – just one minute – and gave the phone his full attention. "Sure. Fire away."

There was a long pause, maybe a little noise in the background, and then, "Is there any chance we'll get together? A... a couple. You and me?"

His eyebrows took a dive and confusion corrugated his forehead. "Erm...I don't know what to say. I hope so, yes." What kind of fucking question was this? Was it a trap? "Is everything alright? Is someone there with you? Is Bronx there?"

And then he heard a low laughter coming over the phone. It sent a prickle across his shoulders. It didn't sound much like Moneypenny's voice. "That's all I needed to hear, Eddie."

Eddie's eyes widened, and he almost dropped the phone. It sounded like...

The phone died.

He looked at the screen – a red screen, with Moneypenny's face smiling at him from the circle in the centre.

"Moneypenny? Moneypenny!"

"I just wanted to know how you two were fixed, see?"

Maggie dropped the phone into her lap and looked at her. She appeared almost normal –three-quarter raincoat, scarf – but Maggie couldn't take her eyes from her face. She wore lots of black eye makeup like a Goth, and her hair was greasy and tangled. The whites of her eyes were red because of all the burst veins in them. Her teeth were held together by a sheet of plaque, gums pale, lips cracked and bloodied.

"You see, Maggie, if there's any chance you and Eddie will pair up... then, well— Will you shut up, I'm trying to— Yes,

I know that!" She looked back at Maggie, not realising she'd skipped a few seconds, and resumed. "If you and Eddie are going to become a couple, then I'll back off, give you two some room." She smiled and the hideous teeth came into view again, stretched lips leaking blood.

"Well, that's very gracious of you." Maggie couldn't work out what her reaction should be. Should she nod and ask her to leave, or invite her to stay for coffee, a light lunch perhaps? Would Eddie realise Alex was here and alert the police? Maybe the coffee was a good idea, just to give them a chance to get here in time.

It didn't matter; her reaction grew automatically. She was scared, and it would be much safer if she didn't invite Alex to stay. "Is that all? Are you leaving now?"

"Do you want me to?"

"I think it best, yes, please."

Alex stood quite still and nodded at some conversation going on inside her head. "Before I do, could I use your bathroom?"

Maggie almost vomited with relief. "Oh yes, absolutely. Top of the stairs—"

"Thank you." She stared down at Maggie. "Back in a mo."

Maggie felt cool with relief, yet she couldn't stop her lower lip from trembling. It was all too much for her to absorb, and the thought of having a murderer in her home hadn't fully materialised yet; for if it had, she would have been through that front door and out of sight before Alex had even reached the top step. As it was, she only stared, and allowed her fingertips to tremble as the cool turn cold.

She looked from the staircase across to the door that would lead to freedom and certain life. It was with something like a shock that she suddenly realised there was a chance of freedom presenting itself here, and she ought to make good use of it. She stood, watched the stairs and tiptoed across the lounge. She grabbed the door handle. But it wouldn't move.

The key. Where was the key?

Confusion lasted only a second or two before she heard Alex on the stairs behind her. Maggie screamed.

Chapter Fifty

The Last Surprise

"Looking for these?" She shook the keys, and the little fob showing a spaniel called Tyrone nodded at her.

Maggie screamed and ran towards the kitchen and the back door, her dressing gown flapping like a flag of defeat in her wake. The terror on her face gave Alex a surge of hot power through her abdomen – anticipation, like the sense of first-time sex with someone, a feeling she'd missed. The anticipation, the trepidation almost – a luxurious mixture that was joyful and yet horrific all in one serving.

Alex walked after her, savouring the moment, yet treating the whole episode as a job of work that needed doing in order to progress to the next step. Nothing special. Just a deed.

"You need to do this slowly. No rush."

"Go away, Dad."

He's got to know that you won't tolerate anyone standing in your way.

"Will you shut the fuck up!"

This is a statement to him. Make sure he understands.

"Leave me alone!"

Maggie screamed. She had reached the back door just as Alex entered the kitchen. The door, as predicted, was locked, and Maggie suddenly had a hand full of Play-Doh fingers and a mind full of misfiring neurons that got everything wrong all in one go. It rendered her useless. She screamed. She turned to face Alex. "You said you'd go!"

Alex tightened her cracked lips as though in disappointment.

"You got what you came for – me and Eddie are a couple!"

Oh, was that ever the wrong way to talk yourself out of this particular corner.

"I kinda lied there a bit. Sorry."

"Alex, there's no need for this."

"There's every need for this. While you're available, he won't give me a second glance."

Maggie's mouth fell open, the scream turned clear and only hot breath came out. Incomprehension blended into understanding. Her mouth closed and the corners turned up into something resembling a smile.

Alex hesitated.

Why is she smiling?

"Is that what you think? That Eddie will want you? You? Are you delusional?" Maggie laughed at her own question before reason made an appearance and shut her mouth for her.

Kill her!

"No one laughs at my daughter!"

Maggie's fear was back. "You can just have him. No need to do this, Alex. I'll go; I'll leave." The quiver strummed her voice, the strength in her eyes leaked out with each new tear, and she pushed herself into the back door as far as she could go.

Alex stepped forward. "After your heart stops..." She came closer. "Your brain still has three minutes before it dies. Did you know that? Fascinating. Three whole minutes to consider how you lived, and what you'd have done differently. Three minutes to wonder if things could have worked out differently if only you'd told Eddie to get lost."

Maggie held her hand out to ward Alex off, but Alex batted it aside as though it really was made of Play-Doh. And that's when Maggie knew it was real; that talking and reasoning were well behind them now. Now was the time for action, and now was the time for Maggie to scream. And she did, like she had never screamed before.

Chapter Fifty-one

Beyond Scary

PART OF HIM SAID it was serious and he should get the hell over there as fast he could, that her life might be in danger. And yet another part of him stood there shaking its head, telling him he was overreacting. Moneypenny was feeling ill and all she wanted was something to look forward to, that she'd enjoyed their brief meeting yesterday and found that she still had feelings for him. Letting her know there was a chance for them made her feel better.

Eddie tried to call time on the two factions inside his head. Do you have any idea how unusual that call was? Do you have any notion of how strange that question was, irrespective of how she was feeling? And did you forget thinking there was someone there with her? Bronx? Maybe Bronx, but maybe...

Was it her? Maggie? Voice rough because of a cold? Or could it have been...

Before he knew it, he was at the foot of the stairs again, in the foyer. Benson took his head out of his hands and looked up.

"What's up?"

Eddie looked at Benson.

Benson stood. "Eddie?"

The first part of him wanted to burst into tears and tell Benson about the fears that were spiralling around in his mind right now. But the second part of him took control. It said, I've changed my mind. Go!

Eddie was out of the door and searching for his keys in seconds. He didn't even see the fluttering scene tape, or the coppers standing by it freezing their tits off. He climbed into his van and reversed along The Calls, far too quickly.

On his way to Moneypenny's house, speed cameras flashing in his wake, he replayed the call over and over again, feeling more and more uncomfortable each time. He was quite prepared to be totally wrong about it all, happy to have misread the situation, but his foot was to the floor, the scenery scooting by in a blur for more than one reason.

The phone on the passenger seat buzzed and Benson's face appeared in the circle. Eddie ignored it, tightened his grip on the steering wheel.

That uncomfortable feeling of déjà vu clapped him on the back as he stood outside her door. He was breathing hard, as though he'd been running, but all he'd done was run across the road from his van. Her car was there, same mud up the sides of the tyres, same rust on the discs.

He bypassed knocking and went straight to banging – quite prepared to apologise for being out of order, prepared to apologise for every problem in the world if only she'd answer the door.

The nerves came on strong then, a prickle right across his back and shoulders that burrowed inside until his whole being was buzzing with anxiety. He stepped to the side, banged on the lounge window, and tried to peer through, but he couldn't see anything – there were net curtains in the way.

Eddie felt bad inside.

Both of his eyes were twitching now. He banged again and could see the glass ripple under his fists. "Answer the fucking door." He stepped to the letterbox and called through it, "Maggie!"

He stood, surprised by that. Whatever happened to Moneypenny? He didn't even realise that he knew her proper name. Still, it was an improvement over what he'd shouted through the letterbox last time.

Panic took over from the anxiety, and Eddie set off around the back just as her neighbour's car pulled onto their drive. He found himself banging on the back door. He stepped up to the kitchen window, cupped his hand against the greyness of the day and peered in, over the sink, looking left and right, but there was no sign.

It's harder to strangle someone than many people think. Assuming, of course, that the victim is not unconscious, and assuming they're not incapacitated in some way – tied up, drugged, physically impaired by a disability. Survival is hard-wired. And most people will fight like they've never fought before if they see death coming at them.

If someone has their hands around your throat and your eyes are bulging ready to pop out of your face and roll down your cheeks, if your heart is beating so fast and so hard that you can feel it pulsing throughout your entire body, if your lungs are screaming for air, if they're on fire, if your vision is clouding... if all these things are happening to you, you will fight quite literally to the death.

In situations like these, when no one else is going to step in and assist, when no one is going to whack the would-be murderer over the head with a frying pan for you, when no one is going to wrestle them away from you so you can gasp your way back to consciousness with a realisation of how fucking lucky you are to be alive, it's beyond scary.

Sometimes, it's just you and your killer. Alone. Fighting over one thing: your life. They want it; you want it.

If you try to strangle someone from the front, you're going to be in the way for fists, nails, knees – even the forehead – coming at you, raining down upon you until that life is gone and they are meat, or until they have secured their freedom. So doing it from behind is always the preferred method: hook an arm around the throat and pull tight, stay clear of the whipping head and the kicking heels, and you're a winner. Doing it from the front is just asking for trouble.

Either way, when someone is literally fighting for their life, things get messy. All secondary considerations go out of the window; life is the ultimate prize, and everything else – broken fingers, gouged eyes, bitten ears, all that stuff – is way down on the list of priorities.

So seeing people who've been strangled covered in welts, developing bruises, cuts, broken bones, nails peeled right out of fingers... it's par for the course, and if those things are absent, then your victim wanted to die, wasn't too bothered about living (there's a difference), or was incapacitated in one form or another.

Apart from the Imodium on the worktop, Maggie Darlington was clear of drugs, and had everything to live for. Eddie still ached from giving CPR; his own heart was still throbbing, his arms still on fire. He stared down at her face and took in the beauty of her green eyes, reddened slightly, lids puffed-up. They were still gorgeous, her eyes. They seemed to be clouding as he looked on.

He smiled at her.

Her lashes were clumped together by tears or mucus. She had snot and thinned-out blood trickling from her nose. It was slow right now, but in time it would get faster, thicker. Her hands were reddened with blood too, from the cuts across her fingers where she'd lashed out and caught them, maybe on the edge of the worktop, or maybe on the killer's ring or belt buckle.

Who knows what happens in a frenzy? But the cuts were a sign of a vicious struggle. And that meant the killer might have significant injuries too. Maggie had nails missing from each hand, and it would be imperative to find those as quickly as possible; the killer's skin cells or even blood might be under them.

But he knew already who the killer was. It wasn't difficult to work out. And the motive wasn't exactly a Sherlock Holmes mystery. She saw Maggie as a threat, as competition, someone standing in the way of her and Eddie getting back together again. He knew Alex had made her call him, and

Eddie, being Eddie, had sealed her fate by declaring there was indeed still a chance they would end up together.

"She must be further round the twist than anyone thought," Eddie whispered to Maggie.

The sirens grew steadily louder. Eddie wrapped his arms around her even tighter, and closed his eyes. She was warm and she was flexible, and as he squeezed, a sigh popped from her mouth. It was as though she was just the other side of life – still within reach – and he wondered if she could still hear him. Perhaps she could feel him near her? He wondered if she was thinking of him as he was thinking of her.

He could recall her smile from the last time he was here – how alluring it was, and how her laugh seemed to lift his spirits. Yes, it was quite possible they would have got together one day, maybe even one day soon. She was his kind of woman; demure—

The sirens stopped.

—and more than a little bit humble. She had a great sense of humour, and she was... she was the first thing he always looked forward to seeing every morning. He nuzzled into her hair—

The banging came. First on the front door, and then, moments later, behind him, on the back door. A head appeared through the smashed window above the sink.

—and breathed in deeply, taking in her scent as he laced his fingers with hers and held her close.

"What the fuck is going on?"

Eddie didn't hear the copper. He just closed his eyes and whispered his love to her.

Chapter Fifty-two

Urgency

CHARLES STARED ON AS Malcolm put the screwdriver down and plugged the TV back into the wall socket. Nothing went bang, and Charles let out his breath.

"There," Malcolm said, standing and brushing dust from the knees of his trousers, and contemplating the scuffs on his posh boots. "Let's give it a whirl, shall we?"

"No." Charles breathed heavily. "I don't have the balls. You do it."

Malcolm took the remote and aimed it. "You're such a wuss." He hit the button. Some crinkly old reporter was halfway through talking about a scene in Leeds where police were gathered and had "closed off the road. Unconfirmed reports suggest the deceased, who hasn't yet been named, works for the police".

"Nowhere is safe these days."

"No, it seems not."

"Maybe Eddie was right, about there being nothing but shit on the TV anyway. It's depressing."

Malcolm's phone began to ring. He pulled it from his trouser pocket and looked at the screen for what seemed like an age. "I got to take this, Dad." He walked away into the kitchen; Charles could hear nothing but whispers.

He stepped closer until he was hovering outside the kitchen doorway, trying his best to look unobtrusive, like he just happened to be there. He saw Malcolm reach for the A5 pad he kept in there to jot reminders and recipes down on, and a pencil.

"Is it still standing? I wouldn't even know how to get there now," Malcolm said, scribbling something down. "Give me an hour. Okay, okay, forty minutes. Best... Yes, that's the best I can do." He shut off the phone and stood up straight with the torn-out leaf of paper pincered between his finger and thumb. He walked out of the kitchen.

Charles ran his hands up the doorframe, caught red-handed. "I think these could do with a fresh coat—"

"I have to go out, Dad."

"What? Where?"

Malcolm didn't even pause on his way out of the kitchen. "Tell you when I get home."

"When will that be?"

"I don't know."

"We're having beef stew tonight. Don't be late."

Malcolm disappeared from view for a few moments and then brushed past Charles on his way to the front door, carrying the bag from his room.

"You are coming back tonight, aren't you?"

Malcolm almost ran to his car.

"Malcolm?"

"I hope so."

Uneasy, Charles watched Malcolm drive away. He closed and locked the front door and found himself in the lounge watching the local weather forecast. It was set to be cold and rainy for ever more.

He turned the TV off, preferring to live day by day ignorant of all the horrors the news people loved bringing into their homes. It was their thing, frightening people, depressing them, perpetually bringing everyone down, concentrating only on the miserable things in life. "Why is there never any good news?"

And what the hell was going on with Malcolm that he had to shoot off like that, and not even know if he'd be home for tea? Really, twenty bloody years he's been away, and he suddenly has business to attend to.

He didn't look too happy about it, mind.

Charles turned the TV back on and went straight for Turner Classic Movies. He found The Great Escape and sank into it for a while.

After an hour or so, while making a fresh pot of tea, the A5 pad stared at him. The pencil stared at him.

"But it would be wrong. It'd be like spying."

Charles unlocked the door and stepped out, a leaf of paper in his hand. He walked around the back of the cottage and into the thick woodland. "Arry," he said. "Are you there?"

"What's up?"

"I can't see you."

"You're not supposed to see me. What do you want?"

Charles peered into the twilight, squinting against the rain that managed to break through the naked branches of the swaying trees around him. Mushy leaves squelched underfoot. "I need to get something to Inspector Benson at Major Crime Unit."

"Ring 101. Now go inside."

"This is important."

"Charles, this is against—"

"Will you bloody well listen to me! Stuff the protocol – this is urgent, dammit!"

Chapter Fifty-three

Not Asking Questions

THERE WAS A PROCESS to follow. And although Eddie went through that process, he wasn't really there for any of it. He was present in body only.

They arrested him. Had to. He was there at the scene of a murder. There had been no way into the house – all doors and windows were secure, apart from the kitchen window he'd admitted to breaking in order to gain entry. And he was found cradling a dead body. A dead body with marks around her neck and petechiae on her face.

So they arrested him.

They took his DNA and his fingerprints. They took his photograph, and they took his clothes and shoes. He sat in an interview room, wearing a grey sweater and jogging bottoms, a pair of paper slippers on his feet.

Eddie found himself alongside a man in a suit chewing a toffee, with two more men in suits sitting opposite him; one had ginger hair, and the other had a goatee. Together they looked like characters from that old board game: Guess Who?

In the corner of the room the tape recorder buzzed, and that's what brought him round. He clocked those present, and then looked down into his lap, not really interested in what was going on. His eyes still stung from the tears and his nose was blocked. He had a headache.

Somewhere in the background he heard them all talking, getting the preliminaries out of the way, the rights, the time, those present, and then, "Your name, Eddie."

He looked up.

"State your name, please. For the tape."

He looked at Goatee, someone he didn't recognise. But then it would be, wouldn't it? They wouldn't let Benson interview him. And rightly so. "Eddie Collins." He stared back into his lap while their words whirled around him in a cloud of shit that his brain ignored.

"We want to get you de-arrested as soon as we can. But we need to know what happened from your point of view."

Eddie licked his lips and looked up into Ginger's eyes – the guy who'd spewed out that last statement. It wasn't a question; it was just a statement. Why couldn't they ask questions? What the hell was wrong with this pair? "What?"

Goatee looked across at his partner, then back at Eddie. "What happened?"

"Someone killed her."

"No, I mean tell us in your own words what happened."

He looked at them – both of them – and repeated, "Someone killed her."

"You're not being very helpful."

"Would you like me to draw it for you?"

Goatee sighed. "We've heard from her ex-boyfriend, Bronx Smith, that you were extremely volatile towards him and Miss Darlington at your birthday party a few evenings ago. You were rude to him and expressed your jealousy."

Eddie laughed. "Smith? That's his name? Smith?"

"Yes."

Eddie laughed more. "What a tool."

"Eddie. Please keep this—"

He stopped laughing, but was glad of the few seconds Bronx Smith gave him. "Seriously? You think I killed her out of a fit of jealousy?"

"Like I said – tell us what happened."

Eddie blinked, and realised he was going to have to pay attention to this charade for the time being before it got out of hand and they started to think he was guilty. That's how a lot of miscarriages of justice were born – carelessness. "I was interviewing new CSIs all morning. I have several witnesses – I can provide names if required. I left the office at a little after twelve to go and assist a member of my staff at a murder scene in Leeds centre. I arrived there at about half-twelve – check the scene log if you want. At twelve forty-five I received a call from Maggie, while I was still in the scene."

"What did she say?"

"If you shut up, I'll tell you." He sighed and continued. "She asked if there was ever any chance of us getting back together."

"Wait a minute. She asked you that? It wasn't the other way around?"

"No, it wasn't the other way around. Start fucking listening."

"No need for that—"

"Every need for that kind of language! Don't try and fit me up by twisting my words – listen carefully, okay?"

"Carry on."

"Thank you. I thought it was a very unusual question to ask. I'd seen her only last night," – Eddie noticed the raised eyebrows across the other side of the table – "and everything seemed okay then. She was ill, had the shits; I went to visit. But otherwise she was okay."

"Then what happened?"

Eddie stared at them both for a moment. Then what happened, indeed? Well, then he got the worries over Alex. "Someone was there. I felt as though someone had prompted her to ask that question."

"Who?"

"At first I thought it might have been Bronx. And then I thought it might have been an escaped prisoner by the name of Alex Sheridan."

"Why?"

"Because she's fucking nuts. She wants me dead."

"Then why kill Miss Darlington?"

"You should ask her when you see her."

"Why do you think she killed Miss Darlington?"

"If she did."

"If she did, yes."

"Because inside her twisted mind, she sees... she saw Maggie as an obstacle to me and us getting back together."

"If she wants you dead, why worry about an obstacle preventing her from getting back—"

"Like I said, you'd need to ask her that."

"And would you? Get back with Alex?"

"Get back... have you heard yourself?"

"Answer me."

"No. I never want to see the mad bitch again!"

Goatee rubbed the designer stubble on his too-big chin and asked, "Some might say you went over there and killed her yourself. It takes two minutes to strangle someone."

"I'd tell 'some' to go fuck themselves. And then I'd tell you to go fuck yourself for being so gullible."

"Calm down, Eddie." This from the bloke sitting next to him.

"Who are you, by the way?"

"I'm your solicitor."

"Aren't you supposed to advise people not to speak?"

"That's not really relevant—"

"Okay, you earned your fee. You can go back to playing golf inside your head now."

"I beg—"

"But before you do, you can spit out that fucking toffee before I poke it down your neck, you annoying piece of shit!"

"Mr Collins!"

"Ssshhh," Eddie lifted a finger to his lips. "These idiots want a go now." He looked at Ginger and Goatee. "Your turn."

"Mind your language, Eddie."

"Up yours."

Ginger sighed and took a breath. "We think she rebuffed you at your birthday party, and you saw this as your first real opportunity to finish her off."

Eddie jerked in his chair, ready to stand, but he remained seated, staring at Ginger, gritting his teeth, top lip curling out ever so slightly. He saw Goatee swallow, and push back his chair a little.

"We got a call from the neighbours," said Ginger in a hushed voice, "who saw you banging on Miss Darlington's doors and windows as though you were angry. They heard glass breaking at the back of the house."

Eddie stared at him. Again, a statement. Weren't these monkeys supposed to ask open questions? This force has gone to ratshit, he thought.

Ginger swallowed again, pawed at some paperwork in front of him. "You understand that we're just doing our jobs here, Eddie? We're just trying to get to the bottom of things."

"You reached the bottom of things ten minutes ago. Now you're through the other side and heading straight into fantasy land."

"Just answer the question."

"What question?"

"You took offence at your party and finished her off today."

"As I said, what question?" He looked from one to the other. "You do know what a fucking question is, don't you?"

"Don't be so rude."

Eddie smiled. It wasn't a pleasant smile. "Well, son, you'd better start being relevant. You'd better start asking questions that make sense. And then I can go home, he can finally watch the hole in one, and you two can get back to kindergarten. Okay?"

"Listen, Mr Collins," said Goatee, "it's our job to explore every avenue. And if that means probing you to see how you react, then that's what we'll do. If it means asking some unpleasant questions, then we'll do that too."

"I'm happy for you. Did you consider Alex Sheridan?"

"We've made a note, yes," he said. "And she will be dealt with at our earliest opportunity."

"Good luck with that, sunshine."

"And—"

"And if you want to continue probing in that direction," Eddie said, "you'd better do it from the other side of that door."

"Is that a threat, Mr Collins?"

"Well done for finally asking a question. And yes, that was a threat."

Ginger continued. "Where's her phone? The one she allegedly rang you from?"

Eddie shrugged. "No idea. If you need proof that she rang, check my phone."

Ginger and Goatee exchanged glances; though they said nothing, there was a widening of eyes, and a slight nod.

"You'll be de-arresting me now then?"

"Maybe tomorrow."

The solicitor finally spoke. "Gentlemen, Mr Collins has answered all your questions. This interview was for the purpose of completing a statement only. It was not—"

There was a knock at the door; it opened and Khan poked his head into the room. Using his eyes only, he gestured Goatee out. Goatee closed the door after him. A moment later, he was back, face slightly red, grinding his teeth. He gathered the slim file, and said, "You're de-arrested. Interview terminated."

"Why?"

"What?"

"What made you de-arrest me?"

"I thought you'd be happy—"

"What made you de-arrest me?"

Goatee tightened his lips and blew through them. "We found CCTV of a woman with blonde hair leaving moments before you arrived. She locked the door and left."

Chapter Fifty-four

A Past Worth Lying For

MALCOLM ROUNDED THE CORNER and stopped the car, staring at the silhouette of The Sheridan Club. How grand the dilapidated structure before him used to be, but now most of the roof was missing, the grey ribs of joists poking into the night sky against the distant orange glow from the city, four or five miles away. He could see webs of scaffolding over to the right, and there were yellow posters everywhere warning people to keep out.

He decided just to give her the envelope and piss off. He wasn't in the mood for a reunion – and anyway, although he'd kept to his promise and not informed the police, he'd make sure they were the first port of call when he showed this place his taillights.

There was no such thing as an easy childhood, he supposed, no matter who you were or what kind of family you sprang from. But he guessed hers was probably worse than most, and it was why she was a terror junkie right now, why she'd turned into a monster – nurture, not nature. Horrible way to end up.

He left sweat marks on the steering wheel as he guided the car around the back of the pile of old stones, chunks of concrete and crumbling memories, looking for a way in, or better still hoping to find her on the back steps, hand out, waiting for her cash. He could just wind the window down, hand over the envelope, and wish her au revoir.

She'd got in touch with him via LinkedIn a few days ago. At first, he thought it was some kind of prank, but when she mentioned the eight grand, he'd known she really was who she claimed to be. She wanted cash, she'd said, a one-off payment to get her out of town – again! The first thing he did was tell her to naff off and leave him alone. But when she threatened to involve Eddie, he grew angry that she should think it acceptable to blackmail him like this.

It caused him to take a week's holiday from work and drive back up to Yorkshire.

Only when he saw her on the news did he take it seriously. After the latest message – last night, when she'd threatened to kill Eddie – the anger had fled with its tail tucked up tight between its legs. In its place was intrigue with a red and flaming vignette. And it was the fear that gave him the sweaty hands right now, sweaty pits too. This was the kind of encounter that scared the living shit out of him – even though this was the one and only encounter of this kind he'd ever had; but he'd read enough crime novels to imagine himself in that position. He hadn't liked the image, and he didn't like the reality any better.

Just hand it over and bugger off again. Quick.

But he might have known nothing was as straight-forward as your positive side might like it to be.

A bit like their childhood. Teenagers who knew everything. They knew nothing. And he supposed that no matter how much advice your elders give you, there's no way of knowing if their advice is correct unless you go in the other direction and find out to your cost that you took a wrong turn. That's what happened to Eddie – straight into some girl's knickers and straight down the charity shop for a pram and a set of bottles. And that's what their mum had tried to prevent.

Mum had thought so much of Eddie that she was prepared to offer that whore eight big ones to piss off and leave young Eddie Collins alone, bruised and with a lesson learned that showed him he'd had the map upside down. Eight grand had been a lot of money; a girl could do a lot with that much back in the nineties. No one had spelled it out directly to her, but the general idea was that she go and pay for a private abortion and then put the rest towards a future where there were no beatings from her father or blatant indifference from her mum. It would have been a decent future, too, with money behind her. More money than Eddie, or Malcolm for that matter, would now get as a inheritance.

But sometimes you just couldn't help people. Sometimes, as in Eddie's case, people had to find their own route and discover for themselves if it suited them or not.

The girl had grabbed the money, and even now, Malcolm could see the regret in her eyes, because taking the cash had meant letting go of Eddie. That was the deal. It was a tug for her, a strain – she clearly thought a lot of him, but in the end the money had won out, and off she went to begin her new life on her own.

After that, everything turned sunny. For a year.

Malcolm's headlights picked up a shape off to the right, near the potholed far corner of the cracked and weed-infested carpark. It waved at him, and slowly became the shape of a bedraggled thing in a long brown coat. As he approached, he wound down the window, felt the packet on the front passenger seat. He swallowed a lump of nerves and it prickled his eyes like the rain prickled his face.

She had her arms wrapped around herself, wet hair writhing in a fierce wind, eyes squinted against the rain.

"Thank God you're here, Malcolm. I didn't think you'd show."

"Man of my word."

"No police?"

He frowned. "I said I was a man of my word."

"Sorry. Just asking."

"Why? Why did you break out of that hospital?"

"Their chips were soggy. Hate soggy chips."

"Seriously, why?"

She smiled at him, oblivious to the rain running down her face. "Unfinished business."

"With Eddie?"

She nodded. "Among others."

He brought out the package and passed it to her. "This says you finally leave him alone. Okay?"

She bent to him and pushed a gun into his throat. "This would fucking ruin the upholstery."

Malcolm went completely rigid, hyperventilating.

"I don't want your money."

He stuttered, eyes closed, lips uncontrollable elastic bands. "Then what do you want?"

Chapter Fifty-five

A One-Way Trip to Hell

EDDIE COULDN'T HAVE HIS clothes back. He'd asked nicely, and he'd threatened them, and they still refused him. He had jeans and t-shirts in the van, and an old pair of trainers. He rustled up a West Yorkshire Police fleece from the bottom of a kit bag and shivered until the cab of his van warmed up.

By the time the two morons playing Columbo had let him go, it was getting dark and the traffic was building as the rain grew heavier. He sat in a queue along Elland Road past the football ground, being blinded by Volvo brake lights all the way to the M621, where idiots piloting Audis cut others up with reckless abandon.

Everything about his life with Alex, right from their first days back in the nineties, had been twisted. And even today, it was twisted, and it was twisted because she was a lunatic. She was a pathological killer, and now—

The phone on the seat beside him rang. He snatched a glance at it as he trundled along at something only a little faster than walking pace. And what he saw almost caused him to shunt the car in front. Moneypenny's face smiled at him from the screen. Moments later the Bluetooth handset kicked in and picked up for him.

"Eddie?"

He swallowed, muting the grief that lodged in his throat and brought anger to the fore. "I'm gonna pull your head clean off when I get my hands on you! You mad bitch!"

There was a slight pause, and then Alex laughed a little. "I've waited for this day for years."

"Where the fuck are you?"

Still with a smile in her voice, she said, "Remember The Sheridan Club?"

The Sheridan Club was the place to be if you liked nightlife back in the nineties. It was just far enough out of town to be off the police radar, and yet close enough to stagger to the nearest bus route or taxi rank. There was a strictly enforced age limit of eighteen, but it wasn't unusual to find school kids in there at the weekend. The Sheridan Club was great if you liked live music – loud live music – and it served real ale too. They hadn't yet latched onto selling cocktails cheaper than bottled water. When it did, in 2005, drugs followed the booze, and that spelled its decline until a few years later when the public smoking laws killed it stone dead.

The Sheridan Club. It was where Eddie's life had changed forever because of her, because of Alex Trafford, now Sheridan. Hell, she'd even changed her name in its honour.

"I'm on my way."

"Make sure you're alone."

"It's just you, me, and a one-way trip to hell."

A smarter Eddie would have stopped and got hold of Benson. A smarter Eddie would have gone up there for the ride and watched from a safe distance as they hauled her arse into the back of a police van.

But this was grieving Eddie; this was angry Eddie. He hung up. He had no intention of bringing the police to this particular party. He was also sure of something else: she meant to kill him there and put an end to the four years of torture since she'd murdered her own father and failed to murder Eddie.

The anticipation alone must have been killing her. She'd escaped Juniper Hill, and he'd ignorantly thought she'd done that to get out of Dodge. But no, she'd hung around, killing anyone who tried to interact with her, or to stop her, and especially those like poor Moneypenny, who had the potential to stand in the way of her focus: Eddie Collins.

So now, he was driving towards her to find out for sure if she wanted to make love to him or to make death with him.

Eddie never fancied himself as the murdering kind, but all it had taken to change that was the needless death of sweet Maggie Darlington.

Chapter Fifty-six

Where the Past Came to Die

SHE MADE MALCOLM PARK the car out of sight, lock it and hand her the keys, which she stuffed into the pocket of Dee's coat. The coat was horrible and looked out of place with her ragged jeans and mucky boots, but it was warm, and it had brilliant pockets – shoplifter's pockets. "Over there." She shone the torch through the rain and nudged him towards a side entrance. "We're going back to The Sheridan Club, Malcolm."

"Why? You've been well recompensed for whatever went wrong in the past. We don't—"

"Recompensed? For what went wrong? Are you having a fucking laugh?"

Malcolm struggled up the two or three steps that led inside into utter blackness. "I don't understand. The past is in the past, we—"

"The past is in the present too. Turn to your left and walk through the kitchens."

She aimed the torch and he followed the stuttering pool of yellow light across a tiled floor, cracked and spewing weeds, piles of pigeon shit, and over towards a rectangle of night leaking in through an open door. "Go on, outside again."

They exited and their echoing footfalls abandoned them among rubble, a whole shitload of it that stretched all the way to the boundary of her torchlight and probably well beyond it too, the darkness seemingly growing more dense, pierced by that incessant iciness of rain.

"What's out here?"

"This is the part those yellow signs warned you about. Where the building is collapsing. Careful now, there's a hole there." She aimed the torch at the edge of a hole that was easily eight feet across, jagged edges welcoming the unwary into an unfathomable blackness. "That's the cellar. Only one way in and one way out – and you're looking at it right now."

He shuffled around it, arms outstretched, choosing his footing as carefully as her light would allow. "Why did we need to go inside to get back outside?"

"This whole area is fenced off with security fencing. No way through it, no way over it, and that door into the kitchen is the only way out here."

"What do you want with me, Alex? I've paid you; I've done nothing—"

"Shut up."

"I only want answers to perfectly valid questions."

Alex hit him across the head with the gun. Malcolm hit the rubble on his knees and let out a yelp. To her surprise, she found that he was crying.

"Why are you doing this?"

"Shut up."

"Please! I just want—"

She hit him again, harder, and this time he just fell forward, his face breaking his fall. There was no crying this time. Alex slid the gun into one of Dee's big inside pockets, next to the tissues and the Polo mints she'd found there, and took out a pair of cable ties. Once his hands were bound behind his back and his feet tied together, one crossed over the other, she dragged him across the sharp rubble to a clearing of sorts, a place she'd spotted earlier in the daylight. It was near the edge of the hole, and there was a clear path back towards the kitchen door.

The scene looked like a poor man's version of the Acropolis. It could almost be a post-modernist film set, dystopian perhaps. It looked somehow poetic in the daylight; weeds threading their way around and through the stone like a rampant madman. Everything recoiled in the cold wind, mud shuddered, water dripped into puddles where dead things lay.

This was the kind of place where the past came to die.

There were just two more things to do and then her preparations would be complete. She took out the revolver and emptied out all the chambers in the cylinder, except for two: one bullet next in line for firing, and the last immediately after that.

Once back inside out of the rain, Alex took out Maggie Darlington's phone and the lovely keyring with the photo of a dead spaniel called Tyrone on it. She studied the image and rang Eddie. He took only moments to answer. "Eddie?"

"I'm gonna pull your head clean off when I get my hands on you! You mad bitch!"

Alex laughed. Eddie was very upset with her.

Chapter Fifty-seven

Ghosts

ALMOST AN HOUR LATER, Eddie rolled the van along Thorner Lane just off the A64 near Scholes. The traffic had thinned and so too had the buildings. Being stuck in traffic had fuelled his rage until he was screaming for people to get out of his way. But now, near-empty roads and a distinct lack of all things rat-race cooled him and made him think about what he was driving into.

For one, she was literally a certified nutjob who happened to be quite proficient at killing. For another, she might be armed. And for yet another, nobody knew he was here – except for the person who wanted to kill him, and who was quite proficient at it.

This was, as far as he could recall, one of the worst decisions his temper had ever let him make. Eddie drove past the cemetery to his right, and The Arium and along towards Thorner.

The Sheridan Club was halfway between Thorner and Scholes. It was a former mansion house set back off the road along its own long single-track driveway with just a couple of passing places. Anyone living there could see you coming as your headlights fanned out before you.

Eddie switched his lights off before he even made the turn. He slowed the van along that two-hundred-yard driveway, trying to get his eyes accustomed to the darkness.

Wind-driven rain and sleet beat at the side of the van as he approached.

Eddie brought the van to a halt. He shut off the engine and as soon as the heater stopped blowing warm air into the cab, he felt cold. Tonight wasn't going to be at all pleasant. He had a feeling that tonight would be life-changing for him – maybe even life-ending, if things didn't go according to plan. And talking of plans... he didn't have one. Eddie was the kind of man who waded into trouble and just hoped he could find a way back out. He never left a convenient branch within grabbing range, never prearranged a rescue... Rescue?

He took a breath and congratulated himself on thinking like an adult.

For once in his stupid life, he thought it might be a good idea to lay a convenient branch before he started wading. He rang Benson but got no reply. He left a short message: Call me.

So was that it? Forget the convenient branch? No, he'd try once more; this time he called Khan and got an immediate reply. "Where's Benson?"

"Hello, Eddie."

Eddie sighed; this was going to be like pulling teeth. "Hello, Khan. Where's Benson?"

"Hey, Khan, thanks for getting my sorry arse out of custody. It was very kind of you considering you hadn't slept all night.'"

"Yeah, yeah, thank you. I appreciate it. Okay?"

Khan sniffled. "What do you want him for?"

"What, are you his fucking receptionist now?"

"Hanging up."

"Wait!"

Another sniffle. "What?"

"I think I know where she is." Eddie could almost hear Khan sitting up straight, eyes springing open, ears on full volume, pen in hand.

"Go on."

"The Sheridan Club."

"The what? Her name's Sheridan, isn't it?"

"Congratulations on playing audio snap. You win a new brain cell."

"Collins, I'm warning—"

"It's up near Thorner."

"Thorner? It'll take me an hour to get there."

"Who said anything about you getting here? Call plod, get them—"

"No, no, no." He was obviously trying to think of an excuse. "I… they'll come in all guns blazing. This needs tact, Eddie. Wait for me; I'll get there as soon as I can – an hour at most."

"Bring a coat. Thanks to you lot, I'm fucking freezing." He hung up, wishing he knew where Benson was, and knowing that Khan would sidestep him and try to snatch the glory – whatever glory nailing a serial killer could bring. But having Khan was better than having no one.

Even so, Eddie wouldn't wait for him – he wanted someone to know where he was, that was all, and he wanted someone to be there to catch him if he fell, or pick up the pieces afterwards – but first, he had an hour to sort it all out. He unplugged a Maglite and stepped out into the biting wind.

To his left was the car park, and he could see what he assumed to be Alex's stolen Mini parked there.

It didn't take too much energy to remember how it had looked back in the day. They had two search lights, like something from 20th Century Fox, out front on the lawn, and under cover of the porch, two spinning mirror balls attacked on all sides by colour-changing lasers mounted on the four grand pillars.

There was always a queue and it always began outside in front of those big oak doors manned by bouncers wearing bow ties and cool-looking earpieces. Either side of those doors were ten-foot potted conifers ringed in state-of-the-art fibre-optic lights. More floods lit up the front façade and if you were walking up the driveway, you were treated to views of people going nuts through the main dance hall windows, one either side of the entrance. There were blasts of coloured light and blasts of music; the pollution of adolescence. The smell of cannabis would sting the air out here, but in the days when Eddie went, there were never any drugs allowed inside. If you were caught dealing or smoking that shit indoors, you were liable to meet one of those bouncers up close and be invited to inspect the gold sovereigns on his fingers.

Weeds were utterly rampant now. The wall lights were long gone, replaced by graffiti and a general air of entropy. It stared at him, windowless, lifeless. Cheerless. And somewhere inside it grazed him, another forlorn reminder of what happens to the things you outgrow as age plunders your youth. Turn your back on them and they decay until all you have left of them are memories. Ghosts.

The front doors had warped and there was a mulch of leaves and detritus at their base. The tarnished door handles were chained together.

Eddie listened to the night but found no clue and no comfort there, just a cold wind with ice for teeth. He pulled his fleece tighter, tapped the Maglite hanging from his belt and took a left around to the side of the building. Bracken, growing unchecked. Glassless windows, smashed roof tiles, and other debris hindered his progress, but eventually he found something that caused him to stop, hold his breath and listen again.

It was an old wooden fire door that showed an arc of grit carved into the stone step. The muck and growth had been shoved back as the door had been pulled open. He risked a quick flash of torchlight to confirm it was recent.

Eddie pulled the door open and gazed into utter blackness. The wind screamed through holes in the roof as though trying to pull it free, howling in failure, whistling in despair. Sleet stung his cheek until he could bear it no longer. He shuffled inside, his heart thudding, expecting her to jump out on him.

He made his way deeper into the building. Entering through the side like this disorientated him. Only when he'd negotiated several damp corridors lined with flaking paint and fungus growing from blackened walls, stumbling over vine-covered floors, slipping on bird shit and fox shit, and crushing the skeletons of rodents and vermin, did he get a sense that he was back in the foyer behind those old oak doors that were chained shut.

The toilet doors were off to one side, the opulent central staircase that was always chained off and led, so rumour had it, to the special guest rooms. And further around, the cloak room, manager's office, and two ornate archways that led through into a pair of high-ceilinged dance floors.

Rain fell straight through from the floor above; if he stood directly under it, he'd be able to make out the hole in the roof above. A damp, acrid smell of decay accompanied the rotting building. More water cascaded through the ceiling at various points, and Eddie's nerves screamed at him to get the hell out. The longer he was here without encountering Alex, the sooner that encounter would come.

A rat scurried somewhere near, squeaking as it ran.

A shiver crawled up Eddie's spine.

This had been her goal all along. She'd made it clear that Eddie was the only living part of her own unholy trinity; the father was dead, the ex was dead… only Eddie to go. And then what? And then she'd be free. Or so she claimed. Cured. Stable. Normal again.

Never!

Suddenly there was a flash of light and an echoing crack.

Silently, Eddie fell.

Chapter Fifty-eight

Thoughts of a Wise Man

CHARLES DIDN'T LIKE BEING alone. There was something cold about loneliness; you could be sitting in front of a roaring coal fire with a glass of whisky, and still you'd feel cold. He snorted a mini-laugh and was shocked by an echo, frightened of it, saddened by it. Eddie would love this, he thought, being alone surrounded by peace and quiet, echoes, would be his idea of bliss.

He swallowed.

Not Charles, though. Charles liked company. He wrapped himself in that suit he kept for days and evenings like this where there was just him and his thoughts, waiting till his boy came home again. Those thoughts were usually happy; Charles was a glass-half-full kind of man. But he wasn't smiling tonight. Tonight, his thoughts were dark and fearful, glass-smashed kind of thoughts. Alex Sheridan kind of thoughts.

That girl's fronds had spanned over twenty years into the Collins history. He honestly thought they'd never see her again after those times when Eddie was at first besotted by her, and then full of venom towards her as she waved goodbye and left for good. Except that "for good" had ended quite abruptly, and the remaining family was back inside her grip.

The wind rattled the windows and Charles shrank into the chair, barely daring to breathe.

She was a murderer. The news told him so. Killed her own father, they said. Killed someone else to get out of the nuthouse, they said. And now that killer was back in Eddie's life. And it didn't take a wise man to wonder why that was: to finish off her life's work, to kill Eddie once and for all.

He shivered and sipped at a cool cup of tea, too afraid to get up and make a fresh one.

It didn't take a wise man at all.

Chapter Fifty-nine

Protected to Death

IT WAS A HELL of a risk. Playing dead while some nutjob with a gun crept up to you. But that's what Eddie did. And here was the nutjob with the gun, creeping up.

But in here, there was no such thing as 'creeping'. The debris on the floor made each hesitant footstep as loud as a New Year's party. And when she was just one more step away, Eddie turned on the torch and pulled her legs out from under her. She hit the floor hard on her back and groaned, winded and stunned.

He crawled on top of her and ripped the gun from her hand.

She began to sob, and then she wailed, kicking her legs, hands flailing, scratching and slapping. Eddie grabbed her shoulders and pinned her to the weeds until she calmed.

Alex laughed at him. "I could have shot you and that would have been an end to it all, Eddie Collins."

Eddie was panting, heart still stuttering as he played that suggested scene in his head. It really had been that close. And that would have been an end to Eddie; no future, and a past already fading into other people's memories of him.

"Let go of me. You're hurting me." Her torch lay nearby, part-buried under creeping ivy, leaching a green light across her face.

"Hurt you? I should kill you."

"Like you have the balls." She tried to stroke his face, but he yanked on her hair. "Let go of me."

He gritted his teeth and leaned forward until his face was next to hers. When she tried to move, he grabbed her hair tighter in his fist until she stiffened against him. He growled, "I really do want to rip your fucking head off for what you did to her. This thing involved me and you; no one else. You can blame your madness all you like, but it was you, Alex, it was you who killed her, you're in charge—"

"Do it! Shut the fuck up, you whining bastard, and just do it, or let me go."

Eddie's eyes opened. He released her hair and sat upright. She wasn't going anywhere.

"Tonight is your last, you piece of shit." She took a long breath. "And then I'm out of here."

"You should have run while you had the chance. You could have got away, Alex." She came in close to his face, licked his cheek, and he pulled away from her, horrified and disgusted.

"If I'd wanted to leave, I would have." She stared up at him, a knowing look in her eyes that unnerved Eddie. "I didn't break out just to go on the run." She cleared her throat. "I have a question for you. Think about it. Consider it."

"What?"

"I want to know if there's a chance for us."

"What? No. Fuck off."

"Seriously. We can run, Eddie. We can be together." Was that playfulness in her eyes, or embarrassment painted over with pride?

"You are so fucking delusional."

"There's no Maggie standing in our way." She bared her teeth and grinned up at him. "She sobbed. You'd have loved it." She laughed hard enough to break into a coughing fit.

He slapped her across the face, and her split lip oozed blood across her cheek. He didn't want to do it, but... Where the hell was his self-control?

She grinned and her teeth were framed red as she ran her tongue over them.

That stench in his nostrils, that damp feeling, that gathering of hatred tumbled into his mind all at once and Eddie grabbed her by the throat and the words he wanted to say sounded pathetic even to him, even as he was spitting them at her. Pathetic. "You killed a good person for no reason. She was a good person. I hate you for doing that."

"Stop it," she said. "You'll have me in tears." She traced her finger down his face and winked at him. "Want to fuck? Old times' sake?"

His thumbs buried themselves in her throat, and his hands squeezed, and though he stared at her, he was seeing Maggie and the petechiae on her face, her bloodshot eyes of green, and the red trail from her nose. He increased the pressure as the tears came. And he saw it, a way to beat the grief, the awful hollow feeling that had burrowed its way inside like a disease. He saw it clearly.

He straightened his arms and pressed down on her throat. Her eyes widened and her grip on his wrists tightened, but he ignored it all; he ignored the feeling that came along too. Sometimes the payback for a loved one is worth the self-hate that revenge guarantees. Sometimes, hate bites so deep that killing someone else is the only way to prise the teeth out of your heart.

But something else was at work here, too. It was nothing audible, in fact nothing even like a thought; it was more a feeling with edges and lines, with colours and shapes – it was an emotion. And this emotion had a sharp point that worked its way into Eddie's thoughts like an arrowhead skewering a heart. It was quite simple: it was an amalgam of fear and depravity. It was the beginning of insanity; it was the beginning of becoming something from which you could never hope to return. It was the turning of a path, a decision, and it was the wrong decision, it was the wrong path.

He stared down at her. She had relaxed, and if he didn't know better, that was a smile growing on her pale face, that was relief in her dying eyes.

"Ecstasy." She struggled for breath, and croaked. "No more misery. No more waking up as me."

Eddie blinked. "That's why you killed her! So I'd wipe you off the face of the earth."

She tried to speak, but the effort appeared too much, and she just closed her mouth and stared into him. He took away his thumbs, eased off her throat, and the colour seeped back into her pallid face.

When she got her breath back, she said, "You liked her. You should have liked me instead, funny man." She watched his eyes, seemed to get off on his pain. "I'm going to turn you inside out. You pulverised my life... I know! Shut up and leave me alone!"

"What?"

She focused on Eddie again. "I really do love you. I always have. Ever since our first meeting here."

Eddie winced. "What? I can't work you out, Alex. Why did you stop taking your drugs? They were there to help you!"

Alex screamed, and tried to pull chunks out of his face. He batted her off, tried to restrain her, and she calmed again almost instantly. This was turning into a night from hell, and he wished to Christ Khan would hurry up.

Tears blurred her black eye makeup. "Eddie, I'm... I can't do this! Please..."

He was confused. "What is—"

"Ever tried to watch TV when there's another TV on a different channel right next to it. And someone has a radio on in the same room? And upstairs someone is having a loud telephone conversation, just as someone else is whispering in your ear?"

"That's what the drugs were for, Alex."

She prodded her head. "It's like that all fucking day in here."

Eddie stared.

"Loud." She shook her head. "Never mind. So kill me if you've got the balls," she laughed, "and avenge your fair maiden."

"Don't take the piss. She was worth a million of you." Eddie leaned his watch towards the light; twenty minutes gone. Forty till Khan and his brand of cavalry rode into town. "You are so twisted."

"I'm the most normal person you could wish to meet. If you had this going on inside your head, if you...I'm sick of fighting."

"Fighting what?"

"You. Me. Life. Unhappiness. You name it; I'm sick of it. I remember what you said, that I'll never be free. Killing Tyler didn't help. Killing my dad didn't help. So that leaves you. Third time lucky, Eddie."

"Aw, diddums. Can't win 'em all."

"Can you let me up, please? I'm getting wet and there are things crawling on me."

"Ah! Déjà vu. I think this is the part where I ask if you'd like your gun back."

"Keep the fucking gun, Eddie; just let me sit on the stairs, for God's sake!"

Eddie took hold of the gun and clamped tight onto his torch. "Where the hell did you get a gun from?"

"Argos. Just let me up!"

"Try to run and I'll put you down again, okay?" Thirty minutes to go.

"You're a spineless bastard, Collins. If I ran, you'd shit your pants." Alex knelt, took hold of her little torch, and stood up, careful not to dislodge the knife hidden in her boot. She sat on the third step up, slapping muck from her clothes, and Eddie set his torch on the floor to point at her face, taking away her peripheral vision.

"How's your brother doing?"

"Malcolm? How do you know Malcolm?"

"I've known him almost as long as I've known you. Remember when we first met?"

"We're not celebrating an anniversary. Cut the nostalgic shit."

"Got any cigs?"

Eddie took out his packet, lit two and passed her one.

She inhaled hard, closed her eyes as the drug danced behind them, and then exhaled a plume into the torchlight. "We were standing right here. Twenty-five years ago. I've been back a couple of times since I left Juniper Hill. Memories, y'know." She rubbed her hands, and then her arms as the temperature dropped another couple of degrees. "Remember how I disappeared not long after that night?"

"Happiest day of my life. And then you spoiled it by coming back a year later."

"Malcolm made me go away." She plugged her ears with shaking hands, and pulled a face as though she was screaming, but she was silent, enduring an agony only she was aware of.

Eddie took a drag. "You are so full of shit."

She panted, but eventually came back down, and blinked as though just arriving in a bright room instead of this dark pit. "He paid me to."

"Can't you just stop talking? Why don't you listen to your voices for a bit, have an internal conversation with them? I'll listen to Wish You Were Here, and we can loathe each other's company."

"I don't loathe your company." She watched him, but he gave nothing back. "I was pregnant."

"I know. You said your dad made you go away." He took a pinch of salt and added it to the bucketful he'd collected already this evening. "Honestly, the lies just fall out of your mouth."

"No. It was Malcolm. Ask him."

"Why would he send—"

"You fucking dumbass. It was your baby."

Eddie's mouth fell open. "What? But we only did it once."

"You don't build a baby fuck by fuck, Eddie. It only takes one go."

"But..."

"How do I know it was yours? I wasn't sleeping with anyone else. I was sixteen. You were my first."

Silence.

"Eddie?"

"Just... Just shut up, Alex."

"I was in love with you. Malcolm paid me to leave."

"You twisted little cow. Why can't you just be straight with people for a change, huh? Why must you be so fucking evil all the time? Christ's sake, take a day off!"

Alex blew smoke out of her nose, and said, "Eight grand to leave town and never let you know."

That opened Eddie's eyes wide. In the torchlight, he tried to study her face – but discerning lies on the face of a psychopath was like trying to find a single drop of water that fell into a pond. But she was right – eight grand went missing, and how else would she know that?

"I think it was a family affair, you know; how he told me to go."

He closed his eyes and took a breath. "Just... please, just be quiet." He tried to bring the past back for further examination, but it was hazy, and the more he grabbed at it, the hazier it became.

"Not interested in your sordid past, Eddie?"

"I'm interested in putting my sordid past back inside Juniper Hill."

She almost laughed. "He didn't say 'I want you out of town'. He said, 'We want you out of town'. We. I thought he meant you. But clearly I was wrong."

"I didn't know anything about it."

"Well, you do now. Long secret, eh?"

"And where's the baby now?"

"Dad didn't make me go away. Dad kicked me down the stairs, remember? There was blood, and... She'd be about twenty-four now. I might've been a grandmother."

"I'm sorry to hear that." Eddie turned his face away, eyes down. This was so fucked up. Where the hell was Khan?

"You are?"

"Of course I am. There's only one monster in this story, and it ain't me."

"They paid me off. They wanted me to leave town and have an abortion, Eddie."

"They?"

"Malcolm."

"And?"

"Your mum, I guess."

"No. That's not right. They wouldn't do that."

Bitterness spiked her voice. "Someone did. Malcolm and your mum. Mums can be very protective of their children, Eddie. I should know."

"I don't believe it." But it made him think, just the same. On the surface, his mum wouldn't do such a thing – she loved children. She loved her children; wanted the best and steered them away from anything that smelled of danger or corruption. He looked up at Alex.

She sighed. "I have nothing to gain by lying to you, do I? And in case it had slipped your mind, you're the one holding the gun."

"I don't get why Mum... I don't understand Malcolm's role in all of this."

"Malcolm said he would have to leave, too. He said your dad would kill him if he found out. Did he ever find out?"

"We thought he'd stolen the cash and done a runner. Drugs or something."

"And he never told you?"

Eddie said nothing, took a last drag and flicked the cigarette end away into the darkness.

"Then he is a true hero. To do that for his family, to leave them in order to protect you, and to keep it secret. He didn't want you to feel bad or guilty."

"If what you say is true..." Eddie gritted his teeth. "A hero? For forcing a pregnant teenager out of town? That's not a fucking hero."

Her voice croaked. "Maybe that's why he ran, then. I don't know."

Eddie was silent. The things running rampant in his mind were not pretty things; they were deep, ugly thoughts of a family he didn't recognise. If she was telling the truth, his family was a lie. "Given a choice, would you have kept the baby?"

"I didn't really have a choice."

"But say you did."

Silence. Then, "Yes." She ground out her cigarette end. "Would you have wanted me to?"

He folded his arms. "Doesn't matter now. It's in the past."

"You asked and you got an answer. So give me an answer, too." She swallowed, watching him. "Would you have wanted me to keep the baby? Our baby?"

"Yes. I would." He swept away silent tears, happy that she couldn't see. "So you took the money anyway?"

"You think they'd have sued me under the Trade Descriptions Act? They just wanted me off the scene, away from you. Out of your life."

"You didn't have to take the money, honey. I would have stood by you."

"Like hell you would."

He thought about it and knew he wouldn't be able to convince her. But he would have stood by her; he wouldn't have let that girl bring up his child alone. Some things were worth breaking away from your own family for. He shrugged, "And yet you came back after a year anyway."

"Why not? I wasn't about to drag you down with a babe in arms, was I? I didn't have a kid any more. So what was the harm?"

"With a new surname too."

"The Sheridan Club was where my life with you began. Seemed like a good choice."

He swallowed and checked his watch again.

"And this is where it will end, one way or another."

"We didn't know about the change of name – to them you were still that little whore. When you came back, things in our house took a nosedive."

"But you didn't see me as a whore? I was a virgin when I met you." She sighed, and her breath shivered out between cold bloody lips. "Why would they think I was a whore?"

"People use name-calling as a defence, or a cover-up for their own failings. Makes them feel superior."

"But one day you rebelled against them. Didn't you?"

"She bawled her eyes out the day I told her that we were back together. Shouting and screaming at me, name-calling. She cried. Continuously. Dad was furious with me. Not because of you, as such. He was furious with me because I made Mum cry; I was the cause of all the upset. He didn't like Mum being upset."

"And that's when Malcolm came back to town and visited me again."

He straightened up, cocked his head in a question.

"I guess your mum called him, told him the little whore was back. He put pressure on me to leave you. But I couldn't do it."

A pause, then realisation. "So you made me do it."

Silence.

He shouted, "You didn't have the guts—"

"I didn't want to leave you! That was all. Guts didn't come into it, Eddie. I didn't want to go."

"So you bit me. You made me dump you. You made me think you were a psycho."

More silence.

"And now that you are one, you still want me to take the lead?"

"I can't live this life any more. I need to get out of it." Alex cried, big sobs that rocked her shoulders. Echoes bounced back to them, pain amplified.

The Sheridan Club was a place of pain after all, not one of joy. He hated it here, wished he'd never seen it.

And Eddie didn't know whether to comfort her or to laugh at her shite acting. But it wasn't acting. It was real; he was sure of it. And it hurt him to see it. How the past haunts you – no, how the past hunts you, how it makes you pay over and over again, never giving you a break, always tormenting, always making you relive it without a chance to change anything; mistakes on a constant loop inside your head. How cruel the past was.

"You dumping me would have a been a relief for your mum. Well, if she'd lived to see it."

"Shaky ground."

"She killed herself because I was back in town."

"No, she killed herself because Malcolm stole all…" And that's where his sentence ended. To find out that your mother killed herself not because of your brother, but because of you and your inability to learn by your mistakes, cracked the foundations of an entire life. It tipped the scales away from self-righteousness and into the black squalid corners of a madman's mind. It changed Eddie's balance, so much that he almost fell off the gyroscope inside his own mind.

"Eddie?"

He whispered, frightened of the consequences. "She killed herself because of me."

"How does it feel to learn you're responsible for giving away your family's savings and your mother's suicide?"

"Shut up."

"It's true."

"Shut up!"

"Deal with it, Eddie. This is what abandonment feels like, remember? This is what being disowned feels like."

"I haven't been—"

"All of your memories are lies. Everything you thought was real is fake. They protected you to death."

Eddie was inside his own mind, looking around, trying to see the lies for himself, trying them on for size, testing them against what he knew. He wondered how many he would uncover.

"Do you hate Malcolm?"

"You needed help, not banishment."

"He's on my list. Did I tell you? He's right next to you on my list."

"You won't kill him; there's no need. It's me you're after." He twitched the gun, letting her know he was still in charge. But even despite that, he had an awful feeling he wasn't in charge at all. He had a feeling he was surrounded by a fog of deceit, and no matter how hard he tried, he couldn't see through it to the truth.

"Fucking watch me. I'm not afraid of killing people, Eddie. People mean nothing to me."

"Obviously."

"Except you."

"Fuck off, Alex."

She snarled at him. Teeth bared, she shouted, "When I kill him, I'll make you watch! When I kill him, I'll crush him, and I'll call the cops myself, and tell them you had the chance to stop it but refused!" Her voice dropped to a whisper. "When I kill him, I'll make sure you live the rest of your life wishing you'd chosen differently."

Silence. Only panting.

"If I suffer, Eddie, so will you."

"Yeah, okay, you fucking freak, dream on." Eddie dared to smile at her. "It's immaterial anyway. You'll never get to him."

The snarl morphed into a grin. "He's not back in town by coincidence, you know."

Chapter Sixty

When Reason Cried

There was nothing in her face, no emotion visible to him, and for a moment, a sliver of fear took away a good-sized part of his bravery. The remaining part insisted he take stock of where he was, and with whom, and it concluded that he was very vulnerable, in imminent danger. It also concluded that, despite him having her gun, she had something in reserve. Somehow, she had the upper hand.

He swallowed. "How did you find him?"

"Can I have another cigarette?"

"How did you find him?"

She shrugged. "It wasn't difficult. He was always a music nut, wasn't he? And well-connected. I tried Facebook and Twitter, but I realised someone like your Malcolm would be on LinkedIn."

Eddie raised his eyebrows in question.

"It's a social site for professional types. He's a music journalist now; obvious when you look at how keen he was back in the day. Anyway, I got in touch using Chester's laptop and credentials. Told him you were in grave danger from me. He didn't bite, so I told him something to convince him he was actually speaking with me and not some chump called Chester."

"The eight grand."

"The eight grand. Yes. Told him I needed one more payment and I'd disappear for good. Told him you'd be healthier if he paid up."

Eddie shook his head.

"Five grand this time. Nothing outrageous. He could afford it, and he could afford to lose it." She spun her tiny torch in her fingers.

"So he came running."

"In a manner of speaking. Listen, can I have a cigarette, please?"

"No."

"There's not long to go before your coppers show up, is there? Unless they're already here? So how about sharing? I could really use one, Eddie. Bet you could too."

There was that knowing look in her eyes again. No matter what he did now, he just knew she was one step in front of him, and he was walking headlong into a trap. Assuming, of course, that he wasn't already in it.

Despite his promise to come alone, she seemed to have sussed him out, worked out he'd called for backup.

He slid the Maglite into his belt loop and took out two more cigarettes. He was about to put them between his lips when she screamed and kicked him hard in the face. Eddie cupped his hands to his broken face and found himself on his back on the crumbling floor, grunting in pain. When he opened his eyes, she'd gone, but he could hear her.

He grabbed his torch and shone it directly at her back. "Stop! Alex! I'll shoot!"

And before he could even get to his feet she'd gone through the door into the kitchen, and the light from her torch had disappeared. Panting, spitting blood, Eddie got to his feet and trotted after her as the door closed with a boom.

He could feel his face beginning to swell already. His nose was on fire, blood running into his mouth. He spat it at the door and shouted, "Alex, you dumb bitch, come out, for Christ's sake and let's stop playing silly fuckers!" He banged on the door, then kicked at it. The damned thing didn't move.

He remembered the layout of this place enough to know that there was only this one door into the kitchen from in here. But there was a door out the back where the deliveries came in. Eddie slid the gun into his belt and let the torch lead him back out through the side door and towards the right side of the building.

When he reached it, his face was throbbing and the pressure behind his eyes was mounting. But even worse than that was the security fence surrounding the part-collapsed building. It was spiked with wire and joined to its neighbour by bolts. It was designed to keep the nosy out and the danger in. And it worked.

Through the rain, he saw a brief flicker of torchlight behind a vague shape in there, maybe twenty yards away. "Alex?"

"Turn on your torch," she called back.

He did – and saw her standing among the fenced-in rubble. Beyond the far fence was another fifty yards of grass, and then an embankment crowded with bushes and trees that shrieked in the wind, swaying back and forth in a frenzy of crashing branches.

And still no sign of Khan and his warriors.

His torch shone directly on her, and the look in her eyes was nothing short of terrifying.

Eddie was the first to admit that he was running dangerously low on bravery right now; it was just above the red line, and the look on her face didn't help. She was snarling at him, and she was screaming at something he couldn't see or hear, yelling and crying out, clawing at thin air.

The next moment, she was laughing. "Look, Eddie!" she called over the wind. "Can you see him?"

"Who?"

"Shine your torch, you fucking retard!"

Eddie shone the torch to where she pointed. He saw a pair of legs, and he saw some fancy boots. He put his hand to his mouth. "No!"

She shone her own pathetic torch, grinning at him. "Gonna kill him, Eddie."

"Alex, no. Look, there's no need for this. He was a dick, but it's gone now, it's so far in the past that—"

"That what? So far in the past that it doesn't matter any more? So far in the past that everyone's forgotten about it?" She was crying, her smudged black eye makeup adding another layer of macabre to the whole scene. "I haven't forgotten. I can't fucking forget." She was weeping still, intermittent sobs kicking her in the back.

And Eddie stared on, tears in his own eyes, blood still leaking down his face, but all of it unnoticed. He clung to the wire fence, fingers cold and wet.

"Did you like Doc Warburton's face? You should have seen it running into the carpet, Eddie. You'd have loved it." She laughed. "If she'd been alive when I poured it...Can't think of a worse death. Can you?"

Eddie stared on, nerves taut, anger mounting.

"I got a gallon of it here." She laughed and took off the screw cap from a plastic bottle, one of those with a built-in handle on the side. Orange warning labels screamed at him. "Can you smell it?"

"No! Stop, stop!"

She looked at him. No smile, just heartbreak. "You gotta let me go, Eddie."

"What? What do you mean? Just step away from him, Alex."

"Only one way you can stop me from melting his head."

Eddie leaned against the fence and shook it. He felt the gun in his waistband and took it out, looked at it.

"Shall I start pouring?"

Eddie brought the gun up, clumsily holding it in one hand and the torch in the other.

She saw it, and her eyes widened. "There's only one bullet left. So you'd better make good use of it. Make it count, Eddie. If you injure me, I can still make a mess of him."

"No!" he shouted. "Please! There's no need for this."

"There's every fucking need for this." She shook the bottle, and some acid sloshed out of the neck. She moved away quickly, looked across at Eddie. "That was close!" She tried to laugh, but it came out sounding like the shriek of a dying animal. Rain fell from her hair, the torchlight picking it out like diamonds falling from the hands of a dead man. Through tears she shouted, "I was never going to win. I was always going to die, and that's fine. I accept it. But it has to be you, Eddie."

"No!"

"Put me out of my misery, Eddie."

"I won't do it. You're not turning me into a killer."

"That's just what you'll be if you let me pour this." She started sobbing again. "Last chance, Eddie," she called over the wind, a pleading in her eyes, hair a maelstrom around her, coat flapping like a flag. "Do it and end it for me. Please!"

"No!"

"My life or his. You choose."

She lifted the bottle and began to tilt it, but the wind took the first few drops of liquid.

Eddie's shaking hands brought the gun up. His finger gripped the trigger.

He saw a muzzle flash and heard three sharp cracks. He was so shocked that he fumbled and dropped both the torch and the gun.

When he picked up the Maglite again, she and her torchlight were gone. The plastic bottle lay on the ground near the fancy boots, glugging its contents across the ground. People ran from the black bushes opposite, suddenly there were torch beams everywhere, shouts bombarding him, and Eddie stood stunned, not sure what the hell was happening.

Benson was among them. He was screaming, "Bolt croppers! Get some bolt croppers now!" He beckoned to Eddie. "Come around this side. Now! Move!"

Chapter Sixty-one

The Search Begins

MIDNIGHT. EDDIE THOUGHT HE'D never get warm again. They'd dried him out at the hospital, but it hadn't made the slightest difference; his teeth chattered, and he trembled as though his guts had turned to ice. His temperature was normal, but he felt about thirty degrees below.

Malcolm hadn't fared quite as well. He'd suffered a severe concussion and a skull fracture, they intended keeping him in for at least forty-eight hours, mopping up his vomit and taking care of his vertigo.

When Benson and his men had rushed down that embankment like Gandalf in The Lord of the Rings, Eddie thought that was an end to it. Put all the emotion on hold while we get the logistics out of the way: scrape the lunatic off the rocks in the cellar, take posh-boots to hospital, that kind of thing, he'd thought.

But when they'd cut the fence and squeezed armed officers inside, under the cover of more armed officers – namely Arry and Twiggy – they found that the acid had run away from him, and into the cellar. They had noticed this before they picked up the bottle and peeled away an orange warning label secured by a length of tape. The manufacturer's label underneath it had declared the contents to be the finest British table vinegar money could buy.

The vinegar, then, had run into a hole. A big black hole. In the bottom of it, partly shielded by some rather vicious-looking rocks, was a small torch shining in the black. It was the kind of thing you could buy at your local petrol station for a couple of quid when you spent a thousand on premium unleaded. The coppers had some big lamps in their vans, but even when they brought them to bear, they still could not see her.

One of the armed officers, a man who looked like a wet version of Butch Cassidy, stated categorically that he had shot her, under instruction from Detective Inspector Benson. But the important part of his statement was that he had shot her. Full stop, mister. No, it hadn't helped that Eddie was blinding him with his torch, and yes, it was strictly against protocol to open fire when Eddie had been standing almost directly behind her, but DI Benson had given the command. And he had hit her, dammit. He had seen her spiral out of control and plummet into the hole that everyone was staring into right now.

Half an hour passed as they tried to force doors inside the crumbling old ruins – doors that might have led to the cellar – without success.

"It'll need MOE." Eddie stared at Benson, humourless.

They even tried to get hold of some rope access specialists, but most of them were out of town, it seemed, at some awards ceremony the rest were on a job in Sheffield.

Only thing to do was get a ladder, shore it up, and find some copper stupid enough to go down arse-first into the blackness where some nutter who might be armed was lurking. Butch Cassidy had his hand in the air like a kid desperate for the toilet. Next to him, Arry stood shaking his bald head at the desperation of one man to be a hero. He looked at Eddie, gave a brief nod of acknowledgement, and got back to disrespecting his colleague.

As an ambulance turned up, so did Khan, who slithered into the crowd, hoping the rain and the wind and the shouting would hide his tardiness, his subsequent embarrassment, and his lack of a suitable coat. Eddie decided to have a word with him tomorrow when the dust had turned to mud.

Eddie missed all the fun. They bundled him and Malcolm into an ambulance and before long he was travelling fast to Leeds General, taking off over every speed bump and thudding back onto the gurney.

En route, and quite suddenly, the emotion Eddie had put on hold for the sake of logistics thundered its way to the front and yanked open the stop valves inside his eyes, and hit the big quiver button inside his chin.

He was in tears and he didn't really know why. The cooing of the paramedic did nothing to help the situation, and in the end he had to ask her to leave him the hell alone. He didn't like being rude to other emergency staff, but he thought if he had to ask her twice, he would have bawled like a kid who just pissed his pants in class.

They had wanted to keep him for observation, but he told them he couldn't possibly get any more handsome no matter how long they looked at him. It got the desired result: they had smiled and laughed, and Eddie had cranked the handle inside his own smile muscles, and they sent him home.

Chapter Sixty-two

The Black Seed of Paranoia

FORTY MINUTES LATER, EDDIE parked the van outside the cottage, but kept the engine running. He lit a cigarette and gazed, a little in awe and a little in fear, at how badly his hand shook. He sipped coffee from the McDonald's cup and wondered why he felt this way.

And how do you feel?

I feel like I got away lightly again. I feel like I've just been attacked by my own personal whirlwind and it beat me to a pulp, and it uncovered some things I never knew. And I don't know how I feel about seeing those things for the first time. It's like pulling the bandages back and seeing all the blood, and seeing how deep the wounds really are, and wondering if they'll ever heal; how big will the scar be?

The biggest question on his mind was this: would you have killed her given the knowledge you now have and the situation you found yourself in?

It was a tough one. It was full of moralistic nuances and legal-speak. It was full of trap doors and one-way passages. It was damnation and it was retribution; it was freedom and it was chains. It was a coin with heaven on one side and purgatory on the other. And the chances of getting it to land on its edge were very slim indeed. Thank God he hadn't needed to make the choice anywhere but inside his own head.

He shut the engine off, grabbed his coffee and took out the keys. Cigarette clamped between his teeth, Eddie made his way across the gravel to his front door, aware there were no armed coppers around. For the first time in a week the cottage was empty except for his old man. Surely, a part of him asked, that should make you feel better? You've punched your way through another torrid experience and, despite the busted nose, have waltzed out the other side looking like you stepped out of a Disney movie – life and soul intact.

Eddie closed the door behind him, threw the keys onto the hall table, shuffled out of his damp fleece and threw it somewhere near the coat-stand, and then stopped dead.

"'Bout time."

Eddie was mesmerised, and not in a good way. He stood perfectly still, letting the scene sink in.

"Your so-called marksmen are shit."

He still didn't respond. His mouth fell open as he stared at her, sitting in his chair, smoking one of his cigarettes, mug of tea on the table next to her. A certain Pink Floyd mug.

"The fuck are you doing here? They're still looking for you in the cellar."

That made her smile. "I didn't think you'd called them. I thought you'd want to fight your battles by yourself." She shrugged. "Anyway, they missed me."

"He didn't call them – I did," Charles called out from the bathroom. He didn't sound too good.

"I dropped the torch down the hole and found my way back into the kitchens, out through the side door while you still had your dick in your hands. Drove Malcolm's car away slowly, stayed off the brakes so no one would see the lights." She grinned. "Home in time for tea." She sat forward, pointed a pair of smoking fingers at him. "Didn't know your old man was still around, let alone that he lived with you. If I'd known that when I set all this up, I wouldn't have bothered getting Malcolm involved."

"We had armed officers here. You wouldn't have got past them."

She snorted. "Really? Like I didn't see him popping out to feed them."

"Tell me you didn't harm him."

"Or what? You'll burst out crying again?"

Eddie winced.

"How is Malcolm?"

"Listen, he's an old man; he doesn't need this."

She sat back, smoked. "He's gone to the toilet." She laughed. "I see you got the pipes fixed; that brought back some memories. I locked the window, just in case he had any ideas about doing a runner." She pulled a hand through her damp hair and crossed her legs. It looked as though she was settling in for the evening. "I was going to tie him to the pipes, like you did with me. But your kettle doesn't have a detachable cord." She grinned. "It was kind of poetic, I thought."

Eddie's nostrils flared.

"So how's Malcolm?"

"You won't be charged with his murder, if that's what you're worried about."

Alex shook her head. "Not worried. Not one bit."

"Fractured skull."

She raised her eyebrows, nodded. When Charles entered the lounge, she ignored him, and said to Eddie, "Not interested."

"Vinegar?" Eddie hoisted his eyebrows.

"No time to get the proper stuff delivered. I had to make do with a threat." Then she clicked her fingers. "Hey, I learned something tonight."

"Really?"

"I thought my dad had killed my mum. I never let on; that's his business— Shut up! I'm talking!"

"Alex..."

She held out a hand. "No, listen. You'll like this. I thought he'd killed her. Kicked her down the stairs like he did me. She was pissed, as always, and he'd had enough, see? Anyway, I guessed he'd got away with it because he was a copper and, you know, you all stick together."

Eddie said nothing.

"Turned out I'd killed her."

"What?"

"Yeah, I know, right? They're both with me," – she jabbed a finger at her head – "all the time. Arguing and trying to encourage me... they were with me when I went to see Maggie.

"Anyway, listen, she told me she'd tried to grab that eight grand off me when I went home to pack." She laughed, shaking her head. "I'd forgotten all this. She tried to grab it and I shoved her down the stairs. Ha! I know." Her face turned serious. She nodded as if in answer to some silent question or comment. "She was pissed. Hit her head on the radiator at the bottom of the stairs. Dink. Dead."

"And you left?"

She shrugged. "I guess so. It's like a mirror of Malcom's life, eh?"

"Oh, girl, you are poison."

Alex grinned.

Eddie marvelled at the story her own demons had fed her. Had she done it? Probably. Who knows?

The ladders of scars across both of her forearms shone, and he wondered and dared to try and imagine what the storm inside her head was like, how it raged all day and whispered all night, laughing at her from behind a hand and nurturing the black seed of paranoia.

He bit his lip in an effort to quell the fire in his chest. Her black makeup had run down her cheeks, creating a freakshow clown with bad intentions. He hated her for what she'd done to Maggie, but the anger he felt couldn't overcome the exhaustion that plundered his body. Not only was killing Maggie a waste of a wonderful life; it was a waste full stop. Alex killed her because of a fantasy played out in her own crazy head.

She licked her lips and cleared her throat. "I realise now there's no you and me." She tried a smile, but it walked off her face deformed and crippled, embarrassed to have existed. "You know what happens next, then. I need you to..."

Eddie was shaking his head.

She began to cry. "Please," she said. "Eddie. You have no idea what it's like up here." She jabbed her head, teeth bared, eyes screwed shut, agony leaking out of the corners. "I have to get away from them."

"I'm not going to kill you." He reached into his fleece pocket and brought out his phone.

"No! No – don't you dare call them!"

"Alex, I have—"

"I mean it, Eddie." The terror turned her voice to a shriek. Tears and snot shone on her face, and when she opened her mouth to speak it strung between her lips like stitches. Her voice thickened, and she pleaded, "I can't live like this any longer. I can't live any longer! This is the fucking end. You wouldn't kill me after that bitch, and you wouldn't fucking kill me when your own brother's life hung in the balance."

Charles flicked a look at Eddie. Eddie ignored him.

"You are in so much trouble, girl," Charles said, shuffling past Eddie into the kitchen.

Alex jumped up and grabbed Charles around the neck. It was like a high tackle, and she tightened her arm around the old man's scrawny throat until his eyes almost popped out of his face. Old man's claws pulled at her scars, trying to wrench her arm away. He flipped his head, flicking tears from his eyes, and he tried to scream but his throat was sealed shut.

An old man he might have been, but when someone's pulling the life out of you, you struggle with every ounce of your being, because it's your being at stake, it's your life, and so you do anything you can. They fell to the floor, writhing.

Chapter Sixty-three

Abandonment

EDDIE STARED ON.

His tongue was stuck to the roof of his mouth and he was trying to part his lips, but the skin was sealing them shut. It was only a slight tension, one easily broken, but he could see it in his mind's eye, and he could also see the loose skin under his eyes twitching with nerves – anxiety animated. On show. Visible.

He could hear her, the strain in her body as she pulled tight on his dad's neck, the groan as she gripped tighter, how it was draining her. And he wondered how long she could keep it up before she had to relax her arm and take a breath. He could hear her grunting, but when she screamed, teeth bared, mouth a black hole, eyes tight shut, he couldn't hear her at all. It was the strangest thing.

And Charles was there, his liver-spotted hands clutching her arm, trying to pull it away, trying to scrape one sliver of breath down his burning throat. His lips were already a bizarre shade of purple. Plum, Eddie thought. Charles's slippered feet slid against the carpet, digging in, trying to get purchase and push his body away from her. It wasn't working; she was far too strong. Madness could do that to a person. It magnified strength.

Even now, as the struggles were reaching their climax, before they began to subside as the oxygen burned away, even now, he could clearly debate the question at the forefront of his calm mind. Why?

Why didn't Charles know about the payoff? He was the man of the house; he shouldn't have distanced himself from a thing of that magnitude, surely? Didn't Mum respect him enough to confide in him? Was he such a wimp in her eyes that he needn't know, let alone be party to a discussion and a final decision? Did he know? Did he sanction it?

Here's eight grand, give it to the little whore, make sure she kills the thing inside her. Make sure she kills my grandchild.

"My baby," Eddie said to himself. His chin quivered and the tears came.

But what if he didn't know? Really, what if Mum thought so little of him that she took the decision herself – in absentia.

But then she killed herself because of me. She abandoned me as a failure.

And he looked at Alex, and her smeared makeup, the black smudges down her face. The snarl of exertion. And he thought of her dad abandoning her, her mother oblivious of her. That had been the catalyst for a ruined life – hers, Alex's – spent with voices tormenting her until she felt nothing for people any more, until the person had been scooped out and burned while some surrogate mind stepped in and got comfy; the mind of a psychopath.

Tears rolled when he thought of her taking the eight grand and flushing the baby out. The ultimate abandonment.

"I would have stood by you. You took the money, honey."

He could see Charles flagging. His fingernails turning pale, tinged blue. And still Eddie stood there, undecided. Weighing up the family lies, the rights and wrongs as his dad slowly died at the hands of a killer; a killer determined to die. It was tragic.

She was crying, her eyes pleading. She was looking at Eddie and she was crying because the old man was dying, and he was her last chance. He knew she was thinking it, and he could see her growing more and more desperate. Her final card was played and so far it had done shit-all for her. There was no next move – this was it; this was all there had ever been. Game over.

She reached down and slid out the knife from her boot.

Eddie dropped the phone and leapt on her. As she brought the blade up, he grabbed her wrist and rammed the knife into her neck just above the collar bone. She stiffened, then relaxed.

Charles rolled out of her grasp onto the floor where he wheezed, raking in a lungful of breath before coughing it back out along with a string of saliva that became a stream of bile and vomit. His nails were turning pinkish again.

Eddie took his hand away from the knife and left it there. There was a steady seep of blood around the blade, and it ran down her chest and collected in the creases of her jeans as she leaned against the sofa. She reached for his hand and he snatched it away.

Her eyes begged.

He swallowed, sobbed, relented, and gave her his hand. She squeezed and she smiled at him. Her eyes lost their venom, and they grew kind again, they grew into those of a fresh sixteen--year-old girl who had fallen in love for the first and last time.

"I love you," she said. "Thank you."

He held her like he'd held Miss Moneypenny what seemed like years ago. He held her and put his face against hers, their tears merging, their aching waning, their lives changing.

"After the heart stops," – she swallowed, gasped – "it takes your brain three minutes to die. Did you know that? Three minutes to think over your life before it switches off and the blackness comes." She looked up at him, and Eddie peered at her, feeling so much emotion he thought he'd turn inside out. "I want to spend my last three minutes with you. Thinking of us..."

"Ssshhh," Eddie managed.

"It's strange," she whispered, "how peaceful it is in here now. They've gone, Eddie..."

She took one last shivering breath, and then relaxed into death. Her three minutes came and went, and still Eddie held her, thinking of what might have been.

PART THREE

Next

Chapter Sixty-four

The Final Act...

– One –

"I LOVE YOU TOO. No, I won't be late. Promise." Benson put down the phone and took the smile off his face; it didn't seem to fit here in the office. A working environment was no place for a happy smile. But it did feel good, he had to admit.

He glanced up; Miriam was watching him from her office window. She beckoned him.

Benson stepped inside and closed the door.

"You look happy," she said.

"Yeah – just don't tell that lot out there."

"Sit down. I want your opinion."

He did. "What's up?"

"How's Eddie been since the inquest?"

Benson looked away. He had no idea how he'd been; Collins didn't wear a placard. He was just Eddie: grumpy, angry and sarcastic. "Same as usual."

"You don't think this Alex job had any effect on him at all?"

"I'm sure it did, but you'll never dig deep enough to find it, and he'll never tell you about it."

"Well, between you and me, I've asked Rebecca from Juniper Hill to give him a few free sessions. Just to see if he's okay... and maybe if he isn't, she can help him."

"And he agreed?"

Miriam smirked. "I found out that Eddie had sent Sid on a course he was supposed to attend, so I kind of had the advantage."

Benson's eyes glided down to his fidgeting fingers.

Miriam sat down. "What?"

"The armed cops on Eddie's house..."

"Go on."

"That evening, I got a call from one of them. Arry. He told me where Alex was – The Sheridan. Said that's where Malcolm had gone, and I figured it's where Eddie would go too." He paused for a while, thinking, then looked up. "I needed them, the armed cops, so I took them off the house."

"You did the right thing, Tom. I read it all in the report, and anyone would—"

"But if I hadn't done that, she wouldn't have got into Eddie's cottage."

"You made the right call."

"She played me!"

Miriam recoiled in her seat.

"I'm sorry. I just... I made a bad call. Another bad call, as it turned out."

"What are you saying?"

"I'm wondering if I fit this job any more. I'm wondering if I should even be here. Perhaps I should learn how to mow the lawn and plant flowers. Perhaps I should give Brenda the life she's waited thirty years for." He sighed, fidgeted some more, and said, "Maggie Darlington died because—"

"Because there was a psychopath on the loose, Tom." She stood and pointed a finger. "If you're thinking of resigning, I do not accept it. If you're thinking of retiring, I will not allow it." She stuck her nose in the air. "Got it?"

– Two –

"How did you feel after the inquest?"

Eddie peered at her over his fists. His elbows were propped on her desk, and it somehow felt comfortable like this, as though speaking from behind a barrier kept him safe and provided a hiding place for the emotions that might play out on his face. "Okay."

Rebecca sighed. "If we're to make any progress—"

"I felt drained. I felt I'd hit the bottom of a fucking pit. I felt like I'd been put through a mill."

"And the decision she forced you into taking?"

He took a long time to think about it, and a longer time to consider speaking about it. "I watched her choking him to death. But I was focussed on our past rather than on his future – or lack of it. I was trying to weigh up whether my killing her outweighed my dad's part in killing her."

"You think he was party to that decision to pay her off all those years ago?"

Eddie thought about how to answer that question. "That's why I hesitated for so long – I couldn't work it out. But I don't think he was, no. I think it was all Mum's idea. And maybe Malcolm's too."

"And if he had been a party to it?"

He took a deep breath, not enjoying being examined like this. "I don't know. Really. I couldn't have allowed her to take retribution even if he did sign her own madness warrant, I suppose. But it says something that I waited so long to dive in and rescue him. And he noticed."

"He asked you about it?"

"Of course. I said I was appalled that they could make a sixteen-year-old girl go through something like that, and with no support. I was ashamed they thought money could buy them a life without a conscience."

Rebecca raised her eyebrows.

"What was his answer?"

She nodded.

"He slapped my face. Hard. He almost moved out – I had to practically beg the silly old fucker to stay."

"By promising what?"

Now Eddie raised his own eyebrows. "You're very astute."

"What did you promise him?"

"That I didn't blame him. I blamed Mum and Malcolm for sending Alex doolally."

"Do you miss her?"

"Alex?"

She nodded.

"No. She and I were never going to make it; we were too different. And besides, she was a fruit loop. I have my own mental issues to deal with, without scooping up someone else's problems as well."

– Three –

"Is that understood?"

"I think Brenda likes me again. I have a chance to make a go of it instead of providing her with grounds for divorce."

Miriam thought for a moment. "Working here doesn't automatically give a spouse ammunition for divorce, Tom. It's not the firm's fault. You can still be a nice person when you're in her company, you can still surprise her and treat her well. You don't have to resign to do those things."

"I know, but—"

"Can I speak candidly?"

Benson shrugged. "Sure."

"You're more likely to divorce her if you spend all your time together; you're absolutely meant to be in this job, Tom." Her smile was genuine. "And speaking from experience, I think the heart of a healthy relationship isn't the quantity of time you spend together, it's the quality." She laughed. "You would go batshit crazy within a month. Gardening indeed."

Her words lightened his mood, and he let them roll back and forth inside his mind. She might have a point.

"Speaking of digging," Miriam continued, "you remember when I had that meeting to go to, you know, on the day of The Sheridan Club?"

"Is that what we're calling it now?"

"It was with a senior departmental manager from Social Services – as was."

Benson sat back, crossed his legs. "Intriguing."

"I managed to track our Alex Sheridan down to when she was plain old Alex Trafford. Sixteen years old. Pregnant."

Benson uncrossed his legs and sat forward. "And?"

"You're not going to believe it."

He stared at her. "Well?"

– Four –

"Speaking of your own mental issues," Rebecca continued, "do you feel any more relaxed since it ended?"

"No."

"In what way?"

He looked at her cockeyed. "Is that even a question? Are you running out of ways to be original?"

"Sorry," she smiled, "I'm thinking ahead."

"Don't. Stay in the present. There's no room for making plans in this life."

"And—"

"And that wasn't a lead-in for some other stupid theoretical fucking question, okay?" He stood. "Did you have to go on a course to be deliberately vague to qualify as a shrink?"

"Sit down, Eddie."

"No," he said. "I've had enough."

"The baby."

He stared at her, then leaned forward. "That is a statement. How would you like me to react?"

"If she'd kept it, how would you have reacted? Would you have wanted to be involved with its upbringing? Would you have wanted to be a parent to it?"

"What do you mean, if she'd kept it? She miscarried. End of story."

She smiled, flicked forward a page in her notes. "Yep, sorry, slip of the tongue. But still, hypothetically, would you have—"

"I don't do hypothesis. I do reality. And in reality, being here was a bad idea. I've changed my mind; I don't want your help. I want to leave. Let me out."

"I think you're making good progress, Eddie."

"Compared to when? I'm not a snivelling wreck; things happened, I'll get over them, and I'm not having black thoughts, okay?" He turned away. "Now put your pen down and let me leave."

"Just...Would you have looked after the child?"

He spun around, meeting her eyes with a snarl. "None of your business. The kid didn't make it; leave it alone. I'm not going to think about it, and I'm not going to answer you. Now let me the fuck out."

Rebecca sat upright, trying to appear in charge. She looked at him for a moment, and finally did put down her pen. "I think your lack of interaction with people is damaging you. I think your anger can be tamed." She stood up and rounded the desk. "I think we can help you, Eddie. You have a form of personality disorder."

"Good. I'm glad you managed to pin a label on me. But to me I'm just me, good and bad me. I like me as I am and I don't want nobody fiddling about with me, okay? I like being angry and I like not interacting with people, because people are arseholes. Now let me out before I kick the fucking door down."

"Sit down."

"I mean it."

"We're getting close."

"I said—"

"That's why you want to leave, isn't it?" That's why you won't sit down. We're getting close. You're almost ready to—"

"Just piss off!"

"Why do you dislike people? Why do you hate being with anyone?"

"Everyone is an arsehole."

"Everyone you've ever known has lied to you."

"I mean it!" Eddie yelled.

"Your mother, your brother..."

Eddie snarled and stepped forward.

"...and everyone you ever loved abandoned you: your wife, your daughter, Ros, Maggie, your mother, your unborn—"

Eddie slapped her. Rebecca rocked and almost toppled. She stared at him, breathing hard, rubbing her cheek. She shook her hair away from her eyes, eventually said, "I'm sorry, I—"

"You can only ever trust yourself," he whispered. "The only people who don't want to fuck you over... they die." He sat down. "Getting close to someone is just asking for a life of pain. I will never be able to deal with that. There is nothing good in this life."

– Five –

Benson leaned forward and gripped the edge of Miriam's desk, quite unwittingly. His nails turned white.

"One Miss Alexandra Trafford gave the baby up for adoption after it was born at St James's hospital in Leeds. When born, the baby – Penelope she called it – was handed over to a professional couple who couldn't have children of their own."

Benson's mouth was hanging open.

"She opened a trust account for her." Miriam closed the file. "And deposited eight thousand pounds."

"You are shitting me." Benson's gaze fell away from Miriam's face and settled on his white nails.

"Do you think Eddie would want to know?"

Benson sank back in the chair, blinking. Eventually he looked up at her, shaking his head. "We can't get involved, Miriam. We can't. We must never tell him."

– Six –

Eddie finally made it to the front of the queue. It was times like these that he wished he were more conversant with technology; he could have avoided the queue altogether, could have avoided having to speak with anyone.

He nodded at the cashier, did one of those flat smile things that people seemed to do these days that served no reason except to indicate they weren't a threat. "I want to set up a Direct Debit to a registered charity, please."

The cashier's eyebrows were cresting the creases in her forehead, and a smile broke loose on the makeup she wore, her actual face catching up with it moments later. "That's great. How much, Mr Collins?"

Eddie gave it some thought, trying to recall how much his salary had gone up since they promoted him. It was a sham, the promotion; it was there just as a little pat on the head to keep him sweet. Still, he'd remembered Miriam's words:

"You'll get the bloody pay rise whether you like it or not – hell, give it to charity, you sanctimonious idiot". And that's exactly what he was doing here.

"Which charity, Mr Collins?"

"Mental Health UK."

Acknowledgments

There's a long list of people to thank for helping to pull this book, and all of my books, into something that reads like it was written by someone who knew what they were doing. Among them is my amazing wife, Sarah, who makes sure I get the time to write in the first place. There can't be too many people who accept "I want to think of things" as a valid excuse to avoid life for a while – but it seems to work!

To Kath Middleton, Alison Birch from re:Written, a huge thank you for making sure the first draft wasn't the final draft – you will always be the first people to read my books, and consequently always the first to point and laugh at my errors. It's because of you that this book has turned out so well, and it's because of me that you had so much work to do to get it there.

Thanks also to my Facebook friends in the UK Crime Book Club, my Andrew Barrett Page, and my Book Group for their constant encouragement – who knew readers could be so assertive, demanding… and kind.

To those who suffer my newsletter (sign up at andrewbarrett.co.uk), a big thank you for helping me shape this book, and for all your encouragement – you haven't a clue how valuable that is.

And to my ARC readers – you're awesome, thank you for being a part of this magical journey!

A special thanks go out to my wonderful beta readers. This is the first novel we've worked on together; our collaboration continues to flourish after our success with The Crew. Your time and effort shine through in the words of this novel, and you've made the difference between a good story and a great story. I am humbled and amazed by your selflessness. Thanks, guys – take a bow:

Shari
Fritzi Redgrave
Wayne Burnop
Alex Mellor
Janette Mattey
Gail Ferguson
Mike Bailey
Patti Holycross

This Side of Death
Is dedicated to David Gilchrist and his daughter Caroline Maston of the United Kingdom Crime Book Club (UKCBC) on Facebook.
Their determination to promote the work of indie authors to their members and the world is nothing short of dazzling; I and hundreds of other authors owe you a debt of gratitude.
Thank you.

About the Author

Andrew Barrett has enjoyed variety in his professional life, from engine-builder to farmer, from Oilfield Service Technician in Kuwait, to his current role of Senior CSI in Yorkshire. He's been a CSI since 1996, and has worked on all scene types from terrorism to murder, suicide to rape, drugs manufacture to bomb scenes. One way or another, Andrew's life revolves around crime.

In 1997 he finished his first crime thriller, A Long Time Dead, and it's still a readers' favourite today, some 200,000 copies later, topping the Amazon charts several times. Two more books featuring SOCO Roger Conniston completed the trilogy.

Today, Andrew is still producing high-quality, authentic crime thrillers with a forensic flavour that attract attention from readers worldwide. He's also attracted attention from the Yorkshire media, having been featured in the Yorkshire Post, and twice interviewed on BBC Radio Leeds.

He's best known for his lead character, CSI Eddie Collins, and the acerbic way in which he roots out criminals and administers justice. Eddie's series is six books and four novellas in length, and there's still more to come.

Andrew is a proud Yorkshireman and sets all of his novels there, using his home city of Leeds as another major, and complementary, character in each of the stories.

You can find out more about him and his writing at www.andrewbarrett.co.uk, where you can sign up for Andrew's Reader's Club, and claim your free starter library.

He'd be delighted to hear your comments on Facebook (and so would Eddie Collins) and Twitter. Email him and say hello at andrew@andrewbarrett.co.uk

Also by Andrew Barrett

Did you enjoy This Side of Death?
I hope you did. Have you read them all? Did you know The Third Rule has been replaced by series opener, The Pain of Strangers? It's already become a reader's favourite.

Try a CSI Eddie Collins short story or a novella. Read them from behind the couch!

Have you tried the SOCO Roger Conniston trilogy?

Also available as an ebook boxed set

Printed in Great Britain
by Amazon

17140873R00210